Esther Campion is from Cork, Ireland and currently lives in north-west Tasmania. She attended North Presentation Secondary School in Cork and has degrees from University College Cork and the University of Aberdeen, Scotland. Esther and her Orcadian husband have lived together in Ireland, Scotland, Norway and South Australia. They have two grown-up children in Adelaide and the youngest at home in Tassie. Esther loves sharing her life on a small property with an over-indulged chocolate Labrador, a smoochy cat and a couple of ageing mares, all of whom she firmly believes are living proof that dreams really can come true. *The House of Second Chances* is Esther's second novel, following *Leaving Ocean Road*.

Also by Esther Campion

Leaving Ocean Road

Esther Campion

The House of Second Chances

hachette
AUSTRALIA

hachette
AUSTRALIA

Published in Australia and New Zealand in 2019
by Hachette Australia
(an imprint of Hachette Australia Pty Limited)
Level 17, 207 Kent Street, Sydney NSW 2000
www.hachette.com.au

10 9 8 7 6 5 4 3 2 1

 A catalogue record for this
book is available from the
NATIONAL
LIBRARY National Library of Australia
OF AUSTRALIA

ISBN: 978 0 7336 3617 2

Cover design by Christabella Designs
Cover photograph courtesy of Trevillion
Author photograph courtesy of Michelle DuPont
Typeset in 12.1/18.6 pt Sabon LT Pro by Bookhouse, Sydney
Printed and bound in Australia by McPherson's Printing Group

 MIX
Paper from
responsible sources
FSC
www.fsc.org FSC® C001695

The paper this book is printed on is certified against the
Forest Stewardship Council® Standards. McPherson's Printing
Group holds FSC® chain of custody certification SA-COC-005379.
FSC® promotes environmentally responsible, socially beneficial
and economically viable management of the world's forests.

To Mary T Coughlan
and all her Barrett boys,
for your courage

Prologue

Midnight was no time to be taking a swim in the Atlantic. The sea was freezing despite the balmy air temperature that had made this sound like a good idea. Aidan had never skinny-dipped in his life. He wouldn't even have thought of it if it hadn't been for Isabella, who was already mostly submerged, having run past him over the smooth stones, moonlight playing on her blonde hair and her skin, golden apart from that semi-circle of white at her bottom.

'Get down quick,' she stage-whispered.

Aidan was in up to his knees, trying to smile as he covered his manly bits and willed himself out deeper into the icy water. He was supposed to be on a stag weekend in West Cork with his mates. Technically he was; he'd just taken a detour. Wasn't it what any single twenty-six-year-old man would do if he met a young, captivating French woman who said she could listen to his accent all day and would love to be shown around by a local? He could get used to this. In fact, the moment he'd laid eyes on her in the pub two nights before, he'd known he'd happily spend the rest of his life getting used to Isabella.

'It's Baltic!' He was up to his hips now, and any physical trace of his masculinity had all but disappeared.

Splash! He dived under, registering the shock to his head and neck, then came up quickly, shaking his hair off his face, gasping for air.

'You're mad,' he said, stroking toward the woman who had made the past forty-eight hours the most exciting of his life so far.

She made to backstroke away, her long legs kicking at the surface, toes pointed like a ballerina. He grabbed her ankles and drew her past him in a circle. Bending her knees, she reached for his shoulder, laughing as she stalled her momentum and pulled herself onto him, wrapping her legs tight around him. The warmth of her slender frame was like a switch, turning the feeling back on in his body.

In the half-lit hush, water droplets traced the curve of her chin. Her eyes danced as she stared at him until he could stand it no longer. Taking her face in his hands, he kissed her and for the first time in his life, he made love in the pure, salty, rippling sea.

Chapter One

Aidan didn't recognise the number when he prised his mobile from the pocket of the jeans he'd only just managed to squeeze into that morning.

'Aidan O'Shea speaking.' His voice bellowed above the strong south-westerly that threatened to stymie his attempts to finish the roof repairs.

'Hello, Aidan . . .'

'Sorry, can you say again? I'm up on a roof in West Cork.'

'Colette,' came the voice louder and clearer. 'Colette Barry.'

'Ah, Colette, what can I do for you?'

'Can you give me a ring when you're down off that roof? Ellen sent me an email. She wants me to help with the house.'

'Oh, right. Will do.'

He looked at the phone. Colette had already hung up. *What the?* Why couldn't Ellen have warned him? Colette was a nice enough girl, a long-time loyal friend of his sister, but what was Ellen thinking, bringing her in on the project? Interior design; what the heck did they need that for? For all he knew, Colette could be a total head case when it came to her work, with way-out ideas like a female Laurence Llewelyn-Bowen. Holy God! Sure wouldn't a few fancy cushions in the parlour and a few bits of decent bed linen do the job? He pushed his slate ripper in place again and began to hammer with a vengeance. Okay, maybe it wouldn't hurt to call her back, just to be polite, but not before reminding his sister to consult him before foisting her pals onto one of his jobs again.

He'd only taken on the project to please Ellen, having managed to avoid this house like the plague for most of the past twenty years. But he'd have done anything for his sister. Taking a few deep breaths of the sea air now, he could picture the pair of them running carefree around his grandmother's beloved garden below and through the foot-worn path between the bright yellow of thorny gorse bushes down to the sandy beach beside the house. Those were the days of their childhood summers, playing with country friends and cousins, when their biggest concerns were whether the tide would be out or in for a swim or if they'd be lucky enough to catch a few mackerel off the rocks for tea. Ellen had always looked up to him, made him the strong big brother, the dependable cousin everyone thought him to be. When she'd left at twenty-one, he'd had no idea how much he would come to miss having her in his everyday life.

Her own life had certainly been a rollercoaster of late, what with losing her husband last year and then Gerry Clancy showing up on her doorstep in Australia, prompting her recent trip home and their romantic few days in West Cork. If it wasn't for those two and their rekindling of old flames, he'd never have started this renovating carry-on. Oh, Ellen would have been there for him too, if only he'd told her his troubles. But that was all water under the bridge. Or at least it would have been if he hadn't put them all first and agreed to this job he'd begun to begrudge. Forty-five years of age, and he still hadn't learned to say no.

The phone pinged in his pocket. He stopped his hammering again and pulled it out. A text from Jane asking if he could have Millie over one Saturday. He texted back, *No problem.* Of course he did.

'Polite,' he huffed. 'Too polite for your own good!'

—

By the time Colette arrived, The Stables was calming down after the lunchtime rush. She hadn't had a break since 8 a.m. when she'd met her first client of the day at her office on the North Mall.

'Ah, Colette. How's it going?' Gerry strode toward her with that broad smile and air of contentment she envied.

'I've been running around like a headless chicken.' She unbuttoned her suit jacket to let some air through the starched white shirt that was better suited to the world of corporate finance than a power walk through lunchtime Cork City. 'Haven't stopped since the dawn.' The aroma of restaurant food sent her stomach to her backbone.

'You'll be ready for a drop of my legendary carrot soup, then,' he said with a wink that took the edge off her mood if not her hunger. 'Sit down there and I'll be right with you.'

As he left her at a freshly cleaned table in a cosy booth, Colette hoped things would work out for him and Ellen. Relationships were tricky enough without being in one with someone on the other side of the world. Gerry could have moved to Australia months ago to be with Ellen if it hadn't been for his brother Donal's fondness for a flutter on the horses that had seen him narrowly avoid jail and Gerry having to work his behind off to keep this place afloat. True to form, Gerry had put his concerns for his parents' financial security, tied up in this business, before his own happiness, and saved his brother's undeserving ass into the bargain. It was the same old story; good people got walked on every day of the week, and they were the ones left to pick up the pieces. It had been the same with her ex-husband. Tadhg wasn't a gambler, but he'd managed to steal from her in other ways. She'd read somewhere, in *The Kite Runner*, she thought, that all crime was stealing in one form or another. She hated stealing. There was Donal Clancy now, serving customers at another table as if he were Waiter of the Year. Unable to bear the sight of him, she took out her phone and flicked through her emails.

'Hi, Colette. Sorry I'm a bit late.'

She looked up to see Aidan O'Shea's formidable frame standing beside her in a tight zipped-up rain jacket, a shock of strawberry-blond hair falling over his forehead and a worn-looking folder under one arm.

'That's okay,' she said. 'I only got here myself.' There was an awkward pause as he stood looking at a loss as to what to do next. 'Have a seat,' she said, gesturing for him to sit opposite her.

Without a word, he sat down and unzipped the under-sized jacket before stuffing it behind him and rolling up the already rolled-up sleeves of a plaster-spattered check shirt. The large freckles on his forearms made him look almost tanned. His hands, though clean, were covered in a chalky residue she could almost taste.

'How are things with you?' he said eventually.

She'd forgotten he was so quiet, but then apart from bumping into him and his sister when Ellen had been home earlier in the year, Colette hadn't seen much of Aidan since they were teenagers. In fact, she hadn't seen much of him then either. Three years older, he'd moved in different circles. Her memories of him from visits to the O'Sheas' house mostly involved loud music coming from behind a closed bedroom door. Ellen always said he was a rock. But back then, Colette and Ellen didn't spend much time talking about her older brother. They'd been too busy dissecting the goings-on in Madden's Secondary School and planning elaborate futures for themselves that involved hunks with whom they'd save the planet before each of them would go on to have three children with beautiful names like Phoebe and Chandler. Life was easy back then. It had been such a lovely surprise to bump into Ellen on what was only her second trip home since she'd emigrated over twenty years before. They may as well have been seeing each other every week such was the ease between them. Big chunks of each other's lives may have been missed out on, but they were still friends. Why couldn't Ellen be sitting opposite her now, making this project an adventure instead of a test of her patience with the older brother? Gerry arrived with the soup not a moment too soon.

'Would you like a drop, Aidan, or will I get you a pint?'

'Just a coffee, thanks Gerry.'

Colette didn't realise she was shovelling the delicious soup into her until she caught Aidan staring. Straightening up, she swallowed a mouthful and dabbed at her lips with a serviette.

'Sorry. I didn't have time to stop for lunch.'

His face broke into an embarrassed smile. 'That's all right,' he said. 'It's just, you're eating like a builder.'

She squeezed on the serviette. 'And how exactly do you think an interior designer might eat?'

He put a hand up in defence. 'I'm only messing.'

A raised eyebrow was enough to make him keep any further comments to himself.

She was grateful when his phone rang and she could eat the remainder of her lunch in peace instead of in the awkward silence that had fallen between them.

Gerry returned with a tray of welcome coffees.

'Great soup, Ger.'

Colette set the bowl on the tray before turning to search in the work bag that had cost her nearly a week's wages. She pulled out three copies of an email from Ellen and placed them in the middle of the table.

―

Aidan couldn't help but notice the crispness of the paper as Colette slid the sheets out of a plastic sleeve. He gingerly took out his own coffee-stained, dog-eared print-out and looked to Gerry for sympathy.

'Well, I have no email to contribute,' Gerry told them. 'If I had my way, I wouldn't even be at this meeting.'

Colette rolled her eyes. 'Easy, tiger, you'll get your visa and you'll be over there before you know it. Anyway, it says here,' she quoted from Ellen's email, '"You can liaise with Aidan and Gerry, but let me know what you've *all* decided before going ahead with any major changes." So, let's get on with it.'

Aidan squirmed in his seat. Not only was Colette going to be a part of this project, she was going to try to be the boss.

'You might take us through the plans then, Aidan,' she said.

Aidan tried to recall the cheery, fun-loving Colette Barry who used to call to the house when they were teenagers, but it wasn't working. From the top of her head of glossy dark hair to the tips of those heels he'd spotted as he'd stood at the table feeling decidedly under-dressed, she was in business mode and may as well have been a different person. He took the sketches from the battered manila folder and began to talk them through his proposed renovations to his grandmother's house. There was a plan for an extension with the kitchen leading into a south-facing conservatory that could serve as a dining or communal area if they eventually turned the place into a B&B. Another sketch outlined the addition of several bedrooms to the upper floor. When he looked up, those soft brown eyes he remembered were fixed on him in a hardened stare.

'I thought to make the plans as broad-ranging as possible to give us options as to what to do with the place,' he explained. 'Not just for us, but for future generations.' There was no budging her serious expression and Gerry's calm wasn't helping. 'Like Louise,' he added, 'if she ever wanted to come home with her family.' The idea of his twenty-year-old Australian niece having children might be hard to imagine, but as the only grandchild, Louise was the last hope for continuing the O'Shea bloodline, his own contribution having been nil.

'A word of caution, if you don't mind, Aidan.' A set of scary ridges had formed on Colette's forehead. 'How is the budget looking on this all-singing-all-dancing dream home of yours?'

He sucked in his frustration and scanned the email for dollar or euro signs. His sister hadn't included Colette in the finances. In the O'Shea household, money was something discussed on rare occasions and only ever with family. Whatever about Gerry, Colette was certainly not family.

'I don't think you have to worry about that, Colette,' said Gerry, finally helping him out. 'Ellen and Aidan will discuss all that with their dad. Let's put the possibilities on the table and see if we can narrow it down to two or three options. Then the O'Sheas can decide how much they want to spend.'

She rolled her eyes. 'I never start a project without knowing the client's budget.' There was silence. 'But I suppose, in this case, I can make an exception.' She tapped her pen on the table cueing Aidan to continue.

'The parlour can be left more or less as is,' he went on, 'but I thought that's where you could come in, Colette. Smarten the place up a bit, modernise it, you know.'

'Surely you want me to work on more than the parlour?' She looked at him as if she'd been mortally wounded.

He counted to ten and cursed Ellen for not giving him full rein. He could have the whole thing finished in a few months and be shot of it. 'Of course. The parlour is just for starters,' he amended.

'I'll have to see it, of course,' she said, regaining her enthusiasm. 'We can make a date for a trip down once you've taken us through the rest of your proposal.'

'Have you started work on it yet?' Gerry asked.

'The roof repairs are in hand and I've done some costings,' said Aidan. 'Other than that, I've had a couple of fellas in to survey the plumbing and wiring. We'll have to install a few en-suites, but the extension is the biggest job. I'll get the boys started on it once we get a few contracts out of the way.'

'I'd love to give you a hand on my days off,' said Gerry.

Aidan almost envied him his enthusiasm. There was no doubt that the house held something special for Gerry. Its association with Ellen? A way to support Louise? When Ellen had told Aidan that Gerry was Louise's biological father, Aidan had been more than a little shocked. Not half as shocked as Louise by all accounts, finding out at nineteen, and the beautiful man she had known all her life as her father hardly cold in his grave. For Aidan and Gerry at least, this project was about more than bricks, mortar and fancy interiors. It was a thought he would need to keep in focus if he wasn't to let some of his own associations with the house get the better of him.

Forcing himself to shut down memories of Isabella, he listened as Colette went on about coordinating bathrooms and bedrooms. By the end of their meeting, he was left in no doubt that he wouldn't have this project all his own way. Gerry, to be fair, was in agreement with him on most of the improvements, but Colette was a challenge. He hoped their trip to West Cork wouldn't be a disaster. If he had to go down on his knees and beg Gerry to take the day off and join them, that's what he'd do. There was no way he was going to be left on his own with Little Miss Changing Rooms.

—

On a cold Anzac Day in South Australia, Ellen Constantin-opoulos dug her hands into the pockets of the woollen coat she'd taken to Ireland in February, and wished she'd worn gloves. Port Lincoln had basked in sunshine over Easter, but today it already felt like mid-winter. She stamped her boots in the grass that turned a blackish green as the sun began its rise out to sea where lights of waiting grain ships twinkled in the half-light. This was Tracey's idea. It had seemed like a good one at the time, but Ellen had to admit the main thing that drove her out of bed at five-thirty on this longed-for day off was the lure of breakfast at the hotel after the ceremony.

Tracey's breath hung in the air beside her as they watched local school captains lay wreaths at the foot of the cenotaph. Nick had thought about going into the army – but that was before he'd been captivated by Ellen, as he used to tell her. Being married to a fisherman, with his long stints away from home in unpredictable weather conditions, had been enough of a worry. She glanced round at the crowd. How many of these souls who'd braved the early-morning drizzle had lost loved ones to war? At least that was a noble kind of death, she mused, not like Nick's; felled by a kangaroo that had innocently bounded onto his road home. Either way, they were all cheated. Short-changed by death, the slippery customer that always won in the end, no matter which way you went. It didn't make living without them any easier. The flash of white as the doves were released brought her back to the moment.

'You hungry?' Tracey whispered.

'Famished.'

They stood in silence for the 'Last Post'. She blinked away a trickle at the corners of her eyes as she inhaled the pungent smell of burning gum leaves; the smell that had reminded the men in Gallipoli of their Australian home, to which so many would never return. As the band launched into 'Advance Australia Fair', with the local ageing sopranos hitting those notes that shot right to the core of the soul, her thoughts turned to Ireland, to Gerry Clancy and how lucky she was to have been given a second chance.

—

'Any news from the old country?' Tracey asked as they sat at a table in the hotel.

Ellen sighed. They both knew Tracey would be the first to know if there'd been any developments on that front. She peeled off her coat as the warm air thawed her hands and feet.

'Will we share the pancakes?' Tracey didn't wait for an answer, but was up and back from the bar in a flash, her auburn curls springing as she went. 'I ordered cream,' she said, plonking back down opposite Ellen. 'You're wasting away.'

'I am not,' Ellen huffed, yanking the scarf from her neck. 'I'm getting on with my life. Working away . . .'

'Has he sorted out that visa yet?'

Tracey was the most caring, loyal friend anyone could wish for, but patience wasn't her greatest attribute and certainly not where the machinations of the Australian immigration system were involved. When Ellen didn't answer, the subject was changed.

'How is it going with the house in West Cork? Will they keep the range in the kitchen?'

It was uncanny how her friend, who'd hardly left the state, had a way of making you believe she'd been over there. Ellen's grandmother's house had been the bolthole to which she had retreated only a few short months ago, when she'd thought her chances of finding love again had been shattered. Finding Gerry Clancy outside The Stables in Cork with another woman had been a hard lesson in not arriving unannounced and expecting someone you loved to know you were ready for a relationship with them, just because you knew it yourself. Thankfully, Colette had been there to support her and had wasted no time in letting Gerry know what they'd witnessed. And Aidan, God love him, had even offered his services as stand-in barman to let Gerry make a beeline to West Cork to explain himself and make good on what she'd thought was a futile trip. He'd be here now if their plans hadn't been scuppered by Donal's shenanigans.

As far as she knew, the renovations were underway. It was exactly what her grandmother's house deserved. Lizzie O'Shea had died when Ellen was still in her twenties, and the bachelor uncle who'd lived with her had been gone seven years. If it wasn't for her cousin, Eamon, and his wife Orla who lived next door on the old farm, the place would never even get an airing.

In her mind's eye, she could see the traditional stone façade, the white sash windows and solid oak door; a place where you'd always be welcome, the narrow hallway leading to the kitchen where the range warmed the room to match the atmosphere. She stopped herself at the wooden staircase and the bedrooms that lay beyond. Today had already been filled with enough emotion without letting memories of loving Gerry Clancy into the mix.

'They're getting on with it,' she told Tracey. 'I don't know about the range, but the place is in good hands. Aidan's a dab hand at anything to do with plumbing, electrics, you name it . . .' She rubbed her thumb over where she used to wear her wedding band. 'My pal Colette's an interior designer. She's on board as well.'

'And what about the man himself?' Tracey wasn't letting it go. 'Has he been voted off the project?'

'It's not an episode of *The Block*, you know.'

'Well, at least I brought a smile to your face.' Tracey nodded toward the windows. 'You've been about as much fun as that weather out there since you picked me up.'

'Ooh, excuse me, Miss Reality TV, but my life, I'm sorry to disappoint you, is far from anything you watch. And God knows that's a lot of television.'

'You arrived just in time,' Tracey told the waitress who was placing the steaming pancakes in the middle of the table. 'I was just about to punch her lights out.'

The young girl hesitated before setting down their mugs of cappuccino. Ellen wanted to explain, but was struck by a fit of giggles and had to hold her sides to contain a convulsion of laughter.

'Just two old farts having a laugh, love,' said Tracey as the girl took a couple of backward steps and left them to it. 'As my mother used to tell me,' she said, turning back to Ellen, 'if we can have a laugh, we know we're alive.'

Since Gerry Clancy had come back into her life, Ellen had certainly felt more alive. The only problem now was getting his paperwork sorted out so they could actually live in the same place. The house in Ireland was like an insurance policy, keeping their options open. For now, her daughter was her priority, which was why he was moving out here, but who knew what might happen if she and Gerry wished to live in Ireland on a more permanent basis sometime in that uncharted water that was their future?

Chapter Two

Ellen woke up on Ocean Road hoping, as she did every morning, that Gerry's visa had come through. Despite the cool of late autumn, she opened the sliding glass door of the upstairs bedroom and stepped out onto the small balcony. There was a welcome green in the paddocks after recent rain, and a watery sun promised to burn off the haze over Boston Bay. Lambs bleated on the neighbouring farm and down on the highway a truck rumbled its way to Port Lincoln. Twelve months ago she'd hardly been able to leave this house. There'd been times when her life hadn't seemed worth living without Nick. And like a godsend, Gerry had changed all that. It was amazing how life turned out. She hugged her arms to her chest and smiled. With still plenty of time before her day in the social-work office would begin, she jumped back into bed and checked her phone. Nothing on the visa front, but emails from both Aidan and Colette. She propped up her pillows and sat back, excited to see how things were progressing in West Cork.

Hi Ellen,

Just had meeting with boys. Have arranged visit to property next week. Will make a comprehensive list of recommendations, including alternatives, for your perusal. Gathering ideas from similar properties both here and the UK. Very excited.

TTFN

Colette

PS You never told me your brother was hard work.

She clicked on the latest from Aidan.

Ellen,

Hope this finds you well. Kindly consult your dear old brother next time you feel like inviting your annoying little interior designer friend onto a project with me. I have agreed to take her to West Cork next week, so wish me luck. Something tells me I'll need it. Love to Louise.

Aidan

How on earth had her brother and Colette managed to get off on the wrong foot? Aidan was so sweet and Colette so much fun. Surely they should be getting on like a house on fire. But it was the house that really mattered. Aidan's building skills and Colette's talent for design were a match made in heaven. Even though she was thousands of miles away, this project was keeping Ellen going. She needed this connection with Gerry, something to share and talk about instead of this unbearable waiting for visas. Her brother and her friend would just have to work around their personalities.

—

Aidan parked his beat-up Land Rover illegally on the North Mall and checked Colette's business card. The three-storey Georgian house looked resplendent, as the photo on the card promised. A black gloss–painted front door, cream façade and bright white window surrounds made a professional state-ment. To one side of the door were three bell buttons like miniature billiard balls set in brass, together with three gold engraved plaques. Fabulous Four Walls was on the ground floor. Aidan checked the state of his boots before ringing the appropriate bell.

'Good morning, and welcome to Fabulous Four Walls.' A tall, impeccably dressed man swung the door fully open and hailed Aidan in with a flourish. Aidan took a hesitant step as he tried not to stare at what his mother, God rest her, would call the get-up of the fellow he guessed must be in his late fifties.

'I'm John.' The man held out a hand to Aidan as he closed the door behind them.

'Aidan O'Shea. I'm here to pick up Colette Barry.' A waft of something expensive pinched at Aidan's nostrils as he took the strong, squeaky-clean hand. He couldn't help but eyeball the cufflinks on the whiter-than-white shirt and the purple silk cravat inside the starched collar.

'Come this way. She's expecting you.'

Aidan followed over the smart black-and-white tiles of the hallway and along a carpeted corridor to a small office where Colette was speaking into her mobile. She beckoned for him to come in.

'Make yourself at home,' John whispered. 'She'll be with you in a mo.'

Aidan caught himself staring at the man as he swept back down the corridor, leaving him standing just inside the door of Colette's office, his hands shoved into the pockets of his jeans and feeling like a fish out of water. He took in the clean lines of her work space. The hardwood floor and off-white walls at least gave some warmth to the professionalism. Shelving, neatly filled with catalogues, lined one wall. Aidan suspected they were alphabetised to the third letter. He thought of his own office, where the walls were covered in plans and out-of-date calendars and you could hardly see the desk for the clutter. Where the hell did she put her paperwork? The desk was as spartan as the room. Apart from a laptop, there were just three miniature plant pots that served as pen holders in a colour that matched the walls. Even a cup and saucer blended in.

Colette swivelled in a luxurious cream leather office chair as she argued with someone, Aidan guessed was a supplier, about the cost of Roman blinds. She put a hand over the phone.

'Have a seat, Aidan. I won't be long.'

He settled himself in one of a matching pair of leather chairs with armrests and allowed himself a swivel of his own to look out over the River Lee, where a watery May sun was trying its best to shine through the clouds above Vincent's Bridge. As he turned back, a series of photographs on the wall behind the desk caught his attention. Before and after shots, no doubt, of renovations to the rear of the building. The area had gone from what looked like a mossy, overgrown walled garden with a large slab of concrete in the middle to a proper car park bordered by strips of manicured lawn and vibrant flower beds. The walls of both building and garden had been whitewashed, and a wrought-iron table and chairs were arranged to one side of the rear door, perhaps for smokers or summer dining.

'I'll await another quote from you, then,' Colette was saying. 'And don't forget, I'm not afraid to go elsewhere.'

Ouch, Aidan thought, *poor bastard is only trying to make a living.*

She ended the call and turned to him. 'All done. Sorry to keep you waiting.'

'I'm illegally parked,' he told her, hoping she didn't notice him having to push on the armrests to extricate his body from the chair.

'Come around the back next time. There's plenty of space.'

'So I see,' he said with a nod to the photos.

She gave a wry laugh. 'Only blood, sweat and tears went into that little project.'

He doubted the tears were hers.

'Come and I'll give you a quick tour.'

She was out of there with her designer bag over her shoulder before he could protest. The last thing he needed was a parking fine, but he followed her to the bottom of a polished mahogany staircase that wound up to the second floor which, she explained, was occupied by a dental practice. The third floor, she informed him, was an English-language school that held most of its classes at night and in summer. The fact that the school had its own side entrance and could be accessed by the lift was a detail she seemed particularly grateful to impart.

'You've met John,' she said as she took him through to the large room at the front of the building where he wondered if he shouldn't have worn sunglasses. The place was like a fruit bowl. A tangerine corner sofa dominated the space, topped with cushions in lime and apple greens, pomegranate pinks, banana and citrus yellows mixed with splashes of white and turquoise in a mixture of fabrics and prints. He could hear the sales spiel now, the over-the-top language these interior designers might use to describe such things. But he took in the room with a degree of admiration, however begrudgingly. An array of the latest decorating magazines was neatly fanned out on a chunky wooden coffee table that held all manner of drawers and compartments. Between the windows, a collection of photographs on canvas were set at angles; a tantalising glimpse of what this business could achieve. There was even a stylish play area for children with paint pots, brushes, sheets of wallpaper samples and crayons. It wasn't his thing, but Aidan couldn't help but be impressed. As he left, he spotted a series of framed parchments and a photograph of John with Colette and another man outside a building he didn't recognise. A third designer perhaps? Surely there wasn't enough money in that line of work to keep three of them in jobs.

'Nice premises you've got there,' he said as they drove off.

'Thanks,' said Colette. It was the height of their conversation as they made their way across town to collect Gerry.

'Not a bad day for a trip to the country,' said Gerry, breaking the in-car silence as he hopped into the back of the Land Rover. 'I brought a couple of CDs.'

Aidan smiled. At least one of his passengers would make the trip easy.

By the time they reached the bustling town of Clonakilty, Colette had had all she could take of the best of the eighties and almost begged for a toilet stop. When she came out of the restrooms at the service station, the lads were loaded up with coffees, sandwiches, crisps and a selection of chocolate bars. *I despair*, she thought, as she purchased a wholemeal salad sandwich, a spring water and a skinny coffee.

'Is that all you're having?' asked Gerry as they made their way back to the car.

'It's plenty,' she answered, glowering at his collection of edible sins. 'And I'll sit in the back, if you don't mind.'

Gerry didn't argue. She left them to their munchies and talk of football and plugged her earphones into her phone.

It was noon when they turned into the O'Shea property in Crookhaven. The farm gate looked to Colette like it might have been left open decades ago and become rooted by the entanglement of weeds that grew about its lower bars. A huge oak stood proud above it, new leaves waving in the sea breeze.

She lowered her window and breathed in the heady scented mix of sea and countryside.

'Here we are,' Aidan announced as they rounded the bumpy dirt track of a driveway and his grandmother's house came into view.

'A beautiful place,' said Gerry dreamily.

Colette was in no doubt his impression of the house was biased by the rose-tinted glasses that were memories of Ellen. Beautiful wasn't the word she'd have chosen, but she kept that to herself. By the time they'd finished with the place, it would certainly be beautiful, but right now, she was looking at a rundown, two-hundred-year-old farmhouse destined to become another ruin in the verdant landscape if some serious renovations weren't undertaken.

'I'll take ye for a look around the outside first so,' said Aidan, pulling on a fleece jacket as he trudged along the front of the house.

Gerry followed with Colette bringing up the rear, cursing inwardly at having worn heels.

'The stonework is in good enough nick,' Gerry observed.

''Tis,' Aidan nodded. 'They were built to withstand the ravages of the wind and the rain. Grand houses as long as they're lived in.'

As they walked past long-discarded flower beds and rounded the gable end, Colette noticed the outbuildings; a couple of stone structures squashed together like mini semi-detached houses, a set of steps running up the side of one.

'What are *they* used for?' she asked, already thinking studio with mezzanine bedroom.

'They would have been used for storage or animals, the likes of a calving cow in bad weather,' Aidan answered.

'I didn't take much notice when I was here with Ellen,' said Gerry.

'Why doesn't that surprise us?' said Colette.

Gerry crossed his eyes at her.

'What are your plans for those buildings?' she called after Aidan.

'I haven't thought that far ahead yet.' He sounded somewhat exasperated. 'I'd prefer to concentrate on the house first.'

'They could be a goldmine, you know,' she persisted. 'They could be turned into self-catering apartments or a kind of studio.'

He ignored her and carried on inside. She would store her ideas for the outbuildings in the back of her mind for a time when Aidan O'Shea might be in better form, or at least open to discussion. She closed the back door behind her, but immediately thought better of it as she took in the small kitchen with its tile-effect linoleum, Formica presses and an ancient range that stood along the wall at the opposite end of the room. The table with mismatched chairs made her want to wince almost as much as the fusty smell made her want to puke. The only appealing feature was an old dresser with a collection of willow-patterned ware.

'All right if I leave the back door open . . . to let in a bit of light?' she asked.

'There's a light switch on your left hand there,' said Aidan. 'We do have electricity.'

She stifled a hasty response. She could hardly be guilty of sounding condescending for wanting to let in a bit of daylight.

'I'd like to see the room in natural light, that's all,' she said.

'Windows were dear things in my grandmother's time,' said Aidan before turning on his heel and proceeding with the tour.

In the narrow hallway, her feelings of claustrophobia only intensified. A couple of black-and-white photographs hung incongruously on the paisley-patterned wallpaper. The light from the transom above the front door allowed her to make out a bride and groom in one, and four immaculately dressed children in another. If she had her way, these relics would be given special treatment with intimate lighting for all to see and remember. These important members of the O'Shea family should be shown off, not left to gather dust in a house that was lost in a time warp.

'Are you getting any ideas?' asked Gerry as they stood in the parlour where fortunately the south-facing window allowed for a lighter, warmer atmosphere than that in the kitchen.

'There's an awful lot we could do here, lads, but it certainly won't be cheap.' Colette eyed the wear around the bevelled edges of the large mirror above the fireplace. 'You could gut the place and completely transform it.' Without turning, she could see Aidan's jaw set and his lips sealed tight. 'Or . . .' she went on, looking his reflection straight in the eye, 'we could try to preserve some of the more traditional elements of the house.' She watched as he breathed heavily, obviously forcing himself to listen. 'Take the fireplaces,' she continued. 'It would be criminal to lose them. I presume the bedrooms have them too.'

Aidan nodded stiffly.

'Oh, they have,' Gerry chipped in.

'Of course you'd know that,' said Colette with a smirk.

'Ah, will you leave me alone,' he laughed.

'Come on. Time is money,' said Aidan, disappearing upstairs.

'He's scared of his life you'll fleece him,' Gerry whispered to her as they left the parlour.

She made a silent 'Sh' at him, not wanting to annoy Aidan further by talking behind his back. But already a list was forming in her mind of all the things in the house that she would like to give the heave-ho, even before they got down to colour schemes and lighting arrangements. Like the sixties sofa in the parlour, plonked completely at odds with the time-worn leather chaise longue and the corner cabinet filled with a brass collection Lizzie O'Shea might have lovingly assembled over years. The threadbare carpet partially covering the steps of the narrow staircase was another case in point; Colette wondered if Miss Havisham herself wouldn't be there in one of the upper rooms to greet her, surrounded by silken cobwebs suspended in the dank air.

She was pleasantly surprised to find a spacious bedroom filled with light from a pair of windows almost reaching the floor from a coombed ceiling. A handmade bedspread was the first connection she'd felt with the former owner of the property. Its patchwork quilting demanded to be touched, and when she ran a hand over the soft fabric, both the quality and cleanliness surprised her. She sat on the edge of the bed and took in the different patterns on the peeling wallpaper behind the iron bedstead. Even the yellowed newspaper once used as lining was a piece of history. She thought to ask Aidan if this was indeed Lizzie O'Shea's marital bed, but sentiment wasn't something she wanted to indulge in with her friend's two-dimensional brother. She was admiring the vanity with hinged side mirrors that stood between the windows when Gerry popped his head around the door.

'The master bedroom.'

'I thought as much. Great lighting,' said Colette. 'I love her taste in accessories.'

She touched the handle of a ewer that sat in a matching basin of white ceramic with a motif of red and pink roses.

'There's probably a chamber pot in the same design under the bed,' Gerry mocked.

Aidan appeared stony-faced beside him. 'Seen enough of this room?'

'Just trying to get a feel for the place,' said Colette. She brushed past the pair of them and went to look at the other bedrooms. Two were a decent size and had room for en-suites, but the small boxroom wasn't the type of room you'd offer a paying customer even after a makeover.

'What's the loft space like?' She took the delay in Aidan's response as his signature resistance to her ideas. 'Can you stand up in it?' she persisted.

His feet shuffled along the landing. 'What do you want to go up there for?'

'Well, I'm thinking if you put a small staircase up through here, it might make a nice living space.' She caught him glancing at Gerry and was grateful her old school mate's open expression didn't waver.

'You'll have this bigger than Ben Hur if you're not careful,' said Aidan, but he took a chair from under the window and, standing up on it, pushed at the hatch.

There was a scratching sound as something ran across the floor above them. Colette and Gerry exchanged a worried look, but Aidan was undeterred. He took a hefty bunch of keys from a belt loop and found the attached torch, which he shone up into the loft space. Colette could see the top of the house. It looked promising, but what would they do with it? Aidan wouldn't as much as give the loft conversion idea a second thought without his sister's say so. Colette needed Ellen to make some decisions.

They moved downstairs to the bathroom off the hallway, opposite the parlour. Colette grimaced at the avocado suite.

'Very eighties,' she said aloud.

'I helped put that in myself,' said Aidan. 'Granny thought she was made once she got the inside toilet.'

Colette turned to see his face redden at the candid slip. Although in her mind's eye, she'd already changed the entire layout and colour scheme of the room, she decided to leave this one for later.

Back in the kitchen, she took out her laptop. 'Can I have your dimensions, Aidan? I can put in the details as we're here, to save time.'

'Give me a sec.' He left to retrieve the manila folder from the Land Rover.

With Aidan out of earshot, Colette turned to Gerry, who was looking through the utensils that hung over the range.

'What is it with that guy?' she asked. 'He doesn't want me involved, does he?'

'Aw, don't worry about him,' Gerry shrugged. 'He's a bit old school. Seen some tough times in the building trade. Probably sees your services as a bit over the top.' He came and sat beside her and looked at the computer screen.

'Is that what you think too, Gerry?'

He put a hand on her shoulder, turned her toward him and looked her in the eye. 'Colette Barry, you and I go back a long way. You know if I thought you were full of shite, I'd tell you. Now get on with the job you're good at and leave Aidan to myself and Ellen.'

She gave him a playful elbow in the ribs and signed in to her design program. When Aidan reappeared with his tattered folder, she had the distinct impression she was being shown the plans only grudgingly.

'C'mon, Gerryo, there's some real work to be done outside,' he said, and was gone before Colette could respond.

'Ignore him,' Gerry told her before leaving her to the work for which the man obviously had no appreciation.

I'm doing this for you, Ellen, she told herself as she began to input all of Aidan's measurements and prepared to add a few of her own. He hadn't thought of things like window proportions, but then she couldn't imagine he'd ever installed a blind or hung a curtain in his life. As she went about the house again, armed with tape measure and camera this time, she began to relax. Work mode suited her. And besides, the house had character. Even if one of the clients was a grumpy bugger, she would do her best to restore the old farmhouse to its former glory.

—

It was after five when Aidan dropped her back to Fabulous Four Walls. There'd been silence in the car since Gerry had jumped out at The Stables.

'Thanks,' she said as she gathered up her bag and camera. 'I'll get some proposals to you as soon as poss.'

'Right,' said Aidan, idling the engine. 'There's no rush. It'll be weeks before we even get the extension started.'

'I'm no architect, but I have a few ideas about the external renovations I'd like you to consider.'

Aidan kept a hand on the gear stick, not bothering to put on the handbrake.

'I'll email them to yourself and Ellen.'

'Right so.' He revved the engine.

—

John was shutting down his computer for the night when Colette came into the office and sank into the tangerine sofa.

'How was your day in the country?' he asked.

'Next question.' She grabbed a cerise velour cushion and hugged it to her chest.

'Oh, like that, was it?' said John. 'I thought this was going to be your pet project, helping out an old friend and all that.'

'My friend is one thing,' said Colette. 'Her brother is another.'

'Anything you want to tell Uncle John about?' He joined her on the sofa.

'Sorry, John. I'm not being very professional, am I?' She cast the cushion to one side and sat up.

'It's not like you, sweetheart. I'm usually the one bitching about difficult clients.'

Colette had to smile. 'Yes, but you enjoy it. I just try to see past their foibles and concentrate on their homes.'

He put a hand on his heart in indignation. 'As do I, Miss Perfect.' When she didn't rise to the comment, he searched her face. 'So, what's so special about Bob the Builder that he's got my little protégé a trifle flustered?'

'Oh, he's just a pain in the butt. Nothing a good ten-k run won't cure.' She stood up and straightened her slim-fitting shirt over her trousers.

'Mm . . . you go, girl.' John gathered his suit jacket and man bag. 'You okay to lock up or will I wait for you?'

'I've got it,' said Colette. 'See you in the morning.'

Returning emails and uploading photos would just have to wait. Colette needed two things right now: fresh air and a home-cooked meal. If it wasn't for her mother, she might never feed herself properly. With the office locked behind her, she went through the rear entrance to the car park.

'Fancy a drink?' came a voice from behind her.

She unlocked her car before turning to tell Declan Byrne for the hundredth time that she was not interested in going for a drink with him or any other man on the planet.

'No harm in asking,' he said as she drove off. The balding middle-aged dentist waved at her as she took the corner at a speed just slow enough to catch his hang-dog expression.

In Mayfield, Colette set down her work bag and threw her jacket over a chair before grabbing a glass and filling it to overflowing at her mother's kitchen sink.

'Tough day at the office?' Her mother picked up the jacket and slipped it on a hanger she'd taken from one of the coat hooks near the side door.

'You can say that again.' Colette tilted her head back and emptied the glass in three swallows. 'Okay if I go for a run before dinner?'

'You know you don't have to ask my permission,' said her mother. 'Haven't even thought about dinner yet. Got caught up in my sewing and lost track of time. Just as well you roared up the driveway when you did.'

'Was it that bad? The neighbours will think I'm a lunatic.'

'Oh, most of them know you of old,' her mother smiled. 'It's only the new ones you'll surprise.'

Barbara Barry had lived in the housing estate all her married life and would die here 'when her number was up' as she liked to tell her daughters. Although she'd grown used to her own company after her husband died, she'd welcomed Colette back into the family home without any demands about how long she might stay or how they might run the house together. In fact, the only time they'd butted heads was when Colette had suggested they upgrade the seventies décor. She'd decided early on to leave the interior designer at work, grateful that her mother was good enough to give her a roof over her head while she sorted herself out.

Colette shook her head as she placed her glass in the sink. Her mother was a tolerant woman. It couldn't be easy living with the more challenging of the two children she'd raised to grow up, move out and have families of their own. That was how it was supposed to happen. The plan had worked beautifully for a while. The girls left school, went to third level, got jobs. Colette met Tadgh, Grace met Ben. Colette married Tadgh, Grace married Ben. Grace and Ben had children and lived happily ever after. At least her mother's dreams had come true for one of her daughters. She gave Barbara a hug.

'Thanks, Mum.'

Barbara patted her arm. 'Don't mention it, love.'

Colette headed out onto Ballyhooly Road to begin her usual loop around the eastern suburbs. Adele songs from the iPod strapped to her arm helped set a pace she could maintain over ten kilometres. As she ran, her training program played over in her mind. Tomorrow would be her weekly pool session, and the weekend would bring at least another run, possibly a half-marathon if she was feeling good. She'd always kept herself fit. In fact, at one stage in the 'desperately trying to have babies' phase of their marriage, Tadgh had accused her of overexercising to maintain her body image at the expense of falling pregnant. With gritted teeth, she took the incline where the road bent past emerald fields before descending into the leafy township of Glanmire. Although her circumstances had changed, Colette ran today for the same reason she ran then, to stay sane.

Chapter Three

Fern Murphy held the palm of her hand to the forehead of her six-year-old daughter who had climbed into the bed between herself and Rob at 4 a.m. She was hot. 'Right, chin up till I feel your glands.'

Aoife tilted her head of damp flattened curls and let her mother move her fingers under her jaw line where her glands were protruding like gobstoppers. Fern let out a deep sigh. There was no way this child could go to school. Spooning another dose of pain relief into her, Fern thought of her desk in the office of O'Shea Building and the to-do list the length of her arm that awaited her. Most of it could indeed wait, but the pays were due tomorrow. None of them, including herself and her husband, would be happy if their bank accounts weren't replenished on time. The mortgage they'd stretched themselves to afford was just one of the many bills that relied on their hard-earned money. Aoife looked pleadingly into her eyes.

'Do I have to go to school?'

Fern put a hand to her forehead again as Rob stuck his head round the bedroom door, their other two children in tow.

'Well, Aoife Chiquitita, are you getting up for school?' His voice was cheery, but he exchanged a doubtful look with Fern.

'No, Dad,' said Fern. 'There'll be no school for Aoife Chiquitita today.'

Rob came to the bed and kissed the pair of them, followed by his shadow, Sinead, who patted her small hand on her sister's arm.

'Have a nice duvet day with Mum,' she said in a tone well beyond her four years.

Their eldest, Liam, too cool to be infected by anything carried by one of his sisters, said his goodbyes from the hallway before telling his dad to get a move on or they'd be late. Rob gave Fern a wink as he took Sinead's hand and turned to follow Liam out the door. He was good like that, Fern mused, caring and capable when she needed to gear down from her usual superwoman speed. She phoned Aidan. There was no problem, he'd do the wages himself, she was to look after *the childeen*. He was a great boss; the best she'd ever had. He might be quiet, even a little gruff at times, but he had a kind heart. Why he wasn't married with kids of his own was a mystery. He wasn't gay. She'd known him to have a girlfriend; that Australian woman with the child she seemed to palm off on him whenever she needed a babysitter. It would have been easier to take a day off if he was a pain in the ass. For a moment, Fern considered whether he even knew how to do the wages on their new computer system, but then looking at Aoife, who had already fallen back to sleep beside her, she put thoughts of work out of her head and relaxed back against the pillows with her phone.

Flicking through Facebook, she skipped over the funny videos and recipes so as not to wake Aoife. Her mother-in-law had posted most of them. It had come as a bit of a shock to Fern that Mrs Murphy was even on Facebook, but the fact that she sat around all day posting didn't surprise her at all. In fact, it hadn't even occurred to Fern to ask the woman to babysit today, such was the big deal she made of any such requests. Jackie O'Flynn had posted a map with a flight path from Cork to London. She must be there again for another appointment with Ronan. They'd met in hospital nine years ago when Fern was having Liam and Jackie was having Saoirse. Ronan would have been two back then. Fern remembered him coming into the hospital; a gorgeous chubby child with the biggest pair of chocolatey-brown eyes she'd ever seen, bounding in and scrambling up onto Jackie's bed for a look at the baby. She could never have imagined him being anything other than perfectly healthy.

Good luck, Jackie, she typed. *Hope all goes well xx.* It felt inadequate, but what else could she say?

Setting the phone on the bedside table, Fern turned toward Aoife and slipped down under the duvet feeling grateful. Days like this were to be treasured. Bonus days together, riding out a passing fever. She said a silent prayer for Jackie O'Flynn. It was a different story having a child sick every day.

It was unusual for Ellen to open a wine bottle in the middle of the week, but the combination of a stressful afternoon spent trying to convince an old gentleman to consider residential care and coming home to an empty house seemed to necessitate the departure. Gerry would be busy with early customers and lunch preparations at The Stables. She tried Louise. No answer. Probably out with her university friends. *As it should be,* Ellen thought, remembering the nightly phone calls her daughter had made from Adelaide for months after Nick died, just to make sure she was okay. It had been a different story when Gerry had first visited and the secret she'd kept from both of them had come out. Louise had taken it hard and had kept her distance. But they'd worked it out. By the time Gerry returned to Australia earlier in the year, Louise had re-opened her heart and made him welcome. Yes, Constantinopoulos or Clancy, it didn't matter; Louise was a beautiful soul. Warmed by the thought, Ellen took her laptop to the sofa, set her wine glass on one of the nested tables and settled down to read the latest email from Colette.

Hi Ellen,

Just visited the property with Aidan and Gerry and have begun to put together some plans on how we might proceed (see attachments). Some of the designs incorporate Aidan's plans for the extension, but I would also like you to consider my ideas for the outbuildings. Although Aidan dismissed my interest in them, I feel their renovation is an integral part of the project. Without having been allowed access, I can't say for sure, but from experience of similar properties, I think they could provide an extra source of

income in terms of accommodation. On purely external assessment, I would guess there's room for two studio apartments if
not dormitory-style accommodation. This would cancel out the
need for extending the house, as Aidan proposes to do.

Please don't think I'm trying to tell you your business, but
at this stage, I feel you should outline the purpose you have in
mind for the buildings so that we can all be clear on what we
are doing and why.

I'm not even sure Aidan wants me on the project. Whatever
the reason, I'd be grateful if you could have a word. If you both
decide not to avail of my services, it won't come between us, Ellen.

Let me know your thoughts when you get a chance.

Colette

Ellen bristled at the comments about her brother, but set
them to one side, eager to see Colette's plans for the house.
She looked over each attachment in turn, a smile broadening
across her face. If Colette Barry could bring these plans to
fruition, Lizzie O'Shea's house would certainly have the wow
factor. Her friend had set up the images so that a photo of each
part of the house could be viewed alongside its corresponding
computer-generated makeover. Without this arrangement,
Ellen might not have believed that the proposed transform-
ations were possible. Decisions about colour and lighting
would all come later, as Colette explained, but already she'd
given a tantalising glimpse of what could be achieved: a tile-
floored kitchen with modern units, an island replacing the
old table, the addition of a conservatory providing ample

dining space with room for extras like an occasional table and a couple of easy chairs. In another slide, Ellen could see that Colette had dispensed with some of the furniture in the parlour. The space created by the changes was tangible. Even the light background of the designs made the hall, stairs and landing look brand new. Ellen was so excited, she wanted to call Colette straightaway and congratulate her. She reread the email. It was Aidan she needed to call.

Aidan grumbled at the computer screen. Fern had certainly picked her day to phone in with another sick child, leaving him to cover the wage payments on top of all the other tasks he'd rather pay someone else to do. He'd decided to let the voicemail kick in even before he took the mobile phone from his pocket, but when he saw Ellen's name on the display, his sense of brotherly responsibility changed his mind.

'How's she cuttin'?' he said, ready for a short, cheery chat to keep open the lines of family communication.

'Don't give me "How's she cuttin'?"' said Ellen. 'I've just had an email from Colette and I'm not happy.'

'Don't talk to me,' said Aidan, scanning the spreadsheet in front of him. 'That woman will have us bankrupt. Did you see the plans she has for the place?'

'Yes, that's exactly—' Ellen started, but Aidan cut her off.

'She even wanted to nose around in the outbuildings to see what grand designs she could do in there. Is it millionaires she thinks we are?'

'Hold it right there, Aidan O'Shea.'

His sister's audible intake of breath was enough to win his undivided attention.

'Are you sitting at your computer?' asked Ellen.

'I am,' he said. 'I'm just doing the wages.' He heard her do the deep-breath thing again and felt an earful coming on.

'Get into Google and type in Fabulous Four Walls.'

Aidan wished he'd let the machine take her rant, that Fern hadn't pulled a childcare day and that he'd never met Colette Barry, but he did what he was told, cursing every letter of the alphabet as he tapped his index fingers back and forth over the keyboard. The website flashed before him. He had to admit it had a professional, visually appealing format. The Georgian house on the North Mall looked resplendent as ever, as did the renovated rooms featured on the home page.

'Click on About Us,' said Ellen.

The familiar face of a smiling, flamboyant John Buckley appeared. Aidan quickly read the bio detailing John's experience in the interior-design industry in England and his move back to 'twenty-first century Ireland' after a long absence. Scrolling down, Aidan saw Colette. The hair was shorter, but the eyes held that steely determination of which Aidan was slightly in awe.

'Looking for a change in direction after many years as a Home Economics teacher,' he read half to himself, 'Colette decided to indulge her passion for home-improvement projects and signed up at London's most prestigious school of interior design. After gaining a diploma and valuable mentorship from lecturer and fellow Corkonian John Buckley, Colette agreed to return to her native city and help John set up shop at Fabulous Four Walls—'

'Right,' Ellen interrupted, 'look in the gallery.'

Aidan had a strong urge to say, 'So what?' after reading Colette's little life story, but didn't want to rankle his sister further. The photos of successful projects wafted across the screen in a slow slideshow of what he had to admit were impressive before and after shots like those he'd seen at the premises. Names of hotels and restaurants he'd been to, or at least had seen in the passing, were subtly placed at the bottom of each image. He let out a low whistle in admiration as a gym his workmates frequented came into view.

'They've even done that new fitness joint,' he began before another finished project appeared on screen. 'I didn't know they did that kind of thing to old people's homes.'

'Now, can you get off Colette's case and let her do her job?' asked Ellen.

Aidan huffed. 'It's still going to cost us a fortune.'

'And it will be money well spent,' said Ellen. 'Anyway, it's not our money. Don't you think we should leave the decision about whether we can afford Colette's services or not up to Dad?'

His sister had a point. 'Right,' he relented. 'I'll take the laptop with me tonight and talk him through her ideas.'

'Lovely. I'll let you get back to your wages.'

Chapter Four

Tracey broke into song as she poured them a wine after their night out at the high-school production of *My Fair Lady*. She swept round the kitchen table, past her son, Alfie, giving his burning cheek a quick pinch before handing Ellen a glass.

'Mum, you're *so* embarrassing,' said the thirteen-year-old.

'Oh come on, Alfie. You were in it. You know all the words,' Tracey pleaded before taking up 'All I Want is a Room Somewhere' where she'd left off.

Pete joined in, winking at his son as he grabbed a beer from the fridge. Tracey took her husband's arm and the pair proceeded round the table in something of a gavotte.

'You old ones are mental,' said Alfie. 'I'm going to bed.'

'Night, Alfie,' said Ellen. 'You were brilliant.'

'Night, darl',' called Tracey, mid-twirl under her husband's arm.

'That's it!' said Ellen. 'Tracey, you're a genius.'

Pete shook his head. 'Not sure what you're getting at there, matey.'

Tracey sent a swift blow to his midriff.

'What is it, Ellen?' They joined her at the table.

'Well . . . you know how I've been struggling with the pressure Colette in Ireland's been putting on me to come up with a plan for what exactly I want to do with my granny's old house?'

They both nodded.

'Well, who just wants a room somewhere? Who doesn't care if there's a golf course within walking distance or a gourmet restaurant down the road?' She watched their foreheads fall into synchronised frowns as they tried to form an answer. 'People who want to get away from wherever they are,' she continued, 'to get peace to do something, like someone writing a book, or someone needing time to themselves to recover from or reflect on something . . .'

She watched as Tracey and Pete looked at each other and then back at her.

'You mean like a cancer patient?' asked Tracey.

'Or someone who was thinking about divorce, but needed space to do it, alone?'

The suggestion earned Pete another nudge from his wife.

'A man might want to ponder it *alone*,' Tracey told him, 'but a woman would want to talk about it.'

'You're both right,' said Ellen. 'People do deal with things differently. But as a trained counsellor, I'd be on hand for the ones who did want someone to talk to.'

Their frowns dissipated.

'The place could be a kind of retreat for people to work through difficult issues in the comfort of a beautiful house,' said Pete.

'That's exactly it!' Ellen smiled. 'A room somewhere, far away from the demands of their day-to-day lives.'

'But how is that going to affect the renovations?' Tracey asked.

Within minutes, the three were huddled around the Pope family's computer, poring over Colette's email attachments. The dormitory-accommodation idea was first to be knocked on the head. They were all agreed the emphasis had to be on calm, comfortable surroundings, conducive to healing and productivity.

'She knows her stuff, your Colette,' said Pete. 'Makes me want to go all the way to Ireland to see the end result.'

'Don't you wish you were there to supervise, Ellen?' Tracey was serious.

'No, Tracey. It's in safe hands with Aidan. My place is here with Louise for now. I know she's in the city, but she still needs me to come home to.' She sipped her wine and shrugged. 'I'm only dreaming out loud. Anyway, can you imagine what it would be like to say goodbye to you two?'

Pete put an arm around her. 'We'll support you wherever you are, Ellen.'

She was indeed blessed to have such wonderful friends. Nick's death had been a wake-up call for all of them, a reminder that one never knew what might happen next.

Aidan stopped short at his father's front door, remembering to ring the bell rather than use the key as he'd always done before neighbour-from-hell Frances Brady had inveigled her way into their family home.

Bill O'Shea came to the door in his slippers. 'Frances is at the bingo,' he said before he'd even closed the door behind them.

'Oh, right.' Aidan tried not to sound relieved. His mother, God rest her, had been a battle-axe, but after years of what might have been widower bliss, Bill appeared to have gone from the frying pan into the fire.

They put the kettle on to boil and sat in the kitchen where Aidan cranked up his laptop and found the file he'd saved with Colette's proposals. Bill was as impressed by the technological advances as he was with Colette's skills in interior design.

'Amazing what they can do nowadays with all the apps and what have you,' he enthused. Aidan wasn't convinced his father knew what an app was, but nodded in agreement.

'Have a good look at the costings, Dad.' He drew his father's attention to a spreadsheet in which Colette had outlined the estimated costs. 'We don't want to be ripped off.'

'I don't think there's any fear of that, son. Colette's a lovely girl. Haven't we known her since she was a nipper?' He put on his reading glasses and moved in closer to the screen.

As he talked his father through the options, Aidan found himself looking more closely at the plans than when he'd first seen the email and had given them only a cursory scan. For each area of the house, Colette had included three alternatives, ranging from cheap and cheerful to better quality durable materials.

'By God, she's thorough, I'll give her that,' said Bill as he continued to scroll down the document. 'The kitchen is the biggest outlay of course, with that conservatory.'

'We don't have to go for top-dollar stuff just because she suggested it, Dad. The more we spend, the bigger cut she'll get from the whole thing.'

His father scrolled down to the bottom. 'Says here she'll charge a fixed fee for her services regardless of what we get her to source for the place.' He removed his glasses and turned to Aidan with a look of satisfaction in his smiling eyes. 'Didn't I tell you she's a lovely girl? One of our own.'

This was high praise from Bill O'Shea, and Aidan knew better than to argue. Now that Colette had managed to win over both Ellen and their father, it looked like he was outnumbered.

'Let's have a cuppa and take another look at the drawings,' said Bill, putting his glasses back on and peering at the computer. 'That Computer Aided Design thing is amazing.'

Aidan sighed and got up to make the tea.

—

Colette took the short walk to the hospital where she'd agreed to meet Grace at the end of her shift, nursing in casualty. She had a spring in her step, content in the knowledge that the job in Crookhaven was hers now that Ellen and Mr O'Shea had come to a decision on what they wanted her to do. *Majority rules*, she thought, putting Aidan's misgivings to the back of her mind.

'It's going to be awesome,' she told Grace as they sat in a nearby café, grateful for the afternoon lull. 'Ellen wants to set the place up as a retreat, possibly offering her services as a counsellor to those who want it, or just a get-away-from-it-all for those who don't.'

'Is she any good, as a counsellor I mean?' Grace asked, ever the practical sister.

'Well, she's a very experienced social worker,' said Colette. 'I'm sure she's come across most of life's issues.' She stirred the froth on her coffee as one or two issues of her own came to mind.

'Ben could recommend her at the surgery,' Grace suggested.

'I'll keep you updated,' said Colette, 'but I think the business is a long-term plan. Right now, she's just happy for us to get on with the renovations.' She looked around the café to make sure no one was eavesdropping. 'To be honest, I'd like to see that job out of the way sooner rather than later.'

'I thought you loved that house.' Grace looked puzzled.

'I do, I do. It's a great project, challenging and everything . . .'

Grace was waiting.

'It's just a few . . . personnel problems,' Colette conceded.

'Who is he and where does he live?'

'You don't know him.' Colette fiddled with her spoon, but Grace's eyes were boring into her. 'It's the builder.'

'Ooh. Sounds a tad tricky to me.' The whirring of the cogs in Grace's brain were almost audible as she cut into her chocolate-laden crepe and drew a forkful to her mouth. 'Isn't he Ellen's brother?' she asked before devouring it.

'Yes, but it's a job,' said Colette, straightening her back. 'I've got to stay professional and just get on with it.'

'Sounds like this project could be all the edited-out bits of *Grand Designs*,' Grace laughed.

'Don't even go there,' Colette warned, her shoulders sinking again. 'We've hardly started, and he hates my guts.'

Grace reached out a hand and squeezed her arm. 'Colette, he might be the builder, but I bet he knows diddly squat about home décor. You show him how it's done, girl.'

Colette smiled. She knew Grace meant well, but the importance of a good relationship between builder and designer couldn't be underestimated when it came to a project like this one, and she and Aidan hadn't exactly got off to the best of starts. She drained her coffee.

'Don't you have kids to collect and a feast to prepare or something?'

'Ben's finishing early today. He's got it all under control. Anyway, I'm allowed time off to keep tabs on my sister, Ireland's rising star of interior design.'

That was Grace, her number one fan. No matter how bad things got, Grace was there to encourage and support her. It should have been the other way round. Weren't big sisters supposed to pave the way for the small ones? No, Grace was definitely the role model when it came to doing life. She'd married a good husband, had three wonderful children, held down a stressful job and managed to make it all look like a walk in the park.

Sometimes, just sometimes, Colette wished her world could be as black and white as her sister's.

Chapter Five

Aidan lay thrown on the couch, watching Man United thrash Arsenal in a football game in which he had only a mild interest. It hadn't always been the case, but these days he found himself disliking television. He'd like to have gone to the fridge and opened a bottle of beer, but Millie would be on her way. *A little early in the day anyway,* he thought. Dragging himself off the couch, he straightened the cushions and gathered up the cup and plate from where he'd eaten lunch at the coffee table. In the kitchen, he washed up the dishes that had been piling up for a couple of days. He cleared open food packages away into cupboards and shoved empty cans and takeaway coffee cups into the bin. Taking a wet cloth, he wiped down all the surfaces until he was satisfied the place was clean enough for Millie's arrival and Jane's approval. As he glanced around the kitchen of the house he'd renovated for himself, the thought of what Colette Barry might make of the place crossed his mind. He shook his head and returned to the game, happy to have driven the fleeting thought from his mind.

—

Fern Murphy turned from the driveway border where she was planting out the petunias she'd lovingly germinated in the warmth above her fridge.

'I worry about Aidan, you know.'

Rob wasn't at all worried about his boss. No, Aidan would be engrossed in the match Rob wished he was watching instead of slaving here, building a bloody deck on a Saturday that felt like a busman's holiday.

'Do you think he'll ever meet someone?' Fern interrupted the steady work of her trowel to look at him when he failed to respond. 'Are you listening to me?' she called in a voice loud enough to be heard by the neighbours.

'Of course, love.' Rob took a pencil from behind his ear and marked his next cut on a length of wood. 'I'm just not sure what you want me to say. Isn't it Aidan's business whether he wants to put himself out there or not?'

Fern put her hands on her hips and blew at a wisp of blonde hair that had escaped its ponytail. 'I'm just wondering, that's all. I can't help wanting the best for a nice fella like him. He'd be great company for someone.' She moved her knee-pad a few feet along and set to work again.

'Maybe he's happy as he is,' Rob offered without interrupting the careful measuring of another post. 'Not all men want to settle down with the wife and two-point-five kids . . .' He didn't need to hear her heavy sigh to know he'd given the wrong answer. As much as he loved her, Rob knew Fern was a meddling matchmaker at heart. Ever since they'd got hitched, she'd wanted the whole world to share in her idea of marital bliss. Aidan O'Shea just happened to be the latest, as yet unsuspecting, subject of her wily ways.

'Why don't we invite himself and Sarah over for dinner?' she asked.

Screams resounded from the back garden. For once, Rob was delighted to go and referee the fight that had broken out between their darlings.

—

Fern bedded the remaining plants, tongue clenched between her teeth in concentration as she thought about Sarah Grainger, the single secretary who worked in the cash-and-carry warehouse along from the builder's yard. She'd wandered along there when she'd started at Aidan's two years before, looking for a female companion to lunch with. She and Sarah took their break together most days and occasionally Sarah would babysit when the Murphy rellies were unavailable. Although Fern did most of the talking over the sandwiches they ate at the back of Sarah's office, she concluded from their chats that her lunch buddy was lonely and looking for a man. So what if she was a bit plain? Fern was a dab hand with a make-up brush. Anyway, it wasn't as if Aidan were Brad Pitt.

—

Jane and Millie arrived just as the match went into penalties. Aidan told himself he'd only been half-watching it anyway as he went to let them in.

'Hello ladies,' he said, winking at Jane, who was looking well in her hotel manager's uniform with a little make-up and a fresh haircut if he wasn't mistaken. He smiled down at Millie, who was holding one arm outstretched to show off a bulging freezer bag. 'That wouldn't be bread for the ducks you have there, Mills?'

Jane stepped through the doorway, stretching up to give him what had become the customary peck on the cheek he'd prefer to have been a kiss. She pushed past him and proceeded to his kitchen to unload her cooler bag before he'd even asked them in.

'So, it's the Atlantic Pond for us, Millie?'

A girl of few words, Millie nodded enthusiastically, a set of loose braids bobbing up and down behind her.

'Come on so till we see what instructions your mam has for me.'

Aidan's heart leapt a little as he felt her small hand grasp his own.

Jane was on a roll as usual. 'I made a quinoa and vege-table bake you can warm up for tea,' she said, holding up one of a selection of plastic containers. 'Sugar-free chocolate cake for dessert if you still have room in your tummies,' she went on, pointing to another. Aidan and Millie exchanged a conspiratorial glance as she gave them instructions on how to cook the veggie sticks she'd cut and coated herself with what

Aidan imagined were the most joyless ingredients known to man. In the three years he'd known her, the fact that he was not vegetarian and never would be had never seemed to sink in with Jane. But it was one of the foibles he'd been willing to overlook in the romantic phases of their on–off relationship. Without the romance, they seemed magnified. He shook away the thought. Maybe one of these nights, he'd cook a vegetarian special himself and the romance would return.

'Late shift tonight?' he ventured when Millie had skipped off to deposit her gear in the spare bedroom.

Jane hugged the empty cooler bag to her chest, letting the air out of it.

'Bryce is over,' she began without looking up. The ensuing silence was broken only by the zip she drew firmly round the top of the bag.

Aidan's mouth opened to say something, but he just stood there, watching her long fingers working the bag into neat folds. She'd appeared with a black eye after Bryce's last visit, insisting she'd walked into a door.

'He's staying at a mate's, but we thought we'd go out for a bit when I'm finished work.'

'Are you sure you'll be okay?'

'He's not that bad, Aidan,' she huffed. 'And anyway, he always gives me a wad of cash to help with Millie.'

Aidan shrugged. Jane Donovan had a life he really knew very little about. The father of her child was back on the scene and he had no right to interfere. The vegetarian special would have to be put on hold.

Aidan smiled to himself as he lifted Millie's feather-like weight from the back seat of the Land Rover and set her and her fairy wings on the pavement. Armed with her bag of bread, she skipped along, telling him to hurry up or the ducks would be gone. He held her hand to steady her as she climbed over the low wall that bordered one end of the Atlantic Pond. The late spring sunshine bathed the lush green oasis, the last of the year's snow drops and daffodils nodding in the breeze. Millie was first to spot a group of mallard ducks riding the ripples at the water's edge. Unclasping Aidan's hand, she started to run, before realising she'd disturbed them and proceeding on tiptoe, carefully opening the bag as quietly as was possible for an excited seven-year-old.

They took turns throwing bits of the stale bread, Millie intent on sharing her donation equally among the birds.

An elderly man passed them with his dog. 'Great day for it,' he said.

'Indeed it is,' Aidan replied. As he watched the man make his way round the contour of the lake, an inner voice nagged at him. *That'll be you, if you're not careful, a lonely old bachelor.* He shook his head. He had no evidence to suggest the man was either lonely or a bachelor, but given the history of his own love life or lack thereof, it wasn't hard to imagine how he himself might fit the bill in years to come.

'Can we watch a movie tonight?' Millie asked as she emptied the last of the bread over the edge, twelve beaks scrabbling for the spoils. Folding the bag neatly just like her mother had done with the cooler, she looked up at him with those piercing blue eyes. 'Can we go to McDonald's on the way home?'

Aidan put on as surprised a face as he could muster. 'Millie Donovan, what would your mother say if I let you eat that stuff?'

She let out a deep sigh. He hoped those tears smarting at the corners of her eyes were from the wind and not from him denying her junk food. God knows, he'd love to go there right now and sink his teeth into one of those bacon burgers, especially knowing what he was facing when he got home.

'Tell you what,' he said, stooping down and taking the bag from her. 'Why don't we pick up some munchies for the movie at the garage? Your mother didn't say we had to eat her dessert.'

She flung her skinny arms round his neck. 'I love you, Aidan.'

He suspected the outburst had as much to do with the uncertainty of the situation with her parents as it did with their own relationship, but he was happy to be there for Millie Donovan in any capacity. It was the closest he'd ever get to a child of his own, no doubt. Yes, his own children were a dream that had died a long time ago. Minding Millie now and then would have to do. That child had him wrapped around her finger. If she'd asked him to hand her down the moon, he'd have had a go.

Rob knew better than to arrive home without having asked Aidan to dinner the following weekend. If Fern had told him once, she'd told him five times that morning as she stood in her pyjamas, hair a-frizz, working methodically through the morning ritual of waking, feeding and organising their children for school and daycare. With an eight o'clock start, he got to work an hour before her. On a good day, he was out on site and didn't see her until the evening. Sometimes Rob wished his boss had given the job to someone else. There was no doubt his wife had all the necessary skills to run the office of a builder's yard, but why did it have to be the one where he worked?

'Did you ask him?' It was her first question when she got out of her car, transformed by make-up and a smart outfit that covered up the ravages her body had endured through three difficult births and what had seemed to Rob like years of incessant breastfeeding. His cheeks burned in a mixture of attraction and embarrassment. At least she hadn't kissed him, which she often did, much to the entertainment of his workmates.

In the van on the way to an extension job in Blackrock, Aidan agreed to the dinner date.

'Ah, you're a lucky man, Robbo. Fern is a gem. If it wasn't for her, I'd have been out of business by now.'

Rob wanted to tell his boss he was being set up, but Aidan was on a roll and Rob hadn't the heart to dash the positive image of Fern.

'They say the best publicity is word of mouth,' Aidan was saying, 'and I know Fern gives our place a good plug whenever she gets an opportunity.'

It wasn't like Aidan to gush, but Rob had to admit he had a point. Fern's optimism was at times misguided, but she always saw the glass as half full. Maybe it wouldn't hurt to have him round. The Sarah Grainger thing might even prove him wrong about Fern's matchmaking skills.

When they pulled into the petrol station on Church Road, Rob couldn't help noticing the two-litre bottle of cola and king-size chocolate bar Aidan purchased in addition to the mayonnaise-laden baguette, all of which had come to comprise his usual lunchtime meal.

'It's not that hard a job, is it?' Rob joked, nodding toward the items in Aidan's hands.

'What do you mean?'

'Calories in, calories out,' said Rob.

Aidan looked puzzled.

'The body is like a car,' Rob continued as they walked back to the van. 'You put in as much fuel as you need to run it. No more, no less.' He could hear the preachy tone he'd wanted to avoid. 'That's what Fern says anyway.' It was a copout, but Fern was more prone to giving advice.

'Oh right,' said Aidan, pulling his jeans over his belly flab before he got in. Rob hoped he hadn't made him feel too self-conscious.

—

At The Stables, Gerry and Colette exchanged news of Ellen while they waited for Aidan.

'The visa could take months,' Gerry explained. 'The paperwork alone was a marathon to complete.'

'It'll all be worth it when you get there,' said Colette. 'I think you're very brave.'

Aidan appeared in his plaster-spattered fleece and took a seat opposite Colette at their booth in the lounge.

'So, how is it all going in West Cork?' Gerry asked.

'I've freed up next week,' said Aidan, 'to spend a few days down there and do that big job taking out the wall in the kitchen to make way for the conservatory.'

Colette bristled. It had been her impression that she would be made aware of the scheduling of any major work well in advance. Her diary was already full for next week, so he would have carte blanche down there.

'Where are you sourcing the conservatory?' she asked, her tone clipped.

Details, that's what she needed, before the whole project ran away from her and she was left with nothing but cushions and curtains. The company he named wasn't the one she'd recommended.

'Yours were a bit dear,' said Aidan in his own defence.

Colette pulled the laptop toward her and found their website before pushing it between them again. 'Let's just check, shall we?'

The burning of Aidan's cheeks was almost tangible. The conservatory he was planning to install was just two-thirds the size of the one they'd agreed with Ellen and her father. For such a significant feature of the house, this attempt at cost-cutting was, to Colette, simply unacceptable. She continued to the website of the company she'd already liaised with and who'd given her reasonable quotes. There was no doubt hers was the superior option. More glazing meant more light. If there was one thing that kitchen needed, it was serious sunlight. Putting anything other than a glass roof on the conservatory wouldn't be worth the effort.

'I'd say that's the way to go, all right,' said Gerry without taking his eyes from the screen.

Colette set her jaw and looked at Aidan. He raised his hands in surrender.

'Okay, I'll cancel it, but your crowd better have their shit together by the time I get the foundations in.'

Colette crossed her fingers under the table, not convinced her contact would have enough time to deliver, but she'd scored a point and besides, everyone knew that delays were inevitable on a building project.

Chapter Six

The smells wafting from the kitchen put paid to any reservations Aidan might have had about Fern's cooking.

'Come and have a drink,' she said, taking his jacket and hanging it on a hallstand already laden with coats and what might be enough handbags to open a shop. She led him through to the open-plan living area where Rob stood in an apron, stirring a pot on an island hob. A woman he didn't recognise sat in a creamy leather sofa. Her electric-blue dress and high heels made him glad he'd worn a decent shirt.

'I didn't know you were a closet Nigella,' Aidan joked.

'One of my hidden talents,' said Rob with a shy smile.

Aidan thought to join Rob and perch himself on one of the smart stools at the island when Fern came at him with a glass of red wine and took him by the elbow.

'This is my friend Sarah,' she said, steering him to the mammoth sofa. Aidan shook hands and surveyed the unfamiliar face. The make-up was similar to Fern's, but only in quantity of application as opposed to enhancement of natural beauty. It reminded him of the eighties when the girls in his class put on that garish eye shadow in blues and pinks for school discos. He didn't think it made an awful lot of difference; the good-looking girls still ended up with the good-looking boys.

'Have a seat there,' said Fern, 'while I give Rob a hand with dinner.'

He did as he was told.

'Do you work, yourself?' he said by way of making conversation with the stranger who up to now had only smiled at him. When she answered, Aidan felt himself having to lean in to hear properly. The word 'mouse' sprang to mind. He wasn't exactly loud himself, but this was painful. He wondered where the children were. They'd have been better company.

'They're at my mother's,' Rob informed him when he gave up trying to get Sarah talking and turned to his friend for conversation.

'We're having a night off,' said Fern, slipping an arm around her husband's waist and puckering up her glossy lips for a kiss.

Aidan examined the pattern on the shag-pile rug at his feet. The hostess had no doubt started on the wine before he'd arrived. *This might be a long night*, he thought as he tried again to engage Sarah in conversation.

'Dinner is served,' Rob announced.

'You've gone to so much trouble,' said Aidan. Glad to be off the sofa, he admired the gleaming white dinner service and turquoise tablecloth and napkins. Even the cutlery was matching, every piece placed in symmetry. Fern was no doubt the driving force in the family, but Aidan knew that Rob was the perfectionist. His attention to detail was why he'd taken him on in the first place. It had never occurred to him that those skills would extend to the kitchen.

The perfectly cooked rice and tender chicken made Rob's curry a main course to die for. With a few glasses of wine in him, Aidan forgot about the strain of trying to be polite in the presence of Sarah Grainger and helped himself to seconds.

'I hope you're not thinking of giving up the day job,' he said to Rob.

'That usually means you're rubbish, Aidan, but I'll take it as a compliment,' Rob laughed. 'Have you enough there, Sarah?'

It was obvious from the barely touched portion on her plate, the woman didn't share Aidan's enthusiasm for the food.

'It's lovely,' she said in a voice that made Aidan want to burst out laughing. He shook his head and reloaded his fork with succulent saucy vegetables before stabbing another piece of the chicken and coating the lot with as much rice as would stick.

'Mm . . .' he groaned with pleasure.

'Don't forget to leave room for dessert,' Fern warned. There was an awkward pause.

'Don't worry, boy,' said Rob. 'It's automatic. She says it to the kids all the time.' He winked at his wife, but Aidan couldn't help thinking Fern had meant what she'd said.

'Come and I'll show you what we've done to the place,' said Rob, gesturing for Aidan to follow him once they'd finished. 'Might even squeeze in a quick game of pool.'

'As if you two don't spend enough time together,' Fern laughed, pouring herself another wine and trying to persuade Sarah to join her.

Aidan wasn't a huge fan of touring other people's houses. Bricks and mortar was one thing, but looking over personal items wasn't something he enjoyed. He cringed as Rob enthused over the wonderful job Fern had done in choosing all manner of light fittings and space-saving devices to furnish their home. There was no doubt everything matched, and it was obvious the woman had done some significant housework to make the home of five look pristine for their guests, but Aidan was grateful to get to the games room and just shoot some pool.

'The kids love it,' said Rob.

Aidan imagined only one of Rob's children could probably see over the table, but kept the observation to himself.

'So, what do you think of Fern's pal, Sarah?' Rob asked when he was a few points up.

'She's nice enough, I suppose,' said Aidan, paying more attention to lining up his next shot than to Rob's query.

'Fern's afraid you'll be left on the shelf,' said Rob, grinning as Aidan missed.

'What is it about women? They can't leave a single man alone.'

As he sized up the table, Rob drew the chalk over the tip of his cue and blew off the residual dust. 'She's got your best interests at heart,' he said before sending a spot swerving past its intended pocket. 'Bugger!'

Aidan leaned his belly on the table and took aim at an awkward stripe.

'You're not getting any younger,' said Rob, as much to psych him out as to help Fern's cause.

'Or any better looking,' Aidan quipped before driving the ball into the pocket.

'Ooh, nice one!' Rob stood back to let his boss take another shot. Fern would kill him if he hadn't gleaned a little information of a romantic nature from this pool game, but right now, they were level. Rob had his male pride to defend. Five matches in with his new toy and he was undefeated. This romance business could wait.

When they came back to the dining table, Fern was moving the fresh flowers Sarah had brought to make space for a sumptuous-looking tiramisu.

'Chaaam-pi-oh-ohn,' Rob cheered as they pulled out their chairs and resumed their positions for dessert. 'Commiserations, bud.' He raised his glass to Aidan.

'Don't mind him,' said Fern. 'Just look at it as an excuse for a rematch. We'll have to have you over more often.' She took a pearly white bowl and served him a portion of the dessert. 'And you as well, Sarah,' she added, looking at Aidan.

He mustered a gracious smile. As much as Fern's efforts at getting him off the shelf annoyed him, it was nearly worth it for the top nosh. He helped himself to cream.

'You two are like the dynamic duo,' he told them. 'You wouldn't get this in Ballymaloe.'

'I've actually done a cooking course there,' said Sarah, 'and I have to say I agree with you, Aidan.' It was the longest sentence she'd uttered all night, a fact that wasn't lost on the other two. They looked at her in awe as she explained what was involved in the week-long course at the renowned cookery school in East Cork.

'No man would go hungry with you around, eh, Sarah?' Fern giggled and sneaked a wink to the men.

'I go more for quality than quantity,' said Sarah with eyes fixed on Aidan, who was helping himself to seconds again. There was an audible silence as the comment cut through the atmosphere like a knife through butter.

'Well, Robbo,' said Aidan, undeterred, 'if the building goes completely to the wall, they might have a job for you down there.' He laughed at his own joke and carried on eating, aware of the look of consternation exchanged between his hosts.

As the couple began to clear the table, Rob suggested they watch a film he'd downloaded, but Sarah made excuses to leave. Aidan caught Fern nudging Rob from behind the island where they were piling the dirty dishes.

'You could give Aidan a lift . . .' Rob began, 'save him paying for a taxi later on like.'

'You wouldn't mind, would you, Sarah?' said Fern.

Left with no great choice, Sarah agreed to give Aidan a ride home. By now, he was beginning to sway a little. 'Thanks very much,' he slurred as he brushed the lock of hair off his face and made a production of hoisting his good trousers over his belly and tucking in his shirt. Just as well he'd loosened the belt when he'd gone to the bathroom halfway through the meal.

In the hallway, Fern helped him into his jacket, which his arms couldn't quite negotiate.

'Thanks for a great night,' he told her, bending down and planting a kiss on her cheek. He swirled round toward the front door where Rob was shaking Sarah's hand and thanking her for coming.

'Have fun,' was the last thing he heard from Fern as he put a hand around Sarah's shoulder more to steady himself than express any particular interest in the woman.

'What's the rush?' he asked as he held on tighter for fear she might get away from him. He didn't trust himself to stay upright if he let her go.

She gave a loud sigh as they got to her car. Aidan leaned against the passenger door of the blue Fiesta and looked back at the house. Rob was giving him the thumbs-up and Fern was gesturing to him like she was trying to herd chickens into a coop. He opened the car door and plonked himself in beside his chauffeur. The whiff of pine air freshener did not sit well with a stomach full of curry, tiramisu and wine. He swallowed hard.

'Where am I taking you?' asked Sarah.

'Your place or mine?' he joked.

'Seriously.' There was an edge to her tone Aidan thought better than to ignore. He gave her his address. God, this woman was hard work. Maybe she could do with a night out with a fellow like him, an honest, down-to-earth builder. As she turned onto Church Road, he thought he might just ask her.

'What are you doing tomorrow night?' he ventured when she stopped the car outside his house.

'I'm busy,' she answered without taking her hands off the steering wheel or eyes off the road.

Aidan shrugged, unbuckled his seat belt and leaned toward her. 'Are you sure I couldn't take you out? For a meal maybe . . .'

She turned to face him, so close that he could see the dark speckles in her amber eyes.

'Aidan, I know you're not like most men who have a one-track mind,' she began.

This sounded promising. His brain began sending messages to his lips.

'The problem with you,' she continued, 'is you have a one-track mind about food.'

He looked at her, his face slowly registering his incredulity. But she wasn't finished.

'Do yourself and the female of the species a favour. Lose a few stone!'

The engine roared as she pressed a high heel on the accelerator. He turned and pulled himself out of the car.

'Nice meeting you too,' he said before slamming the door shut.

Half-watching the Fiesta disappear in the late-night traffic, Aidan staggered in through the small gate and along the path to his home. The key couldn't find the lock quick enough, so he went round the side of the house to pee in the rose bushes before letting himself in the back door and falling in a heap on the sofa. He was asleep in seconds.

—

It was mid-morning when Aidan woke to the sound of his own name being called repeatedly like his mother might have done on a cold wet Monday when a day at school held about as much appeal as watching paint dry. He looked down at his fully clothed body and had a flashback to the conversation he'd had in Sarah Grainger's car. Surely to God, that wasn't her now, coming to apologise.

'Just a sec!' he shouted as he dragged himself from the sofa and wandered to the door, straightening his clothes as he went, just in case.

'Only me,' came the female voice again.

Aidan opened the door to see his pint-sized neighbour looking like Alice in Wonderland beside her Great Dane, Julius. The dog's stripy coat always reminded him of a dirty cur, but Melanie had assured him he was a thoroughbred, having once shown him the papers to prove it.

'He'll be no trouble, will you, Julius?' she said, looking from Aidan to the canine monstrosity. 'It's just for a few weeks. Thank you so much, Aidan.'

It dawned on him that he'd agreed to mind his neighbours' beloved pet for the duration of their holiday; another overzealous proposition made under the influence of drink. Dave and Melanie were good neighbours. They helped each other out with all manner of domestic projects and enjoyed a night out every so often, but minding their child-substitute was, Aidan now reckoned, in the cold sober light of day, above and beyond the call of duty.

'Dave's just bringing his toys, bed, treats . . .'

Aidan stood bleary-eyed as she listed the accoutrements he was expected to keep track of for the next three weeks.

'He'll make himself at home, won't you, Julie-Jules?'

Aidan thought he might still be dreaming and that any minute now he'd wake up in bed in his pyjamas.

'Thanks so much for this,' said Dave, who was coming up the path with the biggest dog bed Aidan had ever seen under one arm and a plethora of squeaky toys under the other.

'Come in,' said Aidan, realising he'd kept Melanie standing there as he'd tried to take in what was happening. She didn't need to be asked twice. Before Aidan could blink, she'd handed him the lead and was herding Dave into the living room to set up the dog bed and arrange the toys as if they were creating a play station at a children's nursery. Meanwhile Julius had set his brindle behind on the concrete step and begun a doleful whine.

'He saw the suitcases this morning,' said Melanie, returning to the hallway, a pained expression on her face. 'He knows we're going.'

Aidan looked to Dave for some sign of shared under-standing that this woman was in fact a tad mad, but her partner only soothed, 'It's okay, Mel, our baby is in safe hands.'

'I've left his food and bowls in the utility room at our place,' said Melanie, matter-of-fact again. 'I thought if you went in a couple of times a day and fed him in there, he'd feel less abandoned, and it would deter thieves to have someone on the premises.'

'Cheers, mate.' Dave gave Aidan a friendly slap on the arm. 'We can't thank you enough for this. Posh nosh and drinks on us when we get back.'

By now, Melanie had coaxed the dog into the living room and was cradling his head and neck at her chest. 'Be a good boy for Uncle Aidan,' she said softly into the dog's ear before tearing herself away. 'He doesn't need a lot of exercise,' she said, and then with a sudden brightness she added, 'but it wouldn't do any harm.'

'Ah, don't worry,' said Aidan, 'I'll walk him every night.'

'I meant it wouldn't do *you* any harm,' she laughed as she pushed gently at his belly.

'Very funny,' said Aidan. 'Get outta here and have a fantastic holiday, the pair of ye.'

Aidan could hardly believe his eyes when he walked back into the living room and found Julius scratching at a spot on the sofa.

'Get off my feckin' couch,' he scolded as the huge dog reluctantly dropped down to the carpet. He pointed to the oversized beanbag that made the room look like it had shrunk. 'That's your bed.'

Sitting back down on the sofa, Aidan cursed the scratch marks as he smoothed them out with his hands and sniffed to test the level of dog odour the creature emitted. He had to admit, Julius seemed like a pretty clean dog, but he couldn't help thinking the low-maintenance bachelor pad he'd renovated to his exact tastes would reek after weeks of canine company.

Man and dog eyed each other from their respective positions. 'Wouldn't do you any harm,' Aidan repeated Melanie's dig. First Skinny Minnie with her cordon bleu qualifications has a go, and now his nearest and dearest neighbour jumps on the band wagon. He took his gut in both hands. The phrase 'pinch an inch' came to mind. By God, there were more than a couple of inches there.

He'd blamed the downturn in the building trade for the extra pounds, but the country was now on the up; it was no longer a valid excuse. There was no denying he'd let himself go. What he hadn't realised was that it was anything anyone would notice. Maybe he should just walk Julius now and get it over with, but the prospect of exercising on a Sunday didn't fill him with enthusiasm. It was hard enough to drag himself round the sites, Monday to Friday, without having to go out evenings and weekends with this mutt. Rob too had commented on his weight. Could Jane have an ulterior motive with her vegetarian delights? What if it wasn't just a bit of extra weight? His mind wandered back to an article he'd read recently in the Sunday paper about diabetes.

'Come on, short stuff,' he said. 'We may as well walk to the garage and get the paper, at least.' Without changing his clothes, Aidan left the house with his new charge.

Melanie hadn't mentioned Julius's energy levels.

'Who's taking who for a walk?' a neighbour joked as he passed. By the time he got home, red-faced and feeling like his lungs might burst, Aidan wondered if this dog wouldn't end up giving him a heart attack. Just to be on the safe side, he'd phone Ben Dineen.

Chapter Seven

'What can I do for you, Aidan?'

Ben Dineen cut a fit-looking figure in a designer polo shirt that showed off his biceps. Aidan imagined the six-pack concealed under the shirt tucked into the belted chinos. *Lucky bastard*, he thought, drawing the sides of his open jacket together to cover the gut that had brought him to this.

'You're not a regular,' said Ben in that diluted English accent of his.

Aidan shifted in his seat, hands still steering the jacket sides from inside the pockets. Ben waited.

'I'm not sure if it's just middle-aged spread or if I might be getting something more serious.' Aidan's face flamed.

'How old are you? Any family history of heart disease? Diabetes?' Ben typed the details into his computer as Aidan answered as best he could. The family ailments whirled round in his head. His mother had died suddenly of a heart attack; took herself off to bed with what she thought was a touch of dizziness and never woke up. He could only wait as Ben settled himself back in his swivel chair and abandoned the keyboard.

'I know you're a builder, but do you get any exercise outside of work?'

'Not lately,' said Aidan. There was no point lying, but he didn't want to sound like a complete slob.

'Okay. To rule out anything serious, I'll get some bloods from you.' Ben turned back to the computer. 'Do me a favour and hop up on the scales behind me there.'

Aidan squirmed as he removed his shoes and jacket and positioned himself on the digital scales. He felt like Dolly Parton as he tried to read the display.

'You could do with losing the weight, all right,' said Ben, smiling as he noted the measurement and swivelled back to type in the offending figure. Aidan pulled his shoes back on and waited for the lecture.

'Did you play any sport when you were younger?' Ben asked.

'I did a lot of swimming, but that was twenty years—'

'Get back in the pool, is my advice,' Ben interrupted. 'I sit here week in week out printing out diet and exercise sheets.' He threw his eyes to heaven. 'I won't bore you, Aidan. Cut your carbs and swim.'

The printer cranked into action. Ben whipped out the blood test form and handed it to him. 'Don't worry, my friend. Phone me Friday for the results, but if I had a euro for every patient I see who just needs to take control of their food intake, I'd be a millionaire.'

Part of Aidan wanted to wait for Friday. Maybe there was some underlying illness that was making him fat. A course of tablets might be required, further tests perhaps. No, he was kidding himself. Either way, he needed to shift this weight. He'd never been what might be called a babe magnet, but Sarah Grainger's rebuke on Saturday night had been a real kick in the teeth. Even his friends were getting onto him, for Christ's sake. It was starting to get him down in more ways than one.

Two days later, Aidan squeezed into an old pair of Speedos and stood in front of the full-length mirror he'd been meaning to attach to his wardrobe.

'Jesus,' he said, staring at his belly, a roll of fat hanging like a gelatinous ring over the tree-trunk thighs he'd barely managed to drag the swimsuit over. 'You need to get a serious grip,' he told his reflection as he took in the bulk of weight he'd been ignoring for too long. He shook his head in despair. 'Things are bad.'

A memory from his swimming days came to him; he was standing on a podium at a pool in Dublin after being placed in the two hundred metre freestyle at the national championships, all triangular with the big shoulders and narrow waist hours of work both in and out of the water had given him. He'd held his shape into his twenties. Isabella had loved it. Letting his mind drift back to that time, he could almost feel her fingers trace the square of his chest, down over his toned core to the vee at the top of his thighs.

There was a whine as Julius pushed the door in with his paw, bringing Aidan back to reality. The mournful sound, together with the doleful look on the dog's inclined face, were all the confirmation Aidan needed that this was not a good look.

'Thanks a lot,' he told the dog. 'What are you doing up here, anyway?' He made to run at the door. 'Get away downstairs, ya scabby mutt.'

He peeled off the Speedos and grabbed a pair of trunks he'd bought in Ibiza a few years before. He cursed the bright white and orange pattern, chosen under the influence of holiday euphoria no doubt, but at least they managed to hide the gut or at least forced some of it off to the sides where it wasn't as offensive. They would have to do. The battle of the bulge began tonight, seven o'clock sharp at the Mardyke pool. He'd paid his money. The thought was enough to send him stuffing the trunks into a gear bag. Money was not something Aidan could afford to waste.

Colette was early for Grace, giving her an excuse to chat to her twin nephews and enjoy a cuddle with her toddler niece.

'See you later, babe.' Grace kissed Ben. 'Be good for Dad,' she told the children as she slung her backpack over one shoulder and hugged each child with her free arm, bending to kiss them in turn, whether they wanted a kiss or not, as was the case with the twins.

'Maybe you want a kiss from me as well,' Colette teased.

'They're saving them all for the girlfriends, aren't you, boys?'

Ben's answer was a punch in the ribs from Tom and a grimace from Sam.

'Don't mind us, lads,' said Colette. 'We're only mad old fogies,' she laughed, placing Sophie back in the crook of her dad's arm.

'Have fun.' Ben and the three children waved as Grace and Colette walked to the car.

The tableau was the same every time, but Colette always felt a twinge somewhere deep inside when she saw it. A strange emotion on a kind of spectrum spanning from jealousy to extreme happiness. Whatever it was, it lay closer to the latter, but there was always an accompanying guilt that she even felt this way. The recent news of Tadgh Caulfield of course heightened the feeling, but that was something she'd tell Grace about later.

'Would you look at your man with that beautiful Great Dane?'

Typical Grace, thought Colette, *looking at bloody dogs*. She glanced across Church Road in the direction of her sister's trance-like gaze and did a double take at the man with the shock of strawberry blond hair who was leaning back, trying desperately to control the massive hound straining at the end of a lead.

'Oh my God!' She stared back at the road and pressed her foot on the accelerator.

'What are you doing?' Grace was turning in her seat to look behind her. 'I was getting a grand look at him. His brindle coat—'

'For God's sake, Grace. That was Aidan O'Shea.'

It took a second for the name to register with her sister. 'The builder that's bugging you?'

'The very one.'

'Well, he's not looking so tough now, is he?'

Colette had to smile. *Not so tough at all.*

It was a busy night at the pool, with sections for swimming lessons and three lanes roped off for the session Aidan had signed up for. After walking Julius, he'd had an urge to throw himself down on the sofa, but he was here now. In a cubicle, he changed into the Ibiza shorts and stuffed his gear in a locker, not sure what to do with the key. He grabbed his cap and goggles and headed to the poolside, where a woman who looked to be in her sixties was writing a schedule on a whiteboard under the heading Fit Swim. *Fat Swim in my case*, he mused as he took in the group of adults diving into lanes, one after another, to start the warm-up.

'I'm Aidan ... eh, I'm just starting ...' he stuttered to the woman who was still copying items from a notepad. She drew back her pen and turned to him.

'Ludmilla,' she said, scanning him from head to toe.

For a split second, Aidan thought this well-built blonde might be an ex-Soviet coach of the push-you-to-your-limits-and-beyond variety. As he considered bolting, a smile broke out across her face reaching a pair of blue eyes that twinkled, making him blush and warm to her at the same time.

'Here to lose few pounds, eh?' she asked in an accent that might have confirmed his worst fears if it hadn't been for that smile.

'Just a few,' he laughed, putting a hand over his paunch.

'You swim laps before?'

'A long time ago,' he said. 'I wasn't too bad. Just very rusty now.'

'Okay, Rusty, you show me what you got. Stop when you want.' She pointed to the board. 'This for regulars. See what you can do.'

He looked over the schedule, an easy-looking three hundred metre warm-up, through a series of complicated drills, then sprints. The bottom line read, 'Total: 2000m'. The session would last an hour. The last time he'd swum that far in that kind of time, Aidan had been in secondary school. Then he could have done more, a lot more, but tonight, after a hard day's work and walking that blasted dog, he thought he'd be lucky to manage the warm-up. He fiddled with his locker key.

'You put here.' Ludmilla pointed to a bowl on a trestle table filled with similar keys. It reminded him of one of those parties. He might get lucky with this fitness drive yet. The silly thought cheered him up as he sat at the edge of what looked like the slow lane and eased himself into the pool.

Four lengths in and he stopped at the wall to let the queue of fitter figures past. What exactly were the symptoms of a heart attack?

'Breathe,' Ludmilla shouted from the deck. 'Then another hundred.'

He did as she said and found the wall again after the second hundred metres. By now, the others had finished the warm-up and were donning flippers for the first set of drills.

'What size?' Ludmilla asked, pointing to her feet.

'Ten,' he told her, hoping he wouldn't have to say anything else through his heavy breaths. He pressed his palms on the deck and hauled himself out onto the poolside. Beached whales came to mind. Flippers on, he got back in the water. This was so much easier. He could even keep up with the others in the lane. Two hundred metres, thirty seconds' rest, another two hundred metres. He was into his third rep when pain shot through his left calf like a vice grips. He trailed the leg as he swam to the wall, threw his goggles on the deck and pulled off the flipper.

'Cramp?' Ludmilla's tone was more casual than concerned.

Aidan grimaced. 'Yeah.' *Just my luck. First bloody session and I'm crippled.* Resting one elbow on the wall, he put a hand under water and held the ball of his left foot and tried to pull it toward his knee to stretch the muscle. Boy, was it painful.

'It's normal,' Ludmilla was saying. 'You get over it. Must relax with flippers.' She waved a hand and went to talk to the swimmers in the fast lane who'd already finished six two-hundred-metre reps. A woman in his own lane pulled up.

'Cramp?'

Aidan nodded.

'I got that when I started,' she told him. 'I think it's the way you hold your leg when you've got flippers on.' As he listened, Aidan wondered how this woman could be having a conversation when he could barely breathe. 'Don't give up,' she continued. 'Try to relax. It gets easier every time. I'm Margaret, by the way.'

Before he could even attempt to comment, she was moving to the other side of the lane to make room for the others. He noticed the tight-fitting trunks on the men. If his face wasn't red from exertion, it would have been puce with embarrassment. He wasn't sure those swimsuits even came in his size.

The cramp began to ease and he set off again, this time without the flippers. As his lane mates lapped him, he wondered if he hadn't bitten off more than he could chew, but despite the setback, there was something about having made the effort that spurred him on. He could have gone home, but he stuck it out till the hour was up and tried not to limp as he went to the showers.

In the change rooms, he battled with the locker. No way would it open. He checked the number on the door against the key. 'Shite,' he grumbled as he realised he had the wrong one.

'Looking for this?'

Standing up from where he'd been bent down fumbling at the door, he took in the toned legs and flat stomach of a petite woman dangling a key from its band. As he looked from the key to her face, her smile gave way to shock.

'Aidan! What a surprise to see *you* here.'

'Colette. How are ya?' He tried to look nonchalant as he stood wishing the ground would open and swallow him.

'I didn't know you did Fit Swim.' It sounded like an accusation.

'Yeah. Just started tonight. I wouldn't have recognised you.' With an upturned palm, he gestured to her swimsuit-clad body, but quickly thought better of it and pulled his hand to his side. Colette had folded her arms under a pair of modest breasts. *What an idiot*, he berated himself. But she was quick enough for him.

'I might have said the same about you.' She smiled now, the shock of seeing him in this state having obviously turned to amusement.

'You tell Rusty we go to pub?' came the booming voice of Ludmilla, who was charging through the change rooms.

Colette didn't say anything.

'It's okay,' said Aidan to save any further embarrassment. 'I've got something on.' He held out the key to do a swap.

'Maybe next week,' she said as she made the exchange, their wet fingers touching.

'Ta.' He bent down to open the locker wondering why she hesitated before her small feet, with their red varnished toenails, walked away.

—

The front bar of O'Brien's was heaving with its usual Thursday night crowd of mostly university students. Mick, the barman, had kept an eye on movement in the back bar as usual and managed to hold a table in the corner for his regular customers.

'Good session?' he asked as Grace and Colette perched on high stools and ordered half pints of beer and packets of peanuts. They nodded. 'And now ye're going to undo all the good of it bating into pints and rubbish.' He gave a wry smile as he drew the Budweiser tap down over a glass.

'Don't you ever tell my husband,' warned Grace, 'or he'll sue you for selling me the stuff.'

'Don't worry, Mick,' said Colette. 'The chances of Ben Dineen darkening your door are very slight.'

'Is that right?' asked Mick.

'Oh yeah,' said Colette. 'Nice fella, but a bit of a health freak.'

Grace chuckled.

'Mum's the word so,' said Mick as he set the two glasses on the bar.

They were still giggling as they took a seat at the long table in the corner where the Fit Swim crowd were gathered. Ludmilla and her triathlete husband were advising the others on upcoming open-water events. It was one of the usual topics of conversation and although Colette didn't take part in many of the events, she relished the fitness chat and the knowledge to be gained from the others' experience. Grace was the competitive one. If it wasn't for her busy family schedule, she'd have been out every weekend competing in some race or other.

'Rusty not make it?' Ludmilla asked, catching Colette's eye.

'No, he had something on.' She felt the eyes of all of them on her as if it were her fault that the new boy hadn't been invited along.

'Who's Rusty?' asked Grace, a little too loudly for Colette's liking.

'A new fella,' Colette began, but before she needed to elaborate, Margaret had begun another thread in the conversation about Aidan's leg cramping which, much to Colette's relief, engaged the group, Grace included, in an animated debate on the subject.

They were hardly outside the pub when Grace set about quizzing her on the mystery cramping swimmer who'd escaped her attention.

'How could you have missed those flowery shorts?' asked Colette.

'Some people take their training seriously, you know,' said Grace. 'And anyway, why would I be checking out the talent when I'm a happily married woman?'

'It has nothing to do with checking out the talent.'

'Then why did your face go red when Ludmilla asked you about him? Ha?'

'I did *not* go red.'

'You did so.' Grace skipped to the car like a giddy teenager.

Colette sat in, worried now that she might indeed have blushed at the mention of Aidan O'Shea, number two on her current enemy list, second only to her ex-husband.

'Well?' Grace looked squarely at her sister and waited.

Colette turned the key in the ignition and went to fasten her seat belt. 'It was Aidan O'Shea,' she said into the belt buckle.

'The builder? With the big dog?' Grace was incredulous. 'That's twice in one night we've talked about that guy. I thought we didn't like him.'

Colette had to smile as she pulled out into the steady night-time traffic. She sometimes envied her sister's simplistic view of the world despite the complexities of her job and family life. People were paying a fortune to life coaches and counsellors to be as happy-go-lucky as Grace. Colette wished more of their mother's genes had come her way.

'Forget about *him*,' she said, determined to keep Aidan O'Shea off the agenda when there was a matter of far greater significance to discuss. Without taking her eyes off the road, she made the announcement she'd been waiting to make all day. 'Tadgh Caulfield's girlfriend is pregnant.'

When she turned, she saw the excitement had left Grace's eyes as tears gathered at their corners.

'Oh, Colette, I'm so sorry.'

'I know.' Colette slipped a hand into her sister's and squeezed. The shock sat in the silence between them, a silence they reserved for only the gravest of news, like when their mother had sat them down and told them about their father's cancer. Words were surplus to requirements. The sisters felt each other's pain.

On his way home, Aidan stopped at the garage for milk. He ran his eyes over the confectionery at the counter and thought about rewarding his efforts in the pool with a chocolate treat. *Cut the carbs.* Ben Dineen's words echoed in his head and he decided against the indulgence. He had to take a minute when he sat back in the car. It struck him how hard it had been to say no and walk away. This wasn't going to be easy. Resisting temptation that was everywhere, coping with cramping calf muscles, and the small but perfectly formed Colette Barry in the same pool as him just to add insult to injury. If it hadn't been for the upfront credit card payment for twenty sessions, he might have packed the whole thing in.

'How're the muscles?' Ben sank his thumbs into Grace's shoulder blades, catching her eye in the bathroom mirror before inclining his head and kissing her gently under the earlobe. 'You smell of chlorine,' he said, looking at her again, but not halting the progress his lips were making toward her collarbone.

'Mummy!'

Grace made to extricate herself from his embrace and see to her daughter.

'I'll go,' he said.

She took a deep breath and loaded up her toothbrush. What a rock. He had just spent the evening single-handedly performing and supervising the cleaning and tidying rituals of their household and he still had the energy to soothe their teething toddler, not to mind spend some romantic time with his wife. She would wake in the quiet of the morning before any of them got up and walk into the kitchen with nothing to do except throw the pre-made sandwiches into the lunchboxes lining the worktop and get herself showered and dressed. She never minded early starts, knowing Ben was more than capable of steering the ship, dropping the kids off before opening the surgery. In his family of eight, he'd told her, it was normal; they'd all mucked in.

'About those shoulders.' He was back, taking up where he'd left off. She threw her head back and laughed a little too loudly.

'Mummy!' It was Sophie again.

'I'll go this time,' said Grace.

Ben sighed and shook his head. '*I'll* go. If you go in there, you'll never come out.'

It was true. Ben had the knack that had the kids eating out of his hand, most of the time. It was what had attracted her to him in the first place. That and the killer smile that had melted her heart the day he'd walked into the ward on his first paediatric rotation. The day would be forever etched on her mind. She wasn't long qualified herself after training in England and securing a job in a hospital in London where she was doing her utmost to carry out her tasks to the letter. The matron was a serious woman from Wexford who demanded the highest standards from her nurses – and even higher ones from those who happened to be Irish. Grace would never forget her words to them, 'Every time you step into this hospital wearing that uniform, you're flying the flag.' They often joked that she must have had the reddest ears in England, such was the mileage they got out of moaning about her in their spare time.

Ben had sailed into the children's ward like a cool breeze on a sweltering summer's day. Hands in his pockets, a confident calm had separated him from the clutch of interns as they stood, huddled in their white coats, around the kindly looking consultant who could have passed for Mahatma Gandhi until he opened his mouth and demonstrated a hidden talent for spitting fire.

'Dineen!' He spat out the name as they stood beside the bed of an asthmatic six-year-old who eyed the motley crew from over his oxygen mask.

'Yes, sir.' The white coats parted as Ben came forward with an exaggerated step, clicking his heels together and tipping the fingers of his right hand to his forehead, head turned toward his superior but mischievous eyes trained on the young boy in the bed.

As the consultant looked down at the patient chart and spouted sharp snippets of medical jargon at his students, the boy watched as Ben took something surreptitiously from his pocket. Grace had to bite the inside of her mouth to suppress the smile that threatened to spring the young doctor and his antics and quite possibly see her reported to Matron.

'I'm waiting, Dineen,' came the next volley from the consultant as Ben dangled a goofy-looking red puppet from where he had half-hidden it behind his back.

Grace willed herself to focus on the details of Ben's assessment of the boy's condition while drinking in the delight on the child's face as the puppet nodded and pulled faces as if in agreement with everything Ben said. Before the group moved on to the next patient, Ben high-fived the boy and gave him a wave of the puppet.

'Thanks, champ,' he said, and then winking at him he added, 'Be nice to that pretty Irish nurse.'

Grace set her toothbrush in its holder and reached into the medicine cabinet. There were still a few left in a packet of the contraceptive pills she was supposed to have stopped taking. *Feck it*, she thought, popping one into the back of her mouth and leaning her head under the tap to wash it down with a drink.

'What are you doing?'

Ben had caught her red-handed.

Chapter Eight

Barbara Barry was up at dawn as usual, humming a sixties song as she went about her morning routine. Colette turned over in bed, wishing it were Saturday. Her arms ached as she pulled the duvet over her head to muffle the sound of the whistling kettle her mother loved. Two men appeared in a half-dream; Tadgh Caulfield with a smarmy smile, rubbing the beach-ball belly of the floozy he'd taken up with, then Aidan O'Shea in those hideous shorts. She held the latter image and examined it. The roly-poly paunch hung over the waistband. But the legs were strong and there was that funny ginger chest hair lying wet against his pale skin. Would it curl in soft swirls as it dried?

Get up, you mad woman, she told herself as the alarm clock crowed like a cock. Fabulous Four Walls took over her thoughts as she stepped into the shower and reviewed the day ahead. Today was a big one. She and John were staging a small hotel for auction. It wasn't often they got to work together on site. Although they consulted each other on individual projects, working together was special. As she towel-dried her hair, Colette thanked God for gay men. John, at least, was straightforward.

The team were gathered at Carlton Manor by eight-thirty, a mix of professional painters and decorators together with a year group from one of the technical colleges who were only too happy to let their interior design students loose for some practical experience. John and Colette's hard work over the past few years had gained them an excellent reputation, and a day like this was a way to keep their hand in with teaching the craft they both loved.

As John briefed them on the day's schedule, Colette had to smile at the navy cravat tucked inside the oversized denim shirt John wore loosely over the closest thing to a pair of casual trousers in his possession. The navy sailing shoes completed the look, which, for John, announced physical labour or at least the supervision of it. She knew the heavy work would be hers, hence the red paint-spattered overalls she'd turned up at the wrists and ankles. Hair tied back and ready for action, she took her charges upstairs where they would paint walls, reupholster furniture, dress beds and finally add finishing touches to a series of rooms that had lost their appeal.

'Let the makeover begin,' she announced as they split into pairs to begin work on their assigned rooms.

An enthusiastic girl helped carry a tired-looking couch to the centre of a bedroom out of the way of a couple of lads who were laying dust sheets on the floor along the walls they would transform from a horrible mushroom to a lovely latte by the end of the morning.

'What about the ugly en-suites?' the girl asked.

'If I were the buyer, I'd replace all the bathroom suites,' Colette explained, setting down her end of the couch, 'but that takes money. All we can achieve today is a clean, fresh look to what's already here. The owner isn't paying us enough to do a complete revamp.'

'Isn't it bathrooms and kitchens that sell houses, though?' the girl persisted as she helped Colette with an outdated dressing table they would probably hide in the shed in the grounds. The others had paused to hear her answer.

'You're right, but you have to remember, it comes down to taste. I've seen people go to a lot of expense buying a new kitchen or bathroom suite to help sell a house, only for it to be ripped out by the next owner.'

'No way,' someone called out, voicing the group's incredulity.

'That's right,' Colette continued as they stripped the bed of its thin mustard duvet cover and matching flannelette sheets. 'I've seen the most beautiful pieces of furniture in skips or dumped at the side of the road.'

'Are we all right to start sugar-soaping?' one of the boys cut in from the doorway.

Colette left the girl to spread the protective sheets over the remaining furniture and went to make sure the boys had everything they needed to start on the walls.

Her next group were preparing to replace the threadbare landing carpet with a functional taupe low-budget one that would give the floor a smart, uniform appearance without breaking the bank. She wished they'd been given the time and money to bring the old oak floorboards back to life. They reminded her of the farmhouse in West Cork. How beautiful those floors would look with a bit of TLC. She pulled her phone from her pocket and typed in a reminder to talk to Aidan about it. Her curiosity as to how it was all going down there was frustrating, but calling him to casually enquire about progress wasn't an option. He'd probably think she was meddling, not to mention charging for her time.

'Everyone happy upstairs?' came the voice of the boss.

Without a strand of his thinning hair astray, John joined Colette on the landing before proceeding to inspect each bedroom. She took one side of the carpet the lads were removing and helped to roll. John emerged from one of the rooms just as they were hoisting it on their shoulders to take it downstairs.

'Great work, boys,' he said as he watched them manoeuvre around the staircase. He winked at Colette. 'What a nice bunch of young gentlemen we have here.'

'Yes, John. Young, willing and able, unlike yourself.'

'Ah, Colette, if you knew me in my prime.' He smiled as he trailed off again, leaving her to help with the painting.

By lunchtime, the young people were starving. In exchange for their labour, John shouted them lunch; the delivery of baguettes and pastries was met with a huge cheer. As they sat outside in the late spring sunshine, the conversations revolved around end-of-year assessments and summer holidays.

'Where are you going, yourself?' one of the boys asked her.

Another quiet holiday with her mother in County Clare was the honest answer. The days of long summer school holidays and Tadgh's quest to find Europe's cheapest destinations were well behind her.

'You'll have to do a bit of surfing at Lahinch,' the boy told her. 'I'm friendly with a fella who gives lessons. I'll give you his number.'

He was already calling out figures as she fumbled in her pocket for her phone, incredulous that this boy half her age could even imagine her on a surfboard. She punched in the details and took his comment as a compliment as opposed to blind ignorance.

Most of the afternoon was spent in a supervisory role giving her arms a rest from shifting carpets and curtains and cutting and covering MDF headboards. The students were good, but she needed to be sure she set the standard. She would ask her mother to rub a bit of Deep Heat into her shoulders when she got home. Aidan O'Shea would be another one suffering today. Whether or not he had anyone to massage him, she couldn't say. She'd never known him to have a steady girlfriend. But what had she known of him, really, since Ellen had left? *Enough of him*, she told herself and got on with the job of assessing the students' work.

Her mobile buzzed in her pocket. It was Gerry. She went to the landing from where she could watch another team tidying up the flower beds and strategically placing extra-large plant pots to hide some messy maintenance jobs they didn't have the time or budget to complete.

'Gerry, what can I do for you?'

'Colette, old bean, my visa came through.'

The excitement in his voice was contagious. Her feet did a happy dance.

'Fantastic news. When are you heading?'

'Week after next. Will you come to my leaving do?'

'Of course I will.'

He filled her in on the details.

'I'm so happy for you, Ger.'

'I know, I know. It's been a long time coming.'

Gerry would not have been much older than the young lads down there in the garden when Ellen emigrated. Twenty years later, their reunion had been sweet and now it looked like it would be permanent. Colette was over the moon for them both. It made her think again how it would be nice to meet someone, but with her luck in the love department, or rather the lack of it, she was probably better off on her own.

'Fifteen-minute countdown,' John called out, bringing her back to the moment and sending the students in to speed bed-making and accessorising.

No better man than John Buckley to finish the day with a flourish. She joined him in helping everyone get finished and packed up. The hotel looked bright and fresh, ready for potential buyers to view and hopefully be sufficiently wowed to make a bid.

'Dinner's on me, if you're free,' he said after they'd seen off the last of the students and contractors.

'That's kind of you, John. And no, I don't have anything on.' She wanted to moan at him about the unfairness of the single life, how the highlight of her week was meeting her sister for a swim or a long run alone at the weekend. But if it was hard for her, it must be even harder for John. She kept her griping to herself.

—

'Are you coming for a pint with the lads?' asked Rob as they finished for the day at the builder's yard.

'I have to feed that bloody dog,' said Aidan. 'I might catch up with ye in The Arms later.'

Fern called out from the office. 'You wouldn't be getting attached to the oul' mutt, would you?'

'Feck it, no,' said Aidan. 'The quicker the neighbours come back, the better.'

'Liar,' she teased. 'Any man who forgoes a pint for the sake of a dog is a gem.'

Aidan's cheeks burned. Fern had a way of seeing right through him.

'Are you sure about that pint?' she said. 'I can always tell Sarah Grainger what pub you're in.'

'Get away outta that,' Aidan rounded. 'The next time you try that matchmaking nonsense on me, I'll be ready for you.'

Rob and Fern exchanged a smile.

'So, what have yourself and Marmaduke got planned for the weekend?' Rob asked.

'Go home to your family and leave me alone, will ya?'

With the place to himself, Aidan sat in the office to spend another half hour on paperwork. His plan for the weekend included the obligatory Sunday lunch at his father's as well as a long run on a beach with Julius. Now that Colette Barry was in the same swim class, he'd need to step up the fitness. No point looking like a complete loser, even if she was the bane of his life.

Chapter Nine

The loud snoring woke Aidan. Lying on his side, facing the window, he watched the sun lightening the sky as he registered the weight along the length of duvet. *What the—* Julius was stretched out beside him, taking up most of the double bed. The dog stirred and jerked up his head, one eye opening, an ear cocked and a dribble hanging from his jowls.

'What are you doing in here?' Aidan bawled. There was a pitiful whine as Julius placed a paw over his nose. Aidan wasn't sure whether to reprimand or cuddle him. 'I must be going soft in the head,' he grumbled, 'sharing my bed with a dog.' Julius let his paw rest on Aidan's shoulder.

'Get off, ya mangy mutt.' He dragged the duvet from under Julius and pulled it round him. It was Saturday. At least he didn't have to go anywhere. Just walk this bloody dog and get some shopping. He remembered his promise to himself and decided on Garretstown.

Julius was sitting up now, hanging on his every word.

'Fancy a walk on the beach, boy?'

The 'w' word was enough to send him into hyper mode, spinning in circles on the bed, stopping every so often to lick Aidan's face with a long slobbery tongue.

''Tisn't a walk you'll be getting if you don't cop yourself on.'

Too late. He'd mentioned the 'w' word again. Julius bounded down the stairs and returned with the lead in his mouth before Aidan was even out of bed.

'Another couple of weeks of this,' he told the dog, 'and you can go back and annoy your owners.'

~

The run along Garretstown beach was harder than Aidan had imagined. The wobble of his belly at every stride reminded him of the arduous task of shifting the excess pounds. He forced himself to stay positive and think of how it would feel when he'd no longer have this weight to drag around.

In the supermarket he bypassed the bread, didn't even look sideways at the cakes and filled his trolley with protein, vegetables and healthy dairy products he'd only ever seen advertised on TV. He even managed to drive straight past the off-licence he frequented every Saturday. *Cut the carbs.* Ben Dineen's words played in his head like a mantra. The GP had kindly called him at work on Friday to assure him the results of the bloods showed nothing untoward, and hadn't missed the opportunity to remind him of the lifestyle improvements he could be making to keep things that way.

A Saturday without giving in to the munchies was nothing short of a miracle. Sunday lunch was the next hurdle. He would take Julius for moral support, to remind him of exercise.

—

Julius strained on the lead as Bill O'Shea opened the door. Frances approached from the end of the hallway, but stopped a little way back from them as she took in the sight of the Great Dane.

'What in the name of God have you there?' she asked from behind Bill.

'Hello, boy.' Bill ignored her and put out a hand to pat Julius. 'Aren't you a beauty?'

Before he could contain the dog's straining, Aidan lost hold of the lead and Julius bounded inside.

'Beauty, me eye,' shrieked Frances as she stood against the wall to get out of the way of the dog, who didn't need any more encouragement from Bill to feel welcomed into the family home. 'Put him out!' she screeched.

Aidan thought he might have burst an eardrum.

'Ah, Frances,' said Bill, ''tisn't every day we have a Great Dane in the house.'

'I hoovered the whole place yesterday. I had it spick and span for you.' She was shouting now as she stormed into the kitchen after Bill. 'I put on the roast for the dinner before I went to mass and I've been peeling spuds since before you even got up out of bed.'

Aidan didn't know where to look. Julius came back and stood beside him, tail between his legs, his stripy skin quivering along his back.

'And you, you savage beast!' She turned and wagged a finger at the dog. 'Don't think you can come in here and undo my good work.'

Julius must have misread the scolding because he launched himself toward her, set his paws on her shoulders and proceeded to lick at her rosy lipstick.

'Agggh!' Frances bolted out the back door with Julius bounding after her and Bill doing his best to follow despite having to stifle a fit of laughter. Aidan made a futile attempt to grab the collar as the dog whizzed past.

In the garden, he saw Frances disappear through a door in the fence. Since when did their fence have a door? It gave direct access to the garden behind. Very handy. He imagined his mother turning in her grave. Standing there for the first time in so long, he remembered Ellen and their friends playing and getting up to innocent mischief. It seemed like yesterday.

'Ah, come on, Frances. It's only a dog,' his father pleaded from the back door.

'Come on, boy,' Aidan called again as Julius trotted up the garden, a dejected Bill O'Shea in tow.

'Sorry, Dad.' He followed his father into the house. 'I should have kept a better hold of him.'

'Don't blame the dog, son. Terry Brady kept dogs all his life.'

Aidan couldn't stand the sight of his father sitting slumped in the kitchen chair after the domestic he wished he hadn't witnessed. He put the lead on Julius and led him to the car. 'Be good,' he told the dog through one of the partly open windows, before going back in the house.

'It's an awful shame to waste the good dinner she's made,' said Bill. 'I'll ring her and tell her you've put him out.'

Within ten minutes, the neighbouring widow was back, serving up Sunday roast with a smile that belied whatever was behind the earlier outburst.

'More roast potatoes?' she offered when they'd run out of weather conversation. Aidan declined, only having eaten a couple to be polite.

'Ellen tells me Gerry got his visa,' Bill was saying.

'Shacking up together? Just like us,' Frances giggled, her face puce as if she'd let slip a well-kept secret.

'Ah sure, 'tis nice to have company,' said Bill.

Aidan bit his tongue as he fought the urge to tell his father he was kidding himself if he thought this relationship with Frances was anything like what Ellen and Gerry shared. No, that was the kind of relationship he might have enjoyed with Isabella well into old age had things been different. He declined dessert and left on the premise that the dog would wreck the car if left alone for too long.

—

Ellen was giddy with excitement. Even the grumpiest clients were a joy to work with today. No one could get her down. Gerry Clancy was booked to come and live with her here in South Australia. Who said dreams didn't come true? Tracey had insisted they celebrate. They sat on Ellen's veranda on a starry Sunday evening in June, rugged up with blankets over their knees and cradling warm glasses of the mulled wine she had long ago dispensed with saving for Christmas.

'How long before he arrives?' Tracey asked.

'I think it's Tuesday week.'

'You think?' Tracey shook her head. 'Is it Tuesday here or Tuesday in Adelaide? What if it's Monday?'

'I'll get the email.' Ellen retrieved her phone from the lounge room and held it between them. They peered at the screen. 'Thursday morning.'

'You'll be playing hookey if you haven't already booked the day off.'

Ellen hadn't thought that far ahead.

'The boss will surely give me time off. It's not every day your . . . well your—'

'Your boyfriend comes from Ireland and moves in with you,' Tracey finished the sentence.

'I don't know about *boyfriend*,' Ellen argued. 'Don't you think I'm a bit long in the tooth for that sort of thing?'

Tracey rolled her eyes. 'Too old? Look how many women way older than us are hooking up with fellas.' She gave a deep chuckle. 'It's not like you're just friends.'

'Ha ha, very funny.'

Ellen sipped her wine. It was one thing to see Gerry for the short stints they'd spent in Ireland and Australia together earlier in the year, but this was long term. She'd been so unsure of how the whole thing would pan out, afraid to give in to her hopes and share them with anyone besides the Popes and Louise. Now it would be official. She'd have to get used to introducing Gerry as . . .

'Partner.' Tracey was emphatic. Ellen tossed the term over in her mind.

'Okay . . . lover,' said Tracey, cracking up at her own joke before draining her glass. 'Mm . . . that was good, but I'd better dash before I'm divorced. What time do you want me on Saturday to help whip the place into shape?'

It was as much an order as an offer. Ellen knew better than to turn down the generosity of the friend who'd helped drag her out of the depression Nick's death had plunged her into a year and a half before.

'Ten okay?'

'Perfect.'

As she watched the Ford Falcon hurtle down the driveway, Ellen knew Tracey was already shelving other plans so as to put preparations for Gerry's arrival top of her list.

—

Rob and Aidan sat down to lunch in the small kitchen at the back of the office.

'How's the diet going?'

'What diet?' said Aidan as he tucked into the bowl of tuna salad he'd prepared that morning.

'The diet you've been on since you went to the doctor last week.'

Aidan set the fork in the plastic container.

'How did you know I was at—' The grin on Rob's face said it all. 'Fern?'

'She's only got your best interests at heart, you know. We were worried about you. Until the results came back.'

'Is there anything you two don't talk about?'

Rob closed one eye and looked up at the ceiling.

'Forget I asked,' said Aidan. 'I know too much already about what you guys talk about.' He took a mouthful of salad and gulped from his water bottle. 'You can tell your good wife I appreciate her concern—'

'But when you need her help, you'll ask for it?'

'Exactly,' Aidan agreed.

'That doesn't work with Fern, I'm afraid.'

The sound of heels on concrete sent them into a fit of laughter.

'You two look like a pair of naughty school boys. I hope you weren't talking about me.' Fern stood with her hands on her hips, her freshly applied lip gloss accentuating her pout.

'No, love. Just boys' stuff,' Rob lied. They watched her leave before letting out another burst of laughter.

'Actually, Rob,' said Aidan when they'd recovered, 'you might be able to help me on my fitness campaign.'

Rob looked at the door to check Fern couldn't overhear.

'Sure, boy. What can I do for you?'

'The thing is,' said Aidan, 'I need to buy a pair of those modern swimming trunks.'

'Oh yeah, for the lap swimming, like?'

'Exactly,' said Aidan, relieved his friend knew what he was on about. 'You see, I'm not sure if they'd have a pair to fit me.'

Rob wiped mayonnaise from the corners of his mouth with the back of his hand.

'I know a fella in Cummins Sports. Very discreet. Will we go in and have a look on the way to that job in the Northside?'

Julius looked unimpressed as he watched Aidan pull on his new jammers in front of the mirror he still hadn't attached to the wardrobe.

'Stop staring, will ya?' He fiddled with the waistline, pinched the stretchy fabric that was catching under one of his buttocks and turned to the side, breathing in and smoothing his belly as he studied his reflection. 'Not too bad, I suppose.'

Julius dropped to the floor with a heavy sigh.

'It's not *that* bad, is it?'

Aidan was grateful the dog couldn't answer. He wasn't at all sure about these jammers or whatever they called them. Better than the Ibiza shorts, maybe, but that was as far as it went. Taking them off again and stuffing them in his gear bag would be too much like hard work. He pulled his trousers on over them.

'Aidan O'Shea, it's been years.'

'Dessie Farrell, how've you been?' Aidan shook hands with the friend he'd trained with in his youth when they'd been keen enough to swim before school and at ungodly hours at weekends. Dessie was right; it had been years. He'd filled out since the old days, but it was obvious he hadn't let himself go. As they walked onto the pool deck, Aidan felt the urge to bolt again, but the memory of how he used to beat Dessie in the sprints gave him the confidence he needed to keep going.

'Rusty, you come back.' Ludmilla smiled at him from where she was putting the schedule on the whiteboard. 'You relax tonight, eh?'

Aidan nodded and slipped into the slow lane. Dessie was two lanes away, pulling on a pair of goggles tied with string. Aidan thought he might have been wearing the same ones the last time they'd swum together.

'I'll catch up with you over a pint later on,' Dessie shouted.

Aidan gave him the thumbs-up and watched as his old friend stroked down the pool like a pro. Would he ever get back to that level of fitness? He pressed his goggles to his face and dived in. *Small steps*, he told himself.

After the warm-up, he looked up at the whiteboard and was grateful to see breaststroke sets next. There'd been a time when he'd hated the stroke. The rules back then meant that despite some respectable times, he'd suffered many a disqualification because he couldn't keep his head above water. Of course, after the invention of what his old coach had liked to call 'Russian Breaststroke', it had been deemed okay to duck under on every stroke. Unfortunately, Aidan had left the sport by then. At least he could do the set now as he pleased. He pushed off into a deep glide.

Margaret was stopped at the wall at the other end. 'Go in front,' she urged him.

He grinned as he pushed off for the underwater stroke. Surfacing, he pulled hard to catch the guy ahead. The fellow let him past. At the end of the two hundred metres, he stopped to check the schedule. Ludmilla took a kickboard from an old milk crate and handed it to him.

'You were good breaststroker, no?'

Aidan shrugged.

'No flippers tonight. Lucky you!' She gave a laugh as she distributed the boards to the others.

'You didn't tell us you were a breaststroker.' It was Margaret's turn to puff and pant tonight. He'd noticed her slightly screwed kick, but thought to keep any advice to himself at this early stage in his Fit Swim career. He looked round to see who would lead the lane on the kick set.

'Go ahead,' said the man he'd passed before. 'Don't let us oldies hold you back.'

Margaret sent a wave of water that splashed in the man's face. 'Speak for yourself,' she told him. Aidan pushed off and left them to it. They seemed like nice people, but he wasn't here to make friends. He was here to shift this spare tyre before it was in danger of killing him or indeed his prospects, if he still had any.

Chapter Ten

Dessie persuaded Aidan to come along to the pub afterwards. 'Lovely crowd,' he'd assured him. 'Into their fitness and living life.'

Aidan didn't mention his theory on people like Colette Barry wanting to make as much money as possible from conning people into tarting up their homes at great expense. He parked the car and joined Dessie at the back bar where he was talking to an older man Aidan recognised from the slow lane.

'You've met Chris?' Dessie introduced them.

'You did better tonight,' said Chris with a nod.

Aidan blushed. 'That wouldn't be hard. I was pretty abysmal last week.'

'Don't be too hard on yourself,' Chris counselled. 'The fitness will come. Just keep showing up.'

'That's it,' Dessie agreed. 'Routine is everything. That's where I lose out with the shift work.'

Aidan relaxed as the men chatted easily about their jobs and families. He was aware of Colette sitting with Ludmilla and some of the other swimmers at the table in the corner, but put the prospect of having to speak to her to the back of his mind. It turned out Dessie too was on the low-carb beer, which made ordering painless. If that had been the lads he normally hung out with, they'd have been slagging him about it for weeks.

Dessie called to a woman who was standing further along the bar. 'Hey, Grace, have you met Aidan?'

As she came toward them, Aidan saw a taller, more robust version of Colette Barry. Same fine dark hair, but cut to just below her ears.

'I'm Colette's sister.' She thrust a hand in Aidan's and shook with an unexpected vigour. 'She's been telling me all about you.'

He cringed at the thought of what Colette might have said about him, but the barman rescued him with a shout to let Grace know her order was ready.

'Nice meeting you,' he managed.

Chris and Dessie looked at him, waiting for that nugget of information that would connect him to Colette. He played it straight.

'Colette's helping us renovate my grandmother's old house in Crookhaven.'

It was enough to set the pair of them off on a tangent about the beauty spots of West Cork and the price of houses. Half-listening, Aidan watched Grace as she made her way from the bar. Just as she passed him, she leaned in, careful to keep the glasses out of the way.

'Come and join us later.'

When the lads ushered him to where the other swimmers were gathered, his plan to avoid the table in the corner and make his excuses after one drink were knocked on the head. Colette smiled at him. She almost looked like a different person with the hooded sweatshirt and still-wet hair tied back off her face; definitely less intimidating without the power suit. But then, as he well knew, looks could be deceiving.

'Colette,' he said quietly, nodding to her as he took a seat with Chris between them.

'And how are you, my dear?' Chris asked her. 'Still enjoying life at Fabulous Four Walls?'

'Grand altogether,' she answered.

'Any difficult clients?'

'We get a few of *them*, all right.' She glanced in Aidan's direction before looking into her glass and taking a drink.

'Well, we still miss you at school,' Chris told her, oblivious to any undertone in the comment. He turned to Aidan. 'Best Home Economics teacher we ever had. Gifted as well as good-looking.' When he winked, Aidan wasn't sure where to look, but Chris was on a roll. 'Never did so many boys do Home Ec at St Colman's as when Colette was on our staff.'

'Go way outta that, you old charmer,' Colette laughed.

Aidan couldn't help smiling at the sound. It was a hearty, infectious laugh, the kind that made you forget yourself. He realised he hadn't heard it in years and thought back to the day they'd gone to West Cork. Was he that serious and uptight that in a whole day with Gerry and Colette, they hadn't had a laugh about something? He listened as she entertained the group with tales of her latest projects. The thrills and spills at Carlton Manor had them in stitches. The antics of the young people who had helped, the suggestion by one of them, 'half her age', that she learn to surf, all had them enthralled. The self-deprecation too surprised him.

'Do you remember that windsurfing course we did out in Farran with the club one time?' Dessie asked him from the other side of the table.

'I do indeed.'

'You had more than your share of wobbles, I remember,' Dessie mocked good-humouredly.

'What about yourself and the time you nearly got knocked out when the boom hit you?' Aidan realised he had the floor and looked sideways to see Colette laughing along with the others. He crossed an arm over his chest and took a drink of his pint. Maybe he could hack this swimming crowd after all.

When Chris got up to head to the bar, Grace declined another drink and said they'd better go. Colette reached under the table to gather up her gear bag.

'I'll get that for you,' said Aidan. As he reached down, his hand brushed hers. She jumped as they both felt the small shock.

'Ow!' Colette pulled her hand away.

He wished the ground would open and swallow him, but he smiled through the embarrassment and set the bag between them.

'Thanks,' said Colette taking the bag in her hands.

He took in her wet hair in its untidy twist that laid bare the curve of her fine-boned face as she stood looking at him.

'Are you going to Gerry's leaving do this weekend?' she asked finally.

'I am.'

'I'll see you there then.' She didn't move.

He tried to think of something else to say, but she got in first.

'You'll have to update me on what's happening on the house at some stage.'

'Definitely.' There was another pause. *Say something, man.* 'I'll see what the next few weeks are like. Maybe we can go down and have another look at the place together?'

'See you Saturday.'

Her hand softly touched his shoulder. He wasn't sure why she'd done it, but he didn't mind.

—

'You're an angel,' said John as he let Colette in the heavy front door and relieved her of one of the coffee cups she'd carried from the car.

'The soy?'

'Yes. I've got the cow's.'

They sat down at the chunky coffee table in the main office and pushed aside the magazines to make way for their notebooks; John's of the paper variety and Colette's the plastic and aluminium.

'Handwriting makes you smarter. Did you know that?'

'So you tell me, John. I like this better.' She flicked open the cover of her laptop. 'Have we got an agenda?'

Colette took their Friday morning meetings seriously. It meant she could analyse the events of the week, plan for the next one and go home at five o'clock and forget about work. If there was one thing she didn't miss about teaching, it was taking work home on weekends.

'West Cork,' said John after their other projects had been discussed. 'How's that coming along?'

'Slowly.' Colette drained her cup.

'Is that builder still giving you a hard time?'

She thought about her parting exchange with Aidan the night before. *Together* was the word she remembered. It was a step in the right direction. 'Actually, I think there just might be a thaw in relations happening on that front.'

'Mm.' John didn't sound convinced. 'Business can be a painful way of finding out who one's friends are.'

'Trust me on this one. I know time is money, but I don't want to rush it.'

'Trust is something you've earned ten times over from me, Colette.' He set his glasses on his chest and looked at her. 'That's why I want to make you a partner.'

She set her cup down. 'Are you serious?'

John smiled and waited for his proposition to sink in.

'Are you sure?' She was sitting up straight on the sofa now.

'Why wouldn't I be sure? You're the best designer I've worked with, darling.' He looked over to the photo beside their diplomas. 'Steve always said you were special.'

At the mention of John's long-time partner, tears welled in her eyes. They'd been her biggest supports when she'd moved to London to study.

'I have to hug you, John.' She threw her arms about his neck.

'Watch the Guccis!' He pulled the glasses with their beaded string out of the way before putting an arm around her and kissing the top of her head. 'If I'd had a daughter, I'd have wanted one just like you,' he told her. 'You're like family to me.'

She'd wanted a daughter too. But this was no time to be maudlin. She had bills to pay, a mother to look after as she got older and, down the track, her own senior years to secure. She'd worked her socks off and would continue to do so. A partnership would just make it more her own.

'Now before we break open the bubbly, I do have some, well, some controversial news to break to you,' said John.

She drew a tissue over the edges of her eyes and sat back against the tangerine velour.

'My sister in Scotland wishes to send her son over here to work for me . . . for *us*, sorry. It's us from here on in.'

'We could certainly do with the help,' Colette began. 'What's he like? Has he skills?'

John took a deep breath. 'He's a bit of a rebel from what I remember. Lovely as a child, but went a bit wild in his teens. Kate says he needs a fresh start, a break from his mates in Glasgow who seem to be leading him astray.'

'Lovely.' The sarcasm replaced her short-lived euphoria. 'Just what we need around here. A charity case.'

'I can say no, Colette. You have an equal say in all decisions now.'

'Has he got a CV?'

'Can I borrow this?' He drew her laptop toward him and logged in to Facebook. 'This might give you an idea.'

From his profile picture, Shane MacKay looked, Colette supposed, like any other teenage boy. She glanced over the page. 'Three hundred and sixty five friends. One for every day of the year. He looks quite—'

'Normal?' John interrupted. He pointed to a recent status and scrolled down to give her a better look.

'"I love sex,"' she read aloud. 'Oh God.' Her eyes rested on a line drawing of a couple having intercourse in a most unflattering position. 'So, what are you saying?' She looked at John, grateful to take her eyes off the screen. 'You want me to take on a sex-crazed juvenile delinquent in a boutique interior design agency?'

'One month,' said John. 'If he doesn't behave himself, I'll send him back.'

She had a sneaking suspicion this would be one of the longest months of her life. *Just when things were starting to look up.*

Chapter Eleven

At seven-thirty, Colette was pretty much ready for Sandra Doyle to pick her up and drive them to Gerry's leaving do. It was a balmy summer's evening, perfect for airing some of the clothes that had been hibernating at the top of the wardrobe. She took another look at herself in the free-standing mirror she'd picked up in an antique shop. The white ankle grazers and buttoned-up sleeveless shirt hadn't seen daylight since the summer before, but they fit just the same. Her mother was fighting a losing battle in her efforts to fatten her up. No, she was a lean, fit machine and that's how she liked it. A last stroke of mascara, and she was ready to face the night.

Sandra wasn't usually late. She'd been as excited as Colette about Gerry and Ellen. They'd all been in school together. Sandra was, in fact, one of a very small number of people Colette could still call friends since her split with Tadhg. As a couple, they'd had a hectic social life, always going out to someone's birthday party or anniversary dinner. When she

went back to being single, the invites dried up. Friends like
Sandra had proved their mettle, just by staying in touch.

The bedroom door opened.

'That's Sandra for you, love.' Her mother handed her the
house phone.

'Sandra!' Colette threw a questioning frown to her mother
as she closed the door. 'Is everything okay?'

After a brief conversation, she went through to the kitchen
and replaced the handset.

'Has something come up, love?' her mother asked.

Colette sighed. 'One of the kids had his tooth knocked
out in a football match. They're in A and E.' She picked up
her red cashmere sweater and tucked a matching clutch bag
under her arm.

'Will you be okay on your own?'

She was touched by her mother's concern, but she was a
big girl, and big girls could look after themselves, couldn't
they? She wished she could say she'd got used to being independent in the years she'd been away from Tadhg, but every
social occasion was an effort. She told herself she'd be fine
once she got there. A nice white wine spritzer in the company
of old friends, and the constricting dread would disappear.

'I'll be grand.'

What else could she say to her seventy-two-year-old
mother. It wasn't like she could drag her along. Barbara Barry
would stand on her head for her daughters, but a heaving
pub on a Saturday night was not even on her radar. Colette
laughed at the idea.

'What's so funny?' Barbara asked as she saw her to the door.

Colette wrapped an arm around the shoulders that were level with her own.

'Oh, just pictured you joining me at The Stables.' She kissed her mum's cheek.

'Not on your nelly,' laughed Barbara as she herded her daughter out the door. 'You don't need your old mother to hold your hand in the midst of all those lusty men.'

'Mother dear, it's a going-away do, not an orgy.'

Barbara threw her eyes to heaven. 'Get out and enjoy yourself.'

—

The Stables was heaving. Colette scanned the crowd for familiar faces as she weaved between groups of drinkers. Heels would have helped. It was impossible to see over anyone in Mary Janes. Just when she was beginning to think she had the wrong night, she was grabbed from behind. Spinning round, she saw Gerry smiling down at her.

'Gerry, I thought you were some creepo!'

'Ah now, I saw you coming in there and I couldn't resist sneaking up on you.'

That was Gerry Clancy all over. With those twinkling blue eyes and mischievous sense of humour, you couldn't stay mad at him for long.

'Are you packed?' she asked.

'Nearly there,' he said. 'I'm not flying out till Tuesday, so I have a couple of days to do all the last-minute stuff.'

She was grateful for his strong hand at her back as he steered her toward the beer garden where some of their old school pals were interspersed with strangers at a long wooden table under a Heineken parasol. Gerry introduced her to everyone. Aidan was at the opposite end talking to Flynnie whom she instantly recognised despite a receding hairline. She thought she might have been imagining Aidan's face going red as they waved to her, but she'd seen the same reaction at the pub on Thursday night. That family were all a bit ruddy-cheeked, she reassured herself.

Michelle Cronin made a space for her on one side of the table.

'How've you been, Colette? Haven't seen you in years.'

Oh God. That would mean filling her in on the very events she'd rather forget.

'I hear you're an interior designer now.'

Thank God. A safe subject. Michelle listened with interest as Colette told her of her journey with John and Fabulous Four Walls. It turned out Michelle had just bought an old church and was in the throes of enlisting professional help with the renovations.

'I know a good builder as well,' Colette heard herself saying. Why she was recommending Aidan O'Shea, she wasn't entirely sure when all he seemed to do was stonewall her ideas.

'Is that Ellen's brother, the fella down there?'

Too late. Gerry must have done the introductions. 'That's him,' she said, trying to smile.

'Drinks, ladies.' A short man, whose midriff looked like something that could bounce its own way to the bar, set three glasses in front of them. 'Gerry said yours was a spritzer.'

'You haven't met my other half,' said Michelle. 'Brian, say hello to an old school friend. Colette, Brian—'

'Well, that wasn't today nor yesterday,' said Brian, laughing at his own joke.

'Listen to the spring chicken.' Michelle took hold of a pint glass and prodded Colette with an elbow. 'Colette, my old pal here, might help us with the house.'

Brian raised his eyebrows in surprise. 'I take it you're not a builder.' He gave a little chuckle again. Colette didn't know if she'd like to kill or cuddle him.

'She's an interior designer, you thicko,' said Michelle. Dismissing her husband, she turned to Colette. 'Have you a website?' She was already pulling her smartphone out of her handbag and searching up Fabulous Four Walls.

Colette smiled at the memories of the Michelle she knew in secondary school – eager to learn and unpretentious, even if a little rough around the edges. Just as well she'd married someone who thought he was hilarious.

'That kind of thing might be a bit pricey,' Brian was saying in an attempt to rein in Michelle's enthusiasm. 'Do you do any foxers?'

Colette forced herself to swallow her pride on this one. She was under no illusion that the services of an interior designer were within everyone's home-improvement budget, but moonlighting wasn't an option, especially now she'd signed a partnership agreement. Torn between a flat no and offering to help the couple out for nothing, she tried to be tactful.

'Not exactly,' she began, 'but I could certainly come and have a look . . .'

'Everyone enjoying themselves?' Gerry had appeared at the head of the table. Glasses were raised as the group chorused in the affirmative.

'Empty glasses down here,' someone shouted.

'Just can't get the staff these days,' said Gerry as he began stacking the empties in a tower in one hand.

Aidan got up and relieved him of the load with the ease of an expert. Colette didn't know if he'd worked in the trade. 'Sit down there and I'll get you a pint,' he told Gerry as he took the glasses inside.

As Michelle and Brian squabbled over what they wanted to do with their property, Colette watched Aidan disappear through the glass door and merge with the throng.

'I'll get the drinks in,' she said, making a grateful escape from the table.

'Colette, hang on.'

It was Harry O'Flynn, a white stubbly chin matching the thinning hair around his lined face. What had happened to the stocky teenager whose mother couldn't feed him enough? They stood side by side at the bar, arms touching in the sardine tin density of people waiting to buy drinks.

'The last time I saw you, you were just back from your honeymoon.'

'Been a while then, Flynnie,' she said, wishing Cork were smaller and you met people often enough to avoid having to explain your life to them. 'You tied the knot yourself, I heard.'

'I did indeed,' he said with a beam that took years off him. 'Have a couple of kids an' all.'

She could only beam back at him. Who'd have thought the Flynnster would have turned into a family man? 'How old are they?'

'Saoirse's nine and Ronan's eleven.' There was an almost visible swelling of his chest. 'I was a bit of a late starter,' he said with a wink. 'Never what you'd call a gigolo, as you may remember.'

Colette couldn't help but laugh. When it came to anything other than platonic relationships, the girls in her class had been unanimous in their allergy to Flynnie. He'd had a name for being the worst kisser known to Madden's Secondary School.

'But we won't talk about that,' he added quickly. 'Not in front of Jackie anyway.'

'Don't worry,' said Colette, 'some things are best shared only with the people that were there at the time.'

'What will you have, folks?' Aidan stood on the other side of the bar, tea towel slung over one shoulder as if he'd been doing this all his life.

'What are you doing serving?' She'd said it without thinking.

'Just giving them a bit of a hand so Gerry can have a break.'

Was he blushing again or was it hot in here?

'Gerry was actually rostered on tonight?' Flynnie was incredulous.

'You have no idea,' said Colette.

'Pint, Flynn?' Aidan asked.

'A Murphy's and whatever Colette's having.'

'White wine spritzer.'

Aidan had moved away to where he grabbed a pint glass and set it under a tap while he poured a glass of house white.

Hadn't he heard 'spritzer'? It was too noisy to shout to him, and anyway, she didn't want to embarrass him when he shouldn't even have had to be helping out.

'Donal Clancy never lost it,' she said, half to herself.

'Is that who owns the place?' asked Flynnie. 'I thought Gerry had a share—'

'Don't talk to me about this place,' Colette interrupted. 'Gerry will be glad to get away to Australia. He's been a slave here since they bought it.'

"Tis great about himself and Ellen all right,' said Flynnie, taking her cue to change the subject. "Twas an awful shame she left when she did. I don't think he ever quite got over it.' He leaned in as if to ensure no one would hear before adding, 'I often wondered if Jessica Sheehy hadn't got pregnant if he'd have up and left and gone out to Australia after Ellen.'

Colette nodded. *Twenty years!* So much had happened between the September her friend had left and the September just gone when she and Gerry had met again. If Gerry's son hadn't done a year's backpacking in Australia, they may never have had a second chance. Despite the failure of her own marriage, Colette had had her own successes in those twenty years, but she'd certainly learned that time was a thing that could easily slip away, if you let it, by holding on to the false hope that people or circumstances might change.

'Your drinks.' Aidan set the glasses down and took the note from Flynnie, who insisted on paying.

With drink flowing in the beer garden, Colette felt herself relax in the easy company of Gerry and his friends. When she found herself beside Flynnie again, she wondered why his wife wasn't with him.

'So, where's Jackie tonight?' she asked. But she wasn't prepared for what he told her.

She'd never heard of Ehlers-Danlos Syndrome. As she listened, her eyes widened. Life for Harry O'Flynn and his wife had become an exhausting schedule of hospital appointments since their son had been diagnosed. The frequency of trips back and forth to London for treatment and their unyielding support for the young boy had her spellbound. She was so engrossed in the story that the arrival of a bunch of drunken middle-aged men almost escaped her notice.

'There's Colette Caul-field!'

She froze at the sound of the name she'd denounced after the divorce. The shout had come from a table at the other side, but the last thing she wanted to do was look. Flynnie had stopped talking.

'Who the hell is that?' she asked, her head bent down over the handbag she pretended to be searching.

'I have no idea, but one of those loud blokes is heading this way.'

'Keep talking.' She chanced a quick glance through the hair that had fallen over her face.

'He's a tall fella with glasses. Greying mousy hair, check shirt ...'

'That's the prick I married.'

Tadhg Caulfield was making his unsteady way over to her, followed by an equally well-oiled Fergal O'Malley, who had been their best man.

'How've you been?' asked Tadhg, boasting a stupid smile, as if it were the most natural thing in the world to bump into her.

'Fine,' she managed, gritting her teeth as he squeezed in between her and a friend of Gerry's she hadn't met before tonight. The friend was no doubt a nice person, but she didn't appreciate his willingness to slide along the bench to give Tadhg room to put his sorry ass beside her for the first time in four years.

Tadhg gave a loud burp. 'Pardon me,' he slurred, putting a hand to his mouth in a futile attempt to cover the wafting smell of half-digested stout. Colette was sure she could feel the bile rising in her stomach. She'd had enough years of the up-close-and-personal with Tadhg Caulfield. Couldn't he just go away and leave her alone?

'I know we didn't part on the best of terms, Col—' he began before being interrupted by Fergal.

'Have you seen Baby Caulfield?' he said.

It was like a blow to the solar plexus. Glancing over her shoulder, she saw Fergal squinting at his phone, pint held in the crook of one arm while he struggled to stand in one spot. Tadhg gestured to Fergal to put the phone away.

'Yeah, I'm a dad at last,' he said, head down, almost apologetic.

Another person might have congratulated him, but Colette said nothing, desperate to maintain her composure. This was Gerry's night. No one here knew the details of her unhappy marriage. She wished more than ever that Sandra's teenager had dodged the ball, that Grace could have been here.

Her head swirled with the sounds of chatter and guffaws of laughter from all around her who were oblivious to her discomfort.

'We weren't so lucky, you and me,' said Tadhg, putting a hand on her thigh.

It was enough to make her snap. 'Get your fucking hands off me!'

There was a collective gasp as she shot to her feet and smacked the red handbag across her ex-husband's face. As she tried to swing one leg over the bench, Fergal set his hefty frame in her way.

'Wha's wrong wit' ya, Col?'

'I think you should leave her alone.' It was Flynnie who had stood up beside her.

'What's this all about, boys?' Gerry was calm, but in charge. 'We don't tolerate any harassment in this establishment.'

'Har-ass-ment!' said Tadhg, shocked. 'Assault, more like.' He held a hand to his face and looked like he might cry.

Gerry grabbed his arm and forced him to his feet.

'We're only wetting the baby's head,' Fergal protested.

'Well, unless you want this pint over your head, you'll get out of my pub.'

'Come on, boys,' Fergal called to the others. 'Let's get out of this hole.'

―

When Colette sat back down, she thought she might throw up. Michelle Cronin had taken Tadhg's seat and had an arm around her shoulder.

'I heard that fella was a prize wanker,' she said.

'You're well shot of him, girl,' said Flynnie.

He was right. They were both right. But she was the eejit who hadn't seen it coming, the complete dough ball who took ten years to cop on. She wanted to go home and curl up under her duvet and never have to set foot in the real world again.

'Get that down you, love,' said Brian as he held out a beautiful brandy glass. It was the shape that made her want to hold it. She slipped her fingers round the tiny stem, felt the ball of the glass in her palm and swirled the amber liquid as she let the comments, the music, the noise swish and swirl around her. She put it to her nose and before the pungent smell had even travelled all the way to her brain, she downed the drink.

'Good girl.' Michelle was rubbing her back as if soothing a sick child.

Sometimes she wished she *were* a child and could start over. She shook her head. 'I'd better go.'

There was a discussion about how she would get home. After several drinks, the car would have to stay put. Flynnie offered to share a taxi, but he lived on the other side of the city. Brian and Michelle were meeting other friends later. Gerry had to stay till closing.

'I'll be fine,' Colette assured them. 'I'm a grown woman. I'll walk home.'

━

Aidan came through from the main bar to see Colette backing away from the table, looking dishevelled. Gerry was running his hands through his hair. The general air of consternation must have had something to do with the bunch of drunken loudmouths Gerry had escorted through the lounge and sent on their way, but what it had to do with Colette Barry, Aidan had no idea.

'Goodnight,' she said as she brushed past him, her face flushed and her hair – well, not as perfect as it was when she'd walked in.

'Aidan,' Gerry called to him.

He joined the group and was about to sit down and enjoy the pint he'd waited over an hour to drink, when Gerry thwarted him again.

'She can't walk home on her own,' he was saying. There was a rumble of agreement. 'Would you go after her?'

The whole group were looking at him. *Oh man!* He'd half hoped he might find the seat beside Colette empty for once and enjoy his pint while actually having a civil conversation with the girl. This was not how he'd planned it. 'Right so.' He grabbed his fleece jacket from beside Flynnie and bid them all goodnight.

Gerry came with him to the door. As they shook hands, Aidan looked him squarely in the eye.

'Hope it all works out for yourself and my sister this time,' he said.

'Thanks, mate. Me too,' said Gerry. 'And mind Colette. Bad judge of men, I'd say.'

He caught sight of her just before she turned onto Patrick's Street. She wasn't hard to spot with the flame-red jumper and the white skinny jeans that made her look like she was in her early thirties instead of her forties. *Genes*, he mused. *Must be the genes*. But then, his own parents weren't heavyweights and look what happened to him. She was going at such a speed, he had to run to catch up.

'That's some pace you're setting, there,' he said, trying to stifle the need for a deep breath.

'Oh, they sent you to babysit me, did they?' She barely looked at him before striding on, her red bag swinging out to one side.

He looked down to see the red flat shoes taking determined steps along the pavement. Her usual heels would have slowed her down.

'I see you're a fan of red,' he said, for the want of something to say.

'Red, the colour of the mood I'm in right now,' she said as she continued to stomp.

'Sorry.'

She didn't respond. They were on Patrick's Bridge before she spoke again. When she stopped and turned to him, he was grateful for the chance to catch his breath.

'Do you have any idea why I'm so mad?' she started.

He shrugged and held up his hands in surrender. 'I just saw Gerry show a few guys the door. When I came back into the beer garden, Gerry's pals were around you, and then you were leaving.'

She threw back her head and laughed, a mocking laugh, devoid of pleasure.

'That was my ex-husband and his cronies Gerry threw out.' She resumed the brisk walk.

'I had no idea,' he said, following her toward the incline of Bridge Street.

'No, most people don't have an idea,' she went on. 'That's the problem.'

Christ, she was fit. Aidan wasn't sure where exactly she lived, but he suspected walking her home might give him a heart attack if it was Patrick's Hill. How the Tour de France types did it legally, he'd never know. He heaved a sigh of relief as they turned onto the gentler slope of Wellington Road.

'I'd have an idea if you told me,' he ventured, but immediately thought better of it. She was mad enough for both of them, whatever she was mad about. 'Sorry. You don't have to tell me anything . . . if you don't want to.'

'Oh, it's about time I told people about that shagger I ended up with.'

The vehemence in her voice made him shudder. She spoke as if he weren't there or at least as if she didn't care that he was. Gone were all traces of his sister's madcap friend. No, this was a version of Colette he hadn't seen before. Recently, when they'd crossed paths again, she was the kick-ass interior designer. At the pool, she was the super-fit, sociable girl he'd forgotten about. But tonight she was someone he hadn't yet met. She was on fire, albeit a drink-fuelled fire.

'You must have seen something in him.' As soon as he said it, he wished he hadn't.

'What would *you* know, Mr Bachelorhood?' she rounded. 'How in God's name would you have any idea what it's like to live with someone you thought you loved, hoped to have children with . . .'

He thought to attempt an answer, but she was off.

'How would you know what it's like to have to shag on demand in the faint hope that you might have a child, actually produce someone who would love you just the same as you'd love them. Someone who thought you were the best thing since sliced bread and loved you no matter what you weighed . . . or what you ate . . . or what kind of people you chose as friends.'

She took a couple of sideways steps and pressed a hand to the stone wall. He wasn't sure where to look as she spewed.

'The demon drink,' he muttered.

She shook her head as she rifled in her handbag and found a tissue. He heard her blow her nose and turned to see her draw the tissue across her mouth.

'It's all your fault anyway.' She stuffed the tissue in her bag as she walked on. 'If you'd given me what I ordered, I'd be fine.'

He shook his head. 'How is it my fault?'

'I was on white wine spritzers until you cocked up my order.'

It came back to him now. At the time, he'd wondered briefly if he'd heard right, but the place was so busy and lots of women drank white wine, didn't they?

'Sorry,' he said. All he seemed to be doing was apologising. If only that bastard husband hadn't shown up, they might be sitting happy in each other's company in the moonlit garden as the evening cooled. *Yeah, right!*

'No, it was probably the brandy that did it,' said Colette. She looked a bit calmer now. 'Remember that couple I was talking to at the start of the night? He gave me one when Tadhg left.'

Tadhg. Aidan remembered a conversation he'd had with Ellen. His sister couldn't understand what her friend had seen in him. A player, by all accounts. But then, there were women falling for the Tadhg Caulfields of this world every day of the week.

In the shop at St Luke's, he bought her a bottle of water.

'You hungry?' he asked.

She shook her head. He could have murdered a chocolate bar, but decided against it. The fitness drive was going well, but after the sprint he'd just done, it was obvious he still had a long way to go. They were standing outside to let Colette get some of the water into her when a group of young men emerged from Henchy's bar, clearly the worse for wear.

'You got lucky tonight,' one of them remarked to him. A roar of laughter went up from the others.

'Be careful out there,' Aidan replied.

One of them made the peace sign as they moved away down Summer Hill.

'We're getting one of them at Fabulous Four Walls for a month,' Colette half-whispered, nodding her head in the direction of the group. 'I'll be tearing my hair out by the end of it.' He watched her shake her hair back off her face before she took another swig. Dark, glossy hair. Silky smooth to the touch maybe. At least the bits that didn't have sick stuck to them.

'One of *those* boys?' He didn't understand.

'No, just a fella who fits the mould. Bit of a juvenile delinquent by all accounts.'

'Those guys are not so bad. Just out for a good night.'

'Yeah, well, when Shane MacKay comes to Cork, I'll have my work cut out.'

She told him about John's nephew as they made their way to Dillons Cross. By the time they turned in to Colette's road, he realised they'd slowed to a stroll.

'Send him over to us if he gives you any nonsense,' he said. 'Rob and the boys will sort him out.'

'Well, this is me,' she said, stopping at the end of a driveway that ran alongside a manicured lawn. 'Sorry you drew the short straw tonight.' She looked down at her shoes and a lock of hair fell on her face.

Without thinking, he reached out and pushed it gently to one side. She raised her eyes and pressed her head gently against his hand. For a split second, there was a flicker of vulnerability in those eyes that made him want to take her small frame in his arms and kiss her.

'Thanks for walking me home,' she said, her eyes dropping to her shoes again.

He drew his hand away as she straightened her jumper and clutched the red bag under one arm.

'I'm sorry you had to see me like this,' she said as she backed up the driveway.

He shook his head. 'Let me know when you want to take that trip down to West Cork.'

'Okay.' She gestured with an outstretched hand like a stop sign. 'Don't worry. I'll be the consummate professional by Monday. I'll give you a ring.' She waved before letting herself in the side door.

Aidan took his fleece from over his arm and pulled it on. He shoved his hands in his pockets and stowed the memory of her silky hair somewhere in the grey matter. *Warts and all*, he mused as he retraced some of their steps before taking a taxi home.

In the downstairs bathroom, Colette threw the dirty tissue from her handbag into the bin.

'Ugh, gross!'

As she washed her hands, she caught sight of herself in the mirror, semi-dried vomit at the edges of her hair.

'Oh Christ!' How could Aidan O'Shea have touched that? *He mustn't have seen it*, she argued. *Ah God, a blind man could see it. In fact, a blind man would smell it*, she reasoned as she leaned down to wash her hair out under the tap. 'God!' She couldn't believe it. After the tirade he'd witnessed, surely he couldn't have been making a pass at her. No, he'd just felt sorry for her. That had to be it.

She brushed her teeth and went upstairs to bed. But she couldn't sleep. Tadhg Caulfield had ruined a large part of her life and now he'd ruined her night. The audacity of him casually coming over to her, the pathetic look on his face when Fergal mentioned the baby, the invasion of her personal space had all made the anger bubble up inside, and boy had it boiled over. She'd really hurt him with that handbag. Physical violence wasn't something she'd ever resorted to before. Nor had Tadhg. No, his style of bullying was the verbal, emotional variety, hitting where it hurt inside her head, and her heart, what was left of it.

Of all the nights for Gerry to have his going-away do. Tadhg's little exhibition had ruined his night too. She'd ring him before he left for Australia and apologise. As tears seeped into her skin, despite her best efforts to fight them back, she put a hand under the cheek Aidan had touched and closed her eyes.

Chapter Twelve

Ben and Grace were preparing the usual sumptuous Sunday lunch when Colette and Barbara arrived in Blackrock. At Ben's offer of a glass of wine, Barbara announced she was driving and on the dry, thanks to Colette.

'Tell us more,' said Grace, who was mixing dressing into a large salad bowl.

'Oh, it was just Gerry's leaving do at The Stables,' said Colette. 'Pretty tame, really.' She tried her best to shoot Grace a dagger of a glance, but it was Grace and her mother who were making faces at one another. 'Stop it, you two. I just had one too many to drive. That's all.'

Colette's stomach had indeed recovered from the effects of last night, but just in case, she would take it easy on the barbecued delights that would be cooked up when they got back from their run and decline her nephews' invitations to join them on the trampoline. Besides, letting her family believe she had a hangover was easier than getting into an explanation of what had actually gone on at The Stables.

'Granny's going to look after you all while we go for our run,' Grace called to the boys when she'd made sure they had everything ready in the fridge for later.

'*We'll* be looking after Granny actually,' shouted Sam, the eldest of the six-year-old twins by twelve minutes, as he liked to tell everyone.

'Oh, that's kind of you,' said Barbara. 'I need looking after at my age.'

'For payment,' said Tom, the *younger* twin, 'we could test your cheesecake for you, Gran.' He made a funny face and promptly fell onto the trampoline and into a fit of giggles.

'Do you think Sophie would like some?' asked Barbara, smiling at her granddaughter who was busy pushing a cart full of furry toys on the decking.

Not even two, but not one to be outdone by her brothers, Sophie toddled over and reached for her grandmother.

'Let's move before she changes her mind,' Grace whispered over her shoulder.

As she ran along the marina with her sister and brother-in-law, Colette marvelled at the beauty of Blackrock Castle looming before them. A team of rowers pulled in unison as their oars skimmed the calm waters of the River Lee. With so many people out making the most of the glorious late morning, they had to run in single file.

'Isn't that your man, the builder?' Grace called over her shoulder.

She looked past Grace and Ben to see the massive dog she'd seen with Aidan. It looked like him walking it, but there was a child with him. *Must be someone else*, she thought and put her head down to keep up with Ben's brisk pace.

'Nice dog,' said Grace.

Colette nearly tripped over her sister, who had slowed down and was swooning over the huge brindle creature. It was Aidan all right.

Colette wished she could make herself invisible and keep running. It would be rude not to stop, she reasoned as she pulled up, putting her hands on her hips and steadying her breathing.

'Hi,' he said, tightening his grip on the lead as the dog approached for a sniff.

'Hi,' was all she could manage as she took in the sight of him, dog on one hand and a small delicate-looking child on the other.

'This is Millie.' He followed her gaze to the girl, who had pushed herself against the side of his leg and hidden half her face in the tails of his short-sleeved shirt.

'Hello, Millie. I'm Colette.' She went to bend down, but the child pushed further into him.

'And Julius of course.' He nodded toward the dog who was straining on the tight leash.

Her brain was in overdrive trying to compute the incongruity of the scene. Ellen hadn't mentioned a child. Neither had Gerry.

'Long run today?' he asked.

Her words from the previous night came rushing back like a pounding headache. Mr Bachelorhood, she'd called him.

'I'm so sorry about last night.' Although her face was already beetroot from the run, she doubted it was much cover as she stood there like a stunned mullet.

'Can we go now Aidan?' the girl asked as she pulled at the freckled hand that looked so big in comparison to her own.

'Yes, Millie. I'm just going to say goodbye to the nice lady.' He winked at Colette. 'We've got a hot date with Shrek, you know.'

'I'd better let you go.' She looked down at the child, who hadn't as much as loosened her grip of his hand. 'It was lovely to meet you, Millie.'

She was rewarded with a smile, one tooth short of a perfect set of milk teeth.

—

Colette caught up with Ben and Grace below the castle.

'When do children start losing teeth?'

'About six or seven,' said Ben. 'The boys aren't far off losing theirs.'

'Remember the Communion pictures?' asked Grace.

Colette had a flashback to her childhood when children used to make their Holy Communion at seven and there were always those unfortunates with front teeth missing in the photos.

'Why the sudden interest in children's teeth?' asked Grace.

As they ran, Colette scanned the houses along Church Road, looking for Aidan's Land Rover. 'Just wondering about that child with Aidan.'

'His niece?' Grace suggested.

'His only sibling is Ellen,' Colette countered. 'Her Louise must be twenty.' She took a couple of breaths before adding, 'And she lives in Australia.'

'A friend's child, then?' Grace offered. 'Maybe he's babysitting.'

'Mm.' It was really none of her business, but she wanted to know all the same.

'A child from a previous relationship?' Ben suggested.

Colette dismissed the idea. 'She called him Aidan.'

'Some people like their children calling them by their first names,' said Ben.

'Go in front, Ben,' Grace told him. 'You're not helping.'

Colette was a little taken aback by the edge to Grace's tone, but she wasn't surprised to see Ben run on. If there was one thing her brother-in-law hated, it was his wife and sister-in-law's conversations about men. Best out of them, he'd always maintained.

'Don't mind him, Colette,' Grace reassured her. 'Aidan O'Shea doesn't strike me as that kind of parent.'

'But what if it was the mother's idea and he didn't have a choice?'

'There's always a choice,' said Grace firmly.

—

Colette flopped down on the sofa beside her nephews.

'Ugh, Sweaty Betty!' they chorused and ran out the back to join their father on the trampoline.

'Oh, the monsters,' her mother laughed as Sophie stirred on the pillow beside her.

Colette reached over and stroked her sleepy niece's tummy. 'Hey, Soph,' she said softly, 'how many teeth you got?'

Sophie bared her tiny teeth before climbing onto her grandmother's lap and closing her eyes again.

'Colette! There won't be a child in Cork safe from your teeth quest.' Grace handed her a glass of water and sank into an armchair opposite them.

'What's this about teeth?' asked Barbara.

'We ran into Aidan O'Shea, Colette's friend.' Grace gave an exasperated sigh. 'Him and his mystery child.'

'Was it he walked you home last night?' Barbara asked.

Colette nearly choked on her drink. 'How do you know he walked me home?'

'Ah now, girls,' said Barbara, 'don't you know a mother's job is never done until her children are all safe in their beds?'

Grace shot her a sympathetic look as Colette sucked in her annoyance at the well-meaning comment.

'Anyway,' Barbara continued, 'I drew back the bedroom curtain and spotted him saying goodnight to you.'

Colette said a silent prayer of thanks her mother hadn't caught them in the throes of a passionate snog. Not that there was any chance of that.

'I recognised him, of course,' said Barbara.

'How?' Colette couldn't believe it.

'Sure didn't he put in the built-ins while you were across the water?'

'That's right,' said Grace. 'I'd forgotten about that.'

'You didn't even see him,' said Barbara with a sideways glance at Grace. 'You were too busy.'

Colette ignored the layers the conversation was forming and focused on the timing of the wall-to-wall cupboards her mother had had installed in the bedrooms. She had indeed been surprised when she returned to Cork after her first year away to find her mother had gone a bit mad on decluttering after reading a book by Marie Kondo. But Aidan O'Shea as joiner; that was a detail she'd overlooked. At the time her mother had said she'd got a nice local lad to do the work. Colette had been so wrapped up in her escape to London, she hadn't had the energy to get involved. A twinge of guilt gripped her now, but the memories of the gargantuan effort it had taken to leave her beloved city and end a safe teaching career reminded her of the headspace she'd been in at the time. Tadhg Caulfield sure had a lot to answer for.

'Excellent worker,' Barbara was saying as Colette came out of her reverie and drank deeply from her glass. 'He must be great to work with.'

She couldn't look at Grace.

'Yeah, he is all right.'

As they ate lunch, Colette knew Grace's nose would be well and truly at her and she'd be desperate to quiz her on how she'd managed to end up with Aidan O'Shea after a night out.

'I suppose we'd better think about collecting my car,' said Colette as soon as she could once they'd eaten. By the time they'd said their goodbyes and made their way to Barbara's Micra, Grace had already sent a text.

Phone me!!

Colette smiled to herself.

'Ben was a bit quiet,' said Barbara as they drove off.

'Between work and the kids, he's probably wrecked.'

Her mother didn't sound convinced, but Colette had other things on her mind. Although the Tadhg episode was still sinking in, her thoughts were being rapidly taken over by her conversation with Aidan. Now, more than ever, she regretted her tirade. Maybe he was more of an authority on a child's love than she'd imagined, and as for romantic love . . . But it was none of her business. She wouldn't go there.

—

Grace looked out her kitchen window onto the small lawn she and Ben had lovingly transformed from a patch of dirt. They'd bought the house as a new build in what had been a quiet cul de sac. In the six years they'd lived here, enough young families had moved in to make the street look like something from *The Little Rascals*. One of the neighbours even owned a friendly bulldog. Grace would have loved a dog. She imagined a golden retriever running after a ball, a long feathery tail held high, eyes fixed on the boys, watching their every move. A dog gentle enough for Sophie to wrap her arms around and cuddle, maybe even sit on now and then.

She pushed the daydream aside and began to stack the dishwasher. Her mother had been in good form, and Colette had a lightness to her that Grace hadn't seen in a long time. Aidan O'Shea seemed like a lovely bloke. She hoped to God something was happening there on the romantic front. At the sound of sobbing, she turned to see Ben carrying an injured Sophie into the kitchen.

'Oh sweetheart, did you fall?'

Sophie reached out her two little arms as Ben handed her over.

'Nothing a cuddle with Mum won't fix,' he said, already turning to the sink and wetting a cloth. Grace set Sophie's bottom on the small island, holding her close and smoothing her silky curls. Ben handed her the cloth and went back to his gardening without another word. He was hurt too. Dabbing at the graze on Sophie's knee, Grace wished his wound could be as easily fixed.

Aidan settled himself on the couch with Millie and helped her work her way through the remote-control buttons to play the movie she so desperately wanted to watch with him. At the sound of the theme music, Julius gave a groan and threw himself down on his bed for a sleep. Aidan could well have nodded off too with Millie nestled against him. It didn't matter how much time passed between visits, she always slotted right back in as if she'd seen him the day before. If only things had worked out better with Jane; they might all be here curled up together. He stroked Millie's untidy blonde hair and kissed the top of her head, wondering how her mother was faring with Bryce Manning. He'd asked Millie about him, but she'd never said much, just enough for Aidan to know she wasn't her father's biggest fan. Children could be so much smarter than adults.

Chapter Thirteen

'Howdy, partner!'

John greeted Colette with his usual flourish as she arrived at Fabulous Four Walls a tad late. A beautiful bouquet of flowers sat on the oak hall stand they'd painstakingly restored together.

'Have you been splashing out again?' she asked, handing him his coffee.

'No, my dear. They're a gift from the previous owners of Carlton Manor.'

'How thoughtful!' She bent to smell the sweet scent of the brightly coloured gerberas.

'By all accounts,' said John, 'they never expected to get such a good price, and they're crediting us with much of the profit.'

'Let's hope they broadcast it far and wide.'

John followed her into her office, signalling an imminent announcement. She set her bag on the desk and switched on her computer as John sipped his coffee at the window and took in the morning view over the river.

'Shane's on his way,' he began. 'Kate rang last night and gave me the details. I'll collect him from the airport tonight.'

Colette sat down. The challenge of keeping a wayward youth meaningfully engaged for a month would require an energy she wasn't sure she could muster.

'Aidan's offered to have him if he gives us any trouble.'

John turned round, his eyebrows raised. 'Bob the Builder?'

She couldn't help but smile.

'Do I take it you're friends again?'

The image of Millie squeezing Aidan's hand gnawed at her brain.

'I saw him at the weekend,' she said, trying to sound matter-of-fact.

John was looking at her as one might look down a microscope. There was no hiding the colour that had rushed to her cheeks at the mention of Aidan's name.

'Always helps to be on the right side of the builder,' he went on. 'We may not require his boot camp services, but it's no harm keeping it up our sleeve.'

She was grateful when he left without further comment. Not much escaped John's notice in the feelings department, but he waited to be consulted on matters of a personal nature. That way, she could come to work and leave such matters at home – most of the time.

⁓

A stop at The Stables had made her late, but she'd had to see Gerry to say a proper goodbye. He'd brushed off her apology with his usual ease.

'Don't mention it,' he said. 'As long as you got home safe and didn't let the incident get you down too much.'

Ellen was one lucky woman. Good looks and humour were only the half of it. Above all else, Gerry was dependable, solid, someone who wanted the best for the people he cared about.

'Aidan got you home all right?'

It was the opportunity she needed to grasp before he left the country.

'I ran into him again yesterday.' She tried to sound casual. 'He was with a child.'

'Millie?'

She nodded.

'Ah, Millie's a dote.' The mention of the child brought a cheery smile to his face. 'Aidan is mad about her, and she idolises him.' He gave a tut. 'A pity the same couldn't be said of her mother.' The smile was gone.

Colette listened.

'He met her a while back,' Gerry said thoughtfully. 'In a way, I can't believe Aidan still sees her.'

'Millie or the mother?' Colette heard herself almost spit the question at him.

'Both, I suppose.' He shook his head. 'No, once Daddy decides to come back on the scene, Aidan gets shafted.'

She closed her gaping mouth to hide her keen interest.

'Handy babysitter is all he is, really,' said Gerry. 'Wasting his time thinking anything else, I'd say.'

'What a shame.'

'A shame indeed,' he said. 'Too nice a bloke for his own good, our Aidan. Loves that child, like she was his own.'

'Doesn't she have grandparents or aunts and uncles?'

'The mother's Australian. No family here.' He paused before adding, 'Aidan is probably the closest thing to an uncle the child has.'

Oh God. Just what she needed. Another reminder of how awful she'd been. How could she ever make it up to him?

━

When John left her office, Colette looked over the week's schedule. There were client visits on every day, design student assessments locked in for Wednesday, a staging on Thursday. The forecast was good for the week. An ideal time to visit West Cork. Surely, she could move the one Friday appointment. She dialled Aidan's number.

'O'Shea Builders. This is Fern. How can I help you?'

The female voice surprised her. For some reason, she had expected Aidan to answer.

'Oh, hello, I, em, I was looking for Aidan.' A strong pulsing in her neck annoyed her. It was a business phone call, for God's sake.

'He's not here at the moment. Can I take a message?'

'It's okay. I have his mobile.'

'Can I ask who's calling?'

She had a childish urge to hang up. 'It's Colette, Colette Barry, from Fabulous Four Walls, the interior—'

'Oh yes. I know who you are. Aidan mentioned you.'

She scratched at the burning in her neck.

'They're in West Cork all week actually,' the woman went on. 'My husband works for Aidan too, you see.'

'Oh, oh right.' So, they were all down there, and she was being kept in the dark.

'You could try him on his mobile,' came the voice again. 'I'll tell him you called.'

Colette wanted to tell her not to bother, that she'd only sound desperate, but thanked her as calmly as possible and rang off. If only Gerry were staying, she'd have an ally. Aidan O'Shea, the enigma – one minute she was feeling sorry for him, the next he was making her blood boil. God only knew how far into the project he planned to go before consulting her. She phoned her client and moved their Friday meeting to Thursday. She was going to West Cork, whether Aidan liked it or not.

—

If first impressions lasted, Colette didn't hold out much hope for her relationship with John's nephew. When there was no answer at Fabulous Four Walls the next morning, she'd been forced to ring Declan Byrne's bell and explain to his none-too-pleased receptionist that John was late and she'd forgotten her own key. It was close to ten by the time John appeared at her office door, his lanky dark-haired nephew in tow. John rolled his eyes at her before gesturing to Shane to go in.

'This is my partner, Colette.'

This long string of potential misery didn't seem to care too much who she was, but Colette was grateful to have been given her rightful title. Being an equal to his uncle might prove an important weapon in an arsenal she stored for future reference. She rose from her desk and stretched out a hand.

The ends of her fingers were barely grasped before the boy's pale hand returned to the pocket of his low-hung jeans. His T-shirt made all the conversation required of the situation. '*Youth well wasted*', it shouted in block letters.

'I've got that appointment I was telling you about,' said John. 'Shane will be fine with you for an hour or so.' He put his hands together in a sign of prayer when Shane wasn't looking.

It wasn't even a question, but the pained look on John's face made Colette reconsider protesting. She'd been more productive than expected already this morning, with suppliers and contractors all on schedule. An hour with Shane might give her a chance to set a few ground rules and maybe even glean a little about his background, if he ever decided to open his mouth to emit more than a grunt. She smiled at John who gave her a surreptitious thumbs-up as he left.

'Have a seat.' She watched the young man slouch into the chair in front of her. 'Have you been in Cork before?'

'Aye.'

Open questions, she told herself.

'So, what has John planned for you at Fabulous Four Walls?'

A shrug in response.

Lovely!

He stretched out an arm toward her desk and took a brand-new notebook from a pile of three.

'All right if I take one?'

'Sure,' she said, seething as she watched him scan the pen holders.

'Would you like a pen as well?' she asked only to get in before he helped himself.

Without answering, he selected a pencil from one of her coordinating pots. She was just about to ask him what he planned to use it for when her phone rang.

'Fabulous Four Walls, Colette speaking.' She went to gesture an apology, but he was ignoring her and scribbling in the notebook.

'Oh, hi, Aidan. Yes, she told me you were down there all week.' Colette swivelled her chair away from Shane in an effort to block out the distraction of the scratching pencil, not to mind the brazen T-shirt. 'I think I could squeeze you in on Friday. I'm down that way seeing a client anyway.' She heard the lie, but pushed the ripple of guilt to the back of her mind. 'I might have Shane with me. John's nephew.'

When she rang off and turned back to the desk, the boy was staring at her.

'Are you married?' he asked.

Good God. What is this boy on?

'Divorced,' she answered, and before she could ask why it was any of his business, he'd returned to his scribbling.

'Right,' she said, getting up from her desk and straightening her jacket, suddenly uncomfortable with whatever thoughts might be going through this young man's mind. 'I'll show you round.'

The notebook was stashed in a back pocket, sending the jeans even further down the blatant boxer shorts. She let him past and pulled the door behind her. Introducing him to the staff on the two floors above would be a precautionary measure; if they knew who he was, Colette reasoned, they'd be able to identify him in the event of any incident. She hoped to God the month would be devoid of anything that would sully the reputation she and John had built, not just with their own clients, but with the staff and customers who used the rest of the building. There were standards to be maintained, and she was damned if this Scottish blow-in would do anything to lower them.

'You'll love working with Colette,' Declan Byrne assured him when they entered the antiseptic-laden space of Byrne and Associates Dental Practice. 'She'll show you the ropes, I'm sure.' He'd winked as he'd said it, making her question the standards she was so keen to uphold.

Edwina and Prudence on the third floor weren't much better.

'I'm sure some of our Continental girls will be seeking you out to practise their language skills,' Prudence told Shane with a giggle that made Colette want to throttle her.

'Don't encourage him,' she whispered to Prue when Edwina had taken him into one of the classrooms. 'He's here for a month. John's sister needs a break, by all accounts.'

'Oh, a bit of a worry, is he?' Prudence raised her pencilled-in eyebrows and eyed the boy through the doorway.

'Let's just say,' Colette whispered again, 'the sooner this month is over, the better.'

In the garden, Shane took a roll-up cigarette from his trousers pocket.

'Got a light?' he asked as if she would just magic a lighter from somewhere on her person.

'I don't smoke the wretched things,' she said.

'What do you smoke, then?'

Ah, very funny. A real smartass.

'You may have time to slowly kill yourself,' she said, opening the door to go back inside, 'but some of us have work to do.'

Chapter Fourteen

Ellen took a last sip of the coffee she'd bought to pass the time in the small regional airport when the delay had been announced. Other people had settled to reading magazines or scrolling on mobile phones, but this waiting was eating away at her. She walked outside into the fresh winter morning and searched the sky for signs of Gerry's plane. Weeks of waiting for him seemed like nothing compared to these unbearable minutes. The house was ready; rooms and furniture had been rearranged, photographs sorted through, all to try and make the man feel welcome. Although she would never forget Nick, now that Gerry had made a commitment to live with her, the last thing she wanted was to have him feel uncomfortable in her dead husband's home.

Tracey had been a stalwart as usual, advising but not pushing, scrapping ideas as soon as Ellen came up with different ones, and as generous with the elbow grease as if it were her own family that were coming. She smiled to herself as she paced along the fence line, peering at the cloudy sky.

Her house always looked better with Tracey's help. Better than any Mr Sheen. There it was, the Q400 from Adelaide, almost an hour late, but here, approaching the runway like an albatross returning to its nest after fishing at sea.

Back in arrivals, she considered a quick nip into the bathroom to have a look in the mirror, but it was too late. Gerry must have been seated right behind the cockpit. The door opened and there he was at the top of the steps, saying cheerio to the hostess and stepping out, rucksack over the shoulder of a waterproof jacket that billowed in the stiff breeze. The skin tingled on her arms as she clasped her hands together to stem the urge to wave frantically at him. He was finally here, on a one-way ticket.

'What happened to the Australian sunshine?' he said, gesturing with his thumb and looking back toward the tarmac.

The feel of the car keys in her coat pocket reminded her she'd stuffed her hands in there as she'd waited for what felt like an age for him to walk through the arrivals' door. What happened to the romantic reunion she'd imagined, like the last time she'd seen him when he'd whisked her off her feet and kissed her?

'Did your luggage come straight through?' she found herself asking as he turned back. Maybe he was having second thoughts, imagining being trapped in South Australia and wondering if he could just run back through the doors and jump on the plane before it took off back to Adelaide.

'Lead on, MacDuff,' he said and followed her to where an airport vehicle was parking a trailer loaded with suitcases to one side of the terminal building. They stood like a pair of business associates who'd never met before and didn't speak the same language.

'There it is,' said Gerry stepping up to the trailer and grabbing the handle of a smart new-looking Samsonite suitcase. He set it on the ground beside him and quickly retrieved an even bigger matching one from further along. As they manoeuvred the cases through the crowd and out to the car park, the reality of what they were doing confronted her.

'How did you manage to take this much with you?' she ventured.

'Paid for every extra kilo,' said Gerry.

The hundred questions she wanted to ask him seemed to back up just behind her tongue. She opened the boot of the Chrysler, the car that, in the aftermath of Nick's death, had sat for months in the shed on Ocean Road. To think if Gerry hadn't come to Australia, both she and the Chrysler might still be up there gathering dust. She watched as he positioned his belongings inside.

'How is the old girl going for you?' he asked over his shoulder.

'Good,' she said, the word escaping like a lone pebble sent to test the depth of water.

He slammed the boot shut, making her jump. He rested a hand on the turquoise bodywork and looked at her. Not the up-and-down intake of her appearance she'd seen him do when he landed, but a look straight in the eye that seemed to reach to her soul.

'Nervous?' he asked.

'Very,' she answered.

'Makes two of us, so.'

He took a step closer and put a hand gently under her chin. When she tilted her head toward him, she felt the familiar lips press against her own. Her hands reached in to touch the shirt under his jacket. The warmth of the space enveloped her, and she was lost in the smell of him as he drew up the hair at the nape of her neck and kissed her deeply.

'Look!' someone shouted. They broke apart and saw a young boy being shushed by his mother. Ellen buried her face in Gerry's shoulder and felt his mouth at her ear as he bent his head to whisper, 'I think we should go before we have to start charging people.'

The sound of her own laughter was like a powerful medicine, rushing through her veins, sending reassurance to every corner of her careful, mistrusting self that this was right, this was absolutely how it should be.

⸺

By Thursday, Colette was convinced it had to be Friday and someone had messed with the dates. Three days of Shane MacKay had been enough to try the patience of a saint. When John had phoned to say he'd be late back from his meeting on Tuesday morning, she'd made the mistake of taking Shane with her to her own appointments. It was either that, or leave him to his own devices. The latter proved a non-starter after she'd left him alone in her office while she went to the loo, only to come back to find he'd taken a pair of scissors to one of her expensive magazines.

'You can't do that,' she'd told him with too much incredulity to sound like a serious reprimand. Anyway, he'd just shrugged and set the scissors back in their pot before stuffing the pictures into his notebook.

He'd then sat his belligerent behind in the car beside her and given monosyllabic answers to all her efforts at open questions. She gave up. Two house calls and she would have happily handed him back to his uncle. Maybe Aidan's offer wasn't such a crazy one after all. But it was early days. She had to persevere, if not for the boy's sake, then for John's. How any sibling of her gentlemanly boss could produce such a disengaged offspring, she couldn't fathom.

Timothy Conway: recently divorced, retired judge, aviation enthusiast. Colette went over the details of her first client as they drove in silence toward the Lee Road on the western side of the city. A proper summer's day, with only the whitest of cloud shifting across blue skies, provided the perfect antidote to her dour driving companion. She hadn't been to the house, but Timothy had implied on the phone that he wished to make some serious changes to the results of his ex-wife's particular tastes.

She parked the car at the kerb of the walled street and loaded Shane up with the box of samples she brought to such consultations. If there was one thing this young man would be good for, it was donkey work. Moss shone an iridescent green on the archway that was the entrance to the property. Stone steps led to a garden, where Timothy was sitting at a white wrought-iron café table. A jug of what looked like homemade lemonade sat on a tray with two glasses. He beckoned to them as he held a mobile phone to his ear. As they followed the paved path, Colette thought to tell Shane that he could leave the talking to her, but there wasn't much danger of him saying anything in the first place.

Timothy ended his call and stood to shake hands with a strong, reassuring grip. Colette had always been careful working one-on-one. This line of work was such a change from the busy school environment, and when she'd started in the business, she'd been so paranoid, she would get John to phone mid-appointment to make sure she was safe. Part of that had been a hangover from the days when Tadhg Caulfield had messed with her head. She'd found ways of managing it, but sometimes it still took some effort.

'Ah, a young apprentice,' said Timothy, putting his phone on the table and stretching out a hand to Shane.

Colette cringed as she saw the boy balance the box with one arm and reluctantly offer the limp digits of his free hand. She willed Timothy to crunch his knuckles a little.

'Shane is John Buckley's nephew. He's working with us for a few weeks,' she said.

'We might all have a drink once you've been through the house?' Timothy suggested.

'That would be lovely, Timothy.' She didn't look at Shane, who, she imagined, would prefer a can of one of those keep-you-awake-forever drinks or something even stronger in preference to homemade lemonade.

'Come through, come through,' said Timothy, ushering them toward the house.

She took in the freshly painted exterior. Glossy white window surrounds dazzled in the sunshine against the cool blue walls, giving the house a coastal look.

'You've made a good job of the outside,' she said.

Timothy paused and glanced over the façade of the three-storey house.

'Better than bright orange, don't you think?'

Although a fan of bright colours, Colette couldn't imagine the refined Timothy Conway living in a house painted in anything garish. She stepped over the threshold, curious to see what exactly he wanted to change.

The narrow hallway – with its claustrophobia-inducing crimson textured wallpaper – gave her a good idea. A retro telephone rested on a seventies table seat with plush green upholstery. A brass umbrella stand occupied one corner. The hardwood flooring was almost occluded by a dark woollen rug that had seen better days. A large chandelier dominated the too-small space, and cornices brought the ceiling in on itself.

In the living room, the same patterned cornices adorned the larger ceiling, but it was the leopard-skin wallpapered feature wall that really stopped her in her tracks. At the sound of a snigger from behind her, Colette turned and glared at Shane, who quickly put a hand to his mouth in mock shame.

'I don't blame you, son,' said Timothy. 'How I put up with it for so long is a mystery.'

'I take it you weren't consulted on the decorating, then,' said Colette.

'I'd come home after a few days away and it would all be done. Started to dread the annual conference for fear of what she'd do next.'

'But the accessories, things like these cushions?' She took a faux-fur zebra-striped cushion in her arms. 'Or the lamps?' She pointed to two ornate brass lamp stands. 'Didn't she want to take any of it with her?'

'Left in a hurry, you see. Ran off to Dublin with a barrister. Used to be a friend of mine.'

It was painful to watch the resigned expression on the face of a man so respected among his peers. He'd tried murderers, for God's sake. But Colette knew only too well that what went on behind closed doors didn't always correlate with what those outside perceived. She took a deep breath.

'Right. Would you like to show me the rest of the house and we can start planning some changes?'

Shane's face threatened to stymie her attempts at reserving judgement on the overuse of animal print. In the master bedroom, the hide of something huge took up most of the floor between the door and the four-poster bed; the absence of a head did nothing to reassure Colette that the item hadn't once been a living, breathing animal. Definitely not her thing, but then to each his own, as she was often forced to remind herself.

After a tour of the house, it was a relief to sit in the garden and taste the refreshing lemonade. Shane had declined the drink despite Timothy having fetched an extra glass on the way out.

'Mm. That's delicious, Timothy,' said Colette. 'Did you make it?'

'Avril never let me near the kitchen, so I'm having fun experimenting.'

The fire-engine red kitchen, yes. That was another room for improvement. Aware of Shane's boredom, Colette glanced around the garden. A wheelbarrow stood at the far wall.

'Is there anything you'd like to change out here?' she asked Timothy.

He pointed a finger and made an arc with his arm. 'Every one of those ugly gnomes will have to go,' he said. 'Hate the bloody things.'

She could feel the empowerment her visit had awakened in the man. It was always the same. Employing the services of an interior designer was like gaining an important ally in a war for change.

She turned to Shane, who looked like he might fall asleep in the late-morning sunshine. 'Would you be so kind as to start collecting those gnomes into that wheelbarrow?'

She held his gaze until the defiance dissipated.

'Thanks, son,' said Timothy, sealing the deal.

She took out a sketchpad and talked Timothy through the rooms, throwing ideas back and forth on layout before turning to lighting and colour schemes. As Timothy browsed catalogues, Colette fired up her laptop and found examples of furnishings that might suit his needs. The only room she'd liked was his study. There was enough flying memorabilia in there to decorate most of the house. But that in itself could be stressful; transforming what must have been his hideaway into a space that could blend seamlessly with the rest of the interior. She had known clients to be disappointed despite her best efforts to strictly adhere to their requests. The colour coordination, accurate measurements and proportions were easy to get right. It was the psychology that challenged her.

'It will be very different when we've finished, you know,' she said. 'I won't do anything you're not a hundred per cent comfortable with, but there's always risk involved.'

He smiled and said, 'My girl, you're doing me a huge favour. I should have taken risks years ago.'

⟶

At their next stop, Michelle Cronin hadn't pulled any punches when Brian took Shane inside the old church and out of earshot.

'How long do you have to put up with that waste of space?' she'd asked.

Colette had smiled despite her attempts at being charitable. 'A month tops, or I'll be in the loony bin.'

Michelle laughed. 'Took a bit of convincing to get Brian to agree to have you come out,' she confided.

Colette cast her eye over the rundown building with its broken stained-glass windows. 'After I met you that night in The Stables, I didn't think you'd hire me at all. What changed your mind?'

There was a high-pitched scream and Shane came running out. When he saw them, he stopped short in the doorway, straightening his T-shirt and grabbing at the back of his neck as if something were crawling over it. Brian came out behind him and leaned against the doorframe, unable to speak as he doubled over, wheezing with laughter.

'What happened?' Michelle asked.

'There's a fuckin' rat in there,' said Shane.

Colette wanted to wash his mouth out with soap on the spot, but the sight of Brian, who by now had tears rolling down his cheeks, made her laugh. Michelle too had joined in.

'Bunch of wankers,' was all they heard before Shane stomped off to the car and left them to the hilarity.

'It'll be a long month if that fella doesn't lighten up,' said Michelle.

'You should have seen his face,' said Brian, gasping in deep breaths. 'It was classic. Ran out of there like a scalded cat.'

The rat was long gone by the time Colette got to the back of the old church the Cronins were planning to turn into a family home. Bought for a song, according to Brian, which was why they could afford someone like her to help renovate it. *Saw you coming, more like*, Colette thought. But she was here now. The place could be amazing if they got it right. She stepped over the rotting timbers and tried to block out the damp stench. It took a stretch of even her vivid imagination to picture the changes the couple and their architect were planning.

'Who's your builder?' she asked, ducking her head to avoid a loose beam.

'Aidan O'Shea,' said Michelle. 'It's funny, after talking to you that night, we phoned him up and he said if we were serious about someone coming in to advise on the home décor, not to go past you.'

'Did he really?' Colette heard the delighted surprise in her voice.

'He said you're doing some work for his family in West Cork,' said Michelle.

'That's right.'

So, despite any reservations he might have about her being a robber, Aidan had actually recommended her. She could almost feel her chest swell, but her delight was short-lived as she realised the pressure she was under to make a good job of the O'Shea ancestral home. If she cocked that one up, he wouldn't be so keen to bolster her reputation in future. If it had been anyone else, she wouldn't have wasted time on such ruminations. She gave herself a mental shake, willing herself to push unsummoned thoughts of Aidan O'Shea to the back of her mind so she could focus on Brian's voice and the job at hand.

Shane didn't speak to her all the way back to the city despite her efforts to console him about the rat and indeed to apologise for laughing at his ordeal. When he threw himself on the sofa at Fabulous Four Walls, feet stretched out, shoes and all, she'd decided to leave him to his uncle and retreat to her office. In a covert phone call when the boy went for a smoke, John explained how he hadn't had a wink of sleep with the volume of the movies Shane had been watching on the internet well into the night. She'd mentioned house rules and John said he'd tried to broach the subject, but by Thursday he'd given up hope of getting the boy to come to work on time. Only that morning, John had greeted her at the door with big dark circles under his eyes.

'You'll be worn out,' she'd told him. 'Honestly, John, you look terrible. I'll take him with me tomorrow to give you a break.'

As Colette stroked down the pool that evening, she berated herself for having been so quick to John's rescue. The West Cork project was contentious enough without the teenager from hell in tow. She caught sight of Aidan freestyling two lanes away and marvelled at his commitment to these sessions if he'd just driven back after a day down at the house. On each breath, as she turned her head, she took in the solid stroke of his arms and the powerful six-beat kick of his legs. In fact, she was so busy watching him, she did two extra laps without noticing.

'Forgotten how to count?' Grace asked when Colette pulled up at the wall to find the others already starting the next set.

She shook her head and glanced at the white board.

'Anything distracting you?' Grace asked.

Colette was glad when her sister pushed off. Grace's voice could be very loud at times.

It was the usual suspects in the pub later on. Colette noticed Aidan chatting with the men he'd known from his old swimming days and those he'd met over recent weeks. Although he couldn't be described as the centre of attention, he was holding his own, and from where she was trying desperately not to make it obvious, she could see he liked this bunch of veteran swimmers.

When they'd all been served, they sat around their table at the back of the bar. Chris from her old school raised his voice to announce that Aidan had something he wished to put to the group. Grace nudged her arm, nearly knocking the glass out of her hand.

'Grace!' she hissed.

'A bit of hush from the terrible two down the end there,' said Chris.

Colette's face turned an even brighter red than Aidan's as everyone fell silent to hear him over the background noise.

'It's just an idea,' he began, 'but I was talking to an old mate of mine the other night. He has a kid with a thing called Ehlers-Danlos Syndrome. It's an awful condition that affects the joints.' He paused to let them take in what he was saying, but no one looked enlightened. 'Anyway, the man is robbed from flying back and forth to London as that's where most of the treatment is done.' He had their attention now. 'I was wondering if we couldn't do a sponsored swim to raise a bit of money for the lad to help with the costs.'

There was a murmuring of concern and amazement as everyone looked to Grace, who was considered the font of all medical knowledge.

'It's a connective tissue disorder,' Grace began. 'Do you know collagen? The glue that holds the body together?'

Colette watched in admiration as her sister gesticulated, explaining the different types of Ehlers-Danlos Syndrome. All eyes were wide. Some of them pinched at their forearms at the mention of hyper elasticity. Hyper mobility had others pushing thumbs back on themselves. The collective sense of gratitude that none of them had to deal with such a debilitating condition was almost palpable.

'In Ronan's type, that's the boy,' Aidan added, sounding more confident now that Grace had helped him explain, 'the joints can dislocate when he's rolling over in bed, opening a door, or even pouring a drink.'

'A fundraiser is a great idea,' said Colette. 'I went to school with Flynnie, the boy's father. They're genuine people. It's been a nightmare for them.'

She didn't meet his eye, but she could see Aidan's shoulders relax.

Ludmilla was enthusiastic. 'Twenty-four-hour swim,' she suggested. 'We do turns. Hour each. How many we have?'

She was off counting heads amid suggestions of others who could be roped in. Colette leaned back in her seat and surveyed the scene. Fancy Aidan O'Shea coming up with that idea. She'd had the same conversation with Flynnie the night of Gerry's leaving do, but the thought had never crossed her mind to actually do something. And here was Aidan blazing the trail, winning the support of *her* friends for a cause they'd never even heard of. Was there no end to the mystery of the man?

He was so immersed in conversation about the fundraiser that Colette didn't get a chance to speak to him about their appointment the next day. When she got up to leave with Grace, she thought to interrupt, but for some reason she lost her nerve as if it was a big deal. God, she couldn't even talk shop to the man. Chris caught her eye and broke off the group discussion to say goodbye to them. Aidan turned and nodded to her.

'See you down there tomorrow?' he said.

'Yeah. I'll be down mid-morning.'

'Right so,' he said with a smile.

That smile. She carried the image of it with her as she walked to the car. Why did he have to give her that smile?

'I loved Aidan's idea about doing a fundraiser,' said Grace as she hopped into the passenger side. When Colette didn't respond she said, 'The fundraiser, what do you think?'

'Yeah, great idea. I wish I'd thought of it.'

'Are you serious? Who cares who thought of it?'

In her peripheral vision, Colette could see the furrows in her sister's brow, a family trait. She huffed and put her foot on the accelerator.

'I don't know what's eating you,' Grace went on.

'Ah, he's just a bit perfect, isn't he?'

Grace turned to look at her in surprise. 'And that's a bit mean-spirited coming from you,' she said.

Ouch! It wasn't like Grace to be so blunt.

—

Mean-spirited. The accusation played over in Colette's mind after she dropped her sister home. She hadn't meant to be negative. It was just that gentle smile of his. The kind of smile that made her melt a little. She didn't want to melt. She certainly didn't need melting. Life had thrown her enough fruit cakes in the men department. Tadhg Caulfield had been the iced-with-a-cherry-on-top kind of fruit cake, the kind you didn't know was laced with arsenic until it was too late. Before him, there'd been the school bursar she'd dated briefly before he was done for embezzlement. And since Tadhg, there'd only been that one time she'd let her guard down and fallen for a man she'd met at a bar in London – well educated, good in bed . . . and married. She might indeed be judging Aidan O'Shea prematurely, but the last thing she wanted was another disaster she hadn't seen coming.

Chapter Fifteen

'Couldn't get him up out of bed,' said John when Colette enquired as to the whereabouts of his nephew whom she'd promised to take to West Cork.

She thought about going without him, but that would be giving in. She'd worked in secondary education for long enough to know all about the slippery slope of wagging school.

'If we let him lie in his bed today, he'll do it for the rest of the month, and what good will that do him?'

John paced the office, worrying at the beads of his glasses as if he were saying a decade of the rosary.

'Kate won't be pleased,' he said.

Colette wanted to phone John's sister right then and tell her exactly what she thought of her son and how he was insulting the generosity of his uncle. But it probably wouldn't help.

'Give me your house key. I'll get him on my way.'

Colette squeezed into a parking space at the top of Blarney Street then walked up and rapped the shiny brass knocker on John's front door. Only dead silence within. She peeked through the letter box. No sign of life. Unlocking the door, she called out, 'Shane, it's Colette. I'm ready to take you on that road trip.'

John's house always put her in a good mood. It was like walking into a *House & Home* magazine, the colours changing with the seasons as if you were turning the pages in slow motion. Even the cat seemed to respect the order of the place. But today it looked different. Shoe marks spoiled the cream carpet John had only just had steam-cleaned in honour of the boy's arrival. A worn hooded jacket was strewn across the antique fireguard that stood to one side of the open fireplace. Rings showed on the inlaid wooden coffee table John had had shipped from Sorrento, the pile of coasters made by Indigenous Australians having been ignored. Colette was familiar with most of John's material possessions. It was she who had shared in the unenviable task of emptying the house in London he'd shared with Steve; she who had helped him in his painful deliberations over what should be packed up and sent to Cork and what should be left behind. It still hurt to remember John's unravelling in the face of shock when he heard Steve had been killed.

'Shane!' she called, louder this time.

A door opened on the upper floor. She went to the foot of the stairs and saw a long skinny shape stumble to the bathroom. As the sound of urine against enamel came from the open doorway, Colette wondered what it would be like to have teenagers. In an ideal world, any children she might have had would be at that stage by now. Her friends all complained of how difficult it was. Whether or not she could have coped any better, she'd never know.

At the sound of the shower, she took heart and headed for the kitchen to wait. There was an odd smell she imagined was from cigarettes, but John was a long-reformed smoker who hated the things. She cast an eye over the compact retro urban space. The slender sixties coffee pot and matching cups and saucers were in their usual place in front of a tin tray bearing the faces of the Beatles. John had once admitted to her that his idea for a business name had as much to do with his love of the Fab Four as it did with interior design. A bunch of bright yellow lilies sat in a large glass vase near the window, their stalks melding with the lawn of the raised garden outside. Many were the evenings they'd spent out there reminiscing about London, poring over plans for Fabulous Four Walls or discussing renovations on the inner-city home. John had turned the once-rundown student accommodation into an exquisite singles' pad. The real estate agents would swoon over a place like this, but Colette imagined that here, close to the vibrant hub of the city centre and not too far from family and old friends, John was happy. At least as happy as he could be without Steve.

As she went to take a closer look at the lilies, the stench became stronger. There, in John's beloved Belfast sink, were stubbed-out cigarette butts. Her immediate reaction was to grab some paper towel and gather them into the bin, and as she was at it, take a cloth to the coffee table and do her best on the carpet. It might make the place respectable for John's return, but it wouldn't prevent it from happening again. She drummed her fingers against the solid wood worktop. Shane MacKay needed a lesson in house rules and she was the one to give it to him.

When she heard the creak of the landing floorboards, she charged to the bottom of the stairs. But as she saw Shane disappear into a bedroom with a towel around his waist, the hard words she'd rehearsed were halted by the sight of the tattoo on his left shoulder blade. The fact that he was dripping water on John's good carpet or that he'd probably left a mess in the bathroom were details now eclipsed by the image of a headstone bearing the words *Alex RIP*.

She went back to the kitchen and despite her better judgement, cleaned up, but when he appeared in an FCUK T-shirt that looked as if it had already been worn out by a previous owner, she felt her blood boil again. Taking a deep breath, she reminded herself they were going to a building site. The T-shirt was the least of her worries.

'All set?' she asked.

He yawned and nodded in agreement. As he took the hoodie from the fireguard and followed her to the front door, she pointed to the hallstand.

'That's where the jackets go around here.'

A tinge of red pervaded his cheeks. It was a start.

—

As she drove out of Cork City and through the lush green of the county, the possible scenarios behind the tattoo weighed heavy on Colette's mind. She trawled her memory bank for any famous people called Alex who had died in the past few years but drew a blank. Surely John would have told her if he'd known of any significant happening in the boy's life. In any event, she couldn't exactly ask him. The boy would totally freak out if she mentioned having seen him half-naked in the first place. And besides, after eating the breakfast she'd bought him in the corner shop, he'd plugged in his earphones and fiddled with his phone for the remainder of the journey, only grunting at her attempts at conversation.

In Crookhaven, Colette did a double take as she drove up the driveway and took in the house with its shiny new conservatory. The light-filled construction made real her ideas for transforming the house from an old farm dwelling into a sought-after twenty-first-century living space. So what if she had to pretend its floor wasn't still concrete and that the skip out front wasn't there. In her mind's eye she could see the green of the foliage she hoped to place inside the glass, the new front door they would order and the dormer windows of the loft conversion from where golden sunlight would stream in over the as yet un-laid wooden floor.

With no sign of Aidan or his workmates, Colette was grateful for the chance to survey progress without him. She led an underwhelmed Shane around the side of the building, explaining the plans for the place as they went. He nodded as she talked about a possible Valentia slate patio on the seaward side and a covered barbecue area further round out of the prevailing wind. At the back of the house, she was saddened to see the range standing like an old farm dog that was no longer fit for work and had been usurped by an agile pup. She took out her phone and made a note to turn it into a garden feature. If Shane was impressed by her idea to both recycle and retain the piece, he didn't let on.

'Would you mind getting my camera from the car?' she asked as much to get a break from him as to give him something to do.

The door to one of the outbuildings was ajar. She let herself into the dark space, hesitating as she stepped onto the stone floor that might, for all she knew, have been covered in the remnants of century-old manure. As her eyes adjusted to the dim light, she made out an untidy pile of old tea chests. She tried the lid of the top one and jumped when it creaked open like a door in a horror movie. But her heart rate slowed as she pulled gently on the treasures that lay within. Chiffon scarves were threaded through an assemblage of hats and gloves, survivors from another era. She tapped the flashlight app on her phone to illuminate a hat covered in fake hydrangeas someone might have worn to a sixties wedding. A black mantilla passed against her skin evoking memories of mass as a child. A pair of the softest leather gloves lined in suede begged to be tried on. There was a broad-brimmed raffia hat that, together with a length of fabric knotted at the back, could have been worn by someone on the *Titanic*. As she tried it on, her phone slipped out of her hand and down into the chest between the layers of yesteryear. Rifling around to find it, she didn't notice anyone come in.

'What are you doing?'

She grabbed the phone, whipped off the hat and held them to her chest.

'Aidan, you put the heart cross ways in me!'

He stood in the doorway, his face stern. She berated herself for not having waited until he'd shown up, when she might have asked permission to look around.

'They were my grandmother's,' he said, nodding toward the gloves she'd forgotten she was wearing.

She quickly pulled them off and returned them to the box, smoothing down the scarves to hide the extent of her curiosity. Closing the lid, she turned to face him, willing her cheeks to cool down.

'I'd like to incorporate some of these old accessories into the house,' she said with what she hoped was a voice worthy of a professional.

He stepped inside. 'I'm not sure . . .'

'Oh, they're brilliant.' She pointed to the other boxes. 'There must be lots of great vintage material here.'

'I couldn't tell you what's in them,' he said.

She heard the exasperation in his voice. *Holy God! Had he no appreciation of these collectables?*

'This could be worth a small fortune,' she said, indignant.

He eyed her for a second, then ran a hand over one of the boxes to shift the dust before lifting the box to the floor. She watched as he went about opening lids and handling the contents with an unexpected reverence. She could only gape at the extent of the crockery and ornaments stored there.

'This stuff is amazing!' She leaned into one box to take a closer look at a tureen she suspected was Wedgwood.

'*Junk* is what my grandmother called it,' said Aidan. 'I suppose she was an original minimalist. Hated to have the place cluttered.'

'A woman after my own heart,' said Colette. She looked around the cool space. God only knew what other treasures were hiding in there. 'And what about these?' She made to walk to the back wall where what looked like frames or pictures were bound in plastic sheeting. She desperately wanted to rip off the dusty masking tape to see what lay beneath, but Aidan was beside her, blocking her way.

'Let's leave those for now.'

His voice was calm but determined enough to let her know she'd crossed some invisible line. She reined in her curiosity and waved a hand round at the boxes.

'I just think some of this deserves a second chance.'

Their eyes met in the half-light. The shock of strawberry-blond hair hung over his eyebrows.

'I suppose we all deserve a second chance,' he said.

Colette could only watch as he set the lids back on the boxes. *What did he mean, 'second chance'?*

'Come on till I show you what we've been up to,' he said, turning away from her and striding toward the house.

She followed him in the back door, where Rob was giving Shane the low-down on how to install a kitchen. The boy stood with arms folded across his chest and legs spread, rocking at the ankles, camera slung around his neck like a pro. Although Colette wanted to tell him he'd strain a ligament, it was the most relaxed she'd seen him since he'd arrived.

'I don't think you've met Rob,' said Aidan.

The tall thirty-something put a pencil behind his ear and stretched out a lean arm making his T-shirt move enough to show a nut-brown tan line.

'You're the one who gets all the nice jobs when we've done the dirty work,' he joked.

A comment like that would normally have turned Colette off for life, but there was something easy about Rob and the way he included Shane as an equal instead of a hanger-on.

'If you could do with a couple of extra pairs of hands, we're willing to help,' she said. She could feel Aidan's eyes sweep over her work suit. 'My *real* work clothes are in the car,' she added, hoping not to sound too keen.

'If you have the time, we'd be delighted,' said Rob.

Aidan looked sceptical. 'Come on, I'll give you an overview and then we might get stuck in.'

There was an altered smell to the place. The fustiness that had almost made her gag when she'd first come here was drowned out by overtones of new-build. The kitchen floor was strewn with the dust and rubble from where the wall had been taken out to add the conservatory. Fresh plaster had been applied to shore up cracks along the walls. The Persian rug had been rolled up and stashed under the staircase. Upstairs, the bedrooms had been partitioned off for the en-suite bathrooms. Colette took in the shapes of furniture swathed in dust sheets, and tried to remember what exactly lay beneath. Aidan could have put much of it in the skip, but she suspected the disposal of his grandmother's possessions wasn't an easy undertaking.

'Are you planning to keep much of this?' she asked, pointing to the covered clumps.

'Well, I thought you could help me decide what to keep.' He straightened up as if to ward off attack. 'It can't all go in the skip.'

'No, of course not.' She tried hard to reassure him. 'A reasonable selection of original pieces will give the place that touch of character, and retain some of the history of the place.'

He looked relieved. In her mind, she was already toning down the more modern of the options she'd first presented to the O'Sheas. There were still Ellen and her father to consider and keep informed of course, but right now, it was Aidan she wanted to please.

—

'That was a great day's work, boss,' said Rob as they motored back to Cork in the welcome stretch of the summer's evening. 'Who'd have thought your one Colette would be such a dab hand at the manual stuff?'

Aidan smiled as he replayed the day's events in his head, only half-listening to Rob's intermittent commentary. Colette had indeed been a revelation, from the moment she emerged from the downstairs bathroom in those red paint-spattered overalls and the pull-on boots that brought her back to her elfin stature when she abandoned the high heels. As they'd hauled old carpet and furniture, errant strands of her tied-up hair had slipped down to frame her face reminding him of the night he'd walked her home. Rob was right. Together, they had emptied the rooms of furniture, stripped the floors back to the original boards, swept up years of dust and started to sand back the imperfections in the wood to a smooth finish. He'd watched her show young Shane how to steam off ancient wallpaper. She could have left the boy to his own devices but was careful to check on progress often enough to offer encouragement while ensuring the job was done properly.

When his cousin Eamon's wife, Orla, arrived in from next door with scones at the tea break, Colette had spoken to her as if she'd known her for years and listened with genuine interest as Orla regaled them with tales of 'Lizzie O', as the locals had called his grandmother. Aidan couldn't help feeling his granny would have been pleased to hear them laugh and reminisce. It occurred to him that the success of Fabulous Four Walls and its fancy website was based, at least for Colette's part in it, on a genuine passion for people and their living spaces. When the lads had gone outside to pack up at the end of the day and he and Colette had sat on the kitchen floor to look once again at the plans, he'd felt for the first time that they were indeed on the same team. God alone knew what she was thinking when she went on about mood boards and whitening the place, but there was a definite building of trust. Later, as he lay on the couch – which Julius was now allowed to share – Aidan sipped a light beer and wondered how soon he could see her again. For the first time, he found himself looking forward to working on the house.

He smiled as he thought of how he'd spooked Colette with the hat and gloves on her like a child delving into a dress-up box. If only she could keep her nose out of those outbuildings. But wasn't it time he manned up and did something about the mementoes that were only gathering dust?

His grandmother certainly wasn't coming back, and eighteen years later, neither was Isabella.

—

Colette thought she might have smiled all the way back to Cork. Even Shane seemed to be in better form, speaking in sentences no less as they talked about the project and the characters they'd met in West Cork. Colette wished she'd known Lizzie O'Shea. She'd never seen Aidan so animated as when he and Orla swapped stories of the old woman. 'A full kitchen,' Orla had said when she walked in with the tray of scones and milk for the tea. 'Just as Lizzie would have wanted. Remember the sing-songs?' And the two of them were off, gesticulating over the new island as if it were the old table where Aidan's grandmother would have baked by day and entertained by night, food and drink flowing if she had it, but always a cigarette and a song. It was the cigarettes that killed her in the end according to Orla, the cancer taking the bachelor son she'd shared the house with too some years later. When Colette ventured to ask why the house had never been sold, Orla looked at her with mild amusement. 'Didn't Aidan tell you?' she asked. 'It was Lizzie's dying wish to keep it in the family.'

'What about that other client you were meant to see?' Shane asked as they neared home.

She'd done a quick think of what exactly he'd overheard in her telephone conversation with Aidan earlier in the week.

'Oh, that was cancelled,' she said of the fictitious engagement.

'Yeah, right,' said Shane. 'Of course it was.'

She could almost feel the smirk on the boy's face and felt the colour rise in her cheeks. 'What do you mean?'

'Conveniently cancelled,' he said.

'I don't know what you're on about.'

'Wouldn't have anything to do with a certain builder, I suppose?'

She didn't like the way his shoulders were shaking with barely suppressed laughter, and his tone, as if he had something over her. She mustered her best teacher's voice.

'You'd do well to remember the favour your uncle is doing you by having you with us at all, Shane MacKay,' she told him. 'Don't be getting ideas above your station, sunshine.'

'I didn't mean anything,' he shrugged. 'Just kiddin' ya on.'

She turned on the radio to cut the conversation short. What had that whippersnapper picked up on in the old house? What could she possibly have done to give him any ideas about herself and Aidan O'Shea? Not that there was anything to get ideas about, of course. Nothing at all.

⌐

Rob Murphy opened his front door to be welcomed by three excited children rushing at him with hugs as if they hadn't seen him in weeks. He'd left his work boots at the door and any cares about building projects out in the van. They'd still be there on Monday morning. The evening ritual was precious. As he lifted each child in turn and tickled and cuddled, Fern waited her turn as she always did, putting the finishing touches to dinner before they'd all sit together and say grace before the meal.

'How was your day, love?' Fern asked when the children had gone to wash their hands. 'I missed you at work. You're not usually gone that long.'

'Ah, it was a long one, all right,' Rob yawned. 'Had that interior designer show up with a kid from Scotland. Nice enough young fella.' He helped himself to a beer from the fridge.

'Not going to the pub?'

'Nah, too long a day,' said Rob. 'Rather be home with you.'

'Ooh, could be my lucky night,' she said, sashaying to the table with a bowl of mashed potato. 'But first, I want the gory details on the designer chick. What's she like?'

'Her name's Colette,' he told her. 'Lovely girl. No stranger to a bit of graft, I was surprised to see.'

'Aidan doesn't rate her, you know?'

'Is that so?' He pulled at her apron strings as she walked past.

'Said she'd cost the family a fortune if he didn't keep an eye on her.'

'Well, I'd say he was doing plenty of that today.'

'Oh?' She took off the apron and put her hands on those voluptuous hips he couldn't wait to get a hold of.

'Ah now, I shouldn't be saying anything. None of my business.' He took a long drink from the beer bottle and relished the look on Fern's face, eyes nearly popping out of her head.

'What's for dinner?' came the chorus. That was it. The three hooligans were back in the kitchen and ready to devour the fruits of Fern's labour. He'd tell her more later, but for now Rob savoured the suspense in which he'd left her.

Chapter Sixteen

Aidan was enjoying a read of the weekend newspapers when there was a loud knock on the door. Julius accompanied him out to the hallway as had become the norm. The dog was like his shadow. He took in the bronzed face and brightly decorated dreadlocks of the woman standing on his doorstep. Julius's tail banged furiously at his leg.

'Melanie!' Although he beamed at her, inside Aidan's heart was sinking. Was it time to hand Julius back already? Surely the mutt he'd reluctantly let into his home wouldn't be leaving so soon. 'How was your holiday?'

Melanie wasn't looking at his fake smile. She was wrapped around her beloved pet, telling him how much she'd missed him and how he didn't have to fret any longer now that she was home. Aidan wanted to tell her he hadn't fretted in the least, but rather had taken up residence in the previously pet-free zone with surprising aplomb. He thought to tell her how the dog had come to share couch, bed, even the odd beer with his temporary master, but he couldn't bring himself to crush her image of a heart-sick hound. He heard the false enthusiasm in his voice, but managed to appear interested as the neighbour swept past him into the house, firing snippets about luxury hotels and sensational sunsets. As she gathered up the dog bed, he wanted to tell her where to shove her sunsets, but reminded himself that she and Dave were good neighbours and the dog only lived next door. He could always offer to take him for the odd walk or have him for the next holiday.

Melanie stood in the living room almost hidden by the giant dog bed she held to her chest. 'I see Julius has whipped you into shape,' she announced.

Aidan looked down to where his beer gut used to be and smoothed his shirt over the shrinking midriff. 'Ah, I've been on a bit of a mission,' he said.

'Well, it's working,' said Melanie. 'You can borrow him any time you like if he's that effective.'

'Oh thanks,' said Aidan. 'I'd like that.'

'If this gets out, I'll be charging.' She laughed and looked him over again, incredulity written all over her sun-baked face.

—

The house was hollow without the dog. Aidan picked at hairs on a cushion and cast them away, berating himself for being such a softie. He went back to his paper, but had lost interest in its stories. Work – that would occupy his mind. He reached for the hard-backed A4 diary and flicked it open. *Skype Ellen* was written across Saturday and Sunday. Yes, he'd planned to Skype his sister to update her on progress. It would be good to see how she and Gerry were doing, and anyway, it was about time they put their heads together and decided on the next stage for their grandmother's house. Colette should be included, of course. The thought of having her here in his home scared him a little. What would she make of the place? Maybe he'd hoover up the dog hairs before she came.

—

Barbara Barry was standing at the sink when Colette let herself in the kitchen door and plonked on a chair to undo her trainers.

'You got a few texts while you were out,' said Barbara.

'Nothing wrong with your hearing, Mam,' Colette teased. She grabbed the phone and went to the downstairs bathroom to shower. Peeling off her sweaty running gear, she checked her messages. Grace wanted her to call; probably something about arrangements for Sunday lunch. Sandra Doyle wondered if she was free one night next week. And Aidan O'Shea wanted her to come over to Skype Ellen. As she stood looking at the last message, she grabbed a towel and wrapped it around her, suddenly conscious of her nakedness. She laid her phone face down and stepped into the shower, laughing at her foolishness at imagining he could see her. Maybe Grace was right; it wasn't fair to judge every man you met by the behaviour of the last man you slept with. She would give him a chance. As she lathered up her hair with the expensive shampoo she'd let the hairdresser con her into buying at her last appointment, she wondered what his house was like and couldn't help speculating as to what else he might have in mind besides the Skype. After all, it was Saturday night.

When she got out of the shower, she texted Sandra to arrange a date, then went to her bedroom to decide on an outfit appropriate to a half-work/half-not-work meeting. It would be great to talk to Gerry and Ellen. Maybe it wouldn't be all work and no play. She texted Grace.

Going to Aidan's to Skype G and E. Wish me luck!

Grace texted back straightaway. *Good luck! Talk tomorrow xx*

—

Aidan had the whole house vacuumed by the time Colette arrived. It felt like a betrayal of Julius to do it so soon, but he couldn't risk anything that might turn the girl off. That also meant putting the toilet seat down and turning the roll the right way round as Ellen had taught him in the days when they were in their teens and such things began to matter, at least to her. He'd washed and put away the dishes, hidden work boots out the back. Even the good serving plate Ellen had bought him as a house-warming present was dusted off. It sat in the freshly cleaned fridge now with a circle of light crackers surrounding a low-fat dip. The place looked straight. It was the best he could do.

As he heard the car pull up, he took one last look around before going to the door. Colette looked amazing as she emerged in a light-green short-sleeved dress buttoned all the way down and belted at the waist. She waved before going to the rear door and pulling out the familiar designer satchel and a small handbag that matched her dress. He hoped the green announced a good mood as memories of the red she'd worn to Gerry's leaving do came flooding back. He took in the wedged mules that lengthened her slim legs. God, she was fit!

'Looking very summery,' he said as she came in the gate and up the path toward him. He nodded at the bigger bag. 'I have a computer, you know.'

'I thought you might,' she said smiling. 'But all my info is on this one.'

He was pleased she waited to be shown through to the living room, and that she stood patiently holding the shoulder strap of her bag while he moved the neat pile of newspapers along the coffee table and invited her to sit on the couch. If there was one thing that irritated him, it was women who barged into a bloke's space as if their gender gave them the right to take over. Jane had begun to do that of late. He couldn't remember when their friends-with-benefits arrangement had lost its spark. Apart from the absolute pleasure that was minding Millie, most of the benefits had gone by the wayside.

'Would you like a drink?' he said, suddenly nervous as if he were sitting a test.

'Just a soft drink is fine. Diet if you have it.'

Diet? He was currently the king of all things diet.

'Come and have a look around if you want,' he called over his shoulder as he went to the kitchen.

'You have it lovely,' she said, looking around the room he'd scrubbed clean.

'You don't have to be polite, you know.' He took a tray of ice cubes from the freezer and ran it under the tap.

'Ah no, in fairness, you've got it well laid out.'

He pushed some ice into a couple of glasses of diet cola and added slices of lemon. He only had lemons because he'd read somewhere that they were an appetite suppressor, but he had to admit the glass looked rather cool as he handed it to her.

'Thanks,' she said, leaning against the worktop.

'It's a bit intimidating having someone like yourself in the place,' he said, folding his arms across his chest and resting against the bench at the opposite side of the small room. 'It's fairly basic. I just wanted to spruce the place up without paying a fortune. You know what some of this stuff costs these days.'

'You can do wonders on a budget.'

He tried not to think what might be a budget in her eyes, feeling the old chip on his shoulder despite having promised himself to behave.

'So, what would you do differently?'

'Some colour would be nice,' she ventured, her keen eyes resting on the overhead cupboards.

'You mean paint over the walls?'

'No. The white works.' Her brow furrowed in concentration. 'It's just a bit samey. Lifeless.' When she looked at him again, her cheeks flushed. 'Sorry, I didn't mean—'

Aidan laughed. 'Go on. Be brutal.'

'I didn't mean to be brutal, but as you ask . . .' She pointed to one wall. 'I'd probably spray-paint those cupboards in a vibrant colour. Like canary yellow or cerise pink.'

He considered the prospect. 'The yellow's a remote possibility, but cerise pink? No chance.'

Her smile was still tinged with embarrassment.

'What time are we Skyping them?' she asked.

Oh right, he thought, *back to business*. 'I said seven o'clock our time.' He looked at the wrist gadget he'd bought to try to keep himself on track with the weight loss. 'We can try now if you like. It's just five to.' As he followed her back to the living room, Aidan couldn't help noticing her taut calves and the slender shape of her hips. He still had a long way to go to get in such good shape himself.

The only woman with any romantic potential he'd had in this house was Jane. He shuddered at the thought of where that had got him. Firmly on the scrap heap of middle-aged men if he were honest. The first time she'd welcomed Millie's absent father back with open arms, it had been enough to knock the confidence right out of him. It was like Isabella all over again. He looked at Colette Barry standing in his living room and wondered if he wasn't wasting his time. Any forays into the romantic realm over the years had either limped into oblivion or ended in heartache, always his. For every Sarah Grainger, there was at least one Aidan O'Shea lying crushed in the gutter of Romance Street.

He set his laptop beside Colette's on the coffee table. He didn't own a dining suite and had thought about sitting on the stools at the breakfast bar, but that was a bit uncomfortable for a guest. There was the desk in his bedroom, but it was a bit early in the proceedings for that.

The buzzing sounded as the call went through and Gerry appeared shouting, 'Greetings from Down Under,' as if they wouldn't be able to hear him from so far away.

'Turn down your volume there, sir,' said Aidan. 'We can hear you loud and clear.'

'Hey guys.' Ellen came in to view. From memory, Aidan reckoned they were on the front veranda.

'Enjoying yourself, Gerryo?' he asked, taking in the coffee pot and mugs on the wicker table where he himself had sat when he'd gone there for Nick's funeral. What a relief to be talking to his sister in better circumstances.

Gerry raved about the wonderful time he was having and adding how Ellen was taking great care of him, in case Pauline asked. Aidan promised to tell Gerry's mother if he bumped into her in town.

'Colette, you're looking great.' Ellen had just noticed her friend, who Aidan had to encourage toward the camera. He found himself looking at her in the small screen in the corner more than at Ellen and Gerry. Her eyes shone with genuine delight at seeing the pair of them. The three had all been such good friends so long ago, but still held that bond shared only by people who've come from the same time and place. He listened as they talked over each other about how things were different in Australia, everything from the stars to the seasons and temperatures.

'Right,' said Aidan, keen to get to the business at hand. He could Skype his sister any time to discuss the weather. 'Let's talk about Granny's house and make a few decisions. My time is precious as you know, and I'll be bankrupt if I spend too much longer on it.'

Ellen and Gerry settled down to hear his update. Although impressed with how much progress was being made in terms of construction, it was obvious they were most excited to hear Colette's input on what the place could ultimately look like. She'd come over all business mode and took them through alternatives for the various rooms, typing notes into her laptop as they went.

'Does Dad have any say in this?' Ellen asked, looking at Aidan.

'Yes, he's one step ahead of you actually. I called up to him Friday night after we were down there. He's delighted to go with whatever we decide.'

'Great man, Bill O'Shea,' said Gerry. 'Easily pleased.' He turned to Ellen with a mischievous smile. 'Like his daughter.'

Ellen shook her head and linked his arm. 'Don't mind him,' she said into the camera.

Colette carried on. 'I'll send you mood boards, Ellen—'

'Mood what?' Gerry was lost.

'I'll tell you later,' Ellen said, nudging him in the ribs. 'Just listen.'

Aidan watched as Colette talked about suppliers and contractors, about paint colours and lighting, feature walls and white-washed floors. He had to admit, he was starting to get excited about the end result himself.

'Purpose?' she was asking. 'Have you nailed that yet?'

'Let's leave it open for now,' said Ellen. 'But definitely guest accommodation.'

She looked non-committal, prompting Aidan to wonder if it wasn't just a little early in Ellen and Gerry's rekindled relationship for that kind of decision. When he glanced at Colette again in the corner screen, she caught his eye. There was the recognition he needed. She wasn't going to push the matter any further. Instead, she went on about the package of textile and paint samples she was putting together and when she'd post it. The feisty professional had a heart after all. There was hope for him.

'Right so, we'd better let ye go and enjoy the sunshine,' said Aidan.

'What are you two doing now?' asked Gerry. 'Isn't it Saturday night your time?'

Ellen looked directly at them waiting for an answer. Had she no cop-on?

But Colette averted any awkwardness. 'We're going out on the tear and then clubbing,' she joked.

'Say hello to Louise,' Aidan added to change the subject. 'Talk soon.'

'Don't do anything I wouldn't—' Gerry began, but Aidan pressed the red button and they were disconnected.

He sat back on the couch and watched Colette tidy away her computer.

'Looks like they're getting on just fine,' she said, head down as she smoothed everything neatly inside the bag.

He smiled. 'It's funny seeing them together on the other side of the world after all these years.'

'They're like an old married couple.' And as if she'd thought better of it, she turned and asked, 'What was your brother-in-law like?'

Aidan drained his glass and set it on the table.

'Sound.'

She watched his face, waiting for more.

'And funny,' he added. 'Ellen needs someone to make her laugh again.'

'Gerry will certainly do that.' She finished tying up her bag, took her glass and sat back against the big cushion he'd done his best to de-pet.

He wanted to say something, but nothing would come. He could have done with a touch of Gerry's wit and humour right this minute. He was grateful when she rescued him.

'So, how's the swimming going? Are you enjoying it?'

Yes, the swimming, something else they had in common besides work. Why hadn't he thought of that?

'It's good. Took me a while to get back into it, but I'm starting to feel a bit water fit after the few weeks.'

'That's great.'

Another silence.

'They're a really nice bunch of people,' she began again. 'And Ludmilla keeps us all on task.'

They laughed at the mention of their coach. Then another silence.

'Can I get you another drink?'

'Yeah. I don't suppose you have a light beer by any chance?'

She'd come to the right house for light beer.

'In a glass or by the neck?'

'In a glass if you don't mind.'

He didn't mind a bit. The only thing he minded was how he might entertain her. Scintillating conversation wasn't exactly his strength, and there was something different about her now that she was here, in his house, something reserved.

When he got back, she was kneeling on the floor, looking through his collection of DVDs beside the television. That was an idea. If they watched a movie, they wouldn't need to talk. He set the beers and snacks on the table and squatted beside her, grateful she didn't comment when his knees cracked.

'Anything you'd like to watch?' It was as casual as he could manage.

'This is an oldie.' She held up a copy of the Tom Hanks movie *The Money Pit*. 'I wonder why you bought this?'

The sarcasm wasn't lost on him.

'We find a lot of them in our line of work, all right.' He took the case from her and put the disc in the player. 'Are you sure you want to watch it?'

'John recommended it to me one time. It's about the couple that bought the house that literally falls down around them, isn't it?'

Aidan switched on the standard lamp and turned out the main light before sitting back down beside her. Why did he feel like a nervous fifteen-year-old? Was there no accounting for age if not vast experience?

Sure, they had a laugh at the antics of the hapless couple trying to renovate their dream home, but Aidan spent the entire time worrying about the disaster the project in West Cork would turn into if he made a balls of it with Colette. She was smart, she was gorgeous, she was here. But Ellen would never forgive him if he stuffed this up. Their grandmother's house could be her ticket home. There were enough half-finished properties in Ireland without adding to the list.

Maybe he'd wait and ask Colette out when Lizzie O'Shea's house was done and dusted.

'I forgot to ask about your dog,' Colette said when the film was over. 'Is he out the back?'

'Ah no, he's not mine,' Aidan said with a yawn. 'I was only minding him while the neighbours were away.'

'That was some ask.' Her eyes widened. 'He's massive.'

'I know. It took a while for us to get used to each other. I thought I'd be glad to see the back of him actually, but the place feels empty without him.' He glanced over to where the dog bed had lain. 'Well, not with you here. You know what I mean.' He was stuttering now. 'I mean it's just that he was a fantastic dog, great company, always happy to see me.' At last a topic he could talk about. 'He was so cute, he'd nearly talk to you . . .'

He realised he'd been talking almost to himself as he noticed her slide to the edge of the sofa and gather up her bags.

'Maybe you should get yourself a dog,' she quipped with menace in those eyes that had turned from liquid chocolate to molten lava. 'I'd better go.'

'Are you sure you won't stay for another drink?' This was a bit sudden. *Holy God*. What was it with women? One minute they were all demure and the next they were on a mission to crush a man's ego. She was already halfway to the front door.

He nearly tripped over the hall table trying to catch up with her.

'It's okay. I'll let myself out.'

'Let me get that for—' As he leaned past her to open the door, he accidentally clipped the side of her head with his half-cupped hand. She put a hand to her hair.

'I'm so sorry, Colette—'

She'd already let herself out and was striding to the gate. He'd seen that stride before, on Patrick's Street when he'd had to run to catch up with her after she'd left The Stables. He thought to run after her now, but his shin was in agony from the collision with the table leg. He threw himself against the doorframe and watched her go. One way or another, he'd made a balls of it.

*

'Aidan's done a bit of a U-turn I see,' said Gerry, pouring them the fresh coffee he'd brewed and taken to the veranda along with a blanket to keep the chill off their knees. Out to sea, the wind whipped up the white caps that eddied toward the shore.

'He was very positive just then, wasn't he?' said Ellen.

'He's better friends with Colette anyway, that's for sure,' he agreed. 'I thought they'd come to serious strife with him all money conscious and her so creative and arty.'

'At least you were there in the beginning. Otherwise they may not even have sat down and discussed the project.'

'I don't think I've ever seen him that animated.' Gerry was thoughtful. 'She must have something, our Colette.'

'You're not suggesting there's something going on there, are you?'

He leaned closer and nuzzled his cold nose under her hair. 'Maybe it's catching.'

'You're mad,' she laughed as his lips brushed across her neck.

He pulled the blanket from her knees, drew it over their heads and kissed her.

'Gerry,' she whispered, pushing him gently away. 'Get into the house before we're arrested.'

Later, when Gerry had fallen into a contented sleep in her arms, Ellen's thoughts turned again to her brother. Colette Barry was like the yin to Aidan's yang, and all the other polar opposites she could think of. Surely, he'd never muster the courage to ask her out. But this was the twenty-first century; Colette could ask *him* out. He'd be perfect for her. Calm, dependable, loving. Why hadn't she thought of it before? She stroked Gerry's warm shoulder and kissed his hair. They both deserved to be every bit as happy as she was.

~

'You're a bit quiet,' said Colette as they set off down the Skehard Road.

'I could say the same of you,' replied Grace.

That was the trouble with being close to your one and only sister; she was like a bloody barometer. Colette imagined her emotions leaking through her pores with the sweat of their Sunday run.

'Just don't go down Church Road, will you?'

She was grateful Ben had volunteered to stay home today as Barbara was nursing a cold. The children were handful enough without trying to mind them when the woman wasn't at her best.

'Well, are you going to tell me what happened last night, or will I just turn into Church Road to spite you?'

Colette turned up the pace. 'It was a flipping disaster.'

'What could that lovely man have possibly done to offend you now?'

'Lovely man, my eye.' She fought the lactic acid building in her thighs.

'Okay, okay,' said Grace, working her arms to keep up. 'Tell me exactly what happened. You went over to his house—'

'First and last time,' Colette snapped. 'All shy he was, until he started talking about the neighbour's dog.'

'So, he's a dog lover?' Grace wasn't getting it.

'Exactly. Might as well just get his own bloody dog.' She inched in front again. Why was she even wasting her breath talking about him?

'Colette, hang on.'

When she looked over her shoulder, Grace was stopped, bent over with her hands on her knees. Colette started back, thinking she might have a cramp, but realised her sister was doubled over laughing.

'First the ex's child, now the neighbour's dog.' Grace held her side and took a deep breath. 'I'm not seeing a problem here. He's even welcomed "Little Miss I've Been Around Don't Mess With Me I'm Allergic To Men" into his home.' She took another breath. 'He's perfect for you.'

Colette just stood and watched as Grace took off past her. Just as well it was only the two of them pounding the quiet suburban pavement in the soft rain that had deterred the usual Sunday strollers. She mustered a sprint to catch up.

'Since when am I allergic to men?' she hissed.

Grace put a hand out to stop her, looked up and down the street and took her by the shoulders.

'Listen to me,' she panted. 'You have been very unlucky.'

Colette looked away, but Grace pulled her chin round so their faces were so close she could feel her sister's breath on her face.

'There are good ones out there too,' said Grace. 'And they're not all a million miles away.'

'He's not even interested.'

'Give him a chance, Colette. Maybe he's just a bit slow.'

Colette tried to smile, but tears burned at the back of her eyes. Grace knew. Grace knew everything. She pulled Colette in close and hugged her. Colette went to say something, but the words wouldn't come. She didn't need to. It was all there, sitting between them; her unhappy marriage, the six miscarriages. After the first two, she'd stopped telling people. It was Grace who finally called her out on all the excuses she'd been making for her husband. Hindsight was a great thing, but she wished she could have got out earlier. She might even have met someone else and had better luck in keeping her babies.

Tadhg had brow-beaten her without raising as much as a finger. 'You're too thin,' he used to say, and he'd take home massive parcels of hot chips on a Friday night and watch her eat them, or cook dinners with mountains of rice and pasta and insist she finish them. It was all a bit of fun at the start when she thought he was trying to help. She never worried about weight gain as she ran regularly and knew she would work off his over-generous portions. And maybe she was a bit thin. It wasn't until he complained about the running that she realised she was in trouble. 'Take a break from it,' he told her. 'It might help.' Another person might have run in spite of him, or timed it so he was none the wiser. But they taught in the same school. They had one car. They left together in the morning and came home together in the afternoon. He'd even had a word with the principal to ask if she could be taken off the roster for the girls' fitness sessions they ran at lunchtimes, pleading the case that she was doing too much.

'Be kind to yourself, sis,' Grace told her now. 'We all just want you to be happy.'

A car horn blew and a shout of something homophobic came from the open passenger window.

'Bastards!' they said together.

'That's my girl,' said Grace.

Colette wiped her eyes on her singlet and jogged on. Aidan O'Shea must think her a maniac.

—

When they got back, Ben had already started the barbecue on the deck he and one of his brothers had slaved over at a time when all Grace could do to help was make cups of tea and offer encouragement. It always made her smile to think how pregnant she'd been when they'd moved back to Ireland after years of travelling and renting, and bought their longed-for family home. A year in a shared house in Western Australia had probably clinched the deal on marriage and babies; by their late twenties, they'd both been ready to settle down. Although Ben's parents were disappointed they didn't make their home closer to Somerset, when Grace showed them the ultrasound with two babies, everyone understood why she'd prefer to move home.

Ben's grandfather on his dad's side was from Dublin. She'd met him once on Ben's parents' farm where he'd lived out his last years. They'd clicked straightaway, bantering about the old rivalry between Cork and Dublin. 'How's the Dub?' she'd ask him. It always raised a smile where mostly pain showed in his watery eyes. The family loved her for it. There were visits back and forth, and every Sunday evening the call came in from England with updates exchanged on how they were all doing. Grace usually folded washing or ironed to maximise the time it took her parents-in-law to get through the news of their other five children. There was always some-body having a birthday or announcing a pregnancy. Maybe it was just that the latter topic was more front of mind in Grace's world than usual, but she sometimes had to grit her teeth and feign enthusiasm.

As she cleared away after lunch, she looked at her mother who was reading to Sophie in one of the sun loungers. How the woman, who'd still been grieving her husband, had managed to do all she had in the madness of getting the twins through those early years, Grace didn't know. They'd always been close, but the military operation of changing, feeding, washing and soothing the lads had given 'close' a whole new meaning. Ben had been hands-on, but with him working his socks off to establish himself at the surgery, her mother's extra pair

of hands had been worth their weight in gold. Colette, God
love her, had been next to useless. She'd tried, but she was in
such a mess when the boys were born; every time she came to
visit, she cried when the boys cried. There were times when
Grace felt she should have been an octopus for all the arms
she'd needed to comfort upset relatives.

Thankfully, times had changed. Here was Colette in the
garden, crash-tackling the twins to the grass and hurling
the rugby ball at Ben, who in his own head was probably
scoring a try in the Six Nations. She brought out a cup of
tea for her mother and a small beaker for Sophie who had
to be just like her Gran.

'You all right, Grace?' her mother asked.

Grace put an arm on her mother's shoulder and raised her
eyebrows. *Wise old crone!* There were herself and Ben keeping
up appearances like two Oscar winners, and still her mother
picked up on the vibes they were trying so hard to suppress.

'Nothing for you to worry about, Mam.'

No, this was between her and Ben. Although she and her
mother didn't always agree, Grace knew it wasn't her way to
interfere. Barbara was there when they needed her, and she
and Ben were old enough to sort out their own problems.
Besides, her mother had enough to do looking after Colette.

Chapter Seventeen

Fern was surprised when she came back from lunch to find Aidan sitting at his desk, chomping on a king-size chocolate bar. The Sudoku puzzle in the newspaper he normally completed in a few minutes lay untouched in front of him.

'They say it's best to reward yourself with something other than food,' she said as she sat down in the office chair inside the door.

'Hmm,' was his only response.

Although Fern thought she knew Aidan pretty well, she'd never known him to be moody. This morning he'd already bitten the head off a young apprentice, and he and Rob had had a rare argument over a job the owner wanted finished yesterday. Her boss usually took it all in his stride, and this health drive he'd been on had been working a treat. She'd started to see him in a whole new light. Just as well she had Rob or she might have taken a fancy to him. No, this was a side to Aidan she hadn't seen. Things must be bad.

'Is everything all right?' she ventured.

'What?' He looked over as if coming out of a trance.

'Aidan,' she said lowering her voice, 'I hope you don't mind me saying, but you're in terrible form.'

He scrunched the chocolate wrapper in his fist and launched it at the bin.

'Is anything wrong?' she pressed.

He shrugged. 'Tell me, Fern, what do you women really want?'

It was the most, if not the only, personal question he'd ever asked her. She sat stunned in her seat. Surely to God he hadn't been unlucky in the love department again?

'That's a bit of a big question for a Monday afternoon in a builder's yard.' She tried to sound jokey, but he didn't raise a smile. Instead he pushed the lock of hair off his forehead and turned back to his computer.

'Mood boards!' he huffed at the email. 'I know where you can shove your mood boards.'

Fern pretended not to listen to the low growling coming from behind her. She was grateful for the distraction when a pimply young man turned into the yard with a large parcel under his arm, looking around for signs of life.

'Can I help you, son?' she shouted.

He strode in past the open glass door and stood watching Aidan, waiting for him to look up. But Aidan was in another world today. The appearance of the youngster went unnoticed.

'What have you got for us?' Fern smiled at the skinny youth in front of her.

'Colette sent me.'

The words, with their Scottish lilt, were hardly out of his mouth when he had Aidan's full attention.

'Shane,' he said, a bit curtly to a boy who was only here on a message.

Fern couldn't stand it. 'Are you the lad who's over helping at Fabulous Four Walls?'

'Aye.' He was still holding the parcel, and Aidan hadn't made a move to take it.

'You're Scottish, aren't you?' she asked.

Shane nodded.

'I'm Rob's wife. He told me all about you. Did you like it down in West Cork?'

The poor boy was red in the face with all her questions, but someone had to be friendly.

'A bit of a quiet place for a young fella like you.' She turned to Aidan who was slumped like a sack of potatoes behind her. 'Aren't you going to open the parcel, Aidan?'

He leaned forward with a groan and stood up. 'Give it here.' It was hardly polite, Fern thought, as she did her best to keep the smile plastered on her face for the sake of their visitor.

'You'd better open them,' said Shane, handing it over. 'She wants me to report back on your reaction.'

Fern wondered if Colette had meant the boy to say that, but he was possibly blabbering on to fill the void of Aidan's silence. She watched as the carefully wrapped and sealed package was ripped open. 'You might want to be careful with tha—' she started.

The look Aidan sent her was enough to make her keep any advice to herself. He reached inside the package and pulled out a set of foam boards. Pushing past them, he stood the boards along the raised counter of Fern's desk. She had only ever seen the like of what lay before her on the pages of Pinterest or in a magazine. Colette had obviously spent hours choosing colours and textures to bring the rooms of that West Cork house to life. Rob was right; between them they would transform the place. But if what she beheld was anything to go by, it was Colette who would make it spectacular.

Each board represented her vision for a room in the house. Fern feasted her eyes on the colours and detail. She could see Shane was waiting for the reaction he hoped to relay back to base. Aidan was a man of few words at the best of times, but this was unbearable.

'What do you think?' she finally asked, daring to reach out and let her fingers play across the textures of the fabrics. 'Aren't they amazing?'

Aidan seemed to finally smile despite himself and with a tinge of pink pervading his cheeks, he shook his head. Both Shane and Fern waited until at last he spoke.

'She's good at this, isn't she?'

Fern wanted to hug somebody. She clasped her hands together as if it were her own creation she'd been waiting for him to praise. Shane's face broke in to a wide grin. He'd got what he'd come for.

'Should I tell her you're happy with them, then?'

Aidan tucked his hands under his arms, thumbs out, eyes still on the boards. 'She's the crankiest interior designer I ever met, but tell her they're great. I'll take them up to my father tonight and get back to her.'

'Are you sure you don't want to give me a run back to the office and tell her yourself?' said Shane.

'Cheeky bugger,' said Aidan. 'Get out in the fresh air and get a bit of exercise before I put you to work here for nothing.'

Shane shrugged. 'I'll be off, then.'

—

The gentle waters of the River Lee glistened in the morning sunshine. Shane strolled along The Mall and over the bridges, taking his time to get back to work. Although he'd visited relatives here often as a child, Cork felt different this time. More his own. The people reminded him of home. Friendly people, like the Glaswegians. Whenever he'd had to stop someone and ask for directions, they'd sooner accompany him personally as tell him which way to go. But he wished he had Alex beside him. A vibrant city wasn't a place to explore alone. They would have had some craic.

His Uncle John wasn't a bad stick. The family had always played down the gay thing, embarrassed by it. Why they were still in denial in the twenty-first century was beyond him. He had gay mates back in Glasgow; as long as they didn't come on to him, he was cool with it. No, he definitely preferred girls. In fact, there was a Spanish chick he'd had his eye on since he'd started with his uncle. He looked at the time display at the North Gate Bridge. They'd be taking a morning tea break soon. Colette could wait. He deserved a smoke break himself.

When he rounded the back of the Georgian building, the courtyard was buzzing with foreign chatter. Prue and

Edwina's language students stood in groups, shouting from one to another, hugging and kissing cheeks and lighting up one another's cigarettes. The dark girl with the blonde streaks stood to one side of the rear entrance, looking somewhat aloof. Shane walked straight up to her, cigarette in hand and asked for a light. As she drew his hand toward her to light the cigarette off her own, he breathed in the heady mix of smoke and whatever she put on her sun-drenched skin. She looked into his eyes and let go of his hand. He took a drag without breaking his gaze. It was conceivable that the pair could have stood like this for eons, communicating their mutual desire in sensual silence if the door beside them hadn't opened and shattered what was possibly the most romantic moment of Shane's life so far.

'Did you get the coffees?' Colette's face was like fizz.

The instructions she'd given him earlier that morning came back to him. *Shit!* If only he'd got the God-damned coffees and left them to it.

'I'll go for them now,' he said in annoyance. The object of his attention just blew rings of smoke toward him without moving. 'Might see you later,' he told her before turning on his heel and heading down the laneway until he no longer felt Colette's angry eyes boring into his back.

When he returned, the courtyard was empty. He let himself in the back door and found Colette sitting at her desk. He plonked the coffee down amongst the perfection of her minimalist accoutrements, spilling a smidgeon of the froth. She looked from her screen to his face, allowing him a moment to make good on the offence, but Shane hadn't forgiven her for spoiling his chances with the Spaniard. She grabbed a tissue from a box concealed in a drawer and wiped it up.

'What did Aidan have to say about the mood boards?' she asked, eyes back on the screen.

'He said you were the crankiest designer he ever met.' It wasn't a lie. Just not the whole truth. The shock on her face as she stared up at him was priceless.

—

It wasn't usual for Colette to run on a Monday. Tonight, however, a run was required if only to pound away the frustration that seemed to come with all things connected to Aidan O'Shea. The man was an enigma. She was damned if she did and damned if she didn't. Best to steer clear altogether, she decided. Well, as far as that was even possible with this bloody project still ongoing. Starting tomorrow, she would contact Ellen, get her approval on the designs and push on with acquiring materials and contracting decorators. She'd do most of it herself if she had to. In fact, she'd already commissioned her mother to make all the bedroom curtains. A money-saving measure. One thing Bob the Builder could not argue about.

—

The email came as another surprise as she sat at her desk on Tuesday morning.

Hi Colette. I showed your ideas to Dad last night. He's delighted with them. Not sure if Ellen wants to change anything or even if they've arrived there yet, but once she gives us the go ahead,

I think we'll press on. Hope you're well. Aidan

She read the email again. On the face of it, it was positive. There was nothing to be worried about. Her ideas passed muster. Aidan liked them. Bill liked them. But that didn't explain the negative comments relayed via Shane, or make up for the fitful sleep she'd had the previous night. And where was that little shit from Scotland, anyway? She could wring his scrawny neck. But didn't they say not to shoot the messenger? She sighed. It wasn't as if she could challenge either of them. Shane could well have made up the comment to spite her, and as for Aidan . . . She'd given him good reason to call her cranky.

It was her turn to take Shane out today. John was so hopeful for his nephew. *Blind hope*, she fumed as she packed her bag. There was still half an hour before she had to leave for her first appointment; an introductory consultation. She'd need to take lots of photos. Sitting back down, she pushed the memory card from her camera into the computer and set to work, scrolling through the pictorial records, deleting photographs she no longer needed, uploading those of current projects or of finished ones with elements she might use again. In amongst them were photos she didn't recognise; curious close-up shots of flowers and grasses and dry-stone walls. A perfectly centred shot of a sparrow sitting on a five-bar gate gave it away. It was the gate between the O'Shea's property and the neighbouring farm that belonged to their cousins. Shane must have taken them when she'd asked him to get her camera from the car, when she'd been dying for a break from the boy and had gone exploring in the outbuildings.

She'd taken courses in photography in recent years to improve on her amateur abilities when she'd decided to change career. But these shots were better than anything she could produce even today. Another male enigma. And they said women were complicated. She packed up and went to the front office, where Shane was scribbling in *her* notebook. Scribbling, sketching? Who knew? Colette wasn't sure she had the energy to find out what talents lay behind the seemingly uninterested eyes of the belligerent young man.

'Come on,' she told him without going in. 'You're taking the pictures today.'

John gave her a questioning look over his glasses.

'Not just a pretty face, your nephew,' she said without smiling.

Shane shrugged as he strode past his uncle, trousers slipping off his hips as he went.

—

On Ocean Road, Gerry was about to serve up another sumptuous lunch as Ellen came home with the package she'd just collected from the post office.

'Don't worry,' he told her, 'I'll keep it warm in the oven if you'd prefer to open that first.'

It was like telepathy, this knack he had for knowing what she was thinking, like he could cut through the quagmire of trying to work out what she wanted, like there wasn't time for such fumbling. She shuddered as the memory of Nick slumped at the wheel of his car flashed before her. Gerry was now the one with whom she hoped to grow old. Very old. He could take all the time he needed to work out what she wanted. She wished there to be no rush.

The box was set on the table and Gerry, now familiar with where everything was kept, pulled open a drawer to retrieve a pair of scissors. It was like Christmas when they uncovered the mood boards and accompanying fabrics and paint cards. Giddy with delight, they debated which room was which, passing swatches of fabric from one to the other. Dark textured sail cloth would cover the old chaise longue. Patterned voile would adorn the double-glazed doors of the conservatory where elements of green would bring the outside in as Colette had said. Ellen could almost see the lime-green leaves fluttering on the billowing voile as a fresh breeze wafted in from the Atlantic. Pictures of a Quaker-style kitchen made her want to book the next flight and move in. Colette had even thought of a folding window from where dishes could be passed straight to the barbecue area at the back. She'd obviously researched Australian gardens and taken ideas for outdoor living. Her optimism about the Irish weather wasn't lost on them, but if they were to live there at some stage, Ellen would need reminders of the South Australian lifestyle she enjoyed.

'Would ya look at that,' Gerry was saying as he held up a sample of Willow patterned wallpaper.

Ellen searched the boards and found a mock-up picture of one of the bedrooms that incorporated the designer paper in a feature wall. 'Wow,' was all she could say. The transformation the house would undergo would be nothing short of the most dramatic yet tasteful of makeovers.

'Would we take the loft or one of the outbuildings?' Gerry asked without preamble. He looked up from his musings over the décor. She tried to read his eyes. Was it fear?

'I don't mean immediately,' he said softly. 'I'm just buoyed up on the excitement, that's all.'

She put a hand on his arm and was grateful when he gathered her to him in a warm, loving hug.

'Let's enjoy our time together, Ellen. Wherever we want to be.' He kissed the top of her head and held her in close again. She knew he was in for the long haul, wherever that would take them.

'I wish Louise was here.' Tears welled as a longing for her daughter surged inside her.

'She'll be here soon,' he soothed. 'And don't worry, I'll give you two plenty of space.'

Ellen squeezed her arms tightly round him. This living together was all still new and a bit daunting, but Gerry was here, and Louise was due to visit. Less than a year before, when she'd told him he was her daughter's father and Louise too had discovered the secret, she'd thought she might have lost them both forever. She hoped Nick would approve. If there was one thing she was sure of, it was that he would want her and Louise to be happy.

Chapter Eighteen

Jackie O'Flynn was sick of sickness. Sick of her son being sick at least; fed up with sleepless nights, hospital appointments, airports, the relentless chaos that had become her life. Saoirse had been such a dream boat; slept all night from three months, passed all the milestones like a textbook child, went to school without a tear, and still went every morning without a grumble. *She probably needs the escape*, Jackie mused as she pulled the suitcase from Ronan's wardrobe. Suitcases used to be relegated to the attic of the O'Flynns' three-bedroom townhouse. That was just one of many things that had changed with Ronan's diagnosis. The suitcases that had only ever been used for rare family holidays could now nearly pack and unpack themselves.

What a horrible thing for an eleven-year-old boy not to be able to play sport or even run around outside for fear of something popping out, not to mention the ensuing pain he was such a trouper to endure. He'd already had one knee operation, he was slated to have the other one done, and now his insides were going downhill. Jackie slumped on the bed unable to fight back tears. She had to stay strong for Ronan, for Saoirse, for Flynnie. Hearing Ronan's laboured bottom shuffle on the stairs' carpet, she wiped her face with her fists. There was a time when Honey, their golden Labrador, would have raced past him and bounded in on the bed on top of her. She could have at least buried her face in Honey's coat and blamed the tears on a feigned allergy. But they'd had to re-home poor old Honey; too much energy for a boy with EDS.

'What's wrong, Mum?'

She'd turned back to her packing, but Ronan could tell she was upset. His legs mightn't be up to much, but his social antennae had always been well ahead of his years.

'Nothing, Ronan, love. Just tired.'

'It's okay, Mum.' He manoeuvred along the bedside table and worked his way toward her in a painful swagger. Resting a pale hand on her arm, he said, 'We'll do some fun stuff with Dad in London.'

She had to smile. Here was a boy who was about to go in for another operation and he was the one trying to cheer her up. Sure, there was a time when they'd combine his treatment at Great Ormond Street Hospital with wonderful trips to tourist magnets like Madame Tussauds, the Tower of London or the football stadia. Not anymore. Even their favourite coffee shop was off limits. A look at London Bridge out the window of a taxi, or watching the activity at the helipad across from the hotel might be all the fun stuff left to them. He'd once walked across London Bridge.

A bear hug was what the boy deserved, but the physio wouldn't thank her after the work that had gone into the last dislocated shoulder. She patted down his sandy cock's comb and stroked the soft velvety skin of his cheek where a scar would always remind her of the time he'd fallen out of a tree and the slow-healing wound that had helped lead to his diagnosis.

'You are one very special boy, Ronan O'Flynn.'

—

'Everything all right?' Grace asked as they drove out along the Western Road toward the pool.

'Don't ask.'

'Too late for that.'

Colette could see the smirk forming across Grace's face. What could her sister's imagination possibly be conjuring out of her misery? She needed to put her straight. And so, as they made their way through the steady evening traffic, she related the whole story of the mood boards and the mixed messages.

'Dilemmas, dilemmas,' said Grace, smiling. 'Oh, to be falling in love again.'

'Ah, steady on, Grace. I barely fancy the fella—'

'Aha! Finally, an admission, a chink in the armour.'

Oh God! Now she'd never hear the end of it.

Grace skipped ahead of her into the sports complex like someone who'd just won the lottery. Colette stomped behind her. It would be no use trying to get out of going to the pub later. Grace would be more enthusiastic than ever about their weekly outing.

'At least someone's happy,' Colette huffed.

'I needed a bit of light relief,' said Grace over her shoulder.

Colette caught up to her. 'Trouble in paradise?'

'Nah,' Grace shook her dark bob, 'nothing major.'

—

Aidan was early for once. After the lapse he'd had earlier in the week, he was determined to get back on track. The fitness was coming back. He'd push harder tonight.

Ludmilla must have read his mind. 'Rusty,' she called from where she was writing up the schedule. 'You go in middle lane. You get faster, no?'

His cheeks betrayed him as he tried to shrug off the encouragement of the assembled swimmers. There was no getting out of this promotion. He pushed the loose hair under his cap and jumped in. Colette took off beside him. If he got any fitter, he'd be in there in the fast lane with her. *Perish the thought.* As he started the warm-up he found himself looking out for her, tracking where she was on the turn, or halfway down the lane when he'd turn to breathe. On the last lap, they turned almost together at the wall. Coming out of the turn, he watched her glide, beautifully streamlined, before breaking into a faultless freestyle, her legs working like an engine at the back. She was pulling away from him. He kicked harder to try to keep pace, but she edged forward. If he was a betting man, he'd have wagered she was doing it deliberately.

At the wall, they were busted anyway. Ludmilla stood, arms akimbo like a drill sergeant. 'You go out too fast, people.' She had a point. His heart pounded way too hard for the end of a warm-up.

Be sensible, man, he berated himself. *You're not twenty-one anymore.*

'Don't run before you can walk, boy,' came Dessie's voice over the lane rope.

Aidan smiled through heavy breaths and glanced at Colette, who looked a bit puffed herself. What was he doing giving himself a heart attack over Little Miss Changing Rooms anyway? He needed to get a grip.

It was quiet in O'Brien's for a Thursday night. That was the advantage of summer holidays. With the mostly student clientele away, you could hear yourself without having to shout.

'Are you still on the low carb?' Dessie asked as they stood at the bar.

Aidan nodded.

'You're looking well on it.'

Grace shot Colette a wink she hoped Aidan didn't see as they queued behind the men.

'Are you on a campaign?' Grace asked, bold as brass.

Colette wanted to hide under the nearest table and deny all knowledge of this woman who claimed to be her sister. She actually felt sorry for Aidan.

'Ah sure, I'm trying to lose the old gut before it's too late.' He looked down at his midriff as he said it. Colette's eyes were drawn to where his check shirt was tucked into his jeans. The leather belt looked like it might have been a family heirloom. She loved the worn look.

'You've gone in a couple of notches on that belt.'

Jesus, Mary and Holy Saint Joseph, did her sister have no shame? Anyone could see the man was mortified with all the attention.

'Too late for what, anyway?'

Colette thought she might kick Grace if she didn't zip it.

'Ah you're only in your prime, Aidan.' It was Dessie who rescued him. 'Isn't that right, Colette?'

If Grace had said anything to Dessie, she'd kill her. They were like teenagers, egging on their friends to go out together. She didn't know where to look. Mick's appearance with their drinks had never been more welcome.

Of course, the only spaces left around the table were beside Aidan. She suspected that had been perfectly engineered by Grace, who'd left her standing at the bar, all too palsy-walsy with Dessie. If those two were in cahoots . . .

'Colette,' said Aidan, acknowledging her as she took the seat next to him.

'Aidan,' was all she could say. *The crankiest designer he ever met* was on auto replay across the forefront of her mind. She needed to think of another topic or this would be unbearable. 'Any more thoughts on the fundraiser?' *See*, she told herself, *you can do this. Act normal.*

'I ran it by Flynnie. He's delighted,' said Aidan. 'But to be honest, that's as far as I've got.'

'That's great. We'll have to do sponsorship forms, of course, and we can put it on one of the donating sites . . .

for the tech-heads among us.' She knew he'd registered the jab, but without missing a beat she took a notebook from her bag, wrote *Swimathon* on a fresh page and pushed it into the middle of the table.

Ludmilla picked up the baton.

'Come on everybody. We need to organise this swimming-thon.' No better woman to call the group to order. 'I already booked pool for end of month. They give us free veekend.'

'You're a legend, Ludmilla,' said Chris. 'We'll need someone to coordinate the swimmers, of course.'

'And collect the money,' Grace pitched in.

'Publicity,' was Margaret's contribution.

'A couple of volunteers to pull it all together would be fantastic,' said Dessie with a hopeful look around the group.

Chris was in like a shot. 'Colette there is a great organ-iser,' he said. 'And sure doesn't Aidan know the family well?'

Colette made to play down the compliment, but they were all murmuring in agreement.

'You single types have a bit more time on your hands, isn't that so?' asked Dessie, with a nudge to Chris beside him.

'Where did you get the idea that single people aren't as time poor as the rest of the world?' she challenged. 'Myself and Aidan work very hard, I'll have you know.' She didn't dare look at Aidan, but went on. 'Since when was it fair to pick on single people?'

With another nudge to Chris, Dessie was on his feet. A quick look passed between the two men and they burst into a version of 'Single Ladies' that would have made Beyoncé cringe but had the group in fits. They were like the oldest swingers in town, hips swaying, fingers clicking, making it patently obvious to all that Colette and Aidan were the focus of their impromptu serenade. When it came to the bit about putting a ring on it, Colette thought she might die of embarrassment.

She leaned her elbows on the table and put her face in her hands. She felt Aidan move closer to her.

'I think Mick should give them a regular gig, what do you think?' He was whispering the words in her hair. It felt so good she wanted him to stay in close and for the crowd to disappear. All she could do was shake her head and laugh.

When the lads had sung all the words they knew, which thankfully wasn't the whole song, Grace took the notebook and drew a grid with spaces for names and time slots.

'Come on till we sign up. I have a home to go to.' She passed the notebook round as Chris and Dessie sat back down and congratulated themselves on their performance, saying they should think about a double act for the next Lord Mayor's concert. Colette and Aidan agreed to liaise on arrangements. Everyone seemed happy to volunteer them.

In the car, Grace wound her window all the way down.

'What are you doing? It's cold,' Colette complained.

'There's enough heat radiating from your face to melt an iceberg.'

'Ha ha, very funny.'

It was true. Her cheeks were still flushed from the episode in the pub.

'I wish he'd just ask you out and be done with it.'

'Like that's ever going to happen.'

Grace blew the hair out of her face and wound the window back up. 'How long before you finish the house in West Cork?'

'Could take months. What has that got to do with anything?'

Grace gave a tut. 'I just think it might be a business-and-pleasure thing with you two.'

'Mm,' Colette replied, looking out the window. 'Maybe you're right.' Yes, maybe when they'd finished the old O'Shea house, there'd be a chance for them. If they hadn't driven each other completely round the twist by then.

———

Grace drove slowly through the city, across the network of bridges where the River Lee wended its way toward the harbour. With the longest day approaching, it was still light. It would soon be school holidays and they would take the boat to England to visit the in-laws. She'd hardly need the pill; with Sophie sleeping in the same room and mostly in the same bed, together with all the activity that went on in the Dineen household, it would be wall-to-wall contraception. This summer, Ben's five siblings would all be descending at once. The place would be like a zoo. The twins loved it, of course; plenty of rough-and-tumble with their uncles and cousins. Ben turned into a big child in his parents' house, throwing himself into all manner of games and family excursions. It wasn't hard to see why he loved being part of a large family. If only those visits to Somerset could satisfy that particular need of his.

As ever, Grace would play along, get stuck in with whatever made for a memorable family holiday. They were nice people, but coming home was like coming up for air. She loved her life in Cork; Ben and the children, a satisfying job, good health . . . Colette didn't have the half of that. She wished Ben wouldn't push for more.

When she got home, the house was quiet. Padding upstairs so as not to wake the kids, she saw their bedroom door was ajar. A soft light washed over the landing carpet. There was a pleasant, tropical smell. Pushing the door open, she saw the candles flickering on the bedside tables. Ben was propped up against the pillows, glasses on, tablet resting on his knees. Even in an old bed T-shirt he was attractive. He looked up and smiled, sending a tingle through her. She knew the signs. He wanted to make up for weeks of barely talking, not to mention zero touching in the bedroom.

'Good swim?'

'Yes. Kids go to bed okay?'

'Only the usual protests.'

She took off her tracksuit top and hung it on a hanger at the back of the door. 'You haven't dosed them up with anything, have you?'

He eyed her over his glasses. 'I administered enough Valium to knock them out for the rest of their childhood.'

She suppressed a loud laugh and closed the door. At least he'd regained his sense of humour.

He patted the duvet. 'Come and look at these with me.'

Climbing onto the bed beside him, she took in the photo of them standing on a beach against a backdrop of reef and ocean.

'Nauru! That's a blast from the past.'

Memories of their visit to the tiny Pacific island and what was possibly the most romantic, not to mention educational, week of their lives came flooding back. Ben put an arm around her as she let her cheek rest on his chest. They'd been determined to travel as much as they could between their stint working in hospitals in Western Australia and going back to work in England. A Nauruan Ben trained with in London had extended an open invitation to him before returning to his island home. As Grace had come to realise, Ben would always go the extra mile for someone he cared about.

Nauru was a magical place, at least for anyone who wasn't living in the detention centre. Dilip had filled them in on the horrors recounted by refugees he treated at the hospital. Grace and Ben had been torn at the idea of holidaying in a place fraught with such trauma and were tempted to try to stay and help, but they'd jumped through enough hoops to work in Australia without getting embroiled in another visa application process. It was a trip that had certainly inspired them to put humanitarian work up there on a bucket list they would eventually get to once their children had flown the coop.

With the reputation of their beloved island sullied by social injustice, their friend and his family had gone all out to ensure that she and Ben had a great experience. Feeding them until they were fit to burst was only the half of it. The entire community must have been worded up as they were treated like royalty at every stop on the one road that looped around the island's coconut tree–lined perimeter.

Grace laughed now as Ben scrolled to a photo of the airstrip. Coming in to land, she'd been sure they would simply fall into the sea. She remembered the obligatory traffic stop when planes landed on the roadside airstrip. Even the guard there had called them by their first names, chatting easily despite the roaring turbofan engines. It all seemed like a lifetime ago.

'That was an amazing night,' said Ben as he clicked to enlarge a photo of an evening they'd spent celebrating with Dilip's family. 'You were looking pretty hot.'

Ben turned to look at her, desire written in his eyes. Yes, there she was in the thick of it, all fresh and carefree in a sarong with flowers in her hair, on a beach somewhere in the Pacific. She could almost feel the sand under her feet again as she remembered the music, the dancing. God, they looked so young.

Ben stroked the still-wet hair off her face and gave her an affectionate kiss on the forehead.

'You still look great,' he told her.

She stretched her hand across his chest and leaned her body in a little closer. This was more like it. She hated falling out with Ben.

'Have you heard from Dilip at all?' she asked, starting to feel sleepy now as she snuggled into him.

He took his glasses off and set the tablet to one side. 'His sister's had another baby.'

'That's good. She was a lovely girl.' She felt Ben's fingers gently brush at her neck and move down over her T-shirt.

'Mm,' he murmured. 'Not as lovely as you.'

He was kissing her neck, his body slipping down under the duvet.

'Wasn't she the one who gave her last baby to their other sister who couldn't have any?'

'Mm.' She knew Ben wasn't thinking about Nauru and its traditions anymore. And if he was, it was about the hot nights under the whirring fan in their lean-to bedroom at the back of Dilip's parents' house.

'Wouldn't it have been great to have given Colette a baby?'

Ben's lips stopped in their tracks to her breasts. He moved off her and leaned on his elbows.

'Are you for real?' His voice held a mix of incredulity and defiance, the tone he usually reserved for commentary on questionable decision-making by rugby referees and politicians.

She was fully awake now, looking into his eyes, his pupils shrinking to pinheads.

'I only meant I wish we had that tradition here.'

'So, what are you saying? That you've thought about giving away one of our children to your sister?' Even if she could have responded, he wasn't giving her a chance. 'One of the twins? Or maybe Sophie. She *was* our little accident. Maybe you didn't really want her anyway.'

She glared at him, speechless and watched him gather himself as he sat up straight against the pillows and pinched at the bridge of his nose, eyes shut. She knew he'd regretted his words the moment he'd uttered them, but they'd been said.

'I'm sorry, Grace. That was totally out of order.' He reached for her hand, but she drew it away.

'I feel as bad for Colette as you do,' he began as she moved away from him. 'I know things didn't work out for her in the marriage and babies department, but she's got a good family and friends who support her. God knows, you go over and above when it comes to looking out for her.'

Grace sat up straight on her own side of the bed, arms tucked around her knees. Ben had orchestrated the evening to ensure they made up, and she'd ruined the moment, spoiled his hopes of the shag that would normally have set them back on track. She could have berated herself for bringing her sister into it, but this wasn't about Colette. She loved her children more than anything in the world. Unlike Ben, she was happy with three of them. Without a word, she slid off the bed, blew out the candle and went to the en-suite, closing the door behind her.

⌁

Shane was happy to leave John and Colette to their overtime when Marguerita appeared at the door of Fabulous Four Walls.

'Hola,' was all she said.

'Hola,' he called from where he'd been tidying away the magazines and papers John had perused with clients throughout the day. After all the filing, photocopying and fetching coffee he'd done, Shane couldn't wait to get out of there and find out what Cork City had to offer on a Friday night. Marguerita looked amazing in her skinny jeans and that top that slipped off her shoulders, revealing thin black bra straps when she flicked her hair away from her olive skin.

'Enjoy yourself,' John shouted after him, but he was already heading for the back door where Marguerita's friends were gathered.

Colette was coming out of her office as they walked past. He nodded out of a sense of duty rather than anything that might resemble warmth. He'd thought she was thawing out that day in West Cork, but that one comment he'd made about Aidan and she'd gone all narky on him again.

'Be careful out there,' she said. 'Keep your phone and money on you.'

That ice queen could keep her advice to herself. Not that she'd need it or anything. Shane doubted she even went out at night.

'Yeah. See ya.' He took Marguerita's hand and left before he might get a full-blown lecture.

―

Colette did in fact have plans that night, which was why Grace didn't drive straight home after her shift ended at 8 p.m. The children would have been in bed, but there would be time for a last cuddle with the boys at least. She could have gone through the motions with Ben, tidying up, preparing for Saturday sport, sharing stories from work before retiring to separate sides of the bed. Instead she crossed the river's north channel and drove to her mother's house.

'Grace!' Her mother took a good look at her before giving her a customary hug. 'I've just put the kettle on.'

Grace's shoulders relaxed a little as she stepped into her mother's kitchen and drew in the sights and smells of her childhood home. Her father smiled down at her from a photo of the four of them taken on a holiday in Portugal the year before he was diagnosed. Even as teenagers she'd looked older than Colette, towering over her sister's petite frame. Colette had hated it when strangers presumed she was the youngest. *Not much has changed*, Grace mused. The responsibility usually reserved for older siblings still applied to her.

'Colette's out with Sandra Doyle,' her mother was saying over the whistle of the kettle as she dried a couple of mugs at the draining board.

'I know.'

Her mother set the mugs of milky tea down on the table and pulled in a chair. 'So, what brings you here on a Friday night after a long week?'

Grace smiled. 'There's no fooling you is there, Mam?'

'Well, I'd be an awful eejit if I'd got to this stage of my life without knowing when my daughters need me.'

Grace didn't want to fall apart in her mother's kitchen. Her sister should have been the most likely candidate to be on the receiving end of any outpouring of her troubles, but in this case Colette was the last person in whom she could confide. Grace couldn't help it. Her lips trembled as tears leaked from the corners of her eyes. Her mother reached out a hand to hers.

'Oh, Grace love. Whatever is the matter with you?'

It all came out between sobs and tears and snot. Her mother listened, located tissues, sniffed back tears herself.

'We don't have it easy, us women, do we?' she said once Grace had offloaded the burden of Ben's refusal to have a vasectomy.

'I shouldn't have to bother you with this, Mam.'

'What bother is it to me, Grace? Do you think I had two children by accident?'

Grace had to laugh.

'In my day, they used to tell us to cross our legs,' her mother said, 'but neither myself nor your father could have coped with that.'

Nurse or no nurse, Grace hoped her mother would spare her the details of her sex life.

'You know I don't like to give advice in matters of a private nature,' her mother went on, 'but I think you know in your own heart if you want more babies or not.'

'But what about what Ben wants, Mam?'

Her mother looked at her squarely now. 'Grace, it's *your* body. I know you want to make Ben happy, but haven't you given him three beautiful children already?'

Grace sniffed and looked down to where she was folding a tissue in her lap.

'Ah,' her mother sighed, 'if only men could have some of the babies. That would soften them.'

At least her mother had cheered her up. She drank down the lukewarm tea, relieved to have offloaded the lead weight of her dilemma.

'How are you, Mam? Are you still managing to stay sane with Colette living with you?'

'Ah sure, we all have our crosses to bear.' Her mother winked at her as she got up to get the teapot. Pouring a fresh drop for them both, she shook her head. 'I'm not one to complain as you know, but if she doesn't move out soon, I'll be old and decrepit, and she'll have to stay to look after me.'

'Oh God, Mam, I can't believe you're thinking about that. Aren't you still in your prime.'

Her mother gave a wry smile. 'Prime is right! But I'm still able to earn a few bob with my sewing work and get about, enjoy my grandchildren.' She smiled, but as she took a drink of her tea, Grace saw her expression darken. 'I worry terribly about Colette, you know. I'm serious about her getting away from me. She needs to give herself a chance.'

'That shagger she married really damaged her.'

'I know, love, but it's been six years.'

As Grace took her mug and went to wash it at the sink, she noticed the dinner dishes piled up beside it.

'Leave those, love. I was just about to wash up when you came.'

It occurred to Grace to ask if Colette couldn't have done the washing up before she went out, but she knew fine well that her mother had Colette spoiled and she was on a good wicket living at home. Maybe Ben was right, and it was time they all stopped dancing around Colette and encouraged her to move on.

'Thanks for the chat, Mam. I'll have a word with Colette. Sow the seed anyway.'

In the nightclub, things were going well for Shane. Great music, big crowd, plenty of opportunity to get close to Marguerita.

She was a good kisser. Shane figured she'd have a few tricks up her sleeve if he could keep her interested enough to take him home later. They were all staying in one of the hostels in the city centre, but there were ways and means of finding a place to be alone together.

They ended up in one of the boys' dorms. Her friends had huddled round him to get past the porter's desk, and they'd all cracked up laughing when they'd shut the door behind them, collapsing on low bunks and spaces between gear bags on the floor. With Marguerita on his lap, her slender arms draped about his neck, Shane reckoned it was pretty cool being here with a Spanish hottie after a great night out on the town. This was what had been missing in the weeks since he'd arrived; people his own age to hang out with. Finally, some action.

When he came up for air after another of the girl's epic snogs, he felt a nudge from the boy beside him.

'You want?' he said, holding out a joint, his words followed by the kind of nod that was more of a command than an offer. Shane hesitated.

'It not bite,' said Marguerita.

Seeing him swither, she threw back her head and laughed. The loud mocking resounded in his already alcohol-fuelled brain. Her breasts swelled in his face. He wished he was alone with her right now, but he'd never get that chance if she thought him a wimp. He reached for the joint and inhaled, the acrid taste assaulting his windpipe. He coughed and spluttered, gasping for air.

Marguerita took it from him. 'Like dis,' she told him, dragging easily on the roll-up, eyes fixed on him with a glint as she let the smoke permeate her airways before pushing it back at him. Her hand pressed on his chest. He tried again. Deeper this time. The choking resumed. What *was* this stuff? He'd smoked joints with Alex, but they'd been much smoother than this.

The joint was passed around the group, but he was the only one coughing. He needed air. He needed Alex. Without a word, he pushed Marguerita off his lap and bolted out the door. The security man, who was snoozing at his desk, roused himself as Shane ran past, but he was out of there before anyone could stop him. Not that any of the Spaniards had come after him. No, they were doubled over laughing. With that laughter ringing in his ears, he thought about where to go. To the right was his uncle's house, to the north side of the city. He took a left and headed south.

Most Friday-night revellers had headed home by the time Shane stumbled across Kent Station. The railway lines lay silent like the exhausted slaves of iron masters. The windows of train carriages seemed to look at him like blackened, lifeless eyes. Tears sprung from deep within his soul. He wiped with his sleeve, but they wouldn't stop. He rammed his fist against the gates and looked for a way in, away from the odd passing car whose occupants would judge. *That delinquent,* they'd say. *That useless lout.*

In the early-morning drizzle, he sheltered under the station's covered entrance, head down on knees pulled up to his chest. The smoke that had seeped into the fabric of his trousers made him nauseous all over again. He threw his head back and shouted, 'God damn you, Alex!'

Chapter Nineteen

The two guards must have tiptoed up to him. He hadn't heard a single sound until they were pushing him awake and pulling him to his feet. He didn't remember falling asleep, but the haze in his brain evaporated once the cool steel cuffs clicked shut around his wrists, and the night's events came into focus.

'We'll have to take you to the station, son,' the less rough of the pair told him. 'Can't have people thinking they can just camp out wherever they want on a Saturday night.'

The reality of what that meant began to dawn on him. 'I'm sorry, officer.'

John would be gutted. His mother would be told. The Cork rellies would surely disown him.

'Would you listen to him, Sarge?' said the other guard. 'Would we be as well to take him home to his mummy and let her give him a clip around the ear?'

Shane sucked air through his teeth. He didn't know which was worse, the handcuffs or the derision of this bastard whose height was surely below the limit for acceptance into the force.

'Where's home, son?' asked the first guard with a look of what Shane hoped was sympathy.

'Glasgow,' he answered.

'And I suppose your father's Billy Connolly,' said the other one, looking up from his notebook.

Shane had to think on his feet. If he gave John's address, he'd be on the next flight home. He couldn't rely on any of his other relations; they were all leaving him to John to sort out, whatever that meant. There was only one other person in the city he could call on. Of all the lousy luck. He took a deep breath and rattled off Colette's name and the phone number he'd only committed to memory one afternoon out of boredom.

—

The Bridewell Garda Station was the last place Colette imagined finding herself at five-thirty on a Saturday morning. So much for the lie-in she'd hoped for after a crazy week. Her shoulders ached as she pulled on track pants and a sweat top; showing off her swimming prowess to Aidan O'Shea had not been a good move. She left a note for her mother and headed into the city centre. The streets were dead, but of course every light was red. Waiting for them to change, she squeezed the steering wheel as she might wring Shane's neck if there wasn't a rock-solid explanation for this unprecedented journey.

'Are you Colette Barry?'

She spun round from where she'd been half-looking at a display board as a tired-looking guard swaggered out from the back offices. Her stomach growled before she could respond.

'You wouldn't be after that Scottish scumbag we brought in, would you?' he asked, clicking at a mouse and frowning at a computer screen.

She let the judgemental comment go. The less conversation this involved the better. She should be at home in bed.

'I'm here about Shane MacKay.'

The guard took his eyes off the screen and looked her up and down.

'What is he to you, anyway?'

She marshalled the inner strength she'd been trying to hold on to since leaving Tadgh and looked him straight in the eye.

'He works for me.'

He nodded and turned back to type something into the computer. The growling erupted in her stomach again. *For the love of God, would he hurry up?* She pulled a business card from her purse and shoved it at him.

'What's happening with the boy? Am I here to collect him or what?'

The guard glanced down at the card and gave a loud yawn. Without answering, he lifted the countertop, took a bunch of keys from his belt, and unlocked a door to an interview room off the foyer.

'You're getting off with a caution,' he called in the doorway to where Shane sat looking dishevelled.

Colette winced at the sound of handcuffs being taken from Shane's wrists. Surely to God he hadn't been bad enough to warrant restraint.

'Thanks,' was all she could say to the guard before turning her back on Shane and leading the way to the car in silence.

—

After a wordless journey to the northern suburbs, Colette showed Shane into the house and directed him to an old-fashioned downstairs bathroom where he tried to clean himself up. In the kitchen, he took a seat at a small circular table as he was told. All he could do was wait as Colette ricocheted between fridge, sink, cooker, making breakfast as if her life depended on it.

The house wasn't at all what he expected of an interior designer. From the pine kitchen, an archway led to a formal dining area where a long table had been taken over by a sewing machine, swathes of fabric and paper patterns. He recognised some of the cloth from pictures he'd seen on Colette's camera, but it was the dummy that stood to one side of the room in what looked like the beginnings of a wedding dress that made him do a double take. He hadn't taken Colette for a seamstress. In fact, as he looked beyond through open louvre doors to a sitting room with its sensible furniture and small television, Shane began to wonder what kind of double life this woman was leading; advising clients on state-of-the-art home accessories and furniture by day, before retreating into some kind of time warp by night.

She set a plate in front of him. 'Eat up,' she said, nodding toward the enormous fry-up. 'You look like shit.'

The smell took him straight back to Glasgow. It was like something his mother would make. He picked up his fork and got stuck in. Colette Barry might be a hard woman, but she made a mean breakfast. As he ate, she sat opposite, assembling a healthy-looking fruit and yoghurt concoction. He wondered when she would read him the riot act. At least he'd have a good feed before she laid into him, or worse still, handed him over to his uncle.

'Tea?'

He took the serviette from beside his plate and wiped his mouth. 'Yeah,' he said and then politely added, 'if you're making one.'

The legs of his jeans were still damp from his night outdoors. He and Alex had done some mad things, but staying out all night in the rain hadn't been one of them. That was one for the long list of things they'd never do.

'So,' Colette began as she set two flowery mugs in front of them, 'why exactly did I just drive to The Bridewell at the dawn of the morning to bail out someone unrelated to me, who I'm not sure I even like?'

He kept his eyes on the single yellow streak of egg he'd failed to mop up with the buttered bread she'd added to the feast. This could go one of two ways. He could lie his way out of trouble and tell her he'd fallen in with a bunch of thugs who'd robbed him blind and forced him into the train station before they'd fled.

'The truth,' she warned, 'or I ring your uncle right now.'

She was onto him. He'd heard she'd taught high school. If she was anything like some of his teachers, she'd see through him like glass.

'It's not what you think,' he began.

'Please don't presume to know what I think,' said Colette. She leaned forward. 'I've been up since five a.m. I've made a breakfast you wouldn't get in Jury's Inn, and I'm in no mood to be told what I think.' She sat back and took a slow, deep breath. 'Be grateful I'm listening.'

It was a fair point. He straightened in his chair, took his hands from where they'd been worrying at the rib of his hoodie, and gripped the edge of the table. The sequence of events was the easy bit. It was his feelings that were hard to express. The scene in the hostel spun in circles in his head: the Spanish students and their designer gear bags; clothes in brand names his parents would need extra jobs to afford, spilling onto the floor like they were ten a penny; the pungent mix of cigarettes, weed, expensive colognes and perfumes; the choking sensation as he'd tried the joint; and worst of all, the longing for his friend, the hopeless wishing he'd been out on the tear with Alex.

'So, how did you end up in the train station?' Colette asked.

Would train stations haunt him forever? Would he always be drawn to them, like somehow they'd lead him to a living, breathing Alex, and everything would be all right with the world as it used to be with him in it?

Colette's expression changed. She could see the tears he was desperately trying to fight back, hear the sniffles that couldn't conceal an emotion he'd carried around for a year; an emotion that had only rarely broken free from the tight wraps under which he'd kept it – and only then in the safety of his room when his parents were working and his brother was away at university. Why did the useless bubbling have to start in this woman's kitchen? She might throw back her head and laugh in incredulity, just as Marguerita had laughed when he couldn't smoke the joint. Just as Alex had laughed when he'd warned him not to lean too far over the bridge at Lenzie Station. But something in the way she looked at him told him she'd already guessed there was more to this than wasting police time in a city with plenty of real crime to contain. She'd bailed him out, made him breakfast. He started talking.

⌐

It was a slow day in the August of the previous year when Shane and Alex had kicked around Argyle Street in the middle of an average afternoon. Glasgow's shoppers went about their business with their fancy bags and occasional dirty looks. Snap-back hats and visible boxer shorts weren't everyone's idea of cool, it seemed. Other friends had summer jobs or proper jobs or had taken off to foreign parts because they didn't need to work. Alex had thought he'd be a shoe-in at ScotRail with his dad there for thirty years, but connections didn't cut it these days, and failing Higher English and Maths severely limited the chances of even a cleaning job. Shane hadn't done much better, scraping passes in all subjects except Art.

They'd been friends since nursery. Life had been a steady stream of school and play dates until Shane's mum went back to work and decided to use the extra income to buy a house in the West End. Shane's new friends were different from Alex and his old mates. Well heeled, his mother said. But Shane and Alex kept in touch, and when school holidays came around, there was always a sleepover or two. Although Shane was sure Kate MacKay would have preferred to have made a clean break from the inner city, keeping to her promise of helping the boys stay in touch had made the move bearable. He suspected his mother had hoped that, in time, he'd forget his old mate, but that was never on the cards.

All the kids in his posh new neighbourhood did sport after school – when they weren't playing piano. Shane wasn't averse to kicking a ball around at lunchtime, but twice a week outside school plus matches every weekend just wasn't his idea of fun. No, the older he got, the longer he liked to lie in, and with his father working away on the rigs, and his mum doing shifts, he and his brother, Mark, were masters of the house. Shane swore to his parents he studied as hard as his brother, but by the time Mark had passed his second year of a law degree with honours in all subjects, Shane had only scraped through his Highers. The only glimmer of hope for his disappointed parents was the B in Art. At the parent-teacher night in third year, Mr Moncrieff had told them their son was capable of an A, citing his contribution to a school mural as proof of his potential. His mother's chest had swelled embarrassingly. She'd always told anyone who would listen that her boy's artistic talent was in the Buckley genes. Her father had been a boat builder, her uncle a carpenter, and there was her brother John who'd started as an architect before channelling his skills and talent into interior design. Ever since Shane had first written his name giving each letter a separate colour, albeit in the wrong order and with a backward s, she'd hoped her youngest child would follow in the family tradition. It was a thread of hope she clung to every time her friends asked what he might do with his life after what she liked to call his 'gap year'.

In Queen Street Station, Alex tapped his father for a couple of free tickets to Lenzie. Bobby Thouless loved to see the boys hanging out and never held it against Shane that he'd moved to the posh side of town. The Thouless household always welcomed him with open arms and massive plates of mince 'n' tatties. It was like a second home. The boys stuffed their tickets in their pockets and headed for the platform.

As the train hurtled north out of the city, Shane waited between carriages as Alex rolled a joint in the toilets. Once the ticket inspector had passed, they pulled down the window and Alex blew out a puff of smoke that threatened to turn back on itself and engulf them before it was whisked away along the carriages coming behind. Alex laughed heartily as he passed the spliff to Shane. It was a silly boyish laugh, about nothing really, or, as Shane now believed, about the simple joy of being together with his mate doing something illegal. Hindsight would make him question Alex's need for the drug; alleviation of boredom, or a little Dutch courage? He'd told Bobby Thouless they were going to visit a pal. How or why Alex had kept his girlfriend and their love child a secret from his parents for so long was something Shane couldn't fathom, but the camaraderie of being the offsider in his friend's clandestine escapades came with a rush he didn't want to jeopardise. If it meant pushing little Lexie round the park in her pram for half an hour while her parents made out like rabbits in the bushes, Shane was in. His loyalty to Alex was without question. And besides, wee Lexie, all of six months now, spent most of their visits asleep.

On the footbridge over the railway, Alex delved into his grubby old rucksack and pulled out a can of spray paint.

'What are you doing, mate?' he asked as Alex stepped to the edge of the bridge.

'Look here,' said Alex, letting the rucksack fall to the ground and straddling the steel frame. As he leaned over and proceeded to spray onto the Glasgow side of the bridge, Shane's stomach lurched.

'What the . . . Get back, man.'

'Take a look!'

Every time Shane replayed the scene in his mind, he remembered his mistakes. A better friend would have held the guy, anchored him while he pulled off the stunt that could have been just that – a stupid young man's crazy stunt. No, as Alex hung over the bridge, waving one arm about, the sound of the spray can only prompted Shane to hoist himself onto his stomach and peer down at the graffiti with which Alex was defacing the bridge – *I ♥ Lex*. Whether it was the din of the oncoming train that had distracted his friend, or his own drug-induced inertia, Shane could never forgive himself for what took seconds to unfold and yet played in his mind, over and over, in slow motion and would haunt him for the rest of his life.

—

Colette blinked back tears as she imagined the scene; Alex falling from the overpass, spray can in hand, screaming the last sound from the voice his friends and family would never hear again; the fact that Shane could only look on as the body of his best friend hit the train before being thrown down onto the tracks in a tangle of blood-spattered limbs.

'I'm sorry, Shane,' she said quietly. It was exactly the kind of experience she'd hoped he hadn't had when she'd seen the tattoo at John's house. 'I'm so, so sorry.'

Chapter Twenty

After dropping Shane home and watching him slip quietly into the house, Colette was overcome with a sense of responsibility. The boy had made her promise to keep the details from his uncle. But he wasn't a boy, was he? Although it ached to see him disappear through the door, she had to respect his wishes. What would he do? Sit in his room and cry his eyes out? What if John was up worrying about him? Would Shane carry on as if he'd had a one-night stand and it was perfectly normal to get home at this hour? As she pulled back out onto Blarney Street, her thoughts turned to St Colman's High School.

Although she never allowed herself to regret her career change, there were times when she missed her old students. She sometimes saw them in town, where they'd give her a smile, or the boisterous ones would call out, 'How's it going, Miss?' At home, Tadhg would complain about mediocre test results and falling standards of behaviour, but Colette saw past the statistics. What mattered to her were those young individuals with all their struggles to fit in, to measure up. She'd recognised them in Shane that morning. It was often too easy to mistake a belligerent teenager for one who was, in fact, lost.

Chapter Twenty

'Thanks for letting me bring him along today.' Colette checked her watch as she and Grace started their Sunday run. She didn't want to abandon Shane for too long with her family, but Ben said he was happy to stay home and insisted the sisters run as normal.

'Ben's a rock.'

'He is,' said Grace. Colette detected a seriousness in her sister's tone, but she wouldn't pry. If there was something up between those two, they'd sort it out in their usual practical, no-nonsense manner. Anyway, she was more worried about Shane.

'I hope they'll all get on okay.'

'Don't worry,' said Grace. 'Ben will keep Shane and the boys busy. Give Mam a chance to have a snooze on the couch.'

Colette smiled. Grace was right. Ben could keep an army occupied and her mother would be in her favourite spot, snuggled into her granddaughter. An image of Aidan and Millie in such a pose came to her. Aidan the stand-in dad, cast on the slag heap of the no-longer-required. She considered his fatherly attributes: strong, reliable, dependable, cautious (which probably made him protective). Here she went again, thoughts swirling into that upward spiral of boosting the bothersome builder to elevated heights. She so needed to rein this in.

'How are the plans for the EDS fundraiser going?' Grace asked, breaking into her thoughts.

The swimathon! Another thing to thwart her plans of avoiding him. Grace didn't wait for an answer.

'Better have something to bring to the table on Thursday, or they'll only speculate as to why the pair of you haven't had time to discuss the matter.' She gave a sideways wink.

'Oh God, why did I ever agree to organise it with him?'

'Destiny, sweetheart.' Grace sounded all too pleased with herself. 'It was meant to be.'

———

Grace thought to raise the subject of Colette moving out on her own. She was in such good form today, but the incident with Shane had thrown her, and her run-in with Tadgh had brought to the surface all those memories of her marriage. No, Grace would bide her time, be kind, give her sister the support she needed. But there was also their mother to think about. It would be such a shame if she never got her house back. She'd done such an amazing job since their dad died, gathering herself and thriving in her independence. Grace tried to imagine herself in later life, rattling around in a house with an adult Sophie, but decided it was probably best to hang onto the image of Sophie as the bundle of cuteness she currently was. Her children were growing up too fast already. They were home from their run by the time she'd worked out how to broach the subject of Colette moving out. Oh well, she'd leave it for another day. In fairness, her sister had probably had enough to deal with for one week.

⌁

Aidan had already made inroads into organising the EDS fundraiser. Flynnie had given them his blessing, and Aidan had cracked on, enlisting his father's help, thinking it would be a nice diversion from the control freak that was Frances Brady. Fern and Rob had agreed to help too. Aidan had to take a few deep breaths as he'd listened to Fern's suggestion of expanding the swimathon to all manner of money-making exercises, from family fun days to slave auctions. As interesting a prospect as winning Colette Barry and having her at his beck and call for twenty-four hours was, he dismissed the latter idea but promised to bring some of Fern's more sensible suggestions to the group. At least he had a few dot points for his reply to Colette's email.

The Barry sisters had put their heads together and come up with a list of sponsors and donations for a raffle. Colette's offer of a room makeover only reinforced his father's opinion of her as one of their own. She was snowed under with work, she'd said, but would see him at the pool. He wished he'd had the guts to take her to lunch and discuss the fundraiser face to face.

⌁

In truth, Colette was having an easy week. So much so that she'd managed to de-clutter the main office and reorganise her own. Shane had lifted and shifted and done whatever else she'd asked of him. Still without too much to say, but at least now he spoke to her with the respect she deserved.

'I've got some magazines in my office I'd like you to take up to Prue and Edwina,' she told him once he'd rid the hallway of Declan Byrne's collection of graphic brochures on dental hygiene that were enough to put anyone off their plans for home renovation.

As he bent down to lift the box of magazines, the notebook came loose from his back pocket and fell open on her office floor. Picking it up, she considered the contrasting images on the pages before her. On the right was a perfect pencil sketch of a baby's face, its innocence seeping from soulful eyes. The harsh geometric strokes on the opposite page sent a shiver down her spine. She recognised the name, *Lexie*, and the whole sorry story Shane had related to her hit home with a renewed rush of horror.

As he took the box away, she slumped against her desk and perused the pages he had wordlessly permitted her to see.

Edwina waved to Shane from where her generous rear end obliterated her chair from sight.

'Oh, you're a darling,' she said, batting her eyelashes in what Shane hoped was a nervous twitch and not for his benefit. 'Pop them over there.' He set the box down on the vacant desk and looked around, aware of her watching him. Voices came from beyond doors bearing the words Beginner, Intermediate and Advanced. Just as he wondered which one Marguerita was behind, Edwina hoisted herself out of her seat and came toward him. Slipping a hand round his elbow, she lifted her multiple chins and looked up at him.

'Are you sad she's left us?' she asked.

As his brain computed the question, his eyes homed in on the white hairs sprouting from one of her chins. He drew away, willing his throat to moisten so he could speak.

'You did know she finished with us on Friday, didn't you?'

The wrinkles on her forehead tightened into a frown. He shoved his hands in his pockets and hoped she wouldn't touch him again.

'I didn't mean to be the bearer of bad news,' she started, her hand reaching to his arm again, 'but I knew you two had a thing . . .'

He was spared from having to respond when a buzzer sounded and the three classroom doors swung open heralding a stampede of students across the foyer toward the stairs. All he could do was stand beside Edwina and wait for it to pass. Among the swinging books and backpacks and 'See you tomorrows', Prue appeared at one of the doorways.

'Young Shane, isn't it?' she boomed.

He nodded, turning even redder.

'He's brought us some magazines, which we will put to excellent use in class, I imagine,' said Edwina.

'Colette's doing a clear-out downstairs,' Shane explained. Students came and went here all the time, he reasoned. Marguerita may never have mentioned she was leaving even if he'd spent the night with her. Something made him glad he hadn't. 'Better go back down and give her a wee hand.'

'Good man,' said Prue as he went to walk away. 'Don't be a stranger. Come and see us any time.'

Turning to thank her, he saw the two women exchange a glance he read as sympathy. Perhaps it was mixed with a tinge of guilt at having encouraged him to socialise with their students. Either way, it felt good to think the two old wifies cared.

—

Colette was sitting at her desk, bent over his drawings. After standing unnoticed in the open doorway for a minute, he let out a cough.

'Shane!'

Her uncharacteristic enthusiasm unnerved him.

'What do you think?' he asked, steeling himself. At least she wouldn't lie to him.

'What do you do with this stuff?' she asked, her serious tone matching the furrowing of her brows.

The question surprised him. What did she *think* he did with it?

'Nothin'.' He shrugged.

'What would you like to do with it?' Her shoulders lowered as she said it. She was less serious now, but still met his eyes in a way that demanded an honest answer. He shrugged again and made to look away, but a tilt of her head said, *Answer the question, buddy*. He took a deep breath, sat in one of the chairs opposite her and drew it in close to the table.

'I want to go back to school and do Art,' he began, his voice low. 'It's the only thing I'm any good at. Probably not even good enough to get any money for it, but I wouldn't mind havin' a go.' He dropped his head and stared at his hands.

'You know I won't bullshit you, don't you?' she asked.

He nodded and murmured in the affirmative.

'Look at me,' she demanded.

He took a deep breath and braced himself.

'You, my dear boy, have talent. Most people just stick to a signature style, like tattoo design or portraiture, but you can draw in a range I haven't seen before.' She tapped the notebook. 'In here, you've dabbled in landscape, graffiti, manga, animal study ... some of these designs could be used for wallpaper or greeting cards.' She smiled at last and relaxed back in her chair. Then straightening up and pointing an index finger at him she added, '*And* you take bloody good photographs.'

At the unexpected praise, a rush of warmth pervaded his body. He sat back and shook his head. He hadn't felt this good in a long while. It was hard to believe he was even having this conversation, especially with Colette Barry.

'We need to show John these,' she said.

'Okay,' was all he could think to say.

Chapter Twenty-one

Calls to the office phone went to voicemail as John marvelled at his nephew's sketches. Shane watched with quiet pride as his uncle's eyes welled up and he had to take down his Gucci glasses and reach for the tissue box. The guilt at having been so ungrateful made him cringe.

'Your grandad would be proud, God rest him,' said John, gathering himself. He looked Shane squarely in the eye. 'If you want to use your artistic talent, I'll back you all the way.' There was silence as he paused. 'You could apply for something at home in Glasgow, of course.'

Shane didn't speak. The thought of returning home didn't hold much appeal. John read his mind.

'You're too late for college here this year, but if you're serious I could help you get the Leaving Cert and you could apply for next year's intake.'

'You mean go back to school?'

'I'd have to check, but I don't think your Highers would stand up. We both know you have the brains to do a lot better.' John's face was kind but serious.

This wasn't the time to muck about. He needed to commit. He looked to Colette, whose furrowed brow and earnest eyes, the way she leaned forward over her crossed legs, said it all. *Take this opportunity, will you?*

He straightened his shoulders. For the first time since Alex's death, he felt positive, like he actually had a future worth fighting for.

'I'll do whatever it takes, Uncle John. But I'd like to stay here, with you.' He hesitated, trying to read John's face. 'If it's cool with you, I mean.'

John's beam couldn't have been wider. 'Get here,' he said, coming round from behind his desk and enveloping Shane in the biggest hug of his life. He thought he caught a tear in Colette's eye. He felt the love. There was no mistaking the sense that this could be one of the defining moments of his life.

'I suppose you'll want to celebrate, ya big softie,' Colette teased John. 'I'll book Scoozi's.'

Shane thought he might have hugged her too, but she was gone with the signature stride of her high heels. She didn't have to tell him if he let his uncle down, he'd have her to reckon with.

A feast or a famine was right. Aidan couldn't remember a busier week. With work coming out his ears, he'd quite happily have stayed in tonight, but if he let the swimming slide, he'd only undo all the good he'd done on the weight-loss front, and besides, there was the fundraiser to finalise.

He made for the slow lane, but Ludmilla nabbed him before he could get in.

'No go back, Rusty.'

She pointed to the middle lane before barking out the warm-up sequence. There was nothing for it but to obey. He pulled his stomach in and hoisted the jammers higher on his hips. Eyeing the whiteboard, he fought the urge to bless himself. Longer sets, less rest. He hoped his performance the previous week could be repeated. As he wiped his goggles and prepared to step up to Ludmilla's expectations, he spotted Grace and Colette walking briskly from the change rooms, pulling on swim caps, laughing about something. Colette always seemed more relaxed in her sister's company. He hoped the joke wouldn't be on him at the end of the session. If he lasted that long. The warm-up was one thing, but twenty one-hundreds would be a killer. *Oh, to be young and fit again.*

'You sore in shoulders tomorrow,' Ludmilla warned them, a satisfied smile spreading across her face.

Grace and Colette were puffed, but still in good spirits when they finished.

'You okay?' Grace asked him across the lane rope.

'Yeah,' he gasped. 'Never better.'

'No going back now,' she said. Like that was supposed to encourage him. Where she got her breath from, Aidan could only wonder. He managed a smile. 'You'll be in here soon,' she said. Turning to her sister, she added, 'Isn't that right, Colette?'

Colette only managed a nod of her beetroot face. At least she looked like it had hurt.

'Two hundred easy.' It was the nicest thing Ludmilla had said all night.

Aidan pushed off the wall. *All this diet and exercise might finally be helping,* he mused, as he leisurely dolphin-dived down the pool.

—

Chris and Dessie loved Fern's idea of a family fun day to follow on from the swimathon and raise even more money for the boy with EDS. Their enthusiasm was enough to galvanise the group and incite a willingness to volunteer even among the most reticent members. The Lee Fields was agreed on as the venue. Someone knew someone in the council. Permission would be sought to cordon off an area in the popular riverside recreation spot.

'Right so,' said Chris. 'We swim from twelve Saturday to twelve Sunday and man the stalls Sunday afternoon. Early finishers can help set up.'

There wasn't a rumble of disagreement, much to Aidan's relief. All he and Colette had to do was bring a few ideas to the table and Chris did the rest. Why he couldn't have done the organising in the first place wasn't addressed, but Aidan knew fine well what he was up to. There was nothing for it but to let the man have his head. A nod to Colette and they were agreed to let him go. It may have been his imagination, but in that brief glance, a calm seemed to settle between them. Made a nice change, agreeing on something for once.

Chapter Twenty-two

They couldn't have booked better weather for the family fun day. Cork's Lee Fields shone in all their grassy splendour, the river wending its way beyond the walking path behind where the hardy swimathoners were setting up for the second phase of fundraising for Flynnie's son. Aidan parked his car across the road and pulled down his sunglasses against the welcome glare.

Despite only having a few hours' sleep, he was pumped. He'd powered through three and a half kilometres between 2 and 3 a.m. and looked forward to telling his sponsors, who had pledged ten euro a kilometre. He'd even managed to keep up with Colette. Chris had been determined to team them up. 'You young singles don't mind the graveyard shift,' he'd insisted when it came to divvying up the twenty-four hours of pool time. Young was a relative term, but single was, unfortunately, spot on. His chances with Colette were still tenuous, but they had managed a few civil conversations in the lead-up to the fundraiser. He'd even agreed with her plans for West Cork and given her the go-ahead on ordering materials and scheduling contractors.

If dressing to impress were anything, no one could say he hadn't made an effort. The new board shorts were two sizes smaller than what he had in his wardrobe. Even the smart T-shirt was large without the extra. He'd been so delighted to downsize, he'd bought the shirt in three different colours and the shorts in three designs. A haircut earlier in the week, a rest from the razor, and he was a new man.

A wolf whistle went up from a group of swimmers busy setting up trestle tables under a marquee. The new look wasn't lost on his pals. Chris and Dessie stood beaming at him from under a pair of matching sombreros.

'Could be your lucky day, Aidan,' said Chris with a nudge to Dessie.

'You look seventeen again, boy,' said Dessie. 'How did you go this morning?'

Aidan was ready for them. 'All right for you boys, in The Land of Nod while we swam our guts out,' he joked.

They compared notes on the swimathon as they got stuck into the work. He was pleased his efforts hadn't been too shabby.

'The sponsorship's been fantastic,' said Margaret as they helped assemble her wheel of fortune. 'Between that and the weather, we should raise a fair bit for your Flynnie's boy.'

'Is Flynnie here?' asked Aidan.

'Here since the crack o' dawn, helping set up,' said Chris, pointing across the oval of stalls.

Aidan found Flynnie unpacking a box onto a table covered in the EDS signature zebra-stripe fabric.

'Can I give you a hand there?'

As they displayed the EDS brochures and merchandise, Aidan heard the familiar laugh. He hoped he hadn't made it too obvious when he spun round.

'How's it going, boys?' asked Grace, one step ahead of her sister, the two of them laden with clear plastic tubs full of what looked like art supplies. Of course, they'd volunteered their face-painting services. Aidan checked his map and pointed to where they should set up.

'Let me take that for you,' he said, taking the box from Colette.

Sunshine looked good on her, he thought, taking in the sheen on her dark silky hair as she placed the box in his arms. He hadn't been able to read her eyes for the sunglasses, but her mouth had smiled at him, that warm smile that made his heart beat a bit faster.

A horn beeped behind them. It was Fern and Rob arriving in the in-laws' ice-cream van, followed by another relative with a bouncy castle. Aidan shook his head in amazement. Fern was a star at the best of times, but she could really push the boat out for a cause.

Grace huffed as she unpacked her box of tricks.

'Can I take that for you?' she mocked. 'There I am nearly buckled under the weight of this lot and he takes *your* stuff.'

Colette had to turn away to hide her smile. It was a bit obvious that he'd helped her over Grace, but it felt good. She'd even dropped her usual *I can manage* comeback, which surprised her.

'Have you noticed a change in him?' Grace was asking. 'A big change?'

'I don't know what you mean,' she lied. There was no mistaking the weight loss, the haircut, or the rusty five o'clock shadow that, combined with the new threads, made Aidan O'Shea look positively hot. Sizzling bloody hot she'd noticed as their hands had touched when she'd handed over the tub – this time without the electric shock, thank God. She pretended to rifle among her sponges for something important.

'We'll have customers in on top of us if we don't hurry up.'

—

Fern pulled out all the stops, quite literally. She'd never sold an ice-cream in her life, but after the short training she'd received from her brother-in-law that morning, she was handing out double twists and ninety-nines to beat the band. Liam, her eldest, would drive *her* round the twist if he didn't stop coming in and out of the van. Rob's mother was supposed to be minding him, but no, there was her mother-in-law, sat like a lump at one of the café tables, indulging in most of the contents of a bag of donuts she'd supposedly bought for the children.

'Rob, get him out of here,' she growl-whispered to her husband, who was flat-out beside her.

'Mam'll be back in a minute to get him,' said Rob, ever the peacemaker and never one to cross his mother.

Fern just rolled her eyes and turned to serve another customer. Thank God it was someone who didn't require a false smile.

'Aidan, what can I get you?'

Any negativity disappeared when she saw who was standing beside him. The lovely Millie he sometimes minded, looked undecided as she sucked on an index finger shoved between the gap of a missing tooth.

'Tell you what,' said Fern, leaning over the counter of the van, 'I'll give you a double twist with a chocolate flake. How about that?'

Millie's smile was infectious. 'Thanks,' she lisped as she took the ice-cream in both hands.

'I thought you'd be busy enough today,' said Fern, taking Aidan's money with a perfunctory nod to the child.

'So did I,' he said. 'Her mum got called into work at the last minute.'

That's the thing about you, Aidan O'Shea, thought Fern, as she watched them walk away hand in hand. *Too soft by half. 'Tis that child's father that should be taking her round the fair.* Millie's mother only had to say 'jump' and Aidan would say 'how high'. It was shameful. But then, Fern had only heard snippets of the story of Aidan and Jane Donovan from Rob, who wasn't exactly a mine of that kind of information. 'If he wants to tell me about his love life, I'm sure he'll do it in his own good time,' Rob had said when she'd suggested he bring Aidan round to the topic over a few beers. *God knows where the father is*, she seethed inwardly as she slapped on a smile for the next customer.

'A ninety-nine, please.'

Fern looked out carefully at the woman from behind the ice-cream machine. She looked exactly like that interior designer Aidan was working with. A pair of expensive sunglasses rested on the head of dark shoulder-length hair. Fern was sure it was her on the Fabulous Four Walls website. The hair was longer, but she took a chance.

'I hope you don't mind my asking,' she said, handing her the ice-cream, 'but are you Colette Barry?'

'I am,' said the woman, obviously trying to place her.

'I'm Aidan's secretary,' said Fern. 'We've spoken on the phone.'

'Nice to meet you,' Colette smiled, holding her spare hand out for the change.

'I love your work.'

'Ah thanks,' said Colette. 'You'll have to get the lads to bring you down to West Cork one day. They're doing a fantastic job.'

What a nice girl, thought Fern as she watched Colette turn from the van and merge with the crowd. *Not at all big-headed or snobbish. Why wouldn't Aidan snap up someone like her? She'd be perfect.* As she swirled the next orders into cones, her mind panned back to the day the young Scottish boy delivered the mood boards. That was the day Aidan had asked her what women wanted. The same day he'd described Colette as cranky. Surely to God his own bad mood hadn't been brought on by that lovely forty-something. She'd ask Rob, but chances were, he wouldn't have a clue. No, she'd have to get her information from the horse's mouth.

The arrival of Barbara Barry with Ben and the children gave the sisters a welcome break from their face-painting duties. While Grace immediately took off with her family, Barbara had to shoo Colette out of the seat from where she had painted more than fifty faces. She was sure she'd be painting butter-flies and Spidermen in her sleep.

At the wheel of fortune, Margaret convinced her to try her luck. The marker flick-flicked quickly at first, then slowed to an uncertain rattle. As Colette moved to let some children get a better look, she caught sight of Aidan heading her way with Millie by the hand. A nervous wave rippled in her belly. She thought she might escape, but Margaret's excitement made her stay to discover the outcome of her bet. For God's sake, she was a grown woman; she didn't have to avoid him. Only a few hours ago, they'd been stroking up and down the pool together. They'd kept pace with each other for most of their stint in the swimathon. It had felt natural, comfortable. Not having to speak, just swim, stroke for stroke. If she were honest, the overriding feeling of being that close to Aidan had been one of safety. What if Grace was right and he was one of the good ones? She needed to give him a chance.

The small crowd held a collective breath as the wheel eventually came to a stop. A cheer went up from a man who won a bottle of whiskey. Colette thought again to leave, but Aidan had seen her and was coming straight toward her.

'Hello, Millie, isn't it?'

The small girl curled against Aidan's hip with a shy smile.

'Your ice-cream.' Aidan gestured to where the white cream was starting to trickle down Colette's cone. There was nothing for it but to lick around the edge to stop it in its tracks.

A delightful chuckle emanated from Millie, who had detached herself from Aidan and was standing with her hands over her mouth and nose, her shoulders shaking with laughter.

'It's not *that* funny,' Colette said, pretending to be mad.

'It is,' countered Aidan.

Millie reached into the frayed silk bag that hung across her body, took out a folded tissue and held it out. Colette glanced at Aidan, who tapped a finger on the end of his nose.

'Thanks Millie,' she said, taking the tissue. 'That could have been very embarrassing.'

She narrowed her eyes at Aidan. Why did he have to be there when she got food all over her face? She couldn't even remember the last time she'd eaten ice-cream. As she stood wondering how best to enjoy her messy treat while holding a conversation, Chris and Dessie showed up. Aidan's help was required to rescue the bouncy castle, which had decided to deflate with a queue of kids ready to go wild.

Colette thought quickly. 'Maybe you'd like to have your face painted, Millie?'

The child looked to Aidan for permission.

'If you're sure.' He looked from one to the other, his comment meant for both of them. There were nods of agreement. He put his big hands on Millie's shoulders and looked her in the eye. 'I'll come and get you when we're done, okay?' Millie nodded again and slipped her hand into Colette's. It felt like a small circle of trust. 'Colette will mind you,' he said. Heading back to her station, Colette felt she might just be walking on air.

—

Millie wanted to be a butterfly. Colette thought she might scream – *Not another bloody butterfly!* – but instead she set to work applying the white base coat with a damp sponge before outlining the wings and body with a fine paintbrush. She'd seen so many small faces today, but Millie's was different. Filling in the gold and silver spaces with the thin ends of her cosmetic wedges, Colette felt a weight of responsibility for Aidan's . . . not daughter, not even step-daughter . . . special little lady, she decided.

For a second, when she held up the mirror to show her, Colette feared the child would cry at the sight of herself, but when the small, serious face broke into a toothy grin, she laughed with relief.

There was no sign of Aidan, but Millie was happy to sit behind them at their table, looking through the books they'd brought along for ideas, sharing them with the other children as they decided what they wanted to be. When Flynnie came along with his family, Ronan steered his wheelchair over to her and chatted while Colette tried her best to make his sister, Saoirse, look like someone out of *Avatar*. The queue never seemed to abate. Barbara and Grace had swapped again, but still there was no sign of Aidan. Millie was such a stalwart, sitting quietly when another child might have pestered and nagged.

'All done,' Colette told her latest charge, reaching for the mirror behind her as she had done countless times that afternoon. Millie had looked up from her books and smiled at each child, an encouraging butterfly smile. But not this time. Colette went to the back of the marquee.

'Millie?'

Grace stopped mid spider's web and shouted after her. 'Is she there?'

Colette tugged at the opening in the canvas and checked in both directions.

'She was just here.'

Grace was beside her, eyes searching the walking trail and bushes beyond. She called over her shoulder to the waiting children. 'Won't be a moment.'

Colette circled the outside of the stall, straining to catch a glimpse of the pink dress, the flaxen hair, anything that would distinguish the girl. In the distance, the bouncy castle wobbled like a set of dancing jelly babies. She glanced at Grace. The nod was all she needed. Grace would keep the show on the road without raising suspicion.

The crowd merged in a blur as Colette dodged balloon-waving children and their slow-moving parents. If only they'd get out of the way, her sandalled feet might make it to their target in time. Panic rose like acid from the pit of her stomach. *Stop it. She'll be there. She's just got bored of waiting and decided to find Aidan herself. Children got separated from adults all the time, mostly with happy outcomes. But what about the ones that went missing? Stop it.*

'Excuse me, please,' she pleaded as she squeezed to the front of the line for the bouncy castle, where Aidan was bent down helping a little blonde girl tie her shoes. Colette's face broke into a smile. Her shoulders relaxed as she let out a deep breath. But her relief was short-lived. The little girl turned and ran into the crowd to a waiting parent. *Damn!* She scanned round. Maybe Millie was perched somewhere close enough to see Aidan.

'Everything okay?'

He'd spotted her before she'd worked out what the hell she was going to say. She tried to sound calm.

'Is Millie with you?' he asked. 'Sorry, I got caught here . . .'

His cheery face transformed with a frown like a shadow falling. 'Isn't she with you?' He looked past her toward the face-painting stall.

'I'm so sorry.' She held out her hands in despair. 'One minute she was flicking through the books, the next she was . . .'

Chris appeared beside them. 'Thanks for giving me a hand,' he said to Aidan. Registering the looks on their faces, he stopped short. 'What's up?'

Aidan pushed past them, leaving Colette to explain.

'It's Millie,' she began.

Behind them children leapt and screeched, oblivious to the crisis while those in the queue looked on, impatient for their turn.

'You stay here and keep these guys happy,' said Chris. 'I'll announce it over the loudspeakers.'

She stood helpless and watched as Chris caught up with Aidan and hurried with him to the information stand. Even from the back, she knew he was distraught.

A man holding a sleeping baby brought her back to the task at hand. 'Are they finished yet?'

She wanted to bolt, but somehow managed to herd one set of children off and the next on. In the changeover, she scrutinised each group for small people in Millie's age range. She cursed butterflies. Why did little girls all want to look the same?

Chris's voice boomed over the public-address system. 'We are looking for a seven-year-old girl called Millie Donovan. She is wearing a pink dress, has blonde hair and has her face painted as a butterfly. If you are listening, Millie Donovan, could you please come to one of the stands. Thanks, sweetheart.'

Colette hoped it would do the trick. Millie was a good girl. She'd hear her name and front up to one of the swimmers in no time. Convinced, she even managed a smile for her oblivious bouncing customers.

As the afternoon sun began to wane, she imagined Aidan treating the child to a hotdog or some lovely warm cinnamon donuts. He'd just forgotten to let her know. It was fine. All this supervising small people and selling paper tickets was for a good cause. Flynnie's son would get the treatment he needed, and Millie would be another child lost in a crowd, reunited with her responsible adult. But when Chris's voice came over the loudspeakers once again, she felt sick. The crowd were thanked for their huge support and assured the funds raised would be very much appreciated by Flynnie, Jackie and their family. Then came the request for people to leave in an orderly fashion.

The police were already at the entrance, checking everyone who went in or out.

Chapter Twenty-three

An eerie calm fell over the crowd. Parents did their best to gently explain to children why the fun had to stop and they had to go home. Looks exchanged between adults were enough to communicate that something serious was going down and that the request to leave meant immediately. A man shouted to three boys who were ignoring Colette's efforts to make them stop jumping around and get off. Colette didn't know him from Adam, but as she watched his cheeks redden and the veins of his neck bulge, she was grateful to him. He stood firm. The boys did as they were told.

The crowd thinned, moving quietly toward the entrance, where police looked over each one in turn. She cursed the butterfly faces that would slow their exit and delay the relief the parents would feel at getting into their cars and safely home. Ticket stubs and food wrappers fluttered in the breeze. She paced the length of the bouncy castle, clutching her upper arms. What now? Should she leave her post? Help pack up? Find Aidan, and see if there was any news?

The balmy afternoon did nothing for her goosebumps. She looked around the wide circle of food and entertainment stands. The band members were packing away their equipment. Margaret's husband was helping dismantle her wheel of fortune. Fern Murphy was selling the last few drinks and ice-creams to those with thirsty, tired children. Most of the action seemed to be centred at the information point. Dessie's and Chris's sombreros stood out in the throng. Aidan would be in the thick of it, God help him.

She'd texted Grace, who was taking forever to come. When she finally came walking toward her, Colette knew the news wasn't good.

'You're wanted over there,' she told her.

As her sister steered her across the grass, Colette wished she would wake up from a bad dream. The cheery sombreros turned as she approached, but the faces under them were anything but cheerful.

'Colette.' Chris reached out a hand and took hers, drawing her close. 'We told the guards what happened. They've acted really quickly.'

She looked past him to where two uniformed officers were pointing in her direction as they spoke with a lean, overdressed man. Despite the rolled-up sleeves and tie loosened at the neck, the man looked like he was overheating as he made his way to her. When he shook her hand, his palm felt sweaty against her own.

'Detective Niall Carmody.' A power in the piercing blue eyes told her she was locked into this situation whether she liked it or not. Her lower lip trembled. Aidan would be close by, watching, willing her to help. For all she knew, he might be blaming her. She dropped her chin and as the first tear trickled down her cheek, the detective led her away to some chairs. From the pocket of his shirt, he took out a notebook and pen.

'I know how upsetting this must be for you,' he began. 'You were one of the last people to see her.'

She tried to breathe. 'I have no idea what happened.' She sniffed and tried the pockets of her sundress. Even before she drew it out, the feel of Millie's scrunched-up tissue made her sob.

Niall Carmody was patient but firm. 'Anything, anything you can tell us will help.'

She made a fist around the tissue, but instead of using it, she wiped her face with the back of her hand. She wanted nothing more than to help, but what could she do or say that might find the child?

'I barely know her,' she began, her voice straining to come out in a level tone. 'I took her to the face-painting stall to mind her while Aidan . . .' She couldn't go on. The thought of what Aidan must be going through right now was tearing her apart.

'It's okay,' the detective assured her. 'I'm sure you've done nothing wrong.'

—

Aidan stood knee-deep at the edge of the River Lee, unaware of the soaking hems of his new shorts. Surely to God, there was no need for the fire brigade or the police divers. Millie wouldn't just wander in for a swim anyway, would she? And she could swim, couldn't she? Standing at the spot where the water gained momentum from easy flow to swirling rush toward the weir, he began to wonder how easy it would be for a slight seven-year-old to be swept away. There'd been talk of swimming lessons, hadn't there? With the sun starting to wane, the water grew darker. He pushed the hair off his face with his sunglasses. If this didn't end well, he would never forgive himself. Jane would never forgive him either.

—

The Australian accent stood out from the commotion that was swirling round Colette like a movie she couldn't stop watching.

'Were you supposed to be looking after her?'

Colette needed no introduction to Jane Donovan as she looked up, struggling to even see the woman through the tears.

'How could you let this happen?'

'Whoa, whoa!' It was Chris who got between them. Just in time, as Jane looked ready to shake an answer out of her. What the hell could she say? Aidan had asked her to do one thing and she'd failed everybody. She leaned over the plastic chair and vomited.

'Can we get some water here?'

Eyes shut, she heard her sister's authoritative voice taking control.

'Give her some room. She's in shock.'

'I'm the child's mother,' said Jane. 'I demand to know what went on here.'

Colette heard the detective intervene and usher Jane away from the group. Again, she squeezed the tissue, refusing to use it.

'It's okay, Colette,' Grace said. 'Just breathe. You don't have to say anything to her right now if you don't want to. The police are with her.' The feel of Grace's hand stroking her hair gave her comfort. She sat straight in her chair and without looking up, she asked quietly, 'How is Aidan?'

'I don't know,' said Grace. 'I think he might be with the divers.'

'Divers?' She spat the word out like snake venom.

'They can't rule anything out, Colette. It's just what they do.'

How her sister could remain so calm when she herself was falling apart, she would never know. It was just in her, as it always had been. Cool under pressure, as their father would always remark when Grace had shown enviable self-control regardless of the drama going on in their lives. Exams, boyfriends, girlfriend fall-outs – Grace had never been one to let life's stresses get on top of her. Colette had fallen in a heap after every exam, after every boyfriend. In fact, she'd strived so hard to gain control of her life after Tadgh, she'd forgotten what that helplessness was like. But this pain surpassed anything she'd experienced. It would take all her resolve not to let this defeat her. But helpless wasn't an option. Helpless wouldn't find Millie. She took the water bottle from Grace and drank obediently. She might have failed Millie, but she wouldn't sit around and wallow. Standing up, she straightened her dress, and went to speak to Jane Donovan.

There was a huddle at the water's edge as the divers regrouped. Aidan could only look on as he waited for news. Their team leader approached.

'No sign of her,' he said.

For a moment, Aidan stood rooted to the spot. Part of him wanted to stay, in the faint hope they were wrong. He could do CPR when they got her out. Anything to save her.

'She mightn't have gone in at all,' the diver was saying.

It was enough to make his feet move. He nodded and turned to re-join the fundraiser group. The swimmers and helpers had packed everything up but were hanging around in what he knew was a show of moral support. He hoped for all their sakes, they would eventually leave with good news. Jane had arrived and was standing a distance away, flanked by the detective and Colette. From Colette's frantic pointing and head shaking, he could imagine how she must be trying to explain herself. In his horror at hearing Millie was missing, he'd completely overlooked the fact that she would be in the firing line. He replayed the events in his head. The first he'd known of Millie's disappearance was when Colette had come looking for her. As he neared them now, he could see the weary look on her face. Her normally even voice sounded strained, at pains to tell her part of the puzzle. Chris, Dessie, Rob and Fern stood together in silence a little away from them, watching as the guards continued their search of the grounds. Jane looked distraught. She was throwing up her hands and turning away from Colette when they locked eyes. The tirade hit him like gunfire.

'What the fuck were you thinking, Aidan?' she cried out. 'You left her with someone she didn't even know!'

If he could just get her to calm down, he could explain how he'd left her daughter in the care of a trusted friend. His sister's trusted friend; somebody he had known forever. Maybe he shouldn't have done it, but it was done.

'Hang on there now, Jane,' Rob had come beside them. 'It could have been any of us. Sure, we've all left our kids with friends for a small while.'

Jane shot him a look of derision and turned back to Aidan.

'You don't even know this woman,' she railed, her voice brittle. 'You've never mentioned her. Is she your girlfriend? Someone you haven't told me about?'

He drew a hand through his hair. He wished he could shout back, tell her to focus on what mattered, but he let her rant. God knows she had cause to be irrational.

'Look!' It was Fern, pointing at a guard who was approaching from the road, her surgical glove holding out a silken handbag. Aidan ran to her, conscious of Jane on his heels.

'It's Millie's,' he said.

Jane went to grab the bag, but the guard drew it away.

'Sorry, forensics will be interested in this,' she told them before taking it to one of the police cars that had by now closed off the road.

It was in that moment Jane Donovan truly lost it. Colette could only look on as the woman whipped round to face Aidan, the shirt of her hotel uniform riding up over the short black skirt as she pushed at his chest, shoving him backward, then grabbing at his T-shirt, shouting at him, demanding he tell her why he left her daughter. He held out his palms at his sides as she pulled and pushed like a mad woman.

Grace reached for Colette's elbow, but she didn't want to leave, not yet. She wanted to intervene on Aidan's behalf, apologise again, reason with this woman. But what reason could she give for allowing her child to disappear?

Aidan's arms came around Jane's back. Colette saw him hesitate and then take hold of her shoulders as he moved in closer. Jane's head dropped onto his chest as his arms enfolded her shaking body like one might wrap a blanket round a newborn baby.

'We should go,' Grace was saying. Colette unclamped her eyes from the scene, but not before she saw Jane dissolve into Aidan's arms, her shouts having turned to mournful sobs and her angry fists relaxing to reach around his neck and draw his face closer to hers. The sobs cut through Colette like knives. As she made to turn away, her eyes met Aidan's, but he closed them. Why wouldn't he? She had no part in this moment. She deserved to be shut out.

Fern too had been watching. As they left, she gave Colette a sympathetic smile.

'They'll find her, love,' she said.

Chapter Twenty-four

Ellen had gone to the airport to collect Louise and Toby, the boyfriend she'd met at university the previous year, leaving Gerry to the dinner preparations. It was only June, but the Christmassy smell struck her as she walked into the house and set down Louise's vast travel bag. In the kitchen, the turkey rested on the bench. Gerry had gone all out. He mumbled a quick acknowledgement as he bent down at the cooker to check the roasted veggies, oven gloves on and an old apron she never wore tied around his waist. She glanced round at the table. The place settings were perfect, the good cutlery gleaming.

'You *have* been busy,' she said, reaching out to give him a hug and a kiss. He responded with the barest touch, too focused on the kitchen door and who was about to walk through it. 'Relax!' She tried to sound reassuring. 'It's only been a few months since you two last met, and that went fine.'

From the kitchen window, she could see Louise leading Toby by the hand toward the paddock.

'Oh God, she's taking a detour to show him round,' said Ellen, exasperation in her voice.

'She's probably as nervous as I am,' said Gerry.

Ellen shoved her shoes back on and strode out to join them.

'Wait up, Louise,' she called. They turned round, but Ellen looked past Toby. It wasn't that she didn't like the boy. Quite the opposite, in fact; she'd seen him in action in Santorini a few short months before when they'd spread Nick's ashes in the Aegean. Toby had been a huge support, lending a hand wherever one was needed without getting in the way. But why did Louise have to invite him when this was supposed to be an opportunity to spend time with Gerry? She smiled at Louise, trying not to look too earnest.

'Gerry's gone to heaps of trouble to have a special meal ready.'

Louise let go of Toby's hand and held out her palms. 'Sorry, Mum. I think I have cold feet. This all feels so . . . permanent.'

Ellen reached out her arms and Louise hugged her tight.

'It'll be good, Lou,' she said gently.

'I've tried to tell her it will be fine, Mrs C.'

It was then Ellen realised Toby had been dragged along for moral support. She wished Louise could have entrusted *her* with that role, but she had spent years hiding Gerry's existence from her daughter. She couldn't take her trust for granted.

'We've come this far, Lou,' she said.

Louise looked deep into her eyes. It was a look that reminded Ellen of the baby she and Nick had held all those years ago. The tiny girl who had grown into this beautiful young woman.

'Dinner's ready, guys.'

The three of them turned to see Gerry smiling at them from the veranda. It was a warm smile, full of hope. Ellen crossed her fingers and said a silent prayer. Louise pushed her fair hair behind her ears and started to walk toward the house.

'Hey, Gerry. How are you goin'?'

Toby was about to fall into step with her, but Ellen put a hand on his arm. He slowed down and the pair of them proceeded a few steps behind Louise, just enough to let her get to Gerry first. On the middle step, Louise paused. Ellen thought her heart might stop. Louise turned and held out a hand to Toby.

'This is Toby,' she told Gerry, who kept smiling despite any disappointment he may have felt at not getting a hug.

Toby stepped up and shook Gerry's outstretched hand.

'Good to meet you, mate,' said Gerry.

'You too, Mr . . .'

Was he about to say Mr C? But Gerry was onto it.

'Gerry will do, son,' he said.

There was a nervous laugh from everybody just as a timer went off in the kitchen, rescuing them from the awkwardness and sending Gerry into chef mode.

'Come on. I don't want those spuds to burn on me.'

He put an arm lightly around Louise's shoulder as he herded them inside. Ellen took a deep breath as she watched them walk in the door, laughing. The hugs might come later.

'Louise tells me you're old school,' said Toby, not even trying to suppress a cheeky grin as they sat around the table happily stuffed after Gerry's roast dinner.

Gerry looked to Louise for explanation.

'You know,' she said, blushing now, 'with the letters you used to write to Mum and everything.'

'Oh,' said Gerry, the reference dawning on him, 'you two think I'm old-fashioned. Is that it?'

'No,' she back-tracked. 'I mean, there's nothing wrong with letters. They're . . .' She paused as though choosing her words carefully, 'They're romantic and all that.'

Ellen was smiling but saying nothing, enjoying watching the debate unfold.

'But you've never been on Facebook or Snapchatted each other?' Louise went on.

'Hang on a sec.' Toby looked from Ellen to Gerry, a mischievous smile spreading to his cheeks. 'Maybe you guys are on Twitter?'

As Louise gave him a poke to shush his mocking, Gerry held up his hands in surrender.

'I don't know, Ellen. Maybe I should get onto Facebook before I turn in to an old fogey altogether.'

Ellen laughed and began to stack the plates. These young ones could be as cool as they liked, but they would never know the intimacy of letters, the joy of reading and rereading handwriting as familiar as your own face.

'Well, if one of you would like to help me tidy up, the other can show Gerry the ways of Gen Z.'

Toby was up like a shot. 'I'll help, Mrs C,' he said. 'That was a great roast. Thanks Gerry.'

'Don't mention it, boy.'

Louise was already heading to the lounge room to the family computer. Gerry glanced at Ellen, a little unsure. She gave a slight tilt of her head and arched her eyebrows, urging him to follow her.

When Ellen and Toby joined them a while later, Gerry and Louise were budged up together staring at a Facebook page.

'What about Uncle Aidan?' Louise was asking. 'Mum told me you're friends with him.'

'You mean in real life?' Gerry winked at her mischievously.

'Gerry, old mate,' she said, emphasising the 'old', 'this *is* real life.'

Gerry gave a hearty laugh. Ellen couldn't help joining in.

'We've sent you a friend request,' said Louise, turning at the sound.

'I'm not sure I even remember my password,' said Ellen. She had abandoned all things social media when Nick died. 'Even Aidan's on it,' she added. 'And I'm supposed to be the adventurous one in the family.'

'Don't worry,' said Louise, 'he's only posted twice in two years.'

—

Gerry lay in bed, head propped up on one hand as Ellen undressed.

'Times have certainly changed,' he said, yawning.

'What do you mean?'

'The pair of them in the room over there.' He nodded in the direction of Louise's bedroom at the other side of the landing.

'And isn't it a good thing?' she said, climbing in beside him.

He stroked the wisps of hair from her face and ran a hand over her shoulder.

'You're a good mother,' he said simply.

'I don't know about that. I just want her to be happy. Toby's a nice boy.'

'I wonder if your mother thought that about me?' he grinned.

'I doubt it,' she said as she wrapped an arm around his warm chest and rested her head against him. Her mother had been a big part of the reason she'd stayed in Australia and made a new life far away from Gerry Clancy. But that was all water under the bridge. She hoped the two across the hall were as in love as she was right now. They would face enough challenges in life without her or anyone else interfering.

—

'I'm going to have another look at that Facebook,' Gerry told her as they woke to a cold winter's morning. She pulled the duvet in tight and listened as he pottered around downstairs, lighting the wood burner and putting coffee on to brew. It was a far cry from winter at home in Ireland, but there'd been hail the day before and there was a definite nip in the air, even inside. But despite the cold, the house had a special kind of warmth, one that came with the presence of loved ones. She drifted off again, happy to no longer be alone.

Ellen struggled to come out of a deep sleep when she felt a hand at her shoulder. Gerry was beside her, telling her something in a loud whisper. Something about Aidan . . . a child . . . missing.

'Hang on, Gerry.' She pushed at a pillow and sat up. 'Slow down for God's sake.'

He sat on the edge of the bed and explained what he'd seen on Facebook.

'Millie,' she echoed, remembering a photo in Aidan's house of the two of them; thick as thieves by all accounts. At least that's what her father had said when he told her Aidan would often bring the girl to visit on a Sunday when the mother was working. Aidan being Aidan hadn't mentioned any of this when she was home, showing more concern for her issues than discussing his own. She shoved back the duvet and went downstairs to the computer. He'd shared the official Garda post. The sweet blonde child smiled from the screen.

It was too late for phone calls to the other side of the world. Ellen and Gerry had planned to have the day off to spend with Louise, but they were no good to each other, hanging around, waiting for news. Instead, Louise had taken Toby to see the Popes while Gerry tinkered in the shed, giving the Chrysler a promised look over. Ellen tried to relax, but the thought of the missing child plagued her. Finally, at six, when she spoke to her brother, his helplessness was audible. With Gerry beside her, she logged onto Facebook to search for Jane Donovan. It wasn't an uncommon name. 'They took the soup,' her mother would have said as a reminder of the desperation of The Great Famine when, in exchange for food, some families dropped the O' and converted to Protestantism. But then, her mother had had an unforgiving streak. Having all but disowned Ellen when she got pregnant, Maureen O'Shea had gone to the grave without having met her only grandchild. The memories simmered in Ellen now, not far from the surface.

After several blind alleys, they went to Aidan's page and checked his Friends.

'She's from South Australia!'

Gerry looked to where she was pointing at Jane's profile.

'Where's Millicent?' he asked.

She was already typing into Google.

'On the way to Mount Gambier, toward Victoria.' They scoured the map.

'The grandparents must be beside themselves,' he said.

'I hope they are.'

Gerry turned to look at her. 'What do you mean?'

'They've never met the child. Aidan said Jane hasn't been in touch with her mother in years. They don't get on, apparently.'

Gerry went to say something to counter her statement, but stopped himself. Ellen looked him squarely in the eye, his own memories of their history registering there. The tears just fell. He drew her to his chest.

'We have to do something,' she sobbed. 'They can't just stand by and let her go through this on her own.'

He said nothing, but squeezed her in close. She took comfort once again in his presence and in the steady beat of his heart.

Colette hadn't been able for work on Monday morning. She'd sent John a text saying she'd work from home, but a sleepless night and trying to stay on the alert for news of Millie made for an unproductive day. She'd downed tools in the afternoon and with the radio news streaming through her headphones she'd run fifteen kilometres and made herself do a gruelling set of crunches and push-ups. None of it helped her sleep. On Tuesday, she dragged herself to work, her head ringing with the countless radio and television reports on Millie's disappearance. The worst part was that the story never changed. They still hadn't found her.

John was kind but knew she didn't want his sympathy. They sat in the front office with their coffees and moved on quickly from the terrible topic. Their plans for the day were much easier to talk about.

'Before you go,' said John, swiping at his phone as he followed her to the door, 'have a look at Shane's Facebook photos from Dublin.'

She paused, impatient to get on with her tasks, but she took the phone. *These had better be good*, she thought, rolling her eyes as she left him. In the sanctuary of her office, door closed, she set her bag on the floor and flopped into her chair. Across the desk, she stared at the empty chair Aidan had occupied only a month or so ago. The day when he'd squashed his bear-like form between the armrests, swivelling self-consciously as she'd fielded a call from a shifty supplier. He'd looked so out of place in her pristine work space, and yet he'd added a warmth that attracted her. Feeling the phone in her hand, she snapped herself out of the reverie and refreshed the page.

Shane's attitude had certainly improved since she'd bailed him out that night, more positive, engaged even. Taking up the offer to visit another of his uncles in Dublin had been a great sign of improvement. She looked at him now, the dark hair that had grown a little since he'd arrived falling around his face in a serious selfie in the quadrangle of Trinity College. *My word*, she smiled. Maybe she'd helped give him aspirations after all. The uncle, the image of his brother John, featured in a couple of photos at Kilmainham Gaol and Dublinia. She silently applauded the man's sightseeing itinerary; exposure to Irish history would be good for his nephew. But most impressive was the caption accompanying a picture of the pair outside the Museum of Modern Art, *Fave so far.*

'That's my boy,' she said as she flicked through the remaining photos, conscious of the phone calls she should be making. Passing her thumb across the device for a last scroll, something caught her eye. She went back to a photo taken at Heuston Station. Turning the phone to see it in landscape, she worked her thumb and forefinger to enlarge it. There, in the throng of passengers waiting on a platform, was a young girl. Colette gripped the arm of her chair and sat bolt upright. Afraid to lose the picture, she ran to John's office. A middle-aged couple sat opposite him at his desk.

They turned to stare as she brought herself to a halt. She couldn't speak. She didn't need to. John excused himself and led her into the hallway then closed the door.

She pushed the phone at him.

'Look,' she urged, enlarging the image once again. 'I think it's Millie.'

Chapter Twenty-five

Aidan hadn't run in years. Not since his teenage days when early swim training was followed by circuits of the sports centre on icy Saturday mornings. But pounding the pavement was somewhat more productive than staring at the bedroom ceiling, trying to crack a case that hundreds of police were no doubt working on around the country. By the time he'd showered and changed and got himself to work, the slump had set in again. Rob took charge of the team and got everyone out on site and out of his hair. Fern was a stalwart, placing a coffee on the desk beside him and an understanding hand on his shoulder.

Niall Carmody had urged him to stay positive. He'd said that most cases of missing children were solved quickly and usually involved persons known to the child, so the perpetrators were easier to track down. *Perpetrator.* He mulled over the word, like one might swirl a glass of dark red before putting it to the nose in a blind-tasting. Someone known, but who?

The detective had paid him a visit. A personable enough fellow. Even gave Julius a pat as the dog barged out the door when Melanie and Dave were leaving. The house had never been so busy, with Chris and Dessie calling in to check he was okay, the phone ringing with calls of concern and support, and then Jane spending the night. She couldn't have got much sleep, but had refused his offer of breakfast, saying she should be at home getting the place ready for Millie's return. He'd watched, helpless, as she strode down the pathway, pausing briefly at the gate to give him a wave that sent some bangles Millie had made her crashing at the crook of her scrawny arm. He wished she'd let him feed her.

'How long have you known Jane Donovan?'

Carmody had sat in one of the armchairs, tie knotted at the top button of his shirt despite the promise of another warm day. His sidekick sat in the other armchair, leaving Aidan on the sofa between them, not sure if he should look at both of them as he answered. He was too exhausted for a tennis match. Carmody asked the question, so Carmody would get his answer. The other suit could do the psychoanalysis to his heart's content if that's what he wanted.

Aidan didn't have a problem remembering meeting Jane Donovan.

'Two years or so,' he began. Carmody leaned back in his chair and set the ankle of one leg on the opposite knee. Aidan was aware of the other man scratching on a notepad, but he continued to face Carmody. He didn't like an audience at the best of times.

'Just give us a picture of how you came to know Jane and Millie.' Carmody gestured with his hands, rolling his wrists with open palms. Aidan took a deep breath and willed his cheeks to cool down.

'I did a bit of work for her . . . Jane,' he started again. 'Fixing up an old wall at the back. Millie would have been about five. She was at school. I didn't meet her until . . .' He paused and swallowed, but Carmody only nodded to encourage him. 'I asked Jane out. It's been on and off.' He looked at the floor and shook his head. More off than on was the honest answer. 'I'm more of a friend really.'

The detective gave a non-judgemental nod. 'And you were close to Millie?'

Aidan smiled as he recounted the first time he'd met the child. He and Jane had been out on a couple of dates. It wasn't going fantastically well. He blamed himself for not being romantic enough and decided to make a bigger effort. He'd booked a table at a little Italian place in the city centre, bought a new shirt, gone to the barber for a haircut and a shave and even shined his good shoes. In truth, he'd been surprised she'd even agreed to go out with him again. Looking back, she probably just needed company. They were both the same in that regard.

Jane was different from the girls he usually met in pubs on his rare nights out with the lads. For a start, she was Australian and a hippy into the bargain. He'd spotted a sewing machine in one of the bedrooms and it hadn't surprised him when she told him she made most of their clothes herself. But when she'd arrived at the restaurant in a vibrant maxi dress with a mini-me in tow, all smiles and apologies, it was as if a dimmer switch had been turned up several notches to illuminate their table in the corner.

The babysitter had cancelled at the last minute, she told him. There'd been a moment when his heart had sunk at what this would do to his romantic intentions. He hadn't spent much time around children. They were like an alien species. A bit like women. But he needn't have worried. After a few minutes sitting in her mum's lap and sizing him up, Millie had agreed to sit in the extra chair the owner had brought to the table and pushed a bejewelled hand in Aidan's direction. He'd done what any decent bloke would do, admired the plastic rings and bangles as if they were Cartier, and basked in her pleasure in the telling of each item's backstory.

He'd been intrigued to know how Jane had ended up in Cork. She told him how she'd fallen out with her mother as a teenager and left home for Adelaide, where she'd enrolled in a hospitality course that would be her ticket to travel the world. And that's exactly what she'd done, heading to London to work, along with strapping compatriot Bryce Manning, whom she'd met on the course. Sharing Irish heritage, they'd decided to travel to Ireland together. They were in Cork when she'd found out she was pregnant. In her own words, 'something changed in her head' and she decided to stay in one spot, at least until after the birth. She was twenty-eight and ready for a rest. Bryce had promised to be there for her. They found work, but a few months after their daughter was born, the arguing became unbearable and she asked him to leave.

The only thing they'd agreed on was naming the child after Jane's home town.

A sucker for a sob story, Aidan had felt compelled to help out. He'd ended up doing a few extra jobs on the flat for free. There'd been more dates, a couple ending in Aidan's bed. To say Jane was looking for a more adventurous lover would have been putting it mildly, but quirks aside, she was a good person who wanted the best for her daughter. His relationship with Millie had strengthened while that with Jane had waxed and waned from lover to friend and, of late, to pal at best.

'So, you say Jane used . . . uses you as a babysitter?' Carmody was taking it all in.

'I don't mind,' Aidan shrugged. 'Like I said, she's a single mum, it can't be easy.'

'And what do you know about the father? He's been back on the scene for a while?'

Not Aidan's favourite topic. 'As I mentioned to you yesterday, he was working in London. Comes over now and then to see Millie . . . to see them.' It irked Aidan that Jane still slept with Bryce Manning, but he reminded himself it wasn't up to him whose bed she shared.

'Have you actually met him?'

Oh, Aidan had met him all right. Jane had sent him to drop Millie off one night and he'd given Aidan the third degree. Standing at his front door, Bryce Manning had looked more like a bearded prop forward than the hippy house husband Aidan had expected. The handshake alone had held more threat than if he'd wielded a broken beer bottle. When Jane had mentioned he'd worked in all the major clubs in London,

Aidan had pictured him as a friendly barman, an Australian Tom Cruise serving cocktails. When he did manage to throw in a few questions of his own, Bryce told him he did security, adding a few less-than-subtle comments about sorting out what he called 'migrant riffraff'. Aidan was grateful Millie hadn't been there to hear the self-promoting monologue, but instead had shown herself into the house that had become a second home. With the shake of a hirsute wrist to check his Rolex, Bryce had drawn the conversation to a close and shoved a Dora the Explorer bag at Aidan, telling him they'd see him later the next morning.

'Do you think he took her?'

At Aidan's question, the other detective gave a sharp cough.

'We're not at liberty to say, Aidan,' Carmody answered. 'At this point in the investigation, it's all to play for.'

Aidan nodded. They'd already quizzed Jane on Bryce's whereabouts, when she'd last seen him. She'd told them he'd returned to London after his recent visit – another failed attempt to get her to move back there together. He'd called her the day before, not speaking for long, as Jane was rushing to be on time for her shift after dropping Millie to Aidan at the fun day. She'd assured Aidan he'd never do anything to harm Millie. Aidan wasn't so sure.

'Colette Barry,' Carmody was saying, bringing Aidan back to the moment. 'How well do you know her?'

Aidan's cheeks burned. The last time he'd seen Colette she'd looked shocked and distraught. If it hadn't been for her sister's support, he reckoned she might have been taken to hospital. He'd phoned that night to see how she was holding up, but she'd just kept apologising and ended up unable to speak for the tears. He'd wished more than anything that he could have been there to comfort her, tell her it wasn't her fault, but he had Jane to look after. She had to be his priority. At least until Millie was found.

He told Carmody what he'd told Jane, over and over, as she'd tried to implicate Colette in Millie's disappearance; Colette was the salt of the earth, he'd known her since high school and trusted her implicitly. What he didn't tell the detective was that although he'd known Colette for most of his life, he'd only recently come to appreciate just how smart, caring and loyal she really was. And how in this fucked-up world where children went missing and men mistreated women, he'd missed his chance to tell her.

—

It was Fern who took John Buckley's call.

'Colette's beside herself,' he told her. 'On her way to the Bridewell now. Detective Carmody's meeting her there. She wanted Aidan to know.'

Fern's thoughts were with her own children's safety as she dialled Aidan's mobile number. Unable to set his mind to any paperwork, he'd jumped in the jeep saying he was heading to Jane's. As she'd tried to get on with her own work that morning, Fern had been distracted by the beeping of his phone with constant messages. Jane would be a wreck. God love him, he had to go to her. But it was Colette Barry she felt for most acutely. Who knew what happened behind that face-painting tent? Whatever went down, it was on that woman's watch, and that was something no one could live with.

—

As a young guard led them through the administration section and into a conference room at the back of the station, Aidan was aware of the pause in the banter between civilian and uniformed staff. If he was looking for sympathy, he wouldn't get it here. Until Millie was found and her disappearance explained, they were all under suspicion. Again, he felt his insides churn with a mix of rage toward whoever abducted the little girl and terror for how she must be feeling. The fear was written on the nameless faces here too.

Hurrying to keep up with the guard, Jane stumbled as she knocked against the corner of a desk. Aidan reached for her hand and slipped an arm around her waist to steady her. She held on tightly. When they entered the conference room, Carmody was there with Colette. They turned to acknowledge them, but quickly retrained their attention on a computer screen where a geeky-looking fellow with sticking-up hair was manipulating an image.

Carmody waved a hand, beckoning them to come closer. Colette shot Aidan a nervous look as she moved to one side so they could see better.

The technician talked himself through a process of altering pixilation and magnification until an image of a young girl dominated the screen. A sun hat pulled down over the eyes did little to fill Aidan with confidence. He and Jane stared together, silent until the man murmured something about angles and zooming in. Aidan felt his hand gripped tighter as Jane gasped. Unable to speak, she stretched a hand past the spiky hair and pointed to the child's mouth.

Colette saw it now. The gap where Millie had lost her front tooth. She wanted to burst into tears of joy at Jane's confirmation of her own thoughts, but any joy was short-lived.

'Get that Shane boy on the phone,' Carmody barked at the junior guard who'd shown them in.

Grateful for a job, Colette scrolled through her contacts and found Shane's number. She went to hand the phone to the guard, but Carmody intercepted it and strode away to an office with the phone to his ear.

With the door shut, they couldn't hear the ensuing conversation. Colette willed Shane to remember. He'd never met the child, and a small face in a crowd wouldn't have meant anything to him. Unlike his quirky angled shots of famous Dublin buildings and funny selfies with his uncle, this had been a random photo of a busy train station. His first impression of Dublin? Something to do as he waited for his uncle to collect him?

The technician excused himself and left the room, leaving the three of them with the young guard. None of them spoke apart from polite refusals when she offered them tea. Colette leaned against a desk, hands dug into the pockets of her business jacket wishing Carmody would come back and put them out of their misery. She daren't catch Aidan's eye. Nor Jane's.

The sound of her gasp had sent a shiver through Colette. A last sighting of Millie by someone connected with her would not do anything to endear her to Jane.

Nodding at the guard, Carmody came back in.

'Not too much to go on there, but I'll need to speak to you again, Jane.' He looked from one to another, like he was choosing who to have on his team.

'Colette, you can go, but give me a ring once the young lad is back from Dublin.'

'I will,' she agreed.

Carmody turned to Aidan. 'If you could just wait outside.'

As Colette turned away she took one last look at Jane, now sitting at the computer, which displayed the guards' logo screen saver, a nudge of the mouse away from the first hope of finding her daughter.

Moments later, Colette felt Aidan's presence as he followed her out of the room.

'Wait up,' he urged as he caught up with her.

She found herself unable to speak as they made their way through the foyer packed with people, and out the automatic doors into the almost gale-force wind.

'Feckin' weather,' said Aidan, zipping his fleece jacket right up to his chin. 'One extreme to the other.'

Whether it was the weight loss or the responsibility Millie's disappearance had forced upon him, Colette thought he looked taller. A hug was out of the question, and yet she craved it.

'At least, they have a bit of a lead now,' he said, and then when she didn't answer, he asked, 'You holding up all right?'

Lying, she nodded. Standing with her hair blowing across her face, she willed him to end the conversation and let her go. As much as she would have liked his comfort, she didn't deserve it. The bones in her legs chilled as the unseasonal gusts whipped through her trousers. She would take back a warm drink and nurse it alone in the office. John would be flat-out covering for them both.

'Better get back to it,' she said finally.

'Yeah,' said Aidan. 'Not much else for it.'

They stood silent for a moment. As the glass doors parted for people leaving the station, Colette felt for her keys and stamped her feet against the cold.

'I'd better go and see if Jane . . .' Aidan began.

She took a couple of steps backwards. 'We'll be in touch,' she said, already wishing she hadn't sounded so business-like.

Chapter Twenty-six

It was a strange week in the Constantinopoulos household. They all went about their business while checking in with Cork intermittently. Ellen headed to work, leaving the young ones to their own devices. Gerry was still looking for work, but most mornings he helped Pete and Tracey out at the roadhouse they owned, to give him some kind of routine. Tracey had tapped into his baking background and reported to Ellen that he had already started to improve the menu in their café, and what she was now calling her own homemade baking was flying out the door. Gerry had been anxious to spend time with Louise, but was nervous about crowding her. It had been Toby's suggestion that they take him surfing in the afternoons, giving them an easy way to be together with lots of fun into the bargain. Ellen had to admit, the boy was like part of the family. It was as obvious as the nose on her face that her daughter was in love, and she couldn't complain about coming home from a long day of meetings, clients and mountains of paperwork to the smell of cooking and the sight of the pair of them working together in the kitchen under Gerry's tutelage.

Nick would be impressed, she thought as she accepted a glass of wine and a kiss from her daughter and left them to it, grateful for nothing to do except throw herself down on the couch.

'Tough day?' asked Gerry, joining her with a beer.

He rested an arm behind, but not touching her. She liked his ease, the way he didn't smother her. She leaned in and kissed him, then let out a sigh. He drew a leg up under him and waited.

'I've been thinking,' she began, cradling the glass in her hands.

A playful grin spread across his face, but still he listened.

'My brother's going out of his mind. One of my best friends is in bits . . .' She looked at him, gauging the impact of what she was about to say. 'I can't just sit here doing nothing.'

He was still smiling at her.

'Gerry, you infuriate me,' she huffed. 'This isn't funny, you know.'

He raised his hands in surrender. 'I thought women just wanted men to listen. That's what I was doing.'

'No,' she said. 'We want them to read our minds.'

'Right,' he said. 'You want to phone that child's grandparents and tell them they should be in Cork, helping.'

'Nearly, but not quite,' she softened. 'I want to go there and tell them myself.'

He pulled his mobile phone from his pocket and tapped on the screen.

'Well, aren't you lucky I've caught up with the twenty-first century and did a bit of homework on that one?'

She couldn't believe it. He'd not only mapped out the route to Millicent, but he'd trawled the online phone book and found the only two Donovans living there. He'd completely understood how much it meant to her to do something to help the Donovans reunite.

'Nice work, Mr Clancy. But do you think I'm mad?'

'Ellen,' he said, leaning in a little and resting a hand on her shoulder, 'where would we be if we didn't take a chance?'

If Gerry had second thoughts about the road trip, he didn't let on. Instead, he was the one coming up with the most practical suggestions. Ellen wanted to jump in the car straight-away, but Millicent was an eleven-hour trip and there'd be no point arriving late Saturday or on Sunday when rural Australia would be on a go-slow. They decided to travel to Adelaide on Sunday and stay at the house Louise shared with Tracey's daughter, Jennifer, who insisted Ellen and Gerry have her room. They would make an early start for Millicent on Monday morning.

It wasn't how Ellen had imagined spending semester break with her daughter, but she was grateful they were together. She'd phoned Aidan to let him know of their plans. Although he couldn't offer much help in finding the Donovans – it wasn't a subject he wanted to broach with Jane – he agreed that any support they could muster would help. All Ellen knew about Jane was that she was in her mid thirties and made her own clothes. Not much to go on, but that didn't deter them. Gerry was first up on Sunday morning, and once the four of them had packed the car, he hit the road like his life depended on it.

A pit stop in Port Augusta gave Louise and Ellen a moment alone.

'I hope we can find the grandmother, Mum.'

'Millicent is a small place, Lou.'

Louise sighed. 'I just don't want you to go all that way and be disappointed.'

'I'd be more disappointed if I didn't try.'

'I love you, Mum.' Louise reached out her arms and enfolded Ellen in a warm hug. Less than a year ago, they were at loggerheads. Those months when Louise hadn't spoken to her after finding out Gerry was her father had been torture. But the experience had brought them closer. They both knew that whatever challenges life threw at them, they could face them together. She didn't know the Donovan women, but Ellen wished with all her heart they could put their differences aside for Millie.

In Adelaide, they said goodbye to Toby, who promised to do all he could to help. Ellen didn't doubt his sincerity. She was glad Louise had found a soulmate so early in her life.

On the dark winter morning, the city hummed into life as Ellen navigated the route from the house back on to Princes Highway. Louise nodded back to sleep in the back seat as Gerry kept an eye on the GPS confirming directions as they went. They were in Tailem Bend before any of them thought about breakfast. At the roadhouse they sat in silence, nursing warm mugs of coffee and chewing on croissants. Three hours from their destination and they still only had a vague plan of what they might do when they got to Millicent. South Australia's magnificent coastline went past in a blur. The Coorong National Park with its famous wetlands, the spectacular surf beaches and sleepy historic towns would all have given Gerry a wonderful insight into the area, but he was no ordinary tourist, and this was no ordinary road trip.

In Millicent they parked on the main street. Ellen pulled her woollen coat around her and linked arms with Louise as they passed the usual collection of small-town premises – a bank, a newsagent, a bakery – scanning signs and advertisements. Outside a supermarket, they peered into a glass-encased community noticeboard with everything from a dog groomer's business card to a poster for a trivia night at a church hall. A yellowed newspaper cutting caught Ellen's eye. It had a photo of two women holding up a large quilt which, the article said, had been raffled and had raised thousands of dollars for a local charity. One of the women pictured was a Wendy Donovan. Ellen imagined the woman resembled the photos of Millie, but she couldn't swear to it.

It was Gerry who spotted the craft shop on the other side of the street.

'This is awkward,' said Louise as the three of them stood on the pavement staring across at the shop window displaying a couple of patchwork quilts and an old Singer sewing machine. 'We can't just stand here.'

Ellen felt all the gutsy determination to enlist the help of Millie's grandparents dissolve inside, but Gerry put an arm around her.

'Just go in and suss out if they know her,' he said softly. 'Louise and I will stroll around. Text if you need us.'

As she watched them walk away, Ellen felt a surge of panic and thought about backing out, but she focused on the photo of Millie she'd seen on Facebook and willed herself to move. Across the street, she let herself into the shop, a bell tinkling above the door as she walked in. A woman behind the counter doing cross-stitch called to her.

'G'day, love. Be with you in a minute.'

Ellen thought of what to say as she looked around at the rolls of fabric and bright arrays of cotton reels and yarn. She ran a hand over a plastic weave sewing box that reminded her of one she'd had as a child. Absently, she opened the looped tie and felt the red silk lining within. It seemed like a lifetime ago when Granny O'Shea had taught her to sew.

'Sorry, love. Had to get that tricky bit done before I lost my concentration.' The woman came toward her, shuffling on what looked like a gammy hip. 'What are you after?'

Ellen took a deep breath. She was a terrible liar. Best to come straight out with her request.

'Actually,' she began, 'I'm looking for someone by the name of Donovan.'

The woman smiled, a bemused look in her eyes. 'Would it be Wendy you're after?'

Ellen swallowed. 'I think it might be.'

The woman shook her head and motioned for Ellen to follow her to the back of the shop. Behind a set of shelving was a large open space where a woman, who must have been in her late fifties, worked a technical-looking quilting machine along a massive piece of fabric.

'Someone looking for you, Wendy,' the first woman announced over the gentle hum of the machine.

There was a nod of acknowledgement from the woman as she kept hold of the handle, moving slowly along the fabric until she came to the end of the line of stitching. When she looked up, Ellen's heart skipped a beat. From the shape of the face and the piercing blue eyes behind the gold-rimmed glasses, there was every chance this woman could be related to Millie Donovan.

'Can I help you, love?'

Ellen willed herself to keep it together and get on with it. She could have spent hours trawling Millicent for signs of this woman, but instead it had only taken minutes to find her. She had a strong feeling of destiny, but no idea what her news would unleash.

'Mrs Donovan, isn't it?' she began.

'Wendy.' The woman gave a small nod and smiled at her.

'My name is Ellen, Ellen Constantinopoulos.'

The name meant nothing to the woman, who continued to smile expectantly.

'I believe you might be Jane Donovan's mother.'

The lines around the woman's lips tightened as the smile disappeared.

'What do you want?'

The friendly curiosity was gone. Ellen would have to tread carefully. 'Is there somewhere we can talk in private?' she asked.

Without a word, Wendy Donovan strode to the counter in the main shop and whispered something to the other woman. Coming back, she beckoned Ellen to follow her into a tiny kitchen at the rear of the shop.

'Has something happened to Jane?' she asked, her face grave.

Ellen swallowed hard. 'I didn't know if you knew, Mrs Donovan, but her daughter went missing in Ireland a week ago.'

Wendy took a sharp breath and steadied herself against the back of one of the chairs at the small table.

'I didn't even know she had kids,' she said, slipping down into the chair.

'Just Millie.' Ellen took the seat opposite and reached out to touch her arm. 'Mrs Donovan, I didn't come here to shock or upset you,' she said as tears glistened in the woman's eyes. 'My brother is a friend of Jane's in Ireland. He often minds Millie when Jane is working at weekends. I don't know Jane, but I wanted to do everything I could to find Millie, and I believe you would too.'

'Jane's in Ireland, you say?' She clasped her hands together on the table. 'Last I heard, she was living in London with that good-for-nothing she left Adelaide with.'

'She is, Mrs Donovan. Millie is seven. The father, Bryce Manning, is a suspect.'

The woman took a long deep breath and looked up at the ceiling. When she didn't say anything, Ellen went on.

'I know you don't know me from a bar of soap, but whatever happened between yourself and Jane, I came here so you might find it in your heart to support her.'

Mrs Donovan looked down at her hands and began to worry at a ring with a garnet stone set in a simple silver band.

'I bought this for her, you know,' she said, stretching out her fingers to Ellen. 'It's meant to keep travellers safe . . .'

Ellen wondered why the heck she'd never given it to her but let her continue.

'Bryce Manning was always bad news. Possessive, you know what I mean?' She shook her head and gave a heavy sigh. 'I pleaded with her not to go overseas. We had a blazing row. I said things I've regretted ever since. I told her it was him or me. Stupid, I know.' She raised her eyes to the ceiling again and pulled at the ageing skin of her neck, sniffing back tears. 'She told me I was jealous, that she didn't want to end up in a small town, lonely like me.'

'I'm sure she'd love to see you now,' said Ellen.

'My grandchild, my own flesh and blood,' Wendy was saying, half to herself. 'That bastard. She should have listened . . .'

Ellen found a tissue in her handbag and handed it to her as she started to sob. 'Mrs Donovan . . .'

'There's no Mrs, love,' she interrupted. 'Jane's father left me the minute he found out I was pregnant. I've had my share of partners, but none of them ever made me Mrs.'

Ellen let the comment settle and gathered herself. 'Wendy, when I left Ireland over twenty years ago, my mother told me not to come crying to her if I got pregnant. I didn't know I was already pregnant, but when I found out, there was no way I could go back.' She stifled the rising emotion and continued. 'My mother died without meeting her only grandchild.'

Wendy looked at her now, the weight of what Ellen was saying beginning to register. 'I've never been out of Australia,' she began. 'I have a bit of money put aside . . . I always hoped she'd contact me, but maybe I should be the one to . . . I don't know how I'll help her find . . .'

At the sound of her tearful gasps, Ellen took Wendy's hand in her own.

'I'm sure she'd just appreciate you being there.'

As they talked about the logistics of getting to Cork, Ellen mentioned that there was always a possibility Jane wouldn't be glad to see her mother. It was a chance Wendy was willing to take.

Chapter Twenty-seven

After cutting short his trip to Dublin and returning to Cork, Shane found himself being interviewed in a police station for the second time in less than a month. He didn't remember seeing any particular child when he'd taken a photo of the busy station, more to capture the vibe of the place than any particular feature. He wished he could have done more, especially when the detective told him his was the only reliable lead they had to go on.

Colette was a mess. When he was in the office, she gave him his tasks and attended to her own, but there was no banter, not even an occasional telling-off for putting supplies in the wrong place as he was wont to do. She just sighed these heavy, heart-wrenching sighs and corrected his mistakes herself. John was taking all their new clients. It was like she was putting things on hold until the child was found.

He decided to cook dinner in Blarney Street for a change and ask John's advice about how he could help.

'The only thing I can think of is that room makeover she donated for the fundraiser,' said John. 'Maybe that would help her find some of her old enthusiasm.'

'Who won it?'

John went to his man bag for his Moleskine diary and flicked through the pages. 'Timothy Conway,' he said, stopping at a list he'd made in the blank pages at the back, 'one of Colette's clients, has the winning ticket.'

'I know him,' said Shane. 'Colette took me up there. He's having her redecorate his whole house.'

'I'm sure he won't say no to a free room,' said John. 'And by the way, this spaghetti bolognaise is delicious.'

Shane couldn't help an embarrassed smile.

'Colette means the world to me, you know,' John continued.

Shane watched as his uncle finished his meal and dabbed at the corners of his mouth with the linen serviettes he insisted on using. *No point keeping the good stuff for special occasions*, he'd said the night Shane arrived.

'If it hadn't been for her when Steve . . .'

Shane heard the lump catching in his uncle's throat, but just sat there, unsure how to react. He'd always thought of John as far away, someone he'd only met a handful of times, most of those at family weddings or funerals to which he and his brother had been dragged across the Irish Sea to attend. John and Shane's mother weren't close. In fact, she'd contacted all her other relatives to take him off her hands before she'd thought of John. And yet, it was John who'd agreed, without hesitation, to host him. Sitting across the small retro table from his uncle now, he was aware of a warmth somewhere in his chest.

'Sorry for being such a twat,' he thought aloud, mortified at the sound of his own candour.

'You're young, son,' said John, softly. 'Don't be too hard on yourself.'

'No, Uncle John.' Shane sat up straight in his chair and pushed his plate a little away to allow him to rest his crossed arms on the table. 'You and Colette gave me a chance. I don't want to mess it up.' He paused before speaking again. There was so much he wanted to know about his uncle, so much he'd never been told. 'If it's not too upsetting for you,' he began, 'would you tell me a wee bit about your life, about Steve and that?'

John raised an eyebrow, clearly surprised at his interest.

'Would you like to see a few photos?'

'Aye.' Shane pushed back his chair and stood up. 'You look them out and I'll tidy away this lot.'

Instead of retreating to his room as usual, Shane spent the evening poring over photo albums to a soundtrack of The Beatles, to which John was determined to convert him. There were holiday photographs taken in idyllic resorts with white sandy beaches and infinity pools where John and his partner had spoiled themselves with the kind of food Shane had only ever seen produced by gourmet chefs on TV shows. John rattled off all the places they'd been to, but Shane hadn't heard of half of them. It was the photographs of projects the men had worked on together that interested him most. As one of London's top architects, Steve had been involved in the design of some of the city's newest buildings. John's pride was almost palpable when he spoke about their collaborative work, where he'd advised on the interiors. They shared a couple of glasses of Baileys as the evening and John's stories went on. Shane was enthralled. It was a window into another world.

When they came to some photos of Colette, John explained how he and Steve had taken her under their wing when she'd arrived in London six years before, still raw after escaping an unhappy marriage. How he'd come across her studying at the design college one evening as he was leaving. She was the oldest student in his class and by far the smartest. He'd figured she was hanging back in the building more for something to do than a need to catch up on assignments.

'When she lets her guard down, she's a riot,' John confided. 'Just don't ever tell her I told you.'

The final few photos were from Steve's funeral. Shane wasn't sure he liked the idea of people taking photos at funerals, but John assured him he'd given a friend permission to take them because he'd wanted to remember. And besides, the media had attended uninvited and taken all the photos they'd wanted. Members of the Buckley family were conspicuous by their absence, but Colette was there. In fact, it was Colette who could be seen at John's side, supporting him as they walked away from the funeral home. Shane felt a wave of shame at how he'd misjudged them both.

—

Timothy Conway told Shane he'd like to donate the room makeover to the family of the young boy with EDS.

The fundraiser had ended so badly for Ronan O'Flynn. It was supposed to have been a fun day with him as the main man, but of course Millie's disappearance had overshadowed his plight, and although they'd raised a substantial amount of money to help with his medical expenses, it hadn't come with the fanfare the boy deserved.

Colette sat opposite Shane in her office, listening to how he'd phoned Timothy Conway and then Harry O'Flynn to get an idea of what books or movies Ronan was into as a possible theme. She had to keep her jaw from dropping as he spoke; animated wasn't exactly his modus operandi. She couldn't help but be supportive of his initiative. They agreed to meet with Ronan and his mum to talk over his preferences and lock in a time to do the makeover.

The excitement on Ronan's face as he greeted them at the front door of the O'Flynns' semi-detached two-storey home was enough to break Colette's heart all over again. The innocent face sent a wave of worry over her for what Millie might be enduring. But she forced that to one side and smiled back at the eleven-year-old.

'Jackie, Ronan, this is Shane.'

They looked past her to where Shane was following with a big sketchbook under his arm.

'Look, Mum,' said Ronan, 'she's brought a professional.'

Colette winked at Jackie. 'That's right. Shane's pretty good.'

Ronan looped his arm in Colette's and led her to a ground-floor bedroom. She felt the weight of him as he leaned heavily on every step, and hoped she was supporting him properly. She glanced at Jackie who smiled her reassurance.

The room had been newly renovated with a government grant for adapting the home. Colette took in the widened doorframe, hand rails and adjustable bed within. There was no cure for EDS. She knew this was a long-term set-up. Jackie showed her through to the bathroom they'd had specially fitted. She noticed the single-level tiled floor incorporating a wet-area shower with a chair she would normally have associated with older people.

'No way! All this for you,' she enthused for Ronan's benefit. His smile spread to his dimpled cheeks. 'What do you think, Shane? Can we give this place the wow factor?'

'Aye,' was the height of the response from her gangly assistant, who was looking over the walls of the bedroom like a blank canvas. Unperturbed by the clinical surroundings, he sat on the edge of the bed and opened the sketchbook.

'Why don't you boys get a few ideas down while I make Colette a cuppa?' said Jackie. She gently helped Ronan up on the bed, settling him against the pillows and pressing a button to adjust the angle of the headboard. As they went back into the hallway she lowered her voice. 'Thanks a million for doing this.'

'It's Timothy Conway we've got to thank,' said Colette, shrugging off the praise. 'And besides, I haven't done anything yet.'

In the kitchen, Jackie dipped teabags into two mugs, pressing them with the back of a spoon.

'If Aidan O'Shea is anyone to go by, you'll do a great job.'

Colette fought the flash of fire in her cheeks as she accepted the strong brew. 'When were you talking to Aidan?'

'We had him over for dinner the other night,' said Jackie. 'Flynnie wanted to do something for the poor guy. He's in an awful state over the missing child.'

Colette held the mug in both hands. 'I know how he feels,' she said.

'I heard the news about Shane spotting her,' Jackie went on.

'That's the trouble,' said Colette. 'Shane didn't know anything about Millie. He just took a random photo that happened to have her in it.'

'Terrible state of affairs,' said Jackie.

They both took a long drink and sat in silence for a moment.

'Aidan tells me you two are doing a bit of swimming,' said Jackie, her tone brighter. 'He used to be a handy swimmer when he was younger. Munster champ, they told me.'

Colette murmured in agreement. She hadn't made it to the pool the previous Thursday. Grace was on night shift; an excuse Colette had used to both her mother and Ludmilla.

'He says you're a bit handy in the water yourself,' Jackie was saying.

'Ah, I wouldn't go that far . . .'

Jackie's face became serious again. 'He's worried about you, Colette.'

Pursing her lips together, she looked into the mug of black tea and saw the wrinkles around one eye reflected there. She wouldn't be surprised if most of them had appeared in the past week and a half. She shrugged her shoulders but didn't meet Jackie's gaze. God knows the woman across from her had more challenges every day of her life than Colette could even imagine.

'I'll be fine when they find her.'

Jackie touched her arm with a firm hand. 'They will, Colette. They will.'

As they went back to Ronan's bedroom, Jackie put a finger to her lips and they stopped to listen.

'I like Black Widow too,' Ronan was saying.

'Ha, she's a scary chick, a bit like Colette.'

Ronan let out a laugh that made Jackie look at Colette with a mortified expression.

'What are you boys up to?' she said, striding into the room.

Shane shot Ronan a sideways glance from where he was standing at the wall. Ronan's eyes met Colette's, a shadow of fear across his face, but she gave him a smile and started quizzing them on progress. They'd made a list of Marvel characters and Shane had called out measurements to Ronan, who had written them down in the sketchbook. Colette couldn't believe Shane had had the presence of mind to slip a tape measure into his pocket before leaving the office. He was definitely learning. The boys agreed to follow each other on social media and exchange ideas.

'Where did you learn to do these murals?' Jackie asked, in awe.

Shane explained to a captive audience how he'd painted murals at school and for friends and family back in Scotland. Colette took it all in, feeling a tad redundant but immensely proud. She would have liked to have given Aidan a ring and assured him his boot-camp offer would not be necessary. If she'd thought she could have done it without breaking down, she might have done so.

—

Grace insisted Colette go to the pool. Avoiding Aidan O'Shea wasn't going to help anyone, she said. Least of all Millie. The police were doing all they could. This was a time for friends to stick together. Hiding herself away would not get her through this. As she shoved her gear in her swim bag, Colette hoped her sister was right.

'Colette.' Aidan nodded to her across the lane rope after the warm-up.

'Hi,' she said, almost under her breath, as she willed Ludmilla to get on with it and write up the first set.

'Stamina work tonight,' Ludmilla finally announced. 'All-day pace.' She looked at Aidan. 'You know what I mean? Like you thrown out of boat, don't know how long you have to swim. Not too fast. Nice steady, you know?'

Colette knew the drill but wished Ludmilla had spared them the analogy. Lost at sea was exactly how Aidan must be feeling. Exactly how she felt. It was all she could think about as she ploughed up and down the pool for the two kilometres. And if she felt this bad, Jane Donovan must be climbing the walls. It had been a long time since Colette had prayed, but by the end of the set, she'd said a whole rosary.

In the pub, the atmosphere was subdued. There was no sign of Aidan, but just when Colette thought he might have stayed away on her account, he appeared with his pint and joined them at their usual table.

'How's it going?' Chris asked with none of his usual cheer.

'Still no news,' Aidan told them, 'but Jane's mother arrived from Australia on Tuesday.'

There was a collective intake of breath as a ripple of hope spread around the group.

'That's huge,' said Grace. 'I thought they were estranged.'

'My sister in Australia went to see her,' Aidan went on. 'Ellen couldn't bear to think of the grandmother down there knowing nothing and not being able to help.'

'Ellen was always lovely,' said Dessie with a nostalgic glaze in his eye.

Goosebumps tingled on Colette's arms as she felt the connections of the group, some of them friends since childhood, others thrown into the mix through friends of friends, or the sheer love of swimming, or just a social event to get them out. None of them could have anticipated that their efforts to help one child would have them caught up in the disappearance of another.

—

Aidan had driven Jane to the airport on the Tuesday. She had no sooner stepped out of the car when she'd asked him to wait as she pulled out a packet of cigarettes from her handbag and proceeded to light up. Aidan had never known her to smoke, but he made no comment.

'I can't believe she's doing this,' said Jane, taking a long drag and letting it work its way down into her before blowing out the acrid smoke.

Aidan moved upwind and leaned against the car beside her.

'Ten fucking years,' she said shaking her head. 'You must think I'm a bitch.'

'Hardly,' said Aidan. 'I'm sure you have your reasons.'

'Yes, but what if they're not very good ones?'

He plunged his hands into his jeans pockets and shrugged. 'You're here now, aren't you?'

She took another drag and crossed her arms, careful to point the cigarette away from him.

'I put that bastard Bryce before my own mother, for Christ's sake.'

He let her rant, hoping the cigarette would help steady her nerves, but not give her time to back out of the reunion.

'I couldn't even wear my handmade clothes when he was around. "Why are you wearing that stupid hippie dress?" he'd ask. "Your mum thinks she's still a teenager," he'd say to Millie.' She spat out the words with a bitterness he'd never seen in her. She looked away into the distance and when she turned back to him, she said in a softer tone, 'Do you think I look old, Aidan?'

Aidan put his arms around her. Weeks of no sleep and little food certainly had her looking older than her thirty-five years, but she was still beautiful to him.

'I know I've been totally irrational since . . .' She halted, the words catching in her throat. 'I don't deserve you, Aidan. I'm sorry I never gave you a proper chance.' She held onto his arm and leaned her head against his shoulder.

'Sh,' he soothed, hugging her to him. 'We both needed company, Jane.' He drew a little away and smiled at her sad face. 'I think we both know, it was your daughter I really fell for.' Somewhere, they found the strength to laugh. It was some comfort as he fought away thoughts of what might happen to her if Millie wasn't found.

An Aer Lingus airbus was coming in to land. He checked the time and pointed to the sky.

'Better be ready when that touches down.'

An exhausted-looking Wendy Donovan pulled an ancient suitcase sporting a wide polka-dot ribbon through the arrivals doors. Jane gave Aidan's arm a final squeeze before walking toward her. When Wendy recognised her daughter, she let go of the case and threw out her arms, enfolding Jane in a huge hug. Aidan could see the tears leaking from behind the woman's glasses as she closed her eyes and held her daughter. When they drew apart, neither could speak. Keeping one arm around her mother, Jane took hold of the case and steered her to Aidan.

He held out his hand to Wendy and introduced himself as Jane's friend. Wendy took his hand in both of hers and shook vigorously. She had a whitened version of Millie's flaxen hair and the same open face. Millie had missed out on this woman who, at least on first impressions, looked like she would be a loving grandmother.

'Your sister told me lots about you,' she said, looking deep into his eyes like she was trying to match his physical presence with what Ellen had told her about him.

'Good things, I hope,' he said, his cheeks betraying his embarrassment.

She looked at Jane, who was shaking with emotion, and put her arms around her again. 'I'm here now, darl,' she said.

Aidan gathered up the case and led them out into the warm summer evening. The effects of Millie's absence couldn't be lessened, but at least Jane wouldn't have to shoulder the burden all on her own.

—

Back in his living room on Church Road, Aidan switched on the TV. Nothing in the news about Millie Donovan. He knew that the police were working tirelessly to find her, but as far as the media was concerned it was like she'd been filed away in the unsolved mysteries cabinet. He could only hope the police were right in suspecting Bryce Manning, and that Jane knew him well enough to be confident he wouldn't harm her. If Aidan ever met Bryce Manning again, he wouldn't be responsible for what he might do to him. But that was futile thinking. Better to focus on carrying on and staying strong for when Millie was back plaguing him to watch another movie or visit Julius.

As he absently flicked through the TV channels, his thoughts turned to Colette Barry. From what her sister and John Buckley had told him, she was barely holding it together. He'd tried to speak to her on the phone, at the pool and afterward in the pub, but she was far too stoic to talk about it. If he were to offer the woman any support, it would have to be of a practical nature. Work. That was the only way to engage with her. He resolved to check his diary in the morning and free up a time for them to move on the West Cork project.

Chapter Twenty-eight

Timothy Conway was thrilled with how work was progressing on his riverside home. Colette's painter and decorator contacts had done another marvellous job, implementing her designs and transforming the house into a space in which Timothy could truly relax.

'Do you know, I couldn't be myself in this room before,' he told Colette as they sat in the living room that had gone from safari to sophisticated, with subtle pinks and dove greys replacing the startlingly garish palette his ex-wife had preferred. Sitting on the linen-covered A-line chair Colette had loved choosing, Timothy looked ten years younger. There was a sparkle back in the tired eyes she'd noticed when they'd first met. The sceptics could say what they liked, but as far as she was concerned a person's four walls were important. How trapped she'd felt living with Tadgh. He'd only ever wanted the furniture and fittings they'd inherited with the house when they'd bought it. Her attempts to refurbish were always deemed too expensive. She'd become adept at recycling, upcycling, covering chairs in end-of-line fabrics, making her own throws and cushions, fashioning lamp shades out of old bottles and driftwood. But instead of praise, he had only ridiculed. It had taken a supreme effort to believe in her talents and enrol in the course in London. Trying to be herself had come at a cost, but it had been worth it.

'Your house must be perfect,' Timothy laughed. She gave a noncommittal smile in response as his eyes wandered over the walls where she'd arranged a collection of his favourite flying photographs. 'I love that old Lancaster Bomber,' he mused, half to himself.

Colette didn't tell clients she'd been living with her mother after an unhappy marriage and painful divorce. Better to be professional and let them believe what they wanted to about her 'perfect' home. Happy customers were her bottom line, and she was satisfied to leave Timothy Conway's home with another to add to her files. On the way out, he invited her to take one last look at the study he now adored.

'This was always my bolthole,' he told her as they entered the cool blue interior with its decluttered desk and neat shelving where a selection of photos were now displayed in a way that caught the attention they deserved. 'Now, it's just a study space,' he said. 'I don't have to hide in here anymore.'

She thought about her mother letting her move back home when her marriage broke down, storing all the belongings she left behind when she moved to London and having her again when she returned. It was always meant to be a temporary measure, but still she hadn't managed to move out. Her mother had never complained, at least not to her, but Colette wondered if it wasn't time to muster the energy to find a place of her own and let the woman have her house back. At forty-two, it wasn't so much the hassle of finding a property that bothered her as the prospect of living alone.

They went out through the hallway that seemed to have doubled in size since the chandelier had been moved to the living room and the retro telephone table had been sold online. The soft green of the walls linked the house beautifully with the garden, where Shane had helped the landscapers do an amazing job of paring the space right back to an easy-to-manage lawn with a low-maintenance border. Not a gnome in sight.

'Your young man has developed a bit of a work ethic,' said Timothy as they admired the handiwork.

'He had no choice,' said Colette. 'It was either that or be sent to work for a builder friend of mine. The lesser of two evils.'

They paused at the top of the garden and looked out over the road to where the river meandered down toward the city centre. Colette felt a sudden chill at the thought that Millie might have gone in there. She gave herself a mental shake.

'Are you all right, Colette?'

Timothy looked worried. The last thing she wanted to do was spoil his delight in the makeover, but she thought she might burst if she didn't say something. Timothy was a pro. A non-judgemental judge, if that wasn't a contradiction in terms.

'I can't stop thinking about the little girl, Millie,' she said, trying to smile and shrug away the weight of her statement.

Timothy took a calm breath and looked down past the garden again.

'I did hear she was with you before she disappeared,' he began. 'But that doesn't mean you must carry any guilt, my dear.'

She shivered despite the warm afternoon sunshine.

'They haven't found the suspect yet, I believe,' Timothy went on. 'That in itself suggests guilt on his part.'

'How likely are they to find her?' She stopped short of adding the word *alive*.

'It's difficult to say, but if she has been taken by the father, he'll face the full brunt of the law when they get him.'

'How long of a sentence are we talking?'

'Seven years is the maximum,' said Timothy matter-of-factly. 'That's why we have the Hague Convention. To see these children returned to their country of habitual residence.'

'But the mother's Australian,' said Colette. 'Doesn't that complicate things?'

'No, they're signed up to it too. And then there's the infringement of the mother's constitutional rights,' he went on. 'Those who choose to abduct are on a hiding to nothing thinking they can get away with these crimes against their own families.'

For a moment, Colette caught a look in Timothy's eyes that made her glad she had never found herself on the wrong side of the law. She hoped in Millie's case, justice would indeed be served, but most of all she hoped Millie would be found, alive.

⌐

On Saturday evening, Fern and Rob were sitting on the sofa glued to the telly. Jane Donovan was on the nine o'clock news, flanked by her mother and the head of the guards, appealing to the public to help find her child.

'Christ, Rob, will they ever find her?'

He squeezed her hand and pulled it onto his thigh. 'They will, love, please God.'

'I don't know how Aidan is managing to keep it together.'

Rob took a deep breath. 'He has to be strong for Jane.'

'I know, love, but who's being strong for him?'

Rob glanced sideways and saw the glistening in her eyes. Unclasping her hand, he reached an arm around her and pulled her close. She was such a caring soul when it came down to it. He thought of their own three tucked up in bed and prayed to God they'd always be safe.

Grace and Ben had just watched the same report. As he opened a bottle of merlot and poured them both a glass, she was grateful to see him depart from his usual ban on alcohol.

'How's Colette holding up?' he asked.

'Not great.'

'You want to watch something?'

She picked up the TV remote and pressed the off button before turning to him from where she sat at the opposite end of the three-seater.

'I think we should talk.'

He let out a long breath. 'You're right. We can't keep ignoring the elephant in the room, can we?'

Grace couldn't stand watching his hard-done-by expression as he stared at the glass he was rolling in his hands. She stood up and went to a drawer in the sideboard to retrieve a notebook and pen. Plonking herself back on the sofa, she opened the notebook and began to write.

'Vasectomy,' she announced, reading it back to him. She drew a line down the centre of one page and continued, 'Pros and Cons.' She underlined each word with a determined stroke of the pen.

Ben sighed. 'I'm not sure it's that cut and dried, if you'll pardon the pun.'

'Come on.' Grace was having none of it. They'd been skirting around the size of their family for months. 'Let's start with Cons,' she said, already starting to write as she spoke. 'Pain.' She scored it out. 'Make that discomfort. Fear of something going wrong.' She looked up briefly. 'You're the GP, you know all about it.' He went to speak, but she continued her list. 'Possible impotence.' He made a face, eyebrows arching over a strained face. 'Pros,' she went on, putting the pen to her mouth for a moment before recommencing. 'More sleep. More time for the children we already have. Time for ourselves. Spontaneity.' His expression changed to a more hopeful one at that. 'No more multiple births. No risk of complicated pregnancy or birth defects. And of course,' she said, putting the last item in block letters, 'HAPPY WIFE.' She made a loud full stop before shoving the notebook and pen into the space between them.

Ignoring the list, Ben turned and bent one leg under him and leaned back on an elbow. She could tell he was choosing his words carefully. God, his calm infuriated her at times.

'Okay,' he said slowly. 'What if I go through with it and you change your mind?'

'Ha!' She threw up her hands and let them flop onto her lap. 'Is that the best you can do? Put it back on me? Haven't you been listening, Ben?' Aware that the increase in volume might wake the children, she lowered her voice. 'I know I'm finished having babies. You, and only you, need to decide if you're with me.'

He looked down at his glass and shrugged. 'It's so final. I can't believe we're even arguing about this. We both love kids, we're healthy . . .'

'Oh, Ben,' she said, taking her glass and walking away, 'sometimes I wish you would just grow up!'

—

Aidan had thought it best to give Jane space to reconnect with her mother, but sitting at home alone on Church Road would only have driven him mad. After a fitful sleep, he'd woken early on Saturday morning, pulled the covers off his bed, chucked them in the back of the Land Rover and headed for the house in West Cork.

He checked his fitness watch and registered the time, having lost all interest in the minutiae it recorded; the steps, heart rate, burnt calories he'd been so keen to monitor were no longer anywhere near front of mind. He wished he could plough on with the work on the house, such was its distraction value, but now, after a six-day week, his back and shoulders ached and he was in need of a break. Eamon and Orla next door had called earlier in the day and invited him for dinner.

They said, as they always did, he was welcome to stay, but although he was keen to take them up on their offer of food, he'd resolved to sleep in the outbuildings. An old mattress destined for the tip would be his bed for the night. He'd had one of the tradesmen wire the place and he'd brought down a lamp. Not exactly salubrious accommodation, but he wanted to be on his own. It was time he stopped avoiding those outbuildings anyway. In fact, it was time he cleared them out.

Gathering his bedclothes from the car, he trudged across the gravel driveway and lifted the latch on the half-door. Crossing the threshold, he stopped short, his eyes adjusting to the semi-darkness, feet rooted to the stone floor. The tea chests stood in piles just where they'd been when he'd found Colette wearing his grandmother's straw hat and buttoned gloves, oblivious to the rest of the world like a child delving into a dress-up box. The spark of joy ignited by the memory was quashed as his eyes were drawn to the plastic-covered shapes at the far wall. Colette, in her innocent curiosity, had torn open a wound that in almost twenty years still hadn't healed.

The phone went in his jeans pocket.

'Yes, Orla . . . I'm on my way.'

Throwing the bundle onto the mattress, he turned on his heel and pulled the door shut behind him.

—

Eamon and Orla had gone all out to feed him up. There would be no small servings tonight, Aidan mused, as Orla piled mashed potato onto a plate already laden with slices of corned beef. He could only look on in disbelief as the cabbage and everything else was drowned in a pool of gravy he knew she'd made from the fat off the meat.

'Is it watching the weight you are?' she asked when he tried to insist he was full after consuming half the contents of the plate.

'Ah you know, Orla, I have to be careful. I'm not getting any younger.'

Orla held her cutlery apart, resting what his mother had always called 'nappy-changing hands' on the table. 'Have you not found anyone at all to look after you, Aidan?'

Eamon gave a cough, but kept his eyes on his dinner plate. It was one of those laugh-or-cry moments. Aidan shrugged and gave a rueful smile, but Orla wasn't letting go.

'That Colette girl seems nice. Is she with anyone?'

'I think she divorced . . .'

Orla's eyes widened as she stared at him, but he was not going to go there. Like Eamon, he concentrated on his food.

'This is a great meal altogether, Orla.'

The comment earned him a grateful smile, but failed to get her off the topic of his love life.

'Do you remember that lovely French girl you used to bring here?'

Aidan thought he might choke. Orla's memory was far too sharp. Remember her? He'd only spent half his life trying to forget her, but that was a story that might have kept his cousin's wife in family gossip for years.

'Sure haven't I still a photo of ye up there,' she said, pointing her fork in the direction of the wall.

'Ah, that was a long time ago,' said Aidan, desperate to stopper Orla's nostalgia, but she was up out of her chair and moving toward a collage of photos she'd carefully displayed in a series of letter-shaped frames that formed the word FAMILY. As she ran her eyes over the A, Aidan took a deep breath and tried to avoid looking. But photo or no photo, he couldn't erase the image of Isabella sitting here beside him.

It seemed like only yesterday he'd met her down in the pub by the harbour, not much more than a stone's throw from the family farm. She'd come to Ireland to teach at Cork's prestigious college of art and design, and although his mother didn't approve, his country cousins had welcomed his exotic girlfriend with open arms. His uncle, still alive then and living alone in the old farmhouse, had been the same; always grateful for the company and happy to open his home when Aidan and Isabella fancied a break from the city. Back then, Aidan had looked at Eamon and Orla, happily married with the first of their four children the centre of their lives, and imagined himself and Isabella sharing a similar future. As Orla prattled on, in his mind's eye Aidan could see their baby boy, now a father himself, sitting in the high chair, smiling and chuckling as if in on the stories that were swapped around the table, as captivated by Isabella as the rest of them. He could hear her French accent, the disregard for 'h's as she spoke about the ''ouse' and how they had gone walking in the ''ills'; the way she'd said his own name, stressing the *dan* instead of the *Ai*.

'There ye are, in front of the Eiffel Tower itself,' Orla announced, stepping to one side but keeping her finger pointed at the young couple who looked destined for a happy future together.

'Aren't you great for keeping all the old photos?' said Aidan, mustering a smile. It wasn't Orla's fault that Isabella had been dishonest.

Satisfied, she sat back down, but before taking up where she'd left off on her dinner, she reached out a hand to Eamon's and, lowering her voice for what could only be dramatic effect, she said, 'Eamon's taking me to Paris for our twenty-fifth anniversary, aren't you, love?'

Her husband patted her hand gently. 'Yes, love,' and with a wink to Aidan, he added, 'or I'll never hear the end of it.'

'Get outta that, you can't wait either,' she laughed. 'Go on, Aidan,' she said, gesturing with her elbow, 'tell him how beautiful it is.'

Not wanting to pour cold water on her enthusiasm, Aidan trawled his memory for snippets of the week he'd spent in what Orla only knew as the City of Love. At the mention of each famous landmark, she tutted and sighed, while Aidan tried desperately to push images of Isabella to one side. Yes, the Champs-Élysées was gorgeous by night, but the illuminated fountains and ornate streetlights were a mere backdrop to the tall slender beauty that was Isabella. He could hear her laughter as he tried out his French. '*Deux bières, s'il vous plait*,' was about all he could say, but he'd loved listening to her speak in her own language, watching her graceful hands accompany her words, but he didn't tell Orla any of that. No, he was on to the Sacré-Cœur, another special place, spectacular by night. Orla didn't need to know about the lazy mornings they'd spent in bed, or how Isabella would bring him breakfast from the nearby boulangerie. Yes, you could go inside the famous church and light a candle. He remembered lighting one for Isabella. When he'd told her, she'd gone quiet. He'd put it down to the atmosphere and forgot all about it as soon as they tripped back down the steps to explore Montmartre. Strolling hand in hand among street artists and peep-show pushers, he'd felt strong and handsome, not in a conceited way, but because of a confidence Isabella instilled in him. Despite the language barrier he felt at home. Over a candlelit dinner in a basement restaurant with gingham tablecloths and Edith Piaf songs playing in the background, Aidan had imagined himself living in Paris at some point in the future with the girl he'd set his heart on.

As Orla shared her thoughts on where she and Eamon might stay, Aidan was taken back to that grand building in the seventh arrondissement where they'd spent the week at Isabella's grandmother's. It hadn't bothered him that Isabella had been given a bedroom in the old-world apartment with its dark antique furniture and crowded tapestries, while he'd been relegated to the attic that had once served as the maid's quarters. The five flights of stairs were nothing to his young athletic body. He paid little attention to the bathroom off the dimly lit corridor where the rust corroded the bathtub and the shower groaned into a cold trickle. Like the rickety old bed with the stained sheets and thin spare eiderdown, it all paled into insignificance once Isabella climbed in beside him in the early hours and they made love under the canopy of stars that winked at them through the slanted window.

'You missed out on a good one with that French girl,' Orla was saying.

Eamon cleared his throat and pushed back his chair. ''Tis she who missed out, isn't that so, Aidan?'

Orla disappeared to the kitchen, refusing his offers of help to clear away. On her return, she proffered an apple tart big enough to serve ten.

'And no news of the missing child?' she said as she shovelled a massive portion into a bowl and set it in front of him.

'No,' said Aidan, 'not yet.'

Orla moved on from the subject of his love life to speculation as to what happened to Millie as per the media reports they'd all seen. Like Eamon, Aidan slowly worked his way through the over-generous portion of dessert while Orla held court. Whether it was the culmination of a long week, the heavy meal, or the weight of the conversation, Aidan felt a longing to lay down his head and shut the world out for a while. He was relieved to have a quiet ten minutes with his cousin over a drop of whiskey when Orla insisted they relax while she washed up.

'Don't mind Orla and her stories,' said Eamon in a soft voice that was in no danger of carrying to the kitchen. 'She means well.'

'Ah sure I know that,' said Aidan. 'The pair of ye have always been very good to myself and Ellen.'

Eamon smiled. 'Isn't it great all the same about herself and that Gerry Clancy fella?'

'It is indeed.'

There was silence between them before Eamon leaned across in his armchair and raising his glass, he said, 'Sláinte!'

Aidan clinked glasses with his cousin and responded with the same wish for Eamon's good health. At least his sister's luck in the love department had given them cause for some small celebration.

—

Aidan took the short cut across the fields toward his grandmother's house. It was a dry night with a full moon lighting his way, but as he was about to scale the drystone wall that separated the properties, he felt a sudden dread at going back to the outbuildings. He wanted to be alone, but not alone where he and Isabella had slept, sharing dreams of how they'd do the place up. 'Love nest', she'd called it, laughing at her command of her second language as her golden hair tumbled over her white bikini breasts. He dug his hands in his pockets and turned his back on the house.

Brow Head loomed from behind the village. He hadn't been up there in years. The strip of grass running up the centre of the steep incline assured him that in twenty years, this part of Crookhaven had hardly changed. Halfway up the three-kilometre stretch, he stopped to catch his breath. Only the low murmurings from the scattering of tents and caravans at the bottom of the hill broke the night's stillness. Out to sea, the sweeping beam from Fastnet Rock competed with the moon to illuminate the scudding of white horses on the navy-blue Atlantic. With the wind picking up, Aidan continued to the top and took the trodden path past the five-bar gate, ignoring the sign to deter trespassers. As the clutch of old ruins came into view, his heart raced. He strode on until he reached a long-abandoned dwelling, where he had to lean against what was left of a wall, partly to recover from the late-night workout, but mostly to slow the mix of memories that churned through his head like a whirlpool. This was where he and Isabella would come in those romantic days he thought would go on forever; where she taught him to paint in among all those other lessons he'd learned that summer. He could see his younger self now sitting with her in the knee-high grass, her hand gently guiding his brush over canvas, his eyes following as she pointed over the hillside dotted with grazing Fresians, doing his best to capture the huge rollers that crashed like wild frothing beasts on the beach at Barleycove.

God, he'd been naïve. It had come back to him at Eamon and Orla's; that Easter in Paris when Madame Dupont had eyed him suspiciously over dinner at the polished mahogany table; how he'd listened without understanding as Isabella and the older woman had engaged in stilted conversation. The frostiness, Isabella assured him, concerned a family matter over which he wasn't to worry. He'd left them to it and turned his attention instead to savouring the delights of pastis and sampling the fancy French cuisine with so many foods he'd never eaten at home; olives and tomato salads, the ubiquitous crusty baguettes and pale bland butter, the tiny desserts . . . but a name repeatedly dropped into conversation by Madame Dupont should have made him take a greater interest. Jean-Claude, as unsuspecting as Aidan, was miles away in the south where most of Isabella's family lived, where she said they would go 'next time'. But there never was a next time.

On their return to Cork, Aidan had made up his mind. The man who'd hardly read a book since leaving secondary school invested in a set of teach-yourself tapes and a French dictionary, determined to propose in Isabella's native tongue. He remembered driving to Crookhaven after work that Friday in May, almost a year after they'd met. Isabella had said she was involved in student exams and would follow him down on the Saturday. In his blind innocence, he hadn't suspected a thing. It was his uncle who gave him the letter. She'd posted it from Cork two days before.

My dear Aidan,

This is the hardest thing to tell you. I have had the most beautiful, the most romantic time with you, but now I have to go back to France to marry my fiancé. I am sorry, but I can only hope that you will find someone. You are so caring and kind. It was very fun, but you and me got too close. I can't say goodbye. This is better. Remember me as your friend.

Isabella

Aidan lost count of the number of times he read that letter. He'd called her flat in Cork to try to talk it out, but her flatmate said she'd taken an early flight. Not that there was anything left to say, the letter had been clear. She'd removed herself from his life as quickly as she'd moved herself in. Had she even loved him at all?

Alone on Brow Head with the moon disappearing behind the gathering clouds, Aidan slipped down the wall of what had once been a full and vibrant dwelling, and like the building itself, he sank into the landscape. Despite his efforts at staying away, this place was etched into his DNA. He'd never really found it within himself to move on from those happy days with Isabella when he'd imagined they were equal players in a love story he'd hoped would last forever. Shadows of the past intermingled with those of the present as he started to sob.

Isabella, Jane, Millie, Colette . . . It was all one big mess.

Chapter Twenty-nine

Barbara Barry couldn't shake off the summer cold she'd been battling, so lunch in Blackrock was cancelled. Colette texted Grace and used minding her mother as an excuse not to go either, but when she couldn't sleep in, she got up and pounded the regular loop of her ten-kilometre run. In the afternoon, she helped her mother with the wedding dress she was working on and when she lost interest in that, she took to decluttering the kitchen cupboards.

'One of these days, you'll have your own place just the way you want it,' her mother remarked from where she was hunched over a hemline at the dining-room table.

Colette halted her tidying. She couldn't say she hadn't thought about it, but there'd never been a time when she'd lived completely alone.

'I always tell Grace,' her mother went on, 'when Colette gets a place, she'll have it so ordered and beautiful, we won't be able to touch anything for fear we'd put it back in the wrong place.' She gave a chesty laugh and coughed into her elbow.

'Are you trying to get rid of me, Mam?'

Her mother made light of the subject, 'Ah no, love. Sure won't you move out in your own good time?'

'I will, Mam. Once things settle down.'

They both knew what she meant. As she scrubbed manically at the inside of a cupboard she'd emptied, her mother got up and came into the kitchen.

'I think I might have a lie down,' said Barbara, putting a hand on her arm. 'Don't be too hard on yourself, love,' she told her. 'You're still young. Get out and live your life.'

Listening to her mother's steady tread on the stairs, Colette looked around the house she'd grown up in. It reminded her of Timothy Conway's study; a bolthole, somewhere she could retreat to and set down her business suit of armour once she'd spent the working week convincing the world she was worthy. Grace had never mentioned these talks she'd obviously had with their mother about her life. But that was Grace – never pushy, always protective. Yes, her sister had been there for her at every turn, up and down. She wondered now if the same could be said the other way round.

—

At work on Monday, Fern didn't mention the television appeal. Aidan was striding round the premises, firing orders at the apprentices and ticking off supplies on his clipboard. He came into the office looking like a man who hadn't slept in weeks.

'Fern, if you have a minute, could you call Colette Barry?' he asked.

'Sure, no problem,' she said, stifling the urge to enquire as to why he couldn't call her himself. The days of playful matchmaking banter were well and truly on hold, with no sign of them returning if the lack of news on that poor child was to continue. It was like they were all operating under a cloud, treading gently around him, tempering everything they said with a quiet consideration of his plight, while at the same time carrying on with business as usual. She was grateful when Rob stuck his head round the office door to ask about a job.

'As you're there, Rob,' said Aidan, going to his desk and flicking at the pages of his diary. 'I know we have a lot on, but could we fit in a couple of days in West Cork at the end of next week?'

Fern knew by her husband's hesitation they were already up to their eyes without pushing back their current jobs by two days. She turned back to her computer to search for Colette's number as they discussed what was left to be done. A couple of days would see the kitchen installed and the flooring finished if they took both apprentices. Young Shane would pull his weight, and by all accounts, Colette wasn't afraid to get her hands dirty. Contrary to what Aidan had suggested when he'd first mentioned to Fern that Colette was on the project, it wasn't only the pretty stuff she was good at. But they'd have to stay over, she heard Rob say, and that would mean sleeping in the van or inside on the floor if they were to keep down the cost.

'Tell you what,' said Aidan, 'ask Colette if she can free up Shane for both days and she might come down on the Friday herself.'

When Aidan turned away to his desk, Fern raised her eyebrows at Rob. He held out a palm and shrugged before returning to the yard. She made the call and tried her best to sound enthusiastic. Colette's response was acquiescent, like she was going through the motions. Yes, Friday would be fine. No, she didn't have much on. John would cover, she was sure. Best to get the West Cork project over and done with. Fern wondered if Colette felt the same about all her projects? She had such a passion for interior design, such a talent. Hadn't Fern only recently seen an article on her in one of those home-renovation magazines, lauding her as the rising star in Irish contemporary design? Surely this tragedy wouldn't throw her off that trajectory.

'That's great,' John said when Colette told him her plans for West Cork. 'A day in the country will do you a power of good.'

'I don't know about that,' she said. 'At this stage I just want to finish it.'

He came around from behind his desk and bid her to join him on the tangerine sofa. She took a deep breath and let it out slowly, waiting for the fatherly chat.

'You're not the only one struggling with this, you know,' he began with an unexpected gravity in his voice.

Colette looked at him. 'What do you mean?'

'Well,' he sighed, 'I know you're devastated about Millie's disappearance . . . but finding her isn't your job.'

She bit her lip. Deep inside she wanted to walk away from this conversation, to storm out in a huff like a defiant child, but she'd never known John Buckley not to talk sense.

'Jane Donovan, Aidan O'Shea and God knows how many other people are equally if not more devastated than you.'

She felt the bile of shame rise in her stomach, but sat silently and let him go on.

'When Steve died, I could have wallowed in self-pity . . .'

At the rare mention of his partner, John had her full, respectful attention. This was not normal Monday morning office chitchat. Steve Severn, her good friend and the love of John's life, had been the innocent victim of a hit-and-run in the London suburb where he and John shared what was to be their forever home. But although incredibly sad, John had not wallowed in anything resembling self-pity. Instead he had gathered himself and his talents, and moved back to Ireland to the support of his family and friends, where he'd done Steve proud in fulfilling his dream of opening his own business.

'Sometimes, we realise our dreams in ways we don't expect,' he told Colette. 'But we never realise them if we don't keep them in our sights and go after them. You made a commitment to Ellen and Aidan. In honouring it, you'll be a much better support to yourself and everybody else than if you let this get to you.'

She sat, head bent over the laptop she was clutching to her chest, tears leaking from her eyes. 'It's just so hard to carry on as if nothing happened,' she said without looking at him.

'That's the whole point, Colette. You carry on *because* of what happened.'

She lifted her head and let a tear splash on the lid of her laptop.

'Like I did after Tadgh,' she said.

'Exactly,' said John. 'Now, muster that old strength, my girl, and do us all proud. That's what we need you to do. That's what will help us most.'

—

Fern couldn't believe it when Colette Barry called less than an hour after she'd been onto her about arrangements for Friday. Afraid she might be cancelling, and never one to be left out of the loop, Fern was direct.

'Is there a problem with Friday?' she asked. 'I can see if the lads can make it another—'

'No, no, Friday's fine. I just wondered if I could speak to Aidan.'

Fern strained her head to look out over her desk. The van was gone from the yard but there was noise coming from the back.

'Give me a second,' she said, putting down the phone and racing into the yard where Aidan was sitting with one of the apprentices, discussing one of the lad's assessments. 'Aidan,' she half-whispered, 'Colette Barry on the phone for you.'

She wasn't sure why she'd lowered her voice, but without as much as a nod to the young man, Aidan got up, strode to the office and closed the glass door behind him, leaving Fern in no doubt that she was expected to remain in the yard until the call was over. When he came back out, Aidan gave her a smile but revealed nothing of the conversation with

Colette as he got back to the job of explaining the maths of carpentry to his student.

—

Enlisting them to work on her projects was the only way Colette could think of to be of some help to Jane and Wendy Donovan. Her mother, ever ready to help anybody, was on board. Aidan would see if Jane was up for her suggestion. All that was needed was for Jane to phone Colette to confirm, and they could proceed.

After the conversation with John, Colette's productivity increased exponentially. She'd ticked off emails and phone calls that had sat on her to-do list for weeks. By the end of the day, she'd squeezed in two home visits, putting the finishing touches to one project and firm plans in place for another. Shane had been dispatched to the O'Flynns' to begin the transformation of Ronan's bedroom. She was on her way back from collecting him when Jane rang. With her phone on Bluetooth, Colette looked over at Shane, who gave her a sympathetic smile as she took the call. There wasn't much point in asking the girl how she was. She cut straight to the chase.

'Hi Jane, thanks for calling me back,' she began, trying to sound as friendly as she did professional. 'Aidan tells me you're not working in the hotel at the moment, so I thought you might like to help us out . . .'

'Yes,' said Jane, 'yes, I'd be happy to get the work.'

Colette heard the quiet self-preservation in Jane's voice. 'Mum and I can take the machine and our gear to your mother's place if that's easier. As long as I have my phone charged, I—'

She stopped.

'I know,' said Colette, a shiver sprinting down her spine. 'I'll text you my mother's details so you can make arrangements. She's never had so much on between weddings and the jobs I pass on to her. A couple of extra pairs of hands would be a real help.'

When she hung up, Colette let out a deep breath.

'You okay?' Shane asked.

'Yeah. I just hope giving Jane and her mother something to do will help keep them sane.'

'It's helped me,' he said with unexpected honesty.

She looked at him as she drove down the North Mall to Fabulous Four Walls.

'And that's saying something,' she smiled, giving him a gentle push.

'Ha! Don't go getting any ideas about giving me more to do.'

They laughed companionably despite the heavy thoughts that lay between them.

Chapter Thirty

Ellen was glad to hear that the renovation of her grandmother's house would give Jane Donovan a source of income now that the media attention had made it impossible for her to face working in the busy hotel. If the photos Colette sent were anything to go by, the input of the three women would have the house looking beautiful. She and Colette had agreed on colour themes for the bedrooms, and even the grey room Ellen had been unsure about was starting to sound decidedly stylish with the calico curtains and brightly coloured applique patterns Wendy had cleverly created and sewn onto plain grey cushions. By all accounts, from both Colette and Aidan, Mrs Barry was doing a tremendous job of helping the two Australian women keep going while the investigation into the missing child continued.

'All okay on the Cork front?' Gerry asked, touching her shoulders and bending down to kiss her cheek as she sat at the computer in the lounge room.

'Mm . . . everyone trying to soldier on, I think.' She put a hand over his and held it there for a moment.

'Mind if I Skype my folks?' he asked.

'No, not at all.'

She got up and went to the kitchen to give him privacy. He was such an easy, undemanding man to live with; a month into what she hoped would be forever, Ellen felt a contentedness she'd thought she'd never feel again. Boiling the kettle, she made them both a last drink for the night. She would bring it into him and say a quick hello to the Clancys. It had been strange talking to them again after so many years. She'd been struck by how much they'd aged, but reminded herself they must have thought the same about her. In every other way, they were the same; Gerry Senior with his dry humour, and Pauline with her make-up and stylish haircut, well preserved if not getting any younger. She thought Gerry might go the same way if God spared him.

There was an unusual quiet as she came back into the lounge room. None of the usual talking over one another as was typical of the three of them, Pauline correcting Gerry Senior on points of family news and Gerry laughing at the pair of them. She went to walk back out, but Gerry turned and beckoned her to come and sit beside him. Pulling up a chair, she could see tears in Pauline's eyes. Gerry took hold of Ellen's hand and interlocked his fingers with hers.

'Dad's not well,' he told her without taking his eyes off his parents. 'You should have told me, Dad.'

'Ellen, love,' said Pauline, her eyes searching the screen for her, 'sorry to be the bearers of more bad news.'

Gerry Senior looked away from the camera and with the aid of a stick Ellen hadn't seen before, hoisted himself out of the chair and moved away to the other end of the room.

Gerry unlocked his fingers and clasped her hand as he gave a heavy sigh.

'It's prostate cancer, Ellen,' Pauline went on. 'He didn't want to say anything with Gerry going out to you and everything . . .' She began to sob.

'I'm so sorry,' said Ellen, her breath catching. She was truly sorry, and also acutely aware of what this meant for Gerry.

—

Ellen watched from the doorway as Gerry paced outside on the veranda, pausing every few strides to kick a dead leaf into the driveway.

'Old bugger never let on,' he said, shaking his head. 'That stick . . . he must be bad.'

He'd have to go home sooner rather than later. Jesus, life could be so cruel. Gerry was just getting used to living here. They'd fallen into such an easy routine. His parents were top of their visitor list.

Ellen brought the bottle of Jameson and a couple of glasses to the wicker table. Although Gerry was never a great one for alcohol, she thought he could do with a stiff drink. In the cool winter night, the whiskey burned a fire in her throat.

'Lousy luck we're having,' she smiled.

He shook his head. 'Mam said it's spread. Not good.' He took a gulp of his drink.

'You just go when you need to.'

He looked across the table at her, all of their history written in the intensity of his eyes. Twenty years later, they'd been given a chance they'd grabbed with both hands. It wasn't something she ever wanted to lose.

'I might have to be like one of those ping-pong Poms after all,' he said, finally finding the humour he was usually adept at adding to any situation.

Ellen sipped on the pungent amber drink. She could sit here and cry over Gerry's father and what he and Pauline must be going through. She could lament what would be the inevitable absence of Gerry from her day-to-day life when he had to go home. Breathing in the smell of the gums on the air, she looked out to sea and let the evening breeze ruffle the ends of her hair. The picture of Aidan and Millie came into her head. None of them were without their troubles. She reached a hand to Gerry and squeezed his arm.

'Let's take one day at a time.'

—

Colette managed to avoid seeing the Donovan women in person, orchestrating it so that they would arrive at the house after she had gone in the morning and left before she got home. Her mother gave her daily updates. Yes, the projects were coming along nicely. The deliveries had come on time. No, Wendy and Jane were no trouble to work with; they even had a few laughs in among the tearful moments and grafting. The best thing was to keep busy, Jane had said. It made the time it took to find Millie go faster. And they *would* find her. Yes, she firmly believed it.

At the pool, the swimmers were taking a similar philosophical approach. If the father had taken the girl, it was only a matter of time before he did something to reveal himself and they'd catch him. Nobody could just disappear. On every stroke, at every turn, Colette willed it to be so, but the missing-persons posters she'd seen at the police station haunted her. It was easier to disappear than people thought.

At work, she forced herself to focus. A bespoke furniture designer she was working with on a hair salon had agreed to refurbish some of Lizzie O'Shea's furniture. She hoped Aidan wouldn't take too much convincing. She could do a job on the kitchen table and chairs and the dresser herself. Might even have a go at whitewashing those floorboards if the painters were too expensive. Taking a leaf out of Jane's book, she decided it *was* best to keep busy. Just as well they had the house in West Cork; July was normally a quiet month with people off on holiday, which meant many of her projects were already wrapped up. She should have been looking forward to what had become the annual holiday in County Clare with her mother, but at this stage, having nothing to do for a whole week was anything but an attractive proposition.

'Nice man, your Bob the Builder,' said John as he accepted his morning coffee when Colette got to work the following Thursday.

She waited for an explanation, not trusting herself to speak amid the conflicting emotions Aidan had aroused in her these past few months.

'Picked young Shane up this morning in that jeep of his. Stayed for a quick chat. Man of few words, isn't he?'

She nodded, but didn't respond.

'I admire people like that. Don't need to say a lot to let you know what they mean.' He eyed her now over the rim of his glasses. 'Asked how you were.'

She smiled, tucking a hand under one arm and holding her coffee cup to her lips.

'Should get a lot done in that house tomorrow,' he went on, pausing for a moment before looking back at the papers on his desk. 'Long way to go for a day's work.'

'Mm . . .' Colette wasn't sure where this was going. They'd agreed she could be freed up to go down there. He knew they needed to get on with it, especially now the forecast was good.

'You might take an overnight bag rather than drive home late.'

She raised her eyebrows. Since when did John Buckley have to tell her when she could drive home? *Gratitude*, she reminded herself. He was only looking out for her.

'Yes, John. And I'll drive safely.'

'No point wasting these opportunities.' John was still looking at his papers, but a mischievous smile crinkled at the corners of his mouth.

'Is there something you're not telling me here, John?'

He stood up tall and pulled the glasses a little way down his nose. Looking at the photo of them both with Steve, he gave a heavy sigh. Colette hoped he wouldn't choose this moment to unravel. If he wobbled now, they might as well shut up shop for the day, because her nerves were only just holding together.

'For me there'll never be a "someone else",' he began, as much to the photo or the memory of Steve as to her. 'I'll get to my deathbed knowing I was once truly loved.' Turning to her, he went on. 'That's what keeps me going, you know.' There was a small, brave smile Colette tried to match as she listened. 'You haven't found it yet.'

Yet! The word jarred in her head. *Finding that kind of love at forty-two after her experience with men ... snowball's chance in hell.* But she respected John enough not to interrupt. Over his glasses, his eyes looked extra piercing.

'If that's not something you aspire to, that's fine, Colette. But if it is, why would you stop searching?'

She wanted to ask what the heck he and Aidan had talked about. And since when had he ever offered advice on her love life? But in their very uncharacteristic nature, John's words were all the more pointed. Maybe, despite everything, it was time to reach out.

With her car packed to the gunnels, Colette set off for West Cork at the dawn. Even Clonakilty hadn't woken up when she drove through, picking up a quick breakfast at a service station. In Schull, she made another stop at a bakery so as not to arrive empty handed to a bunch of hard-working builders. With every kilometre, her stomach tightened another notch like a coiled spring at the prospect of working with Aidan and his team. Mentally, she went over the plans for the house

and envisaged lists of tasks to tick off, but as she neared
Crookhaven, the stunning coastal views eased her tension.
A light breeze rippled through swathes of wild grasses at the
roadside where foxglove and fuschia reminded her of the
Sunday drives of her childhood. She was definitely a city girl,
but there was something about the sea and countryside that
helped reset the equilibrium even in the height of her troubles.
Maybe they could bring Jane and Wendy here. Maybe one
day they'd all come, Millie included. One day, if this nightmare ever ended.

It was all systems go when she got to the house. Aidan's
jeep, the work van and that of a local painter and decorator
were all parked in the driveway ahead of her. Through the
open windows came the chorus of drills and hammers and
the shrill sound of a circular saw. The ducks had certainly
lined up with supplies arriving on time and workmen on site
as agreed. The front door opened as she was pulling on her
boots and overalls. Aidan appeared in jeans and one of his
signature check shirts with the sleeves rolled up.

'Colette,' he called, striding toward her.

She took the bag of cakes from the passenger seat of the
car and held them out to him.

'I thought the troops might have these on a break.'

'Ah you're very good.' He took the bag and nodded to the
open boot of her car. 'I see you've come prepared.'

She tied the fasteners of her overalls and shrugged. Maybe
it was the flat work boots, but she had an overwhelming sense

of shrinking in such close proximity to his broad frame. She imagined herself in high heels and drew back her shoulders.

'So, how is it all going?'

'Good, yeah . . . really well,' he said, leading the way around the side of the house and in the back door.

Understatement of the year, she thought as she took in the Quaker kitchen Shane and Rob were almost finished installing.

'Awesome job, lads!' She walked around the island, running her hand over the marble worktop, registering the cupped handles and detail in the drawers and cabinets, delighting in the butler sink and the perfect lime green she'd wanted for the splashback.

'Many hands make light work, as they say,' said Rob. 'Young Shane here's been a great help.'

Shane blushed, but as she caught his eye she knew by the shy smile, he was grateful for the praise.

'Colette's spoiling us with cakes for the tea break,' said Aidan, setting the bag on the island. 'I'll get the lads down from upstairs and we'll have a regroup over a cuppa.' He looked at Colette and gestured toward the hallway. 'Come on. I'll update you on progress.'

Colette could hardly believe her eyes. The hall and parlour floorboards she'd cleaned and sanded on her previous visit had been whitened to exactly the beachy washed-out look she'd envisaged. She couldn't help a gasp escaping.

'How did you . . .' she began, unable to fathom how they'd managed to get it done.

'That floor took me most of last weekend,' he said. 'The painters did the rest.'

The parlour was pristine. Empty of furniture, it was like a canvas with the background painted in, ready for the detail that would bring the work to life. The walls had been painted in the lemon tone she'd recommended and the ceilings in a warm white that gave a cosy feel. She couldn't wait to get to work on filling the beautiful space.

Aidan was waiting for her at the door of the downstairs bathroom. Walking across plastic sheeting, she caught glimpses of where the hallway and stairs too had been painted.

'You'll like this,' he said, opening the door wide and extending a hand to let her in ahead of him.

Transformation was too small a word. Gone was the ugly avocado suite. She was almost dazzled by the bright ceiling-to-floor tiling, the gleaming white suite with that sumptuous free-standing bath, the elegant tap system she'd ordered, the soft-grey floor tiles. And this was only the downstairs. She had an urge to wrap Aidan in a full-body hug but resisted, sucking in her excitement. The poor man had enough reasons to think her unhinged.

'Come on.'

He continued up the stairs, which had also received the treatment, the banister glowing with a stain that enhanced the natural hardwood and contrasted perfectly with the white treads. The sisal stair mats she had on order would be just the thing to finish off the look. In the bedrooms, the painters were hard at work, bringing her ideas to life. The pale aqua in one and pebble grey in another were already giving the empty rooms the soothing seaside feel Colette had wanted.

The en-suites were to die for; their compact size offset by the fresh simplicity of porcelain and chrome.

'Right, lads,' Aidan called out. 'We'll take a break and have a bit of a chat if that's okay.'

Colette heard drilling behind the door of the boxroom. 'What's happening in there?'

Aidan paused in what she thought might be his usual exasperation at her curiosity, but then started toward the door. Following behind, she almost bumped into him when he stopped and rapped his knuckles on freshly sanded wood.

'Close your eyes,' he said.

Her mouth opened to ask why, but she thought better of it and did as she was told. As the door opened, she heard a hammer cease some way above them. She sensed Aidan beckon to someone. There were a few quick strides, a whooshing of plastic being pushed across the floor.

'You can open them now.'

Whether it was the emotion attached to the whole project given recent events, or just her own insecurity, Colette had to stifle a tear at the sight that met her eyes. Aidan's two apprentices beamed from either end of a beautiful pine spiral staircase. He had listened to her ideas. And not only listened. She took a few steps into the room and looked up into the loft, where top-quality insulation was visible in a last open section that would be covered in plasterboard. She held a hand to her mouth.

'You wouldn't be speechless, Miss Barry?' asked Aidan.

Oh that man! She could kill him and kiss him at the same time. The chuckling from the apprentices confirmed what she'd imagined him telling them about her. Yes, she was demanding, 'cranky' even as he'd probably told them, but look at what could be achieved when her expectations were met.

'You've done a fantastic job, lads,' she said, smiling from one to the other. Then turning to Aidan, she added, 'So far, so good. Can't wait to see it when it's finished.'

'See, lads. What did I tell ye?'

She knew he was joking when he shook his head. The colour in his cheeks gave away the pride she knew he must be feeling at her reaction. Maybe she could invite him for a celebratory drink when all of this was done and dusted.

—

After a quick lunch of sandwiches provided by Aidan's cousins, Colette went to her car to check the phone she'd deliberately left in there that morning. There were emails that could wait, but she had a missed call from Ben, who rarely rang her.

'Ben, is there anything wrong?' she asked the minute he answered.

'Colette, wait a sec . . .' She heard him saying goodbye to someone and then a door closing.

'Hey, Col, sorry. I was just finishing with a patient.'

His voice was a near whisper. She waited.

'Listen, I need your help . . . on two fronts, actually.'

'Anything, Ben. What's going on?'

'First, do you know of any dog breeders?'

Her mind raced. Was her brother-in-law finally agreeing to the dog her sister desperately wanted? Dog breeders? Sandra Doyle had just bought a puppy.

'I can ask a friend. She got a Retriever a couple of weeks ago.'

'Could you ask her where she got it, have they any left?'

He was speaking quickly, with none of his usual calm. It occurred to her that he might have a queue of patients waiting, but he'd taken the call.

'No bother. I'll phone her tonight. What was the second thing?'

'Well,' his voice lowered again, 'I need someone to mind the kids next Wednesday. It's school holidays'

He paused as she thought of what work she had on next week.

'Can't Mam—' she started, but he cut her off.

'You know I love Barbara to bits, but this is something I don't really want to share with her.'

He had her guessing now. Something told her this other issue had nothing to do with the dog.

'Are you all right, Ben? In your own health, I mean?'

'Yes, yes, Colette. Perfectly fine. But I may not be so cocky once I've had the snip.'

It took a second to register what he meant. 'That was a terrible pun,' she said, unable to keep in the laughing.

'Laugh all you like, but if you want to stay my sister-in-law, I've got to brave it.'

What the heck did he mean, if . . . At the serious turn in their conversation, she let herself into the outbuildings. She was surprised to see a double mattress with an untidy heap of bedclothes taking up space in the middle of the floor, but skirted round it.

'Are you and Grace okay?'

'Oh, I'm sure she's told you how stupid I've been,' he began.

'Ben,' she said in a low but determined voice, 'Grace tells me nothing. I thought you two were fine.'

She heard him tut at the other end of the line and imagined the shrug.

'That would be Grace,' he said almost to himself.

'Why didn't she say anything?' Colette was thinking aloud. 'It's not like we don't see each other.'

She paced along the perimeter of the cool space as she listened. Grace was worried about her, wouldn't want to upset her, give her anything else to drag her down, after all she'd been through, the sore subject of babies ... and now the missing child. As he'd spoken, Colette had stopped at the plastic sheeting at the back wall and fidgeted absently with the sticky tape running along the top. By the time Ben was finished, she'd loosened the wrapping so that it had started to slip down to the floor uncovering a breathtaking seascape.

When Ben rang off, she was grateful for the distraction. She would talk things out with her sister when she got back to Cork. God love her, Grace had never once mentioned any of her troubles, and she herself offloading to her all the time. It was enough to make Colette want to cry her eyes out, but there'd been too much of that in recent weeks. She had a job to do here, a focus. Flicking through the canvases, she was sure these paintings would complete the house. They could put one in each room. The theme was perfect; windy blustery scenes with white summer clouds buffeting across the sky, long grasses bending in the wind, waves scudding about the lighthouse and surf crashing onto rocks. For a second, she thought to rush out and find Aidan, but weren't these the very paintings he'd been at pains to steer her away from the first time she'd been in here? She lifted one up to take a closer look and sure enough, in the bottom right-hand corner were the letters AOS. There was definitely more to these than met the eye. She would bide her time.

—

Apart from helping her cart furniture outside, Aidan hardly saw Colette for the rest of the day. She'd said she was going to work on distressing his grandmother's dresser and other pieces of furniture he couldn't bring himself to discard. There was definitely trust developing if he was letting her loose with the collection of hand tools she'd borrowed, not to mention the supplies she'd brought down. He hadn't bargained for this kind of rufty-tufty approach when his sister had enlisted Colette, but he wasn't complaining. If their project were to pay for itself, they'd need to wrap it up sooner rather than later with as many willing hands as possible. As generous as his father was being with the budget, Bill O'Shea had his own retirement years to enjoy with his hard-earned money, not to mention with Frances Brady. For the first time, Aidan envied his dad in that regard. His own future wasn't something he was sure he had the mental capacity to consider with Millie still missing.

—

Shane couldn't remember ever working so hard or achieving so much in his life. Even his most carefully crafted art projects hadn't received this level of grafting or indeed the sweat and muscle soreness that were beginning to make him yearn for a long soak in the Blarney Street bathtub. Colette showed no signs of such fatigue when he went outside to let her know they were nearly finished and would be heading back to Cork.

'Jeez oh!' was all he could say.

In the course of a day, she had single-handedly transformed Lizzie O'Shea's kitchen furniture from traditional farmhouse to modern beach getaway. He had seriously landed on his feet with Fabulous Four Walls and their associated tradespeople. He'd learned so much. There was no going back now. At least not yet. At some point in the future he would go back, pay his respects to Alex's family, maybe even reconnect with Lexie and her mother. For now, he could do a lot worse than stay in Cork.

'Just packing up here,' Rob told Fern. He always phoned when they were finishing a job and heading back. The quizzing had begun. 'No, I presume Aidan will take him back . . . Looks like she's still hard at it . . . I presume she'll go home as well.' He lowered his voice and let himself out the back door as he heard Aidan's voice in the hallway. 'Jesus, love, I don't know what they want to do.'

'God, Rob, you can be so thick.'

Yes, she'd often said as much, but he let her go on.

'Take Shane home in the van and let Aidan and Colette have a bit of time together.'

He made a face he was grateful she couldn't see. Was there no end to the woman's attempts to get Aidan a woman?

'Right, love. I'd better get on the road . . . Love you too.'

Aidan joined him in what was shaping up to be the barbecue area.

'Everything okay?'

'All good,' said Rob. 'Just checking in with the other boss.' He did his best to hide his exasperation with a laugh. How in the name of God did Fern expect him to engineer a romantic interlude for Aidan and Colette? He pretended to inspect the newly laid Valentia slate.

'She might be right about the barbecue area, our Colette.'

Fern had told him only a few weeks ago to speak positively about her, to get Aidan to see Colette in a good light. Rob liked the girl, admired her vision and work ethic, but he wasn't one to gush.

'She was right about a lot of things,' said Aidan. 'I'm even thinking to do up the outbuildings. A Phase Two.' He gave a wink and added, 'Just don't tell her.'

'Don't tell her what?'

Rob flushed as Colette rounded the corner from where he'd thought her well out of earshot. Aidan dug his hands in his pockets and gave her a guilty smile.

'Ah, Colette,' he said. 'Had enough for today?'

She pulled down her protective face mask and dabbed her forehead with the back of her hand.

'I'm not far from finishing the last of the chairs. I'm happy to stay on.'

Rob waited for Aidan to respond. If the man had any sense, he'd stick around. But he couldn't do a Fern and suggest it.

Aidan looked at him and shrugged, the ruddy cheeks betraying the man's embarrassment. Maybe Fern was right about these two.

'That's grand,' said Aidan. 'Rob, you'll be okay to take Shane and the lads, won't you.'

'Absolutely.' He might be a few brownie points to the good with Fern after all.

'I was planning on staying for a while yet anyway,' said Aidan.

Rob suppressed a smile. *Yeah, sure you were.*

Chapter Thirty-one

Jackie O'Flynn checked the time on her daughter's tablet: 3.30. The gadget she'd thought an extravagance had paid for itself a hundred-fold between letting Saoirse keep up with homework when she had to miss school for their trips and the entertainment value it had provided in the endless hours of waiting for her brother. Jackie set her book on the small circular table and looked around Great Ormond Street Hospital's roof garden. The modern green space in among the piles of glass and concrete of hospital buildings was nothing short of miraculous, and she for one was grateful for the respite to be gained from the tiny square of lush beauty above the relentless buzz of the city.

'Look, Mum.' Saoirse pointed to where a child stared down at them from the window of one of the wards. Jackie smiled and they both waved at him. Or was it her? She couldn't always be sure of the pale, bald children she saw here, tubes in their necks or noses, dark rings around their exhausted eyes. The child's mother appeared and exchanged a sympathetic smile with Jackie. Like foot soldiers in a war on rare disease, they were the parents and guardians whose lives had been turned upside down but who never gave up the fight; transporting, medicating, soothing, cajoling – whatever it took, whatever the slim odds were of seeing their children well, or at least making the best of their shortened lives.

Jackie's phone buzzed in her handbag.

'Better get a move on,' she said.

Ronan was beaming when they found him and his dad telling the occupational therapist about his room makeover. He'd been in this hospital for over a week between another consultation about the second knee operation he would need and all his usual treatments and therapies. Yet here he was, still smiling. Life was certainly a rollercoaster for the O'Flynn family, but as they always maintained, any day with Ronan in their lives was a great day.

Jackie felt her son's infectious smile spreading to her own cheeks. It was their last day in London for now. They would face the arduous task of getting from Heathrow to Cork tomorrow, but there was time for a couple of hours as tourists before they'd return to their hotel and settle Ronan as best they could for the night.

They caught a bus to Oxford Street. The Tube was no longer an option, but as with everything else, they adjusted. Taking turns to push Ronan in the wheelchair, they ducked in and out of a few shops where Saoirse had been promised a browse and some new clothes. Heading toward Soho, they wandered past their favourite chocolate shop which had now been relegated to the long list of 'off limits'.

'Can we just look?' asked Ronan.

Jackie thought her heart might shatter, but she wheeled Ronan to the shop, remembering the times he'd walked in by himself and even managed the stairs to the café on the first floor. Her stomach rumbled at the memory of the decadent cakes they'd enjoyed among the red velvet furniture and lavishly decorated lampshades.

'Back in a sec,' said Flynnie, giving her a wink as he and Saoirse walked up the steps and into the shop.

Ronan grinned up at her. It was no secret that she was the biggest chocoholic of the family. Even though his failing insides could no longer tolerate wheat or dairy, she was grateful for his generous heart; he wouldn't begrudge her the treat with which Flynnie would no doubt emerge. As they waited, she took in the cosmopolitan vibe of the street. Despite the reason for their frequent visits, she'd always loved that feeling of being part of a bigger world that London gave her. They moved a little to one side to let a group of Indian women in the most beautiful saris get a picture in the doorway of the chocolate emporium. Behind them, a man with a child made no secret of his impatience. Jackie shook her head and looked away.

As the women went on their way, she felt Ronan grip her hand. Turning back around, she followed his gaze to where the child with the man was looking back at him from some way down the street.

'It's her, Mum.'

It took her a moment to compute, but with her son looking like he might try to jump out of his wheelchair and run after the child, Jackie pushed hard, her steps striding as she weaved as best she could between the oblivious passers-by. She thought about Flynnie and Saoirse in the shop. Should she have got Flynnie to do this? But time was of the essence. If Ronan was right and this was indeed Millie Donovan, she could explain later why she took off like a mad woman.

She pulled her handbag off her shoulder and thrust it into Ronan's arms.

'Phone nine-nine-nine,' she told him, her breath heavy as she kept her eyes on the man and the girl heading toward Piccadilly Circus. She cursed the zigzag way people walked on the pavements. Why couldn't they stick to the side, like on escalators? *Bloody let us pass!* She could still see them. Her muscles were telling her to slow down, but she willed them to work harder.

'Hey lady, look where you're going,' an American shouted from where she'd nearly knocked the map out of his hands.

'Sorry, it's an emergency,' she called back to him as she swerved Ronan past the next clutch of pedestrians and kept up the pace.

'Police,' Ronan was saying into the phone. 'We're following Millie Donovan. She's been missing.'

With her heart pounding in her chest, Jackie called out to the man who by now was just metres away.

'Hey! Excuse me. Excuse me, there!'

The child turned, but the man held her hand tightly and began to walk faster.

'Excuse me!' Jackie called again. The girl was running alongside him now, but she'd seen her. The hair was shorter, darker than what Jackie remembered from the photos, but the elfin face, the beginnings of a new front tooth visible as she'd opened her mouth as if to call back to them . . . It was her. It was definitely Millie.

She spotted a policeman a distance away, speaking into a device on his chest as he scanned the crowd.

'There, police!' Jackie screamed, taking her hand off one of the handlebars and waving. She was running now. People were stepping out of her way, some telling her to slow down. She hoped this wasn't too rough a ride for Ronan who was still on the phone, telling the emergency services to hurry up and send someone. The man had Millie in his arms now. Jackie waved frantically. Surely the policeman would spot her. Yes. He was moving swiftly, asking shoppers to move aside, but in the blink of an eye, the man and the girl disappeared. Jackie looked past the throng. They were nowhere to be seen.

'Oi! Oi, stop there! Police!'

The policeman was moving toward her, but he cut off, disappearing down the steps of an Underground station. Jackie came to an abrupt halt. They could go no further. She stood at the top of the stairs, registering the death grip she had on the handles of her son's wheelchair. An elderly woman stopped and asked her if she was all right. It was too much. She let go of the chair and leaned on her knees, her lungs gulping in the polluted London air like her life depended on it.

'It's okay, Mum. The policeman will find them.'

She couldn't look her son or the kindly woman in the eye as she stood shaking, tears streaming down her face.

Chapter Thirty-two

There was no sign of the gentle sea breeze that had wafted onshore all day, keeping Colette cool and helping dry her handiwork. She thought she might melt as the evening turned balmy, reminding her again of the summers of her childhood. Those summers when she and Grace had been so carefree, safe in the loving company of their parents, sharing dreams and grand plans for adult lives that had seemed way off in a fanciful future. It had never occurred to her that she might end up on her own. As a young adult, she'd imagined herself a strong, independent woman who could cut it without a man, yet here she was, even after the horrors of her marriage and divorce, on some level still craving companionship. But her early forties was no time to be getting it wrong. She'd already made enough mistakes and paid the price. Maybe her mother was right, and she should bite the bullet and get a place of her own. She realised now how much her family had been tiptoeing around her, trying to be kind. She had a lot to be grateful for. It was time to give them a break and concentrate on taking as good care of them as they had of her.

She pulled her overalls down to her waist, twisted her hair tighter in its band and leaned in for the last coat of silk paint on the dining table. There were still so many jobs to get done. She could spend at least half the day here again tomorrow installing curtain rails and blinds and hanging the curtains her mother and the Donovans had made. The new beds would arrive next week and the furniture maker would have the chaise longue repaired. But she couldn't do it all on her own. She would need to ask Aidan for help.

—

When the growling in his stomach wouldn't stop, Aidan set down his tools and abandoned the job of installing the built-in wardrobe and desk units Colette had had delivered to the site. Anyone trained in carpentry could assemble flat-packed furniture in their sleep, but on an empty stomach, even Aidan struggled to keep his lines straight and levels exact. He would come back later and finish the job before camping down in the outbuildings – but first he had to eat. Confining himself to three healthy meals a day had certainly helped shed the pounds, but there was no way he could have run on less.

In the yard, he found Colette stripped down to a singlet, the sleeves of her overalls knotted at her waist. She was bent over the table, her face a frown of concentration.

'You're a hard worker,' he called over an Adele song playing from a Bluetooth speaker she had set on a window sill.

Reaching into her pocket, she took out her phone and turned down the volume.

'Hey,' she said, keeping the brush moving swiftly to cover the surface evenly.

'You planning on working all night?'

She laughed and set her brush down on the paint pot. 'I don't think so. I'm pretty wrecked.'

She stood with her hands on her hips and ran a critical eye over her work.

'It's really good,' said Aidan, taking in the collection of furniture she'd managed to make over since he'd greeted her that morning. It made him wish she were a builder. With her work ethic he'd hire her on the spot. 'I was just going to get a bite to eat at the pub. If you want to join me . . .'

'I haven't even started on the curtains and . . . I thought I could do them tomorrow. Are you coming back?'

He thought of the mattress he'd thrown down in the outbuildings. Even if he offered to sleep in the car, it wasn't exactly something he could imagine Colette laying her beautiful head of glossy hair down on.

'Don't worry about that. You can leave the materials here and we'll do the installing for you.'

She raised her eyebrows, but didn't say anything.

'Ah, you don't trust me, is that it?' he asked.

'Let's just say, I like to do some things myself.'

His stomach gave a loud rumble that made her laugh, a spontaneous laugh that banished the seriousness from her face. He realised he'd missed that sound, had just begun to enjoy hearing it when—

'Give me a sec,' she said. He watched as she strode off to retrieve a bag from her car before disappearing into the house.

A hot shower and a shave might have turned dinner with Colette Barry into something more promising than an after-work necessity, but there was no time for that. He pulled at the top of his shirt and took a quick sniff of his chest. The forty-eight-hour deodorant was in for the acid test after all the lifting, shifting, hammering and drilling he'd done today. He hoped Colette wasn't undergoing too much of a makeover in there or he'd look an awful sight next to her. When she emerged from the house with the overalls draped over one arm, dressed in the singlet and shorts she'd come in, he realised she didn't need a makeover. Even in the pull-on work boots she looked amazing, her fit body making him suck in what was left of his gut. All she'd done was brush her hair.

'It's just up the road, isn't it?' she asked when he went to open the door of the Land Rover. 'You're not going to drive?'

'Are you trying to kill me?' he laughed. 'We're not all super fit, you know.' He looked to where the driveway met the road into the village. She was right. It wasn't that far. 'Come on, so.'

Thankfully, it was a flat stretch of road, nothing like the night he'd walked her home from The Stables.

'You're looking pretty trim these past few weeks.'

She'd noticed.

'Fell off the wagon a bit when Millie . . .' It was so hard to say in front of her. John Buckley had told him how much she was blaming herself. She didn't need to feel guilty for his weight gain as well. 'I'm onto it again now, though.'

'She'll be running to keep up with you when she comes back.'

He smiled but kept his eyes on the road. He'd been checking his phone on and off all day. It was a habit at this stage. Still nothing.

In the pub, they squeezed in amongst the Friday night crowd and managed to shout out an order to the barman over the music and the banter. Colette sipped on a diet cola and kept her eye on a couple who were finishing their meal at a table by the window. She pulled at Aidan's sleeve and whispered her plan to inherit their spot. The behinds of the pair had no sooner left their seats when, like a cat pouncing, she moved in on the table.

'Sorry,' said Aidan as the woman pushed past him.

He shook his head as he sat opposite her, looking mortified. 'Are you always this determined?'

'I wish,' she answered.

She was grateful when their meals arrived. They'd tried to make conversation about work, but the earlier mention of Millie had settled between them like a lead weight. They ate in silence, the din of the pub resounding around them.

'We could have one for the road and take it outside,' Aidan suggested.

Despite their lack of conversation, she didn't want to leave him. Even if she had unwittingly contributed to the disappearance of his friend's child, he was at least trying to be normal around her. As he made his way to the bar to order, she went out, avoiding the crowds milling around picnic tables, and sat on the low wall by the small harbour. In the evening shadows, the moored boats bobbed on the incoming tide. That's how she and Aidan had been, she thought, just keeping afloat, afraid to go anywhere until conditions improved.

'One white wine spritzer,' he said with a wry smile.

'Ah, you got it right this time.'

He flushed at the sarcasm and sat beside her, the quiet settling again as they each took a drink. She wanted to be able to have a regular conversation with the man, but every time she tried to open her mouth, there was only one word on her tongue.

'Colette,' he said, turning to her, a hand tucked under his armpit, pint in the other. 'I don't blame you for what happened to Millie.'

She sucked in a breath. He'd said it for her. 'That means a lot to me, Aidan.' She couldn't meet his eye, but focused instead on the glass where the bubbles fizzed in the evening light. 'The problem is,' she said slowly, 'I blame myself.'

He didn't dismiss her statement or try to correct her. He didn't shake his head or move away. Instead he leaned in a little closer and in a low voice, he said, 'I think we all do.' Taking his pint glass in both his hands and setting it in his lap, he went on, 'You, me, Jane. There are no winners here.'

She felt the tears pooling in her eyes. A few short weeks ago, she'd fantasised about getting this close to him, undoing the buttons of that shirt and running her hands over the rusty chest hair beneath. The course their relationship had taken couldn't have been more different. It was all supposed to hinge on the success of this project. She would wow him with her interior-design skills. The project was nearing an end. Despite early reservations, he'd followed her advice to the letter. From the big jobs, right down to the light fittings, he'd come on board. She'd earned his respect, that was clear. But she'd hoped for so much more.

'I don't know how Jane copes,' she said, the tears beginning to leak. 'If I could just turn back the clock. If I'd kept a better eye . . . looked back to see—'

'Sh,' he soothed, putting a hand on her shoulder and gently squeezing. She wanted to cave, to lean into him and let him comfort her, but what right did she have to his kindness?

'Sorry, Aidan,' she said, drawing away from him. 'I should go.'

As he went to stand up with her, the phone went in his jeans pocket.

'Just a sec,' he said, taking the phone and checking the screen. 'It's Detective Carmody.'

Colette walked away to give him some privacy. Surely the detective didn't have more questions for the poor guy this far into the investigation. She felt a warm but urgent grip on her arm. Aidan was still on the phone, but pulling her with him toward the pub. She watched his face as it broke into a smile as bright as the light at Fastnet Rock.

'We will,' he was telling the detective. 'We're on our way into the pub now. Thanks. Thanks so much for all you've done.'

On the steps, Aidan stopped and took both of her arms. People jostled past, but he made no effort to get out of the way. He looked into her teary eyes.

'They found her, Colette.' He searched her face as she took in what he was saying. 'Come on, they're about to give a press conference.'

Inside, Aidan pushed past the drinkers, nothing like the quiet, unassuming man she'd just had dinner with. 'Can you switch the telly on?' he shouted over the bar.

The barman put a hand to his ear and shouted back over the crowd.

'You want the TV on?'

'They found Millie Donovan, the missing child,' said Aidan, straining between the crowd at the bar. A few of the customers on bar stools turned to look at him.

'Quiet down, now,' said one of them, then raising his voice, he shouted, 'Will ye quiet down?'

A hush descended as all heads turned to look at the TV on the far wall. Colette held her breath as she saw Niall Carmody and Jane Donovan enter what looked like a hotel function room. Willing the barman to hurry up with the volume control, she realised she had a vice-grip hold of Aidan's arm. When Jane started to speak, he cupped a hand around one of hers. Out of her peripheral vision, she saw his eyes glisten.

They'd found Millie in central London. Bryce Manning had tried to board the Tube with her after being spotted by a Cork boy in a wheelchair who had recognised the child and phoned police. Ronan! Colette couldn't believe it. A huge cheer went up at the mention of the Cork hero. The swimmers would be thrilled. Millie was found safe but obviously traumatised, the report went on. Police in Ireland were alerted and had contacted the mother, Jane Donovan, for formal identification. Mother and child had spoken via Skype and would be reunited in Cork later this evening.

'Miss Donovan, can you tell us exactly what's been happening to Millie during the past three weeks?'

Colette braced herself for the answer. It was Niall Carmody who spoke.

'We believe the father of the child had no intention of harming her. At this stage, we believe the motive was to hurt her mother.'

'What happens to the accused now, Detective?'

'That's a matter for the courts to decide, but negotiations have already begun for his extradition to Ireland. As you'll all appreciate, Miss Donovan has been through the wringer and is anxious to get to Cork Airport, where I'm sure you'll all give her the space she and Millie deserve for a happy reunion.' He looked to Jane as reporters fired a few more questions.

'I'd just like to thank everyone,' came the shaky voice as the camera zoomed in on Jane. She looked like she'd run a marathon, exhausted but elated. The bar was silent again as the Australian accent commanded their attention. 'The police who worked tirelessly to find my daughter, everyone in Cork who supported me, and my mother who came from Australia to be with me in these past few weeks. I can honestly say, they were the worst weeks of my life.' Her voice trailed off as she broke down. Turning to Carmody, she uttered one last comment. 'Thank you for finding Millie.'

There wasn't a dry eye in the pub, Colette imagined from where she was nestled against Aidan's shoulder, his strong arms holding her tight, his cheek resting on her head. When they drew apart, he wiped the back of his hand over his eyes. She did the same. The cheering gave way to speculative conversations about the relationship between Jane and Bryce and then to cold cases of missing children. Colette needed fresh air.

'Let's go,' she said and walked out of the pub, smiling at people she didn't know but who shared her relief.

Outside, they made frantic phone calls; Aidan rang his dad, Rob and Ellen, while Colette phoned her mother and Grace. As she waited for Aidan to finish, the warmth of the evening struck her.

'Look at that sky,' she said, pointing to where a swathe of dark cloud had moved in over the harbour. They both heard the low rumble of thunder out to sea. 'The furniture!'

'Come on,' said Aidan, putting a hand to her waist and herding her toward the road. 'Best get your hard work under cover before that breaks.'

As the first rain droplets started to fall, they broke into a run. Colette felt her heart rate quicken as she kept pace with Aidan. By God, he had been exercising. At the house, he ran to the outbuildings and opened the half-door, securing the latch. A light came on from within and she carried in two chairs. The sight of the double mattress with its crumpled sheet and rolled-away duvet made her stop.

'Come in, come in,' he said, gesturing with his hand. 'Sorry about the mess. This is where I've been sleeping when I've come down on weekends doing a bit of work.'

Feigning surprise, she pushed past to an open area to set down the chairs. They worked quickly, taking opposite ends of the table and dresser and moving the pieces safely past the door and out of the rain that was turning into a steady downpour.

When they finished, he went to the paintings that were stacked uncovered against the wall, just as she'd left them that afternoon.

'I'm sorry, Aidan, I came in to make a private call and I couldn't help . . .'

He shook his head. With his back turned to her, she couldn't read his face.

'I know you have your reasons for not wanting me to see them, but they're really good. They'd work beautifully in the house.'

He lifted up one of the paintings and stood staring at it. His silence unsettled her.

'I'm sorry,' she said again. 'I should have asked.'

'It was a long time ago,' he began, his voice hoarse. 'I was in love with a French art teacher, you know.' He gave a low laugh as he set the canvas back down and covered it in the plastic sheeting. 'Best year of my life, or so I thought until she told me she was going home to her fiancé.'

Colette didn't know what to say. This was a story she'd never heard mentioned in all the years she'd known Ellen and their mutual friends. 'I had no idea,' she began. 'Did Ellen know?'

'None of the sorry details anyway.' He turned around but didn't look at her. 'Time I moved on, really.'

As she stood taking in what he'd just told her, Colette berated herself for misjudging him. Aidan O'Shea wasn't a childless bachelor by choice. Whoever that French woman was, she'd been the one on whom he'd pinned his hopes and dreams and ultimately, the one who'd shattered them. She made to walk around the mattress toward the door.

'This was all wrong,' she started. 'I've overstayed my welcome. They've found Millie. I should be leaving you to celebrate. Instead I've only opened old wounds.'

She stopped short in the doorway and peered out at the lashing rain. A thunderbolt rumbled somewhere close and a fork of lightning lit up the sky over the main house.

Aidan came beside her and said what she was thinking herself.

'You can't drive home in this.'

'I'm sure I'll be fine,' she lied. 'I'll just . . .'

'Colette . . .' He stood beside her, his fingers in the tops of his pockets, thumbs resting on his belt loops. 'You don't always have to act so tough, you know.'

She took a deep breath and pushed a strand of wet hair behind her ear.

'That night I walked you home, I'd hoped to be in with a chance.'

She bit her lip, remembering the touch of his hand on her cheek, the longing it had awakened in her battered soul. A longing she thought she would never allow herself to feel again. She felt it now, standing close enough to touch. Grace's voice played in her head, *There are good ones out there . . . they're not all a million miles away.*

'You're a good man, Aidan,' she began. 'But you were probably right about me being the crankiest interior designer you'd ever met.'

Aidan looked at her, puzzled, but as the lines dissipated at his forehead, she could see the reference dawning on him.

'Shane told you that?'

She nodded.

'Word for word?'

She nodded again.

'I'll wring his scrawny Scottish neck . . .'

She held her hands out in front of her, palms facing him.

'I don't blame him. I was pretty tough on him too.'

He leaned back against the limestone masonry of the doorway.

'Do you ever let your guard down?'

She looked down at her soaking wet work boots and shook her head.

'I just wanted to do you all proud with this,' she said, gesturing to the house. 'And then Millie was taken . . . I thought that when this was finished, when Millie was found . . .' God, why was this turning into a heart-to-heart? She should have just gone home like the others. But this was her chance. She'd waited long enough for it. 'I thought, then, we might . . .'

Aidan stood tall and stretched out his hands to her waist. She hesitated for a moment, feeling the weight of them before reaching for his forearms to keep them there. She raised her chin to look at him. The lock of errant hair had fallen over his eyes, but between the parting strands, she could see they were black with desire. She let her fingers find their way over his chest and shoulders, pushing herself up on her toes. Keeping his eyes on her, he slipped his hands around her bottom and lifted her off her feet. She clasped round his waist with her bare legs as he pressed her to the cool wall in the body-hug she'd wanted to give him earlier in the day. As they held back for the barest moment, their noses brushed, then their lips met. She pulled the shirt out from inside his jeans and breathed in the smell of him. Sweat, paint, plaster, undertones of something manly. She kissed him harder, her body in overdrive at the feel of him. Kicking the door shut, he carried her to a pile of tea chests and set her down. Slowing the pace, he gently pulled off her boots, peeled off her soaking wet clothes and stripped down to his honest humble forty-five-year-old naked self. She wanted all of him. Unable to wait a moment longer, she pulled him in close and guided him inside her.

It was the most natural, most spontaneous love-making she'd had in a long time.

'I'm glad I got a bit in shape,' he laughed as they lay on the mattress after they'd made love all over again.

'You didn't have to go to all that trouble,' she said, running her fingers through his chest hair. 'You had me at the lockers in those awful loud shorts.'

He burst out laughing.

'You're definitely full of surprises, Colette Barry.' He stroked her hair and looked into her eyes. 'And I might as well tell you now . . . cranky or not, I love you.'

Later, with the rain battering the corrugated-iron roof, Colette drifted off to sleep in his arms. Apart from the sheer ecstasy, there was another feeling she had never experienced with a man. It was freedom. With Aidan, there was no agenda. They'd just wanted each other. For the first time, maybe ever in her adult life, she felt precious, beautiful, and truly loved.

Chapter Thirty-three

With the last of the curtains installed and the house locked up, Colette and Aidan set off for the city in convoy. Jane had called Aidan to tell him Millie was asking after him, and that Colette was welcome too.

When they got to the house, Millie ran straight into Aidan's arms. Although Colette had heard the reports on the car radio, she was taken aback at the sight of the once-flaxen hair the child's father had cut and dyed in an attempt to evade capture as he'd taken her on trains, buses and ferries to steal her from her mother.

'Hi Colette,' the little girl said when Aidan turned her round.

'Welcome home, Millie,' she said, emotion threatening to unravel her. 'We missed you.'

She couldn't believe it when the child reached out and touched her wet cheek.

'Don't be sad,' Millie said, 'I'm home now.'

Jane's mother gave a hearty laugh.

'Yes, the boss is home,' said Wendy, 'already telling Nanna what to do.'

Colette knew that Wendy was putting on a brave face for her granddaughter's benefit. It would be a long time before Millie would understand the full extent of what they'd all gone through. As long as Bryce Manning lived, a shadow would always loom over them. But for now, it was enough to let the small child have her innocence and believe that yes, she was home, and all could indeed be right with the world.

On the following Wednesday, Colette did as she and Ben had arranged and drove to Blackrock to babysit her niece and nephews. He was on a mission when she arrived, snacks and lunch all ready for them, bag packed for his procedure. 'You'll be fine,' she reassured him as he walked nervously to his car, crossing his fingers as he waved back at her.

She had a wonderful day. Baking, painting and bouncing on the trampoline with the children like a mad eejit did her a power of good. She couldn't remember the last time she'd taken a day off mid-week.

In the afternoon, when Sophie went down for a nap and the boys chilled out in front of a film, she set about planning the holiday she and Aidan would take after her mother had insisted they make use of the house in Clare together. Before she could talk herself out of it, Colette found the number for the surfing instructor recommended by that young student, and booked a couple of lessons into the bargain. She trawled the local real-estate websites and saved a couple of two-bedroom places she hoped to have a look at. She wouldn't tell Grace today, but she also booked a night for her and Ben at a spa hotel in West Cork. It would be good for them to spend some quality time together once he'd recovered. After the day's success, she was sure she could handle minding the kids. In fact, the day had made her realise how much she'd missed out on as their aunt. Yes, there was a lot of catching up to do, and she was going to enjoy every minute of it.

—

Ben arrived back in a friend's car just as Grace was getting out of hers. Colette watched from behind the computer as Ben cautiously manoeuvred himself out of the passenger side and grinned at his wife. Although she couldn't make out what her sister was saying, the look on Grace's face was enough to convey her incredulity. Colette turned away to allow them a moment of privacy. She would soon leave them to their evening and join Aidan for dinner.

The twins were sitting together on the sofa, oblivious to the decisions their parents were making about the future of their family, making Colette think back to her visits to the O'Shea house when she and Ellen had been blissfully unaware of the challenges of adulthood. If she had known Aidan would turn out to be such a dependable man, she might have been spared the bad choices she'd made and the heartache she'd suffered. But maybe it was because of all she'd been through that she appreciated him now.

—

'The house is finished,' Ellen shouted to Gerry. 'Come here and look at the photos from Colette.'

Gerry ambled in from where he'd been sweeping away fallen leaves from the veranda. Huddled together, they pored over each image, taking in what they'd only been able to imagine from mood boards and digital designs. Lizzie O'Shea would be proud. It was stylish and beautiful in a way that kept the feeling of a comfortable home. *Welcoming*, Ellen decided. She drew a little away and turned to Gerry.

'It feels more real now, doesn't it?'

He nodded and leaned back in his chair. She saw the twinkle in his eye. That man couldn't hide his excitement if he tried. She took a deep breath. The house was ready for its next chapter, but what was hers going to be?

'It would be a shame not to take the opportunity,' she began.

His face broke into a smile, but he put his hands out as if to rein in the enthusiasm.

'Up to you, my love. I'm not going to try and talk you into anything.'

'Hold the champers. I'm only talking about a few months' trial. Like a season. Do you think Louise would be okay with that?'

'You'll have to have that conversation with her, but she might be keen to be part of it.'

Ellen knew he was bursting at the possibilities running the house would bring for spending time with Gerry Senior and introducing Louise to them all. There were his visa requirements to think about. God and Almighty, there was tonnes to think about. But the house was there, ready. It was a chance she couldn't let go by.

——

On Church Road, Aidan was cooking up a storm. He had to admit, he liked the healthier version of himself even if Colette told him he didn't have to change. Anyway, it wasn't just his body that felt lighter. Since he and Colette had finally got together, he'd felt another kind of weight had been lifted off him. He had a new energy, a sense of looking forward he hadn't felt in a long time. If things worked out, they'd have the rest of their lives ahead of them. But he was happy to take it one day at a time. Tonight was dinner, and in a couple of weeks they'd go on holiday together. She was already planning surfing lessons for the pair of them. He was sure life with Colette would be full of surprises, but he had a few surprises of his own to spring on her. In fact, he wondered, as he tossed the stir-fry in his newly acquired wok, had she ever skinny-dipped in the Atlantic?

Acknowledgements

Thank you so much to anyone who has read this book. I really hope you enjoyed it. As much as writing is a solitary pursuit, bringing this story to you involved a small army of helpers. Rebecca Saunders, my publisher at Hachette Australia, you have championed this book, giving me thoughtful feedback at every step. This is a story I felt passionate about and I am grateful for your belief and guidance in enabling me to tell it. They are all fantastic at Hachette. Alex Craig, for your support and guidance, particularly in those last crazy days of preparing final proofs! Karen Ward, thank you for understanding my style of writing and for extending deadlines when life got in the way. Christa Moffitt, you are a genius, thank you for the beautiful cover. Claire de Medici, I am so grateful for your insights even if you had me tearing my hair out (don't worry, I've got heaps, no one would notice). Pam Dunne, thank you for being thorough. To the wonderful Cathy Kelly, thank you for your endorsement. My writing tribe who are like oxygen, including Diane

Hester and all at Eyre Writers Inc. The wider writing community, especially Romance Writers of Australia, Tasmanian Writers Centre and Devonport Writers' Workshop. Thanks to Fay Forbes for your enthusiasm and ongoing support. Aileen Pluker, thank you for your generosity in sharing your stories of Nauru. Sue Thiel, for inspiration and specifics on quilting. Billy Thomson, my son, for keeping me right on all things Marvel and DC. Cyril Moriarty, for your quick response when I was stressing about visas. Lisa Sanderson, Irene Svendsgaard, Paula Weeks, for conversations over cocktails and cappuccinos (what happens in Hobart, stays in Hobart). My swimming family, you are all very special to me and are woven in to the pages of this book. My lifelong friend, Mary T Coughlan, what can I say? Your unfailing love for your family and your resilience in the face of Ehlers-Danlos Syndrome are an inspiration and the reason why I kept at this project. I hope it helps in some small way. The O'Flynns of Bishopstown, for your generosity in sharing Crookhaven with me. My friends and family for cheering me on and keeping me going on this writing journey, especially my husband, Mike, thank you for always encouraging me.

Also by Esther Campion

Twenty years ago, Ellen O'Shea left her beloved Ireland to make a new life in Australia. Now, living in a small coastal town and struggling to cope with the death of her much-loved Greek husband, Nick, Ellen finds her world turned upside down when an unexpected visitor lands on her doorstep.

The arrival of Gerry Clancy, her first love from Ireland, may just be the catalyst that pulls Ellen out of her pit of grief, but it will also trigger a whole new set of complications for her and those she holds dear.

'A heart-warming, positive tale about the journey
everyone takes to find their own beloved place in the
wide, wide world'

Better Reading

'Joins the captivating Maeve Binchy in the pantheon of
popular Irish novelists'

Irish Scene